after all this time

JESSICA SYDNEY

AFTER ALL THIS TIME

SUNSET COVE BOOK 1

ISBN: 979-8-9902197-0-0

Cover Illustration and Design: Jessica Lynn Draws

Editor: Elaine Richards

Published by Jessica Sydney

after all this time

SUNSET COVE
BOOK 1

JESSICA SYDNEY

content notes

After All This Time is intended for adult readers (18 and older). This book contains explicit language and on-page sexual content that may be offensive to some readers. Please continue on at your own discretion.

After All This Time contains the following content:

- Anxiety (on-page)
- Panic attacks (on-page)
- Death of a parent (past, off-page and on-page)
- Depictions of grief
- Blood

author's note

Some of you have asked me how I came up with the concept for *After All This Time* and I can honestly tell you I have no idea. When I was brainstorming ideas for this book, I immediately knew I wanted to write characters that we'd both be able to see ourselves in.

I'm a reader just like you. I love to escape reality and dive into a world that isn't my own. There are so many incredible characters that exist within the pages of books I love, but I couldn't relate to them as much as I wanted to. I couldn't see myself in most of them which is totally okay. Sometimes you're not going to see yourself in a character you read about, but there's something magical that happens when you do see yourself in a character you read about.

The main characters in this book are Noah and Dani. There's something I have in common with both of them which is the fact that I have anxiety.

I experienced my first panic attack when I was in sixth grade.

Middle school was a rough time in my life, not just for me but for my family as well. I was at a low point, feeling utterly and completely alone.

After I finished writing *After All This Time*, I realized how similar I am to Dani, so similar I believe we're the same person. Like Dani, I'm a chronic overthinker. My mind loves to constantly put me in an endless spiral of chaos for no reason. The way we experience anxiety and panic attacks are eerily similar.

I know having anxiety and panic attacks is different for everybody which is why it's challenging to talk about what it feels like. It could feel like a rollercoaster that never ends or a wave that never crashes onto shore for some of you. That's how it feels for me most of the time.

Please remember you're not alone. I thought I was. But *you* are not alone.

Noah, Dani, and I are always here if you need us.

I hope you love Noah and Dani like I do and see pieces of yourself in them.

Thank you so much for reading,

Jessica Sydney

playlist

Difficult — Gracie Abrams
Take Care — Beach House
What You Know — Two Door Cinema Club
Brain Damage — Pink Floyd
ur so pretty — Wasia Project
Sweet Child O' Mine — Guns N' Roses
My Mind & Me — Selena Gomez
Friday I'm In Love — The Cure
Loverboy — A-Wall
Buddy Holly — Weezer
93 Days — Grace Gaustad
shut up — Greyson Chance
No Control — One Direction
Bridges — Erthlings
Peachy — Bad Suns
Everything Has Changed (Taylor's Version) — Taylor Swift feat.
Ed Sheeran

I'm In Love With You — The 1975
invisible string — Taylor Swift
Say You Won't Let Go — James Arthur
all-american bitch — Olivia Rodrigo
Unsteady — X Ambassadors
Snow on the Beach (feat. More Lana Del Rey) — Taylor Swift,
Lana Del Rey

To those of you who are in a constant battle with your mind.
Remember you are not alone.
You are so much more than your anxious thoughts.

CHAPTER ONE

"This is bullshit!" I say to myself.

Slumped in my swivel chair with my arms resting on the handles, I stare down the blank screen of my laptop like it's mocking me.

Writer's block is a bitch.

I was hoping sitting here with music flooding my eardrums would help me brainstorm some ideas, but so far, it's not helping. It's surprising because music typically helps me get into the world I'm writing about.

As I let out a deep sigh, I managed to type out one word on the page.

Shit.

Leaning back in my chair, I cross my arms and scrutinize the word as if it would sprout friends if I glared hard enough.

Instead, it sits there and tortures me until I ultimately decide to slam the laptop shut—I'll only frustrate myself more than I already have. The clapping sound of my laptop closing echoes in my room and rings in my ears.

Maybe I should just stick to my job at Sweet & Salty.

Sweet & Salty is the romance-only bookstore here in Sunset Cove.

I started working there regularly throughout my high school years, up until I started college. And now summer seems to be the only time I can fit it into my schedule.

My mom's lifelong best friend, Laura, opened the store back in the early 2010s. She wanted a place for romance readers to call home—I've been lucky enough to call it my home for the last several years of my life. I'm grateful Laura opened this place because I'd be lost without it.

If only my life was a romance novel, everything would be easier.

I'd fall in love with a guy who'd treat me like a princess, take care of me, buy me books, support me, and maybe be an avid reader like myself.

But, unfortunately, this is reality. It'd be a miracle if I found a guy who could sweep me off my feet.

The creaking noise of the door has my head spin towards it which brings me back to reality.

Bella's head pops into view, her face lighting up until it dims like a faulty night light. "Dani, what the hell are you doing?" she asks. "Did you stay up all night again?"

"Maybe," I reply.

"And how are you functioning right now?"

"Who says I'm functioning?" I quip, pushing away from the desk like it's the worst thing to exist.

She stands there, narrowing her eyes at me and folding her arms across her chest. She's interrogating me with her look alone.

I stand up, stretching out my arms and lower back. "It's called survival mode," I tell her, trying to rub the fatigue off my face. "You know me better than anyone, *Bella Castillo-Ryder*, which means you know I'm running on nothing but shit."

Bella shakes her head at me and laughs. "Okay, let's pull you out of survival mode and get you fueled up. I'll whip something up for us for breakfast."

"Sounds good to me," I smile. "What were you thinking of making?"

She shakes her head. "Nope, I'm not telling you. It's a surprise."

As I shuffle to the bathroom, I can almost hear the pep talk I need speaking through the tiles that line the backsplash.

"Hey, don't take too long in there!" Bella calls after me, her tone playful yet commanding.

"Yeah, yeah. Whatever," I say.

Bella and I have been best friends since we were toddlers. We're practically sisters, even though we're not blood-related. She was there for me when my father passed away, letting me stay at her house with her when I couldn't bear the thought of stepping into my own house.

She always puts other people's interests before her own, and never asks for anything in return. She deserves the world, especially after everything she's been through.

I look at my reflection in the mirror and notice dark, puffy circles under my eyes that take me out of my thoughts.

I'm so exhausted.

I spend a good twenty minutes brushing my teeth, washing my face, and fixing my hair.

Hearing the sound of someone's throat clearing, I find Bella standing behind me.

"Can I help you with something?" I ask her, my eyes widening.

"Breakfast is almost ready, Madame." She curtsies, bowing her head down.

I laugh. "Thank you for letting me know."

"You're welcome." Bella giggles and leaves the room, heading back into the kitchen.

Once I finish up in the bathroom, the smell of onions frying shoots straight up my nose.

As I walk out of my bedroom and into the kitchen, I see Bella working two skillets. One has scrambled eggs, white onions, and tomatoes. The other has two small flour tortillas in it.

"You amaze me sometimes," I tell Bella, standing in the entryway to the kitchen area.

She turns towards me with a dirty look taking over her face. "Sometimes?"

"I'm kidding. How are you not used to my sarcasm by now? You've known me for years."

"Well, you can take your sarcasm over to the tortillas and flip them over. If they're golden brown, take them out."

"Aye-aye, captain." I walk over to the pan and grab a pair of tongs, flipping the tortilla over. Both sides are golden brown and it smells so good.

My mouth is watering from the combination of scents happening in here.

Bella cuts the heat from both sides of the stove.

As I sit onto my chair at our small kitchen table, she slides equal amounts of food onto two plates with the finesse of someone who'd grown up in a kitchen where food was seen as a form of love *and* art.

Bella grew up in a Mexican-American household. Her love for cooking stems from her mother and Abuela. I've learned so much from all three of them about Mexican cuisine, it's opened my eyes in ways I could've never imagined.

A vibrating sensation through the table takes me out of my daze. I peer down at my phone.

SAGE

SAGE

how's writing going?

ME

do you really want to know the answer to that question?

SAGE

like shit, right?

ME

and you are correct!

honestly, i'm amazed i'm functioning at all right now

SAGE

what's that quote from alice in wonderland again? "we're all mad here" it's not just you

shit, i got to go

my roommate needs my help with something. please remind me why i decided to have someone live with me?

ME

is it because you're in desperate need of attention and constantly feed off other people's energy?

SAGE

screw you

ME

you know you love me

SAGE

no, i tolerate you

there's a difference and what you just said is absolute bullshit BTW!!!

ME

oh, really? i had no idea

SAGE

bye, bitch

ME

bye, loser

Sage is one of my best friends, I've known her since high school. We've always had the kind of friendship where we're not afraid to be brutally honest with each other. She doesn't hold anything back, except her own feelings. Mostly because she's had this storm cloud that's been following her for several years.

Bella inserts a forkful of food into her mouth. "Eat up. You need brain food to tackle that novel of yours."

"It's not polite to talk with your mouth full." I press my lips together to stop myself from breaking out into laughter, but it doesn't work.

She fakes a laugh, scrunching her face. "Well, I can say that sitting at your computer screen for several hours isn't going to help write your book."

"Yeah, I know. Also, you're not the one going into overtime with writer's block." I manage a grin, leaning in my seat.

"Good thing I don't write fiction," she spits out.

I stick both of my middle fingers up at her. "Thank you for that."

"Sorry. Unlike you, I was never drawn to books or writing them."

"And that's okay," I say before taking a bite of eggs and a piece of fried tortilla. "Holy shit!"

She whips her head around and back. "What?"

"This is so good."

"You scared the crap out of me."

"I think you missed your calling to go to culinary school."

"Right. Be sure to tell my mom that. Back in high school, she looked like she was going to pass out when I told her I wanted to write about fashion and beauty, so I could add some experience to my résumé. I thought she was going to have a heart attack when I told her I wanted to do this for the rest of my life."

A breathy laugh escapes my mouth. "Yeah, I remember that. And for the record, you're going to be the best digital news journalist the industry has ever seen. They have no idea what's coming," I reply, cracking a smile.

She purses her lips together just enough to make a small frown combined with a smile appear on her face.

I believe in her, even if she doesn't believe in herself. She doesn't realize how strong and incredible she is, and I will spend every day for the rest of our lives reminding her.

Suddenly, my phone rings. The caller I.D. flashes Mom in bold letters with a picture of me and her on the front.

"Hey, Mom, what's up?" I answer.

"Hi, Sweet Girl. What are you up to this morning?"

"I'm just having breakfast with Bella."

"Good. That's good." Her voice comes out in a hushed tone, barely a whisper.

There's a long pause which is starting to make me nervous.

"Is everything okay?" I glance at Bella, who's pausing mid-bite and watching me closely.

There's a heartbeat of silence before she responds. "Dani, there's been an accident."

I freeze as the room stills around me. "What?"

"There's been an accident, and it's really bad."

My grip on the phone tightens as my breathing gets heavier. "Mom, what do you mean by *an accident*?"

"Ben and Lizzie Kaplan got into a car accident earlier this morning. I'm at the hospital with Laura."

The next words she says have me in complete shock. And suddenly, everything around me begins to fade.

I shake my head violently from side to side.

This can't be happening. Not again. This isn't real. No, no, no.

I look down and notice the breakfast Bella spent so much time making is now all over the floor and the table.

Everything around me is suffocating, sticky, and puffy.

Oh God, I can't breathe.

It's like middle school all over again.

My breath comes out in short, ragged gasps, each inhale feels like the air is getting sucked right out of me.

"Dani, what's going on?" Bella asks beside me, her face concerned and worried.

I feel like I'm going to cry, but the tears are at a standstill.

My vision starts to blur and that's when I lose it. "It's...Ben and Lizzie."

Have you ever felt like your entire world is falling apart?

That moment when the world somersaults and here you are, trying to figure out which way is up while your lungs are constricted in an unexpected state of panic.

Yeah, that's me right now.

My hands are shaking.

Everything is a blur.

All of this brings back the memories I wanted to store away forever, but they always seem to rise above the surface no matter how deep I shove them down.

When I was fourteen years old, my mom called my school to pick me up early. She told me that my dad got into a car accident on the way to work and passed away due to the impact.

I remember how I couldn't move or speak the entire drive home. All I wanted to do was curl up in a ball in my bedroom and never come out. I couldn't go to school for a month. I couldn't get out of bed. I could barely form cohesive thoughts.

Goddammit.

I can't help but think about Ben and Lizzie.

They're my found family, the kind you piece together like a puzzle and fits perfectly together.

Ben did everything he could to make sure I had a father figure in my life after my dad passed away.

He'd congratulate me when I got a good grade on a test.

He'd give me constant motivation to continue writing my book.

He'd always be there if I ever needed someone to talk to.

It seems like normal things to do, but the smallest gestures that he did meant the world to me.

Ben's relationship with Lizzie has always reminded me of the relationship I had with my father. He'd always take care of her when she got sick or hurt. He'd always be there for her if something bad happened at school. He'd protect her as if his life depended on it.

I didn't just have Ben as my protector.

I had Lizzie too.

Growing up, Lizzie was like an older sister to me.

We were inseparable when we were younger, despite her being five years older than me. If I wasn't hanging out with Bella, I'd be with Lizzie. We were two peas in a pod.

I loved it so much when she'd team up with me to take down her younger brother, Noah, when he was being a prick to me.

No matter what happened, I knew I'd always have a home to go to.

Them.

And now, it feels like my home is shattering like broken glass.

I hear snippets of Bella's voice from time to time.

All I can concentrate on is how heavy my body feels. The weight of it crushing me and all that I am.

Bella sits on the floor next to me, wrapping her arm around me. "Dani, I talked to your mom. She told me to remind you to breathe." She scoots in front of me. "But I think we should head to the hospital."

When anxiety takes over my mind and body, I forget how to function like a normal human being. Bella knows how I get when I have a panic attack.

I can't focus on my surroundings. My hands shake. My lips get dry. My mind loves to focus on the bad instead of the good.

I'm grateful she's always there for me when this happens. She knows how to calm me down by permeating her warmth through me.

I violently shake my head. "I c-can't."

"There is *no can't*, only can."

"You sound like Yoda," I breathe out.

This isn't the time for jokes.

"Shut up and start packing," she insists.

She helps me up off the floor as we both assess the damage I caused.

I frown. "What about the mess I made?"

"I'll clean it up while you pack."

"I love you." I hug her tightly for a brief moment before releasing her.

She looks at me and smiles. "I know."

Rushing into my bedroom, I grab some clothes, shoes, and a few books, basically anything I can put in my suitcase. I'm stuffing everything in there at supersonic speed. I have no idea how long I'm going to be staying.

I put on a teal tank top that flares at the bottom and cotton gray shorts followed by a pair of Skechers because comfort is vital.

Once Bella is done cleaning up my mess, I see her walk into her bedroom through the crack of my door.

Like The Flash, she comes out of her room with her phone in her hand and her purse over her shoulder.

She's wearing a pink tank top with denim shorts that have small rips on the right side and her high-top white Converse.

I wish I could rock the color pink, but I'll settle with Bella rocking it for me.

Dragging out my giant suitcase, I roll it into the living room area of our apartment and take a deep breath.

It's going to be okay. It's all going to be okay. It has to be. It needs to be.

My body doesn't feel as heavy as it was, and I don't hear my heart beating as loud as it was before.

"Are you ready to go?" Bella asks as she walks towards me.

"I just need to get my bag." Grabbing it from one of the nearby chairs, I sling it over my chest.

I do a mental checklist.

Phone. Check. Chargers. Check. Wireless earbuds. Check. Wallet. Keys. Suitcase. Check. Check. Check.

I meet Bella's gaze. "Okay, let's go."

She nods her head up and down, snatching my car keys out of my hand.

"Hey! What the hell?" My anger starts building.

"You didn't think you were driving, were you? Do you not recall what happened in the last half an hour?" She makes me relive the sadness and agony all over again.

I lug my suitcase out the door with Bella following me.

I stop suddenly. "Wait, why didn't you pack a suitcase?"

"I have everything I need at home. I just want you to be okay. You're all I care about right now." The sincerity in Bella's voice nearly takes me out. "Do you want me to tell Sage what's going on or do you want to do it?" She looks at the door to the apartment, twisting the knob to double-check that it's locked.

"I don't have the energy if I'm being honest. If you want to tell her, be my guest."

Bella gives me two thumbs up, signaling she understands me.

I drag my suitcase to our favorite place.

The staircase of hell.

Hightower, our off-campus apartment complex, is notorious for not having elevators. Unfortunately, our only option is to go up and down these stairs.

Bella and I both look at each other, rolling our eyes and groaning at the same time.

I feel beads of sweat forming on my forehead by the time we reach the first floor.

Bella grabs my suitcase, booking it for my Honda CRV.

I try to keep up with her, despite how out of breath I am.

When it's summer in Florida, it doesn't matter if I lift weights or not. The mix of sweltering heat and humidity makes for a deadly combination.

I reach the car, taking a deep breath. Climbing in, I put my purse by my feet and lean my head back onto the headrest.

Bella gets in, throwing her purse in the back behind the driver's seat. "I put your suitcase in the h—are you okay?" She tilts her head, a smile forming on her sweet face.

Fuck, I'm such a mess.

"Just breathe," she adds. "You're going to be okay. You hear me?"

I nod as a silent response because I'm not in the mood to talk right now.

All I can think about is how Laura's feeling.

Scared.

Sad.

Angry.

Confused.

Everything in between.

This is how I felt when my dad passed away.

This is different though.

This is her husband and daughter.

I can feel the tears swelling up in my eyes again.

Get your shit together, Dani.

She opens Spotify on the car dashboard and hits play. The angelic voice of Gracie Abrams blasts through the speakers.

On a normal day, I'd keep the music on, but I'm not in the mood to listen to anything right now—I turn the volume all the way down.

Backing up slowly, she shifts the gear into drive.

As we hit the road, all I can see are an infinite amount of giant billboards that advertise injury attorneys and endless patches of dying grass.

"Moo!" Bella shouts as she sees a small herd of cows ahead of us to the left.

Ignoring her, I stare out the window.

All I can think about is getting to the hospital, and the thought is making my stomach do flips.

Eventually, we exit I-95. While we're waiting for the traffic light to turn green, I feel Bella's gaze burning a hole through my head.

I know that she's mentally assessing if I'm okay.

No, I'm not okay.

Sunset Cove Hospital comes into view.

I can't wait to get out of this car.

Bella turns into the hospital lot and finds a parking spot. She pulls into a spot closer to the front entrance.

Getting out of the car, I sling my bag across my chest while Bella slides the window down. "I'm going to drop your suitcase off at your house. And then, I'm going home. Dani, you're one of the strongest people I know. You're going to get through this. I'll be here for you every step of the way."

"Thank you," I tell her, my voice cracks like flames in a fire.

"For what?" Her eyebrows sink lower on her face, and a grin appears on her face.

"For being you," I say.

She smiles at me, gesturing to back away from the car and head inside. The window rolls up and she drives off.

Speed-walking over to the sliding doors, I make it through security without any hassle.

I place my visitor sticker on my chest as I walk over to the front desk.

"How can I help you today?" A younger woman seated behind a computer asks.

"I'm looking for two people who were admitted here. Their names are Benjamin and Elizabeth Kaplan. I need to know where they are. Please," I beg.

My heart is pounding as my throat grows tight to the point where I'm starting to lose my breath.

"Breathe, honey. Let me look at my computer here."

My foot starts to tap rapidly against the laminated flooring. My patience isn't wearing thin because it doesn't even exist right now.

Rubbing my eyes with my hands, I let out a deep exhale.

What feels like an eternity is actually two minutes before I'm given any information.

"They're in room 409."

"Thank you," I say.

Once I make my way over to the elevators, the doors open. I step inside and press the number four button.

As I make my way down the hallway, I see my mother standing in front of Ben and Lizzie's room.

Laura's nowhere to be found.

I take a moment to study Mom.

Her dark brunette hair is tied up in a high ponytail. She looks tired with dark circles underneath her eyes and she can barely keep them open.

"Mom," I say.

She turns around and runs towards me, pulling me in for a hug. "I'm so happy you're here, Sweet Girl."

My mom and I have always been close. We grew even closer after my dad passed away.

I'll never outgrow her hugs. They're comforting in a way that's difficult to describe. They make me feel safe. She makes me feel safe.

"How could I not come?" I can taste the salty tears streaming down my face.

"Laura has been pacing up and down the hallway for what feels like forever. I don't know what to do."

Right as Mom says this, Laura appears frantic and exhausted at the same time.

My heart.

When she sees me, it looks like she's going to have a heart attack. She runs over to me. "Dani Girl. You're here." she pulls me in for a tight, extended hug.

I'm starting to lose feeling everywhere, but it's okay.

I'm just happy to be here for her.

"God, I'm so sorry, Laura. I don't—"

She cuts me off before I can say anything else. "Thank you. I don't know how this happened. I'm living a nightmare. I'm happy you're both here." She releases me from her grasp, gesturing to my mom.

Mom guides Laura to a chair that's in front of Ben and Lizzie's hospital room while I'm standing in front of the row of chairs.

I turn and face the window straight ahead.

"God, I *wish* I got here sooner," I mumble to myself.

"I *wish* you weren't here at all," a deep and raspy voice says.

Turning around, I see a tall, muscular guy with a full head of wavy dirty blonde hair and ocean blue eyes you could get completely lost in standing in front of me.

I guess it makes it easier for me to not lose my breath around him, knowing he has a shitty personality.

He looks different, and somehow also the same.

I guess that could be because I haven't seen him in five years.

CHAPTER THREE

Noah. Fucking. Kaplan.

The last person I expected to see. And in a hospital out of all places.

My childhood rival.

The king of all assholes.

God, I can't stand him.

I told myself I was done with him. I thought I'd never see or speak to him again.

Five years ago, my mom planned the day before my high school graduation. I didn't know what she had up her sleeve. All I knew was that we were going to the Kaplan's house, which I dreaded because there was a good chance I'd run into Noah. When Mom told me there'd be chocolate cake from Marina's Diner, I couldn't resist because I love that damn cake.

That all changed when Laura suggested we should have a final game night.

"I figured we'd have one last family game night. What do we think?"

Laura is sitting in between my mom and her husband, Ben, on the sofa in the living room inside the Kaplan family's house.

Lizzie is sitting next to me on the chair bed.

Noah is sitting by himself on the plush chair across from Lizzie and I.

I've tried everything I could to avoid Noah since sophomore year, but somehow our parents thought it'd be a good idea to put us in a room together after everything that happened.

"Have you guys prepared your arguments for what game we're going to play tonight?" Ben asks, looking at Noah and shifting his attention to me.

I shake my head. "Well, considering I had no idea we were even doing this, no I didn't prepare my argument. In fact, I have no interest in taking part in any of this."

"Dani Girl, will you please stay? For old time's sake?" Laura pleads, her pupils dilating the longer she keeps staring at me. "This isn't spontaneous. I planned this. Noah didn't tell you?"

I grunt. "No, he didn't."

Lizzie's breath is on the edge of my ear. "Don't worry, I'm here if you need me as backup to whoop Noah's ass."

"I heard that," Noah says.

"You were meant to, dickhead." Lizzie flips him off, rolling her eyes.

My eyes lock with Noah's.

There's nobody who brings out my anger like he does, even more so now than before.

I can feel a fire starting in the pit of my stomach, desperately trying to escape and torching the shit out of him.

He gets up off the chair, standing in front of all of us.

Noah's eyes land on me. "I did prepare my argument, but there's no sense in me presenting since I don't have anyone to compete against." He licks his lips. "I mean you think a smart person like Dani would've figured out we'd have a final family game night before we go off to college. I guess she's not as smart as you all thought she was."

I'm staring at the wall and attempting my best to keep cool.

"*Maybe that's because she never was smart.*" *He pauses.* "*Maybe it's all a bullshit persona she conjured up in her head.*"

"*That's enough son,*" *Ben says.*

It was hard enough to be in the same room before, but it's more intense now. My feelings towards him have intensified. My feelings of hatred and irritation, to be specific.

"*That's funny.*" *I pause.* "*Tell me something, Kaplan. Do you get off on being a prick or does it just come naturally to you?*" *I tell him all this without making contact until I say the last few words.*

He marches over to me. "*Get up.*"

"*Fuck you,*" *I say.*

"*You want to make a scene in front of our families? Or are you going to listen to me like the good girl I know you can be?*"

I blink my eyes repeatedly. "*What did you just say to me?*"

"*Don't act dumb. I know you heard me.*"

Lizzie shakes her head, rubbing her eyes with her index and middle fingers.

"*Alright, everybody, let's calm down,*" *Ben says.*

Getting up off the chair bed, I stand in front of Noah. "*You're not the boss of me.*"

"*Are you sure about that?*" *He challenges, inching closer to me so there's a sliver of a gap between us.*

"*Oh, I'm positive,*" *I say.*

"*Fine,*" *he says.* "*You wanna air all our shit out? Then, let's do it. Right here. Right now.*"

"*I don't think this is a good idea,*" *Lizzie says.*

Laura turns to her. "*It's not, but we're going to just go with it because they're not going to listen to us.*"

I place my hand on my hip. "*What the hell is wrong with you?*"

"*I think you're asking the wrong person that question.*"

"*Why didn't you tell me tonight was our last family game night?*"

He raises an eyebrow. "*Uh, was I supposed to?*"

My eyes widen. "*Did you not hear when your mom said you were supposed to tell me?*"

He clears his throat. "I must've blacked out."

"You could've told Lizzie." Then, it hits me. "Oh, you did this shit on purpose."

"Why would you ever think I'd be capable of doing something like that?" He smacks his lips together.

I back away from him, pacing in a small circle with my hands on the temples of my forehead. "You're unbelievable." I point a finger at him.

"Don't tell me something I already know." He winks, giving me a wicked smile.

"It's not a compliment, dumbass." My chest heaves. "God, I'm so tired of this."

"Tired of what?"

"This!" I point to myself, then at him. "I swore to myself I'd never talk to you again after what you did. I was at peace and you had to fuck it all up, didn't you? Didn't you?" I take a moment to catch my breath. "I'm done with this. And I'm done with you."

He narrows his eyes, scoffing. "You're done with me?"

"After tonight, I never want to see you again. I never want to speak to you again. I just want to move on. Please, let me move on. Please," I beg.

Tears are cascading down my cheeks as I swallow a lump down my throat.

"Then, go. Leave. I don't give a shit what you do, Dani."

"I hate you!" I shout, straining my voice in the process.

I sprint out of the house before he can say anything else to me, stopping outside to collect myself.

I don't look back.

I've never felt so free, and I can finally move on.

For five years, I've been able to live my life without the constant need to prove myself to a man I despise.

Five fucking years.

And now, here we are.

Noah's sitting in a chair in front of me with a dumb smirk plastered all over his face.

I stand in front of him, feeling the temperature of my body increasing within seconds.

I want to punch him in the face so badly.

He tilts his head slightly, folding his arms in front of his chest. "Why don't you take a picture? It'll last longer."

"Usually when a person takes a picture, it's something they want to remember. I don't need to remember how much of an asshole you are."

"And I don't need to remember how much of a bitch you are."

I roll my eyes, sticking my middle finger up at him. "Fuck you."

"I don't think that would be appropriate. We are in a hospital."

"It's a figure of speech."

"To you, maybe. But, it's not to me."

Our moms decided to hang out at the end of the hallway. All so Noah and I can hash out the last five years of pent-up anger in peace. I mean if you want to call what we're doing peaceful.

A small smile appears on my face. "Aren't you going to ask me why I'm here?"

"You know, I was..." He pauses for a brief moment. "Then, I realized I don't give a shit."

"That's fine, just know I'm not leaving."

His eyes work up my body, starting at my legs and landing back on my face.

What is he doing? He needs to cut that shit out.

I raise an eyebrow. "What the hell are you doing?"

"There's been something that's been bothering me for years."

"And what's that?"

"How can you look like this when you're made of stone on the inside?"

"Funny, I could ask you the same thing." I grin, blinking my eyes and staring at him afterward.

He sits there, not moving a muscle and allowing the awkward air to rapidly surround us. He notices I'm staring at him. "What the hell are you looking at?" He crosses his arms in front of his chest.

"You kinda froze there. Oh my God, are you malfunctioning?" Sarcasm is present in my voice.

"No, I'm not malfunctioning. I'm not a toy. I'm a human being," he says with a straight face.

I laugh. "Yeah, you keep telling yourself that." I breathe out through my nose. "God, why are you like this?"

"Like what?" He presses his lips together, studying my face.

"It's like you have your humanity turned off. Your mom is showing enough emotions for ten people. Guys can show their emotions too. It's okay, you won't look weak." My chest rises and falls.

"Just because I'm not showing how I feel physically doesn't mean I'm not losing it mentally. I need to be strong for my family. Don't assume things you don't know."

"Why? You did it to me all the time. What makes this any different?"

"I've changed. I've grown up. I can't say the same about you."

I point at him. "See. You just made an assumption about me. You don't even realize you do it."

"Neither do you."

"Oh, shut up." I scrunch my face.

Noah rocks from side to side in his chair, gripping the side of it with his hands to balance himself. He places one hand over his chest as his eyes roam around.

I lower my eyebrows to express my confusion. "You are malfunctioning!"

"Fuck off," he says with a straight face.

"Someone took their cranky pills this morning."

He's not looking me in the eyes, but he's not avoiding me. "If you're just going to be a p-pain in the ass, leave. You're not fucking h-helping."

His lips are twitching.

His hands are shaking.

His chest is rapidly heaving.

"Sit down," I say.

"I am sitting down!" He grunts, staring at me intensely. "Dani." His tone is stern rather than upset.

I pull up a chair, moving it in front of him. "You're having a panic attack, aren't you?"

"No, of course not." He pauses for dramatic effect. "Yes, I'm having a fucking panic attack."

Here I am, letting my guard down to help a guy I've hated since I was a kid.

I know what it feels like when you have nothing but the worst thoughts cycling inside your mind and when it feels like they don't want to go away. It's the only excusable reason.

"Look at me," I demand.

He ignores me, staring at the floor.

"Noah, will you look at me?" I roll my eyes, shaking my head. "I'm *trying* to help you."

He picks his head up and his eyes lock on mine. "I don't need your help," he bites out, his breath staggering.

"I'm going to need you to do some basic breathing exercises. Can you do that?"

He nods and closes his eyes, raising his chest and letting it fall.

When his chest heaving slows down, he opens his eyes and examines his surroundings. "What the hell just happened?"

"It's a technique I learned from my therapist. She taught me that breathing helps get you out of the depths of your mind." I clear my throat. "I have anxiety. I get panic attacks, too. I bet you don't remember because you were always so busy in Noahland."

"Noahland, huh?"

"You were always wrapped up in your own world. You didn't give a shit about anything, or anyone, outside of it."

"And there you are making assumptions again."

"I'm not making an assumption. It's a fact."

"You just stated an opinion which is much different than stating a fact since facts are usually backed up by evidence."

"Okay, we're not in science class, dumbass." I burst out into laughter.

He narrows his eyes. "What the hell is so damn funny?"

"You know, you could thank me. I could've let you have a full-on panic attack in front of everybody here."

He chuckles, licking his lips. "I mean you kinda did."

A small smile tugs on the corners of my lips as I lean back on the chair. "Whatever."

"Not that you probably care, but I do remember you have anxiety. I may have been an oblivious asshole, but I did pay attention to some things outside of my time in Noahland. Just putting that shit out there."

If he's known I've had anxiety all this time, why would he keep that to himself? God, why am I wasting my time on this? Why am I wasting my time on him? This is ridiculous. No, he's being ridiculous.

"You're still an asshole," I fire back.

"And you're still a bitch," he says.

"This is exactly why I didn't want to come here."

I get up, rubbing my eyes and leaning my head back.

"And what reason is that?"

"I knew I'd have to deal with you."

He gets up off his chair, walking closer to me. "Dani Solomon never backs down from a challenge, though, right?" He stands taller. "She *never* admits defeat."

"Don't put words into my mouth. And don't talk about me in the third person."

He rolls his eyes. "Yeah, like I'll listen to you."

"I expect nothing less."

CHAPTER FOUR

We've been at the hospital for hours now.

Don't ask me the specific number because I have no idea what that number is.

I mean, I'm at the hospital, anxiously waiting for news about Dad and my sister. I never imagined I'd be here. At least, not for something like this.

It's moments like these that make me re-evaluate what I've been doing with my life and not take things for granted.

I've spent the last several years working on a book I believed would never see the light of day. My dad is the one who convinced me I should publish it. He convinced me I should share my talent with the world which is fucking terrifying, but it's worth it if I'm able to connect with readers.

Not taking things for granted is something I don't think about often, mostly because I've never been in a situation where I didn't have to think about it.

Until right now.

Mom fell asleep next to me which doesn't surprise me because I could tell how exhausted she is. She's been running on a never-ending hamster wheel since we got here this morning.

Celia fell asleep next to Dani with her head nuzzled into her neck.

One of the nurses brought over a couple more chairs for them to sit on.

I turn to my right, noticing that Dani is glaring at me.

"What?" I say in a whisper.

She rolls her eyes, puckering her lips out. "Nothing."

"No, please, enlighten me. I beg you."

"I forgot how irritating you are.

"Oh, I'm irritating. That's funny. You're the queen of being irritating."

I love annoying her because the look on her face is always priceless. I wish I could take a mental picture and store it in my brain forever.

Her bold eyebrows furrow and her cheeks turn a rosy color. "God, I hate you."

"Well, I'm glad we're on the same page about something."

She fakes a laugh, rolling her eyes and sticking up her middle finger at me.

Before we can say anything else, a woman in her thirties walks over to us. She's average height with dirty blonde hair tied into a low ponytail and blue eyes.

"Hi, I'm Dr. Caitlyn Miller. Are you Benjamin and Elizabeth Kaplan's family?"

Breathe, Noah. Just breathe.

I lightly rub my mom's shoulder to wake her up. "Mom. The doctor is here."

She jumps, practically flies, out of her seat like something just bit her on the ass.

We all stand, getting up from the chairs we've all been sitting in for hours.

"I'm sorry. What was your question?" Mom asks Dr. Miller.

"Are you Benjamin and Elizabeth Kaplan's family?"

"Yes. I'm Benjamin's wife and Elizabeth's mother." She puts her arm around my shoulder, pulling me to her so hard it makes me lose feeling in my body for a few seconds. "This is my son, Noah. We've been here for hours and nobody has given us any updates."

"Here's the good news. Your daughter is unconscious, but she will make a full recovery. The impact didn't severely damage any vital organs, but she has a long road to recovery ahead," Dr. Miller explains.

Thank God.

I can see some relief wipe across my mom's face. As Mom releases me from her grasp, I can breathe.

Celia seems relieved too. She walks over to my mom, wrapping her arm around her. My mom rests her head in the crook of Celia's neck.

"What about my husband?"

"Mrs. Kaplan, your husband suffered severe damage to several vital organs. He's still in surgery," Dr. Miller tells us.

Fuck, fuck, fuck.

My mom's facial expression quickly shifts from hope to hopelessness.

Tears flow from her eyes and her breathing is heavy. Celia guides her back to a chair and sits down next to her.

Dani stands there, staring at the wall in front of her. It's like she's immobile and frozen in time.

A nurse puts a thumbs up in the air at Dr. Miller, signaling to the doctor that she's needed back in the surgery room.

I can't form cohesive thoughts in my head because none of this feels real. I'm living a nightmare. One that I can't wake up from.

Let me wake up. Please. I'm begging you.

I can see my mom. Celia's fingers are red from how tight my mom's grip is on her.

Dani stares off into the distance, her hands intertwining in her lap and her legs are shaking.

I'm sitting in between her and my mom.

I turn my head towards Dani. "Will you cut it out?"

"Am I annoying you?"

She knows that my buttons are incredibly easy to push right now. I hate that she's trying to pick a fight with me right now after the doctor told us my father is still in surgery.

I huff. "Honestly, you are. Are you just here to screw with me? Because if you are, you can walk out of this hospital right now. My dad is in surgery. My sister is unconscious. My mom is an emotional wreck. I'm not in the mood for this shit!"

Getting up from my chair, I storm off before she can say anything else that will piss me off.

I end up pacing down a small corridor for what feels like forever.

Three hours have passed by since my dad was taken in for surgery.

I can see some of the nurses sitting at the giant desk area in the middle of the fourth floor occasionally glancing at me.

I'm officially losing my mind.

Oh, the irony.

"Noah." I hear Dani's voice call my name from the other side of the room.

I glare at her when I walk past her and continue to pace. When I come back to complete another lap, Dani's standing in front of my pathway.

"Noah, stop pacing. You're making me dizzy."

Tough shit. I don't care about making you dizzy. I care about my dad making it through this surgery.

Just as I turn my back, she grabs my wrist. Her thumb gently rubs the inner skin in a windshield wiper motion.

What the hell is going on?

I stretch out my hand to express my discomfort, but she doesn't let go.

Her face softens as she meets my gaze. "I'm sorry, okay? You don't have to accept my apology. I wouldn't if I was you." She takes a deep breath. "I'm not here to be a thorn in your side. I'm here because I love your mom. I love your dad. And I love Lizzie. They're like family to me. Your mom means the world to my mom. I'm hoping you know all this." She takes a deep breath. "I can tell how much you don't want me here and I don't want to cause you any more stress. And yes, I know I said you couldn't make me leave, but things change. If you really want me to go, I'll go."

Why do I feel like I just got punched in the face without actually getting punched in the face?

She waits for a response, but nothing comes out of my mouth.

"Okay, then...Well, I'd say it's been nice to see you, but we both know that's bullshit." She heads back to the chair she was sitting in to grab her bag.

Just as Dani is about to reach the elevators, Dr. Miller walks by her. She's walking towards my mom with a surgical mask slung around her neck. Sweat is dripping from her forehead down to her temples.

I'm running back to my mom like a bat out of hell.

Dani hangs back a bit, but enough to overhear the conversation between Dr. Miller and my mom.

Dr. Miller pulls Mom aside.

Celia has her arm around my mom, her thumb rubbing my mom's shoulder.

"Mrs. Kaplan." Dr. Miller's tone is firm and gentle, but her eyes say something entirely different.

"Dr. Miller, how is my husband?" My mom's voice is frantic and searching for Dr. Miller's face for a physical response.

"Mrs. Kaplan, I'm so sorry, but your husband didn't make it."

This is a fucking nightmare. This isn't real. This isn't happening right now.

I see my mom drop to the floor on her knees with her arms covering her face. Her wailing is piercing through my heart.

Celia gets on the floor, hugging my mom tight to comfort her.

Dani's shoulders are rising and falling, but she's not making any eye contact with me.

She's numb.

Just like I am.

"I wish there was more we could do," Dr. Miller says before she leaves us.

I shrug my shoulders, shaking my head. "What the hell is she talking about? What is she apologizing for?"

"Ah, the denial phase is setting in," Dani says to herself out loud.

"Oh, shut up, Dani," I reply.

"I'm not trying to be a bitch. I'm being serious."

Celia cuts our tizzy short. "It's your dad, Noah. H-he's gone."

My jaw trembles before I start laughing. "You're lying." I point my finger at her, my hand shaking and slightly realizing Dani's right.

I am in denial.

I try to put my left hand on the wrist of my right hand to stop it from shaking.

Why can't I stop it from shaking?

I attempt to find one of the plastic chairs in front of the wall and just barely make it. I look around my surroundings.

The room is spinning.

I can't breathe or move.

Fuck, it's happening again.

"Hey, look at me." Dani pulls one of the plastic chairs and places it in front of me. She sits down and delicately places both of her hands on my thighs. "Noah. Look at me."

I take my time, but I look at her.

"I'm not going to sugarcoat this all for you. I'm going to be brutally honest with you, which shouldn't surprise you. The next several months are going to be challenging as hell. But you're going to get through them. You're going to get through this. I know everybody says this. Everybody said this to me when my father passed away." She takes a deep breath in and out. "I know we fight a lot. I—I just want you to know how much I admire your strength. You never back down from a challenge. And you always persevere no matter how difficult things get. You'll get through this."

She gets up, but I reach out to grab her hand before she can walk away.

I forgot how soft her skin is. Wait, what the hell am I saying?

"Stay," I whisper.

She looks down at my hand intertwined with hers, glancing at me.

I've hated this woman for most of my life, but right now, I hate her a little less.

"Stay," I repeat, my voice coming out as a breathy whisper. I run my tongue along the inside of my mouth.

"Are you sure? Because there's no turning back if you change your mind later. Just saying."

"Don't make me regret this, Solomon." I'm laughing when I should be bawling my eyes out.

I need this. I'm laughing so hard that my stomach starts to

hurt and the realization that my dad just passed away hits. The laughter fades away and turns into tears.

She doesn't say anything. Instead, she sits down next to me and holds my hand. She's looking up at me with those big brown eyes of hers.

This is when I realize I don't hate Dani Solomon.

CHAPTER FIVE

Noah's head is resting in the crook of my neck.

How the hell did we get here?

Hours ago, I was ready to punch him in the face and here I am holding his hand.

He fell asleep on me. I can barely look over my shoulder because the weight of his head is holding it down.

My arm has gone completely numb.

My hand is sweaty.

I swear I'm not complaining.

The thing is I know what it feels like being told that the person who raised you and loved you endlessly isn't here anymore.

The shock and fear of the unknown.

And not having any idea what's going to happen next is nerve-wracking.

I still have nightmares about the day my mom told me Dad passed away. They're not as vivid as the ones I had years ago, but they're enough to scare me awake.

There's one nightmare in particular I'll always remember.

I'm in the car with my dad and I see a car coming

straight at us. I'm shouting at him to turn around and watch out, but he doesn't hear me. The car slams directly into us, causing my dad's head to hit the steering wheel before the airbag deploys. I can't wake him up, even though I'm shaking him and screaming at the top of my lungs.

I wish these nightmares would stop, but my mind loves to torture me.

Unfortunately, I've gotten used to it.

My mom took Laura to the bathroom thirty minutes ago.

I unlock my phone and find my mom in my text messages. I start texting her with one hand, discovering it's not as easy as I'd thought it would be.

MOM

ME

are you guys okay? i'm starting to get worried

MOM

We're fine. I'm just helping Laura get some air

ME

why didn't you tell me you were going to do this before you left?

MOM

I'm sorry, Sweet Girl. Laura was freaking out in the bathroom, so I suggested we go outside for some fresh air. I think it's helping a little

How's Noah?

ME

sleeping like a log

MOM

He's been so wired today. He deserves to rest. Alright, we'll be back up soon

ME

okay

I glance over towards the window down the hall.

The sky has turned pitch black and all the desks are lit up thanks to desk lamps.

I've been here since around one in the afternoon, while Laura, Noah, and Mom have been here for several hours. Still, we're all ready to drop at any moment now.

"Did I fall asleep?" Noah asks, his sleepy eyes looking right up at me.

"Yes, you did."

He takes his head out of the crook of my neck and sits upright, rubbing his eyes with the knuckles of his index fingers. "Was I snoring? Please tell me I wasn't snoring. That would be so embarrassing," he says.

"You weren't snoring."

He's looking down both sides of the hallway for Laura. "Where's my mom?"

"My mom took her to get some fresh air. They'll be back up here soon."

He nods his head slowly, puckering his lips out.

After twenty minutes, our mothers make it back to us.

Laura looks so exhausted, it breaks my heart just to look at her. Her eyes are sunken in with dark circles underneath and her face is partially covered in red splotches. She can barely keep her eyes open. Her mascara has melted around where her dark black eyelashes start.

"I'm going to stay overnight with Lizzie," Laura says.

"No, you've been here all day. You need to get some rest," Mom tells Laura.

"Well, if my mom isn't staying, then that means I am." Noah's tone is confident.

"No, I'll stay. You've all been here for hours," I tell them.

Laura looks like she's going to say something, but doesn't. She's too tired to argue with me.

Noah stands there, staring at me.

I can't get a read on him and it's driving me nuts.

"Are you sure, honey?" Mom places her hand on my shoulder, tilting her head.

I nod. "Yes, I'm sure."

Gesturing to my mom and Laura to go, they do so without a fight.

Noah walks up to me and a breeze blows his minty scent my way. "Thank you."

Why does he have to smell so good? Why the hell am I paying attention to how he smells? Get a grip, Dani.

"For what?" A confused look appears all over my face.

"For what you did for me earlier and what you're doing for my family now."

"Oh, now you thank me. How sweet of you." I roll my eyes, crossing my arms in front of my chest.

"Sorry it took me so long."

"If only you apologized for all the other shit you've done, we'd be in a much better place. Also, you never have to thank me for helping your family. And you didn't have to thank me for what I did earlier. I'm just busting your balls." I lightly punch his arm.

I hear a sound come out of his mouth.

Licking my lips, I giggle. "Oh my God, did I hurt you?"

He shakes his head, squinting his eyes with his eyebrows furrowing. "No."

"You can tell me the truth. I heard you moan," I tease.

He walks closer to me. "Trust me, when I moan, you'll know," he whispers in my ear.

Oh, hell no. Not today, sir. Not ever.

I swallow and clear my throat. He takes a few steps back. We're at an arm's length away from each other now.

"Well, you're full of shit," I blurt out.

"Seems like I'm always full of shit when it comes to you." He rolls his eyes. "Good night, Dani." His jaw flexes, his Adam's apple bobbing up and down.

I grin, raising my eyebrows. "Yeah, good night."

I honestly have no idea how long Lizzie is going to be in the hospital for. I just know that I'm going to be here for all of it.

No matter how long it takes.

As I watch Noah leave, I wonder how these next few weeks or months are going to be.

We didn't kill each other which says a lot about the both of us.

I've changed.

He's changed from what I witnessed today.

I mean he's still an ass, but it doesn't annoy me to look at his stupid face with his annoyingly perfect features.

There's something about Noah Kaplan I can't put my finger on.

And it's bugging me.

I'm in Lizzie's room, trying my best not to stare at her too long, so I don't cry. It doesn't work. My eyes are glassy, and I can't stop the tears from falling.

She's lying there.

Her chest rises and falls.

The beeping of the machine that shows her pulse is something I will be hearing in my nightmares tonight.

Looking around the room, I can't help but feel the soul-sucking air swirling around me.

Lizzie's bed is against the back wall, leaving enough space

for the doctor and nurses to make their way around the machines and do what they need to do.

I walk over to her, delicately placing my hand on her shoulder. "I know you can't hear me, but I want to let you know I'm here. You're going to wake up. I love you so much, Lizbug."

Walking away from Lizzie, I find a giant cushy chair hanging out near the window with a blanket on the table across from it.

That's not a hospital blanket.

I graze my hand over the soft and plushy material.

It's a blanket from home.

How did she know?

Mom had to have known I'd show up because she wouldn't have brought this with her otherwise.

I used to use this blanket all the time when I was younger.

Nostalgia floods through my brain like old DVDs playing on an endless loop in a DVD player.

Snapping out of my nostalgic acid trip, I grab the plush material with both hands.

There's a pajama top gently folded on the big, long desk across from Lizzie's bed. Something else I know my mom left for me because she's that kind of person.

I make sure no one is coming in before I remove my tank top.

My bra is next.

Slinging both of them over the back of the chair, I put on the pajama top. The soft cotton feels so nice against my skin.

Sitting down on the chair, I drape the blanket over my body.

Before I know it, everything fades to black.

My eyes slowly open and it takes a bit for everything in my view to appear clear.

I lightly rub my eyes, stretching my arms out wide.

The sunlight is breaking its way into the hospital room.

"Good morning, Sleeping Beauty." A deep voice says to me.

I lower my head and see Noah standing in the room with what looks like drinks from Kailani's Cafe in his hands. I can see the green logo with two pink hibiscus chilling on the front of the cup.

Kailani's is the hotspot for coffee and snacks in Sunset Cove.

"I *don't* drink coffee," I reply in a hushed tone.

Slowly getting up from the chair, gravity takes the blanket off for me.

Noah studies my face and body, making me feel uneasy and uncomfortable at the same time.

"I *know*. I got you an unsweetened iced tea," he says, handing me the drink.

I raise an eyebrow. "Thank...you." A sliver of a smile appears on my face because this guy just gave me caffeine.

He remembers I don't drink coffee. Interesting. Very interesting.

Noah bites down on his bottom lip, staring at my tank top.

Why the hell is he biting his lip?

He starts singing out of nowhere. "Who's the leader of the club that's made for you and me?"

I look at him like he's crazy, tilting my head and lowering my eyebrows.

He walks a little closer to me and points at my shirt which has all the classic Disney characters on it. "M-I-C-K-E-Y M-O-U-S-E!" He raises his voice.

Oh, hell no.

I shake my head, flattening my lips. "If you must know, my mom brought this shirt from home. It's actually quite comfortable. And soft."

"I bet it is." He takes a long pause, scanning my tank top. His eyes are staring deep into my soul. "It's cute." He smirks.

Are you kidding me? I can't handle this shit.

Awkward silence fills the room. This is when I realize I'm not wearing a bra. It's slung over the chair.

Seriously, how could I forget I'm not wearing a bra?

No wonder why his eyes keep wandering to my breasts. Panic mode sets in. Wrapping my arms around my chest as quickly as possible, I can hear the sound of a slap from my hand landing too hard on my arm.

He's still staring at me.

"Do you mind turning around?" I gesture to him with my finger in a circular motion.

I can hear his heavy breathing which makes chills appear up and down my arms. I swallow deeply.

I take a glance at the back of Noah's body.

Damn, his back muscles are impressive.

My eyes wander down to his ass.

What the hell am I doing?

My heart is pounding and adrenaline kicks into high gear.

Biting my lip, I put on my shirt and the shorts I wore yesterday. They're all I have to wear right now so they're going to have to do for now.

"You can turn back around," I say.

He turns back around, placing his iced coffee on the desk. His gaze meets mine as he walks closer to me. "Were you just checking me out?"

Does he have eyes in the back of his head?

"What the hell would make you think that?"

He's so close to me I tense up a bit.

He crosses his arms over his broad chest. This makes his muscles flex even more than when his arms are hanging by the sides of his body.

Why am I paying attention to these things?

Those goddamn black thick-framed glasses he's wearing are doing things to me. He looks like Buddy Holly. An insanely attractive version of Buddy Holly.

Snap out of it, Dani.

"It's okay if you were," he says, smirking.

I roll my eyes, grinning at his smug face. "In your dreams, Kaplan."

His mouth finds my ear. "If we're telling the truth here, I totally wasn't checking you out either." He winks his left eye as he pulls away.

Gulping a lump of saliva down my throat, I look away to avoid any eye contact.

What the hell was that?

He steps back more, so there's a good amount of space between us.

I don't get it. I was dreading coming here because I knew I'd run into Noah. It was inevitable considering he's part of the family. What I didn't know was that I'd be losing my mind over his toned muscles. And his constant staring.

Those ocean blue eyes of his are going to kill me.

CHAPTER SIX

Of course, I was checking Dani out.

How could I not?

Why would I tell her that I was? That's just weird.

When she got up from the chair, I nearly lost my fucking mind. She was wearing nothing else underneath her tank top. Her hard nipples kept peaking through.

Fuck, I can't stop staring at her. Okay, this is not the time nor the place for this right now.

Before I can say anything, Celia walks into the room.

She goes over to Dani, placing a hand on her shoulder. "Good morning, honey. How did you sleep?"

"Like shit. It's hard to sleep when nurses are coming in every hour to check on Lizzie. But, it's okay. She's more important than sleep."

This is when my eyes pull towards the hospital bed my sister is lying in.

God, I hope she wakes up. She has to wake up.

Dani has been a nice distraction from everything going on because I'm trying hard to not focus on the chaos. It's not because I'm in denial and I don't want to accept what happened.

Life is easier when you ignore the bad shit and live in a world where positivity is the only thing that exists. That's why I've been living in Noahland all my life because it's easier. I get to make the rules and I'm able to turn the world off when it's necessary.

And right now, I want to shut everything off.

Celia nods and turns to me. "Can I steal you for a moment?" Her voice takes me out of my deep thoughts.

I lightly furrow my eyebrows. "Sure."

She gestures to Dani to go wait out in the hallway.

Once she leaves, Celia stares at me with her big, brown eyes that look like her daughter's. "I need you to stay with Dani. I know this is a lot to ask of you since you two don't get along, but I don't know who else to ask. I just don't feel comfortable leaving her alone in the vulnerable state that she's in. When Jacob passed away, she was knee-deep in anxious thoughts. It got so bad to the point where she missed half of her freshman year of high school. I don't want that to happen again."

There's no goddamn way.

"Uh...I don't think that's a good idea." I say.

"Noah, I'm going to be honest with you right now. I care about my daughter's mental health and maybe it wouldn't be such a horrible thing for you two to spend some time together. Maybe, you'll actually get along for a change. I'm going to stay at your house to help out your mom. I want to be there to help her out when Lizzie wakes up."

I roll my head around, exhaling. "Fine, I'll do it."

I highly doubt we're going to get along.

"Thank you, Sweet Boy," she says, placing her hand on my shoulder before she walks out of the room.

Dani peeks her head into the room. "Grayson is here and there's another guy I don't know who's with him."

I rush out of the room and see my best friends walking towards me.

Grayson looks like he just rolled out of bed with his tousled dark hair and wrinkled shirt compared to Xander's perfectly placed dark curls and wrinkle-free shirt.

They look tougher than they are with ink covering both of their arms—Xander with significantly less than Grayson, his tattoos popping against his tan skin.

It's not that it didn't occur to me to text them and tell them what was going on. A lot of shit has happened in the last twenty-four hours.

These guys are like my brothers, especially Grayson. I've known the guy since we were in elementary school. It wasn't until high school that Xander joined our trio.

We're family.

"Dude, I'm so sorry about your dad," Grayson tells me, his voice full of concern. He hugs me and lovingly taps me repeatedly on the back with the palm of his hand.

"Your mom called us because she thought we'd want to know what happened. Why the hell didn't you tell us about this yesterday, man?" Xander asks, meeting my gaze.

"This is why." I gesture to their faces full of pity. "Look, I'm happy you guys are here, but I need some time alone, okay? I-"

I get cut off when their heads turn towards Dani coming out of Lizzie's hospital room.

Grayson crosses his arms across his chest, sticking his tongue out enough to wet his lips. He glares at me, shaking his head.

"Holy shit! Well, if it isn't the famous Dani Solomon!" Grayson shouts as he goes over to her, picking her up.

Her body is stiff, barely moving and her eyes are widening so much they might pop out of her head

Why is he picking her up like that? Why is it bothering me so much?

"Put me down!" she demands, slapping his back and flailing her arms all over the place.

He gently places her back on the ground before she smacks his arm.

"So, you need some alone time, huh?" he whispers, smirking and raising his eyebrows at me.

I shush him, telling him to cut it out by narrowing my eyes and doing a swiping motion under my neck to make him stop.

Dani's eyes meet Xander's, her face softening and becoming full of intrigue. "I don't think we've met before."

"We haven't, but I have heard a lot about you." He sticks out his hand. "I'm Xander."

She slides her hand into his, their hands interlocking for a shake. "Nice to meet you. I'm Dani."

I roll my eyes, placing my hands on the temples of my forehead.

She walks away from Xander and leans up against the concrete wall opposite my sister's room. She observes our conversation, studying my facial expressions and body movements.

This is making me uncomfortable.

"Is there anything we can do?" Grayson asks, sincerity cutting through his voice like a sharp knife.

"I think you guys should stay for a little while," Dani suggests. "It would be good for Noah to be surrounded by some *testosterone* for a couple of hours or so. I mean he's been around women for the past twenty-four hours."

Xander raises his eyebrows.

Grayson opens his mouth. "She's not wrong."

She walks over to me. "I'm going to go home. I desperately need a shower."

Now I'm picturing her naked body in the shower. Make it stop.

"Tell the guys how you feel. It doesn't hurt to share your

emotions once in a while," she tells me, walking towards the elevators.

She mouths "breathe" to me, then the elevator doors open and she steps inside. The doors close 30 seconds later and she's gone.

When I turn around, Grayson and Xander are staring at me with the same smug looks written all over their faces.

"What?" I ask, narrowing my eyes.

"When are you finally going to tell Dani you're in love with her?" Grayson blurts out.

Ugh, not this shit again.

Xander chuckles softly, he covers his mouth in an attempt to hide the fact.

I grunt, rolling my eyes. "What the hell are you talking about?"

"You're so full of shit, Noah. You've been crazy about this woman since we were kids." Grayson pauses. "You continue denying your feelings buddy. I hope you know that burying them only makes it worse."

"I don't know what the hell you're talking about. I don't have feelings for Dani. I never have and never will." I point to the hospital room behind me. "Do you see the room behind me? My sister is in there, lying on a bed unconscious. My dad passed away yesterday. This shit with Dani is irrelevant right now. Can we drop it...please?" I beg.

He puts both of his hands up. "Alright, I'll shut up about it."

"Thank you," I say through a deep breath.

"You do know he's never going to shut up about this, right?" Xander adds, the right side of his mouth curving up to form half of a smile.

"I know," I say.

This is exactly why I didn't call them. I knew Grayson would lose his mind over Dani being here because he's convinced I'm hopelessly in love with her.

I'm not *hopelessly* in love with her. I have no idea what I'm feeling, but I know it isn't love.

God, my brain doesn't feel like it's connected to my body anymore.

Yesterday didn't feel real, none of this does.

It's a nightmare that I can't escape.

I wish I could go back in time and be the only one in the car. Dad would be alive. Lizzie wouldn't be lying in a hospital bed. I would be. Or better yet, I wish I was in Dad's place. Sounds morbid, but I do.

Dad had so many more years to live.

It's not fair some asshole decided to cut his life short.

Maybe Grayson brought up the whole "love" thing with Dani to get my mind off everything that's happened in the past twenty-four hours.

But the reality is my dad passed away.

He's gone and he's never coming back.

Get your shit together, man. You need to be strong for Mom and Lizzie.

"What exactly happened yesterday?" Grayson asks, pulling me back to reality while loosely combing his fingers through his dark brown locks.

"It's a long story," I reply.

"We've got time," he responds.

"Yeah, we do," Xander echoes.

I sit on one of the chairs against the wall in front of Lizzie's room while Grayson and Xander are sitting across from me.

I tell them how Dad and Liz ended up here at the hospital, the car accident, Dad passing away, and how my sister's recovery is going to be a long one.

They listen intently, allowing me to pour out my feelings which is something I don't do often.

Xander opens his mouth and says, "I'm sorry the last twenty-four hours have been so shitty for you, man."

"We're just happy that you weren't alone through all of this. If you were, we would've run a marathon to get here." Grayson adds. "Next time something bad happens in our lives, we need to tell each other."

I nod. "Agreed."

Xander gives us a thumbs up. "You got it, dude."

Grayson has this look on his face I can't describe, but I have a feeling that I know what's coming. "Can we acknowledge the elephant that left the room? The pretty elephant, might I add." He tilts his head, raising his eyebrows over and over again

She's a lion, always ready to go in for the kill.

"Dude, she's not an elephant. And I told you to stop talking to me about this." I stand my ground.

"Sorry, bad analogy." Grayson blinks his eyes. "Noah, I've known you since we were kids. I've known Dani since we were kids. I've never seen you two in a room together without looking like you were going to murder each other. The energy felt different when Xander and I got here. Care to enlighten us, bro?"

He's so adamant about this it's getting on my damn nerves. I know what's going to happen if I don't talk about it though. He's going to bother the shit out of me about it until I do, so I cave.

"Fine, dumbass. I'll enlighten you. I thought Dani being here would be annoying as hell, but it turns out it isn't. So. Far."

Xander grins while Grayson has this smug look on his face I want to slap off. I don't know why they're both looking at me like that. "What?"

"Nothing," Grayson says. "Nothing at all."

Xander clears his throat so loud that the nurses at the front desk stare at us for a solid minute.

"Just say it." My sarcasm is present because I want this interrogation to be over already.

Grayson turns towards Xander. "Do you want to take this or should I?"

"I mean you've known him longer, but let me take this one. You deserve a break," Xander says as he stretches his arm to pat Grayson on the back.

Grayson crosses his arms over his broad chest and gets up to move his chair against the wall. He leans against the concrete wall. "Take it away, man."

Xander gets up and moves his chair on the left side of me against the wall. Now, I'm in the middle of these two dumbasses.

"I know I just met Dani, but I've heard you talk about her non-stop throughout high school. You guys weren't even talking anymore by the time we became friends. From what I just witnessed here today, I can say with confidence that you, Noah Matthew Kaplan, are undeniably in love with this woman."

I stare off into the distance ahead, my mouth partially open and my eyebrows furrowing to express my annoyance. I close my mouth and whip my head in Xander's direction.

My annoyance shifts into laughter, vibrating down to my stomach. "You literally just met her. How are you so confident about this? Wait, I see what's going on here. Did Grayson put you up to this shit?"

A small smile appears on Xander's face. "No, he didn't. It's just an observation I made."

Just an observation, my ass.

"Let's change the subject. You told us everything that happened. You didn't tell us *exactly* what happened to your dad. Does the doctor know *how* it happened?" Grayson takes in what he said and rephrases. "Sorry, that didn't come out right. What I meant was—"

I cut him off. "I know what you meant. Dr. Miller told us his organs shut down due to the impact of the accident. Some asshole side-swiped them," I say with a straight face, feeling my insides crushing piece by piece.

Xander walks over to me, arms spreading out until they

wrap around me. At first, it makes me uncomfortable since I'm not the biggest fan of physical touch. Not right now anyway. But, I don't mind it.

I hate when I'm in situations that are beyond my control.

I freeze with my arms pinned straight down both sides of my body. Eventually, I defrost my frozen, cold-hearted exterior and sink into the embrace. Our hands lightly pat each other's backs.

Grayson is standing there with this sickeningly sweet expression written all over his face, tilting his head to the left and nodding.

"You're an idiot," I say.

Grayson smiles at me, laughing. "Hate to break it to you, but we're both idiots. We're founding members of The Idiot Club."

"Hey, why am I not a part of The Idiot Club?" Xander is appalled at the idea that he wouldn't be considered a founding member.

I beat Grayson before he can say something sarcastic and dumb. "You've always been a part of it. You just don't want to accept it."

I pull away from Xander's hug and give him a playful punch below his left shoulder.

Xander rolls his eyes. "Oh, shut the hell up."

"Okay, we've made it abundantly clear we're all proud members," I tell the guys. "I have to go home and pack. Celia wants me to stay at the house with Dani because she doesn't feel comfortable leaving her alone."

"I'm sorry. Come again. Dani's mom wants you to stay with her? At her house?" Grayson's tone is full of sarcasm.

I roll my eyes. "Yes, dipshit."

"Oh, this is going to be *interesting*," Xander adds.

"Yeah, yeah, whatever," I say.

"Look at you with your big boy words. You really are a

writer, aren't you? Aren't you?" Grayson rushes over to me, scratching the top of my head like I'm a human-sized dog.

Luckily, Xander comes to my rescue and I'm able to escape Grayson's grasp.

Slapping Grayson's wrist, I proceed to fix my hair and try to put certain tendrils back into place afterward. "You really are an idiot."

"Haven't we already established this?" Grayson puts his top lip over his bottom one, shrugging his shoulders.

"I don't know if Lizzie's going to wake up, and I don't want to miss it if it happens." My thoughts come out as one messy sentence.

Xander walks towards me and places his hands on my shoulders. "We'll stay here. I'll text you if something happens."

"We both know there's another reason you want to go home. We also know the reason isn't at your home, but at another home down the street. The home you're being forced to stay at where a particular brunette resides." Grayson's idiocracy is on full display yet again.

What a surprise.

"What?" Xander and I say in unison.

Grayson opens his mouth again and I just know it's going to be something sarcastic and stupid. "Say hi to Dani for me, will you?"

"Do you ever just think to yourself, 'Wow, now might be a good time to shut the hell up and not say anything'?" Xander punches Grayson on the upper part of his left arm.

"Death makes me uncomfortable." Grayson shrugs his shoulders.

I check my back pocket to make sure my phone, car keys, and set of keys for the house are in there. And we're good.

I glance into my sister's room to see if she might wake up.

She's lying there with her eyes shut, chest rising and lowering itself back into place.

God, I hate seeing her like this. It breaks my heart.

"We got this, bro. Go!" Xander pats my back.

"Thanks. Bye, losers." I walk away from the guys, heading towards the elevators.

The button for the elevators lights up as I press it.

Here I am standing at the hospital.

I'm about to go pack up my stuff and drop it off at my childhood rival's house. All because her mother is forcing me to stay with her.

I know I could've said no, but the look on Celia's face was genuine. I could tell she was genuinely worried about Dani.

But, at the same time, what the hell is Celia thinking?

Why did she think having me stay with Dani would be a good idea?

It's a horrible idea.

The doors to one of the elevators open.

I'm so exhausted. My eyes are struggling to stay open and my body feels sluggish. I think I ended up getting three hours of sleep last night. Honestly, I don't know how anybody sleeps after going through a traumatic event like that.

When I reach the lobby, I take a deep breath and walk out of the elevator.

I debate on whether or not to run to the bathroom. Ultimately, I decided against it and headed towards the sliding glass doors. They open when they sense me approaching them.

Once I make my way into the parking lot, I search for my Subaru Forester.

You know how you forget where you park your car in a giant parking lot? Yeah, that's what's happening to me right now.

It takes me a solid three minutes to find my car—the Sunset Cove University magnet I have on the back helps. It stands out with the school's signature teal, accompanied by a palm tree and birds.

My body goes into autopilot as I pull the keys out from my back pocket to unlock the car. Getting in the driver's seat, I put my phone and house keys in the cup holder. The sound of silence fills the car as I turn it on and back out of the parking space.

The hospital is a fifteen-minute drive to Crystal Harbor, the neighborhood Dani and I grew up in.

Even with everything going on in my head, I can't help but think about her the entire drive home.

Is she okay? What is she doing? Why the hell do I care? No, seriously, why do I care so much?

This is the woman who'd steal my shit when I wasn't looking. The woman who would try to crush me at *War of Words*, but would unfortunately fail at it.

She's the kind of woman who never admits defeat, and I can't help but admit that it's a quality I've admired about her since we were teenagers.

Either way, I can't imagine any of this is easier for her.

Part of me wishes I could go back and be there for Dani. I'm just not sure if she would've wanted me there for her.

I wouldn't if I was her.

CHAPTER SEVEN

BELLA

ME

hey bells, can you come pick me up?

i need to go home and take a nice, hot shower

I stare off into space.

All I can think about is Noah. I want to know what's going on that head of his which is covered in that thick, dirty blonde hair.

Wow, what is going on with me?

The elevator dings and the doors open, snapping me out of my staring contest with the interior of the doors in front of me.

BELLA

I'm in the car. Do you want to talk about what happened?

ME

i'd rather talk to you about everything in person

Walking down the hallway of the main floor of the hospital, I drag my feet along the way. I'm about to reach the sliding glass doors when I realize I need to go to the bathroom. Turning around, I push the door open to enter the ladies' room.

Strutting out of the bathroom stall, I look up at my reflection in the mirror as I wash my hands.

My eyes are a little red and glassy.

I really didn't get enough sleep last night to function like a normal human today, but I don't care.

I'd do it again.

For Lizzie.

I walk towards the sliding glass doors and feel the warm, humid Florida air slapping me in the face. I stand a little toward the left of the doors near a bush full of pink Jessica Pentas until I hear a buzzing noise and run away like a child.

I don't like anything that crawls, moves, or flies.

Never have and never will.

BELLA

For the record, I would never text and drive.
I'm speaking into my phone

ME

that's still texting and driving

BELLA

It's speaking and driving. there's a difference

Bella's Jeep Wrangler turns into the hospital entrance.

She pulls up in front of me, rolling the window down. "Hey, what have I missed?"

"Uh, where's my car?"

"Oh, you know me, I can't stay away from this baby for too long." She slides her hand down the steering wheel and turns her head towards me. "I took yours home, it's waiting for you. Anyway, fill me in on what's going on."

I turn my sarcastic charm on. "Oh, you know, just your basic run-of-the-mill stuff. My mom's best friend's husband passed away. And her daughter has a long ass road to recovery ahead of her. No biggie."

I get into the passenger seat, placing my purse in front of me on the floor and buckling my seatbelt in. I close my eyes and take a deep breath.

There's an underlying look of concern that takes over Bella's face. "Dani, I'm so sorry." She pulls me in for an embrace that's squeezing tears out of me. "How's Laura?"

"She's a mess."

"And how are you?" she asks, her eyes searching for an emotional response from me.

"I'd say about the same."

"Dani, I know this is hard for you. I also know how much Ben meant to you. Please talk to me."

I bring my legs up to my chest.

God, I hate talking about grief. It's a vicious never-ending cycle.

I'm staring at the dashboard because I can't make eye contact with her. "I've known Ben since I was a baby. *A baby, Bella.* Losing him feels like I lost Dad all over again." I pause for a brief moment. "When my dad passed away, Ben became a father figure for me. He was my personal cheerleader. During the remainder of my high school career, he'd cheer me on. Whether it was for academic achievements or progress I made on my novel despite his son's disapproval and the fact that we stopped talking altogether. When mom called the Kaplans to tell them I got accepted into SCU, I could hear him cursing and screaming like crazy." I catch my breath as tears continue streaming out of my eyes. "Watching the way Noah completely shut down after Dr. Miller told him Ben passed away, it felt like I traveled back in time to when Mom told me about Dad passing away."

Bella looks at me tenderly. "I don't know what it's like to lose a father. *Not that way.* But, I do know this, you're going to blame yourself. Even if it's not your fault. I know you did this when your dad passed away. It's unfortunately become some-what normal for people who lose their loved ones. Even if they don't *actually* pass away. Even if they just *leave.*" Her lips quiver, eyes blinking to stop the tears from forming. "Dani, you're one of the strongest people I know. You're going to get through this. And I know your relationship with Noah hasn't always been *the best.* But, you're going to have to put your animosity aside. He needs you."

He needs you.

Her words hit me straight in the chest, shooting into my heart.

She switches gears on me. "While we're on the subject of Noah, how was it seeing him for the first time in five years?"

Confusing as hell. Can we just go?

"The same. He's still the same irritating piece of shit. Nothing's really changed."

She squints her eyes at me. It's like she knows I'm lying and telling the truth at the same time. "Yeah, yeah, that's great and all. Not surprising he hasn't grown out of his 'I'm an asshole and I don't care' phase. I want to know what he looks like compared to the last time you saw him."

I lift one of my eyebrows up, expressing my confusion. I hesitate before asking this, but I end up blurting it out anyway. "Why?"

She looks at me, puckering her lips out and her eyes start looking around in different directions. "Oh, you know, for research purposes."

I roll my eyes, giving her my best sarcasm-filled laugh. "Right, sure. For research purposes." I wink at her, shaking my head.

She raises her eyebrows up and down and a wicked grin appears across her face. "This is important information. Now, spill it."

I let out a breath. "I don't know. He looks the same. Just older."

"Well, duh. Of course, he looks older. You're going to need to be more specific. I can say if he looks anything like he did five years ago, you're in trouble. Deep. Trouble."

Not helping, Bella.

I close my eyes, letting silence consume the car for a couple of minutes, there's no way I could look at her right now.

Bella takes a quick glance at me, her mouth opening wide

despite trying to keep her focus on the road. "Danielle Solomon, are you telling me he got even more attractive?"

I place my hands on my warm cheeks. A half smile appears on my face, eventually turning into a full smile. "This is ridiculous."

She smirks. "He did, didn't he?"

"I can't confirm, nor deny."

"You're so full of shit. C'mon, tell me. I'm dying to know. You didn't text me at all yesterday to rant about him or anything. Something's obviously changed."

"To be completely honest with you, we were able to be in the same room without murdering each other for the first time in...*forever*. When I was in the elevator going up to the fourth floor, I was dreading having to see his stupid face again. That all changed when he had two panic attacks."

Her mischievous facial expression transforms into one that reeks of motherly instincts. "Oh, Dani."

"I saw too much of myself in him both times and it freaked me the hell out. I knew I had to help him. I mean, I was helping Noah—a guy I've hated since we were kids. A guy who always tried to crush me at everything. Whether it was school or a dumb board game." I pause to catch my breath. "I ended up holding his hand. He fell asleep in the crook of my neck. That's not even the crazy part, though."

Eagerness is written all over Bella's face. "There's more? Please tell me there's more!"

"Oh, there's more...I slept over at the hospital last night to keep an eye on Lizzie. He brought me an iced tea this morning because he knows I don't like coffee. He sang the Mickey Mouse March song to me. I haven't heard that song since I was a kid. Anyways, my dumbass forgot I took off my bra the night before. He kept staring at my breasts!"

"Oh, shit!" She brings her hands to her mouth, covering it as the white part of her eyes gets bigger.

"I put my clothes on so fast. My eyes may or may not have wandered to his ass to get back at him." My lips pucker out towards the right side of my face and I shrug my shoulders.

"Okay, so let me get this straight. You were checking each other out?" A psychotic laugh comes out of Bella's mouth, catching me off guard so much it makes me jump.

I nod my head. "Uh-huh. Well, at least, I think so."

Hearing myself say all this stuff out loud to Bella makes it even more real.

It terrifies me because Noah has never been "sweet" to me. He's always been egotistical, annoying, and a total dickhead. He never used to compliment me, or dared to stare at my chest.

He was just a shitty human being.

He's not so shitty anymore.

"You never answered my question from earlier. Is he more attractive than he was five years ago?"

I cross my arms as my cheeks grow warm. "I can say without a doubt Noah Kaplan has gotten more attractive since the last time I saw him." My voice is full of sarcasm.

Why the hell did I just admit that out loud?

I tilt my head, raising my shoulder up a bit, so my head touches it.

Bella licks her lips. "I say this because I love you, and I want to be honest with you," she tells me as she puts the key into the ignition. "You're so fucked."

"Thank you for that. There's just something I don't understand. Why did all this have to happen now? Why did I choose now to do this?"

"Choose now to do what? Realize you might actually have feelings for Noah? Like, romantic feelings? Not the kind of feelings where you want to punch him in the face?"

I shrug.

As we drive, Bella stops bugging me about Noah as I take in the views of Sunset Cove.

It's a picturesque coastal small town with beaches and palm trees. The water is crystal clear blue with giant waves constantly crashing onto shore. The palm trees are standing proud and tall.

Our town is a hub for artists of all kinds and has been for decades. The art community keeps growing every single year. That's why Sunset Cove University offers so many incredible art programs for its students. As a creative individual, I'm very thankful I have access to them.

I'm grateful I was able to grow up in a town where I could walk to Loggerhead Beach from my house. Not a lot of people can say they had that. I am one of the lucky ones that can say they did.

Loggerhead opens a floodgate of memories.

There's one in particular I will always remember.

It was my seventh birthday.

Dad thought it would be fun to take Mom and me to the beach. The Kaplans joined us, including Noah. Probably because his parents forced him to go.

Lizzie and I built sandcastles for hours. We had our plastic shovels and molds to help us out.

Noah was miserable until he decided to run over our sandcastle masterpieces.

I was devastated. I gave him the dirtiest look while he was laughing like a villain from a cartoon movie. I got up and chased him a good distance down the beach until he just stopped running. He stopped right in front of me and stuck his tongue out at me.

For that, I punched him in the face.

His nose was bleeding.

I got yelled at.

He got yelled at.

Over the years, our teasing became dubbed as War of Words. We'd just obliterate each other with words. I looked forward to it, especially after my dad's passing. It distracted me from the grief-filled thoughts that consumed me every single day until it all came to a sudden halt.

Five years to be exact.

We're not those seven-year-old kids anymore.

Sometimes I miss being that age. It would be nice to not have to worry about responsibilities and hone in on a career that will help me live a stable life.

When you're a kid, everything seems so easy. You don't have to worry about paying bills, searching for a healthcare plan, or going to work to be able to afford rent and other necessities.

I'm pulled out of my memories as Bella pulls up to the front of the house. I didn't even realize how long I zoned out.

You can't get any more beachy than the Solomon family home.

It's a mid-sized two-story Colonial with an exterior that's covered in light grayish blue shingles, white detailing, and multiple shades of gray that make up the roof. What ties it all together is the front porch which overlooks a zoomed-out view of the ocean.

The front of the house is lined with an eye-catching variety of flowers. I missed seeing a home full of life and color. High-tower has nice landscaping but it doesn't compare to the magic Mom is able to create.

I haven't been home since Hanukkah.

That was six months ago.

I've had no reason to come back home because I've been so busy working on my debut novel and my coursework.

I've had no time to see Mom in person. There's not a day that goes by where we don't talk, whether it's through texting or FaceTime.

Bella turns to me. "Are you okay?"

I stare at the house, turning my head and peeling my eyes

towards her direction. "I know six months isn't a long time to be away, but it's strange being back here."

Bella switches positions, turning more in her seat to face me. "Six months is a pretty long time to be away from home, Dani. Especially when you only live an hour away."

I don't want to talk about how I'm feeling right now. I just want to go inside and take a shower. I need to wash off everything that happened over the last twenty-four hours.

"You don't need to come in with me. I'll text you when I'm done with my shower."

She nods. "You text me if you need anything. Not only when you're done with your shower. Okay?"

"Okay," I say.

Opening the car door, I slip out of Bella's car carefully since it has some height to it and I'm pretty short.

She waves at me as I slam the passenger car door shut. I hear the sound of her car driving away as I walk up to my front door.

When I unlock the door, I'm immediately overcome with emotion.

Dad's presence lingers throughout the house.

I can still picture him sitting on the sofa, watching TV. I can hear his laugh bouncing off the concrete walls and the sound of his voice.

That's the real reason why I haven't been back here. It's still hard to come back home and be reminded that he's not here. He'll never be here.

It's been almost an entire decade and I'm still not over it.

I don't think I'll ever be over it.

A year and a half after my dad's passing, I tried to convince Mom we should move. It would've been a fresh start for us. But, she didn't want to leave. She couldn't leave because leaving would've felt like abandoning Dad. Plus, she couldn't bear the thought of living more than five minutes away from Laura.

It's not just that, though.

Laura and Ben took care of us and supported us.

On the day that Dad passed away, Laura held my mom for hours on our sofa. For hours. Across them, Ben sat on the ottoman, holding her hand.

Lizzie and I spent countless hours together, laying in my bed and sharing my earbuds. We listened to *Pity Party* by Melanie Martinez, *Summertime Sadness* by Lana Del Rey, and *Cigarette Daydreams* by Cage the Elephant on repeat. It might have not been the best idea, but I needed some kind of a release.

Bella graciously offered for me to stay with her for a few months until I was ready to go back to my house. It was so hard for me to step foot in there. Way more difficult than it is now.

Her mom, Teresa, is the most generous and kindest human in the entire world. Her older sister, Valerie, is a year younger than Lizzie. She's one of the coolest human beings I've ever met.

I owe the entire Castillo-Ryder family so much for everything they did for me back then.

Noah had no idea what was going on during that time. He was living in his own world. Not giving a shit about anything or anyone for that matter.

I hate that he wasn't there. Not because I'm here for him now. It would've been the courteous thing to do, regardless of how much we hated each other. It just would've been nice if he was there.

If he was the one to hold me and not his sister.

If he was the one to hug me, and never let me go.

If he was the one to help with my panic attacks, read to me, hold my hand, and tell me it's going to get easier.

Unfortunately, that's all a fantasy inside my head that will never come true.

I shake my head, remembering where I am.

I'm home.

I take in my surroundings and try not to lose it. I'm emotionally vulnerable right now.

I see a small orange fuzzy thing run towards me.

It's Archie, our three-year-old short-haired ginger tabby.

He's meowing up a storm and rubbing my legs.

"Hey, little guy. I missed you," I tell him, picking him up with both of my hands.

He kisses me on the tip of my nose.

"Come on, buddy. We're going to take a shower. Well, me. Not you. Mom would kill me if I did that. And you would definitely hate me if I did that to you."

I grab my suitcase, and head to my childhood bedroom.

It's still the same as it was six months ago and even six years ago.

The walls are painted teal. The comforter on my bed is a mixture of different shades of blue with thick cream-colored blankets hanging on a diagonal towards the edge of my bed.

I gently throw my purse on my bed, turning around to face my bookcase.

My personal library is my favorite part of my entire bedroom because it's full of books from my adolescence.

Books have always been an escape for me.

I love that I'm able to dive into an alternate universe that isn't my own. And I'm lucky I get to experience that same feeling with writing. It's why I want to publish my own books.

I want to make readers feel every single emotion that exists by writing characters they can relate to.

After I examine my library, I go to my closet and grab a tank top and shorts.

Heading into the bathroom, I search for a couple of towels. I'm able to find a towel for my head and a towel wrap for my body—the kind you can wrap around with velcro across the top—in the small linen closet next to the door.

God, I'm so fucking tired.

After I finish combing any tangles out of my hair, it nearly doubles in size into a wavy frizz ball from all the humidity that decided to cling on to it.

I remove my clothes and throw them in the corner behind the door.

It's time to wash all the pain and worries away.

noah

The drive home is peaceful.

I'm singing along to one of my favorite songs by Guns N' Roses on my favorite Spotify playlist the entire time.

I belt the song out from start to finish. It's liberating since nobody is in the car with me complaining about my terrible singing voice. I'm incredibly off-key, but I couldn't care less.

I'm playing my imaginary guitar when I'm waiting at the traffic lights, not even worried if anybody's watching me.

Once the song is over, a smile forms on my face.

I feel free.

It's hard to not think about Dad when I listen to this playlist.

God, he had the best music taste.

He loved alternative and rock music and shared his love for those genres with me when I was a kid.

Pulling up to the house, I grab my phone and house keys out of the cup holder.

I turn the car off and close the driver's side.

Gently slamming it closed, I walk up to the front door.

It's like Sammy knows I'm home because there's a barking noise piercing its way through the door.

Sammy is our ten-year-old golden retriever and my best friend.

His nose nudges me in the ass, making me jump. He sits in front of me, tongue out and ready to attack me out of pure excitement. He knocks me down, making me land pretty hard on the floor.

He's just happy to see me, but I've had enough of his slobber and stinky breath. "Okay, that's enough. Down boy."

I get up off the cold, light gray wooden floor and study the interior of the house. It's bright from the white walls and open floor concept. There are windows all over. Sunlight reflects off the furniture in the living room, causing them all to glisten.

All I can think about is Dad.

His scent greeted me when I walked through the front door.

We used to sit and watch basketball games with Grayson on the sofa.

I can still hear him through the walls, the sound of his voice piercing through my eardrums.

And his laugh.

The clunking of his shoes when he'd come home from work.

You came here for a reason. Just do what you need to do and get out.

Walking into my room, I head straight for my closet and take out one of my suitcases. I pack it to the brim with clothes and other shit. Zipping it up, I roll it out of my room and stand in the middle of the house.

Sammy runs up to me, breathing heavily and sticking his tongue out.

"Be a good boy while I'm gone, okay? I'm going down the street to stay with Dani. You remember her, right? She was the girl I always had screaming matches with. And still do. I'll come and visit you. I promise."

He tilts his head like he understands what I'm saying.

"I know. I can't believe what I just said either," I say, petting the soft, thick golden fur that sits atop his head.

Sammy follows me to the door.

"Sit."

He sits down right on his butt, wagging his tail back and forth.

"Stay."

He doesn't move.

The look he's giving me right now is killing me. As much as it pains me to leave him alone for several more hours, I have to.

Twisting the doorknob, I wave goodbye to Sammy as I make my way out of the house.

My car key jingles in my hand until I unlock my car. I plant my ass in the driver's seat and turn the car on. The cool air conditioner blasts in my face, causing me to close my eyes and smile. The heat in Sunset Cove this summer is no joke. You go outside, and you're already sweating your ass off.

The heat is the least painful thing I have to think about since I have to wrap my head around the fact I'm going to be staying with Dani for who knows how long.

Why did I agree to this?

As I'm washing the body wash off myself, I can't help but think about Lizzie. How the hell did I get any sleep knowing the state she's in? I could barely look at her yesterday because I've never seen her in such a vulnerable state before.

And Ben.

Goddammit.

Breathing in and out, my eyes are getting glassy, but I don't let any tears fall because I'm so tired. First, my dad. Now him. It's not fair.

Life isn't fair.

God, poor Laura. The way she ran to me broke my heart. She's always been such a positive and upbeat person. Seeing her broken like this feels as if she's a different person. This isn't the same Laura I spent so much time with growing up.

So much for washing the pain away. It's seeping its way deep into my bones now.

And then there's Noah.

I didn't want to come here because I knew I'd risk running into him. I mean how could I not when this is his family we're talking about?

It was inevitable.

There's something I can't seem to wrap my head around. The way I let my guard down to help him when he had his first panic attack in front of me.

His ocean eyes were hypnotizing the shit out of me more than they ever have before. The way his hand intertwined with mine and how warm his body was against mine made me feel things.

Snap out of it, Dani.

I turn off the shower, and grab the towel hanging over the towel bar, hunching over so my head is upside down. I wrap it tightly around my head so it stays in place. Concealing my naked body in my towel wrap, I make sure the velcro is lined up correctly.

Stepping out of the shower, I notice how steamed up the mirror is. I can't see my reflection.

Maybe that's a good thing.

I wipe my hand across the mirror to reveal myself in my current state.

My face doesn't look like a zombie anymore. There's color in my cheeks. The bags under my eyes seemed to have disappeared.

The irony is that I'm fucking exhausted. I guess hot shower water is a miracle worker.

Looking at my reflection, I see a young woman who's going through a similar experience she went through when she was fourteen.

When you go through a traumatic experience like losing a parent, it changes you. It alters your brain chemistry in ways you could never imagine.

I genuinely believed I'd be miserable for the rest of my life. That I wouldn't feel anything ever again.

I'm not the same fourteen-year-old girl anymore. Although it's been several years since Dad's passing, I still struggle with it.

The way I look at it is I'm here and I'm alive.

That's what truly matters.

Shaking my head to enter back into reality, I gently remove the towel from my head, letting it fall on the floor next to me.

Twisting the doorknob, I see a ball of ginger fluff sitting on my bed. Archie has his long arms stretching straight out, blinking his eyes at me. He looks like he was asleep, so I try to be as quiet as I can so he can get back to being the cute and lazy boy that he is.

"Archie, why are you sitting on my clothes?" I ask, folding my arms and sticking my leg out.

He's not looking at me. Instead, he rests his head on my underwear and bra.

I grunt in response.

Walking over to him, I pull my clothes out from under him. "Why do you do this?"

As I'm raising my arms to put my white tank top on, I slip it on as I hear a strange noise coming from the living room.

My heart starts pounding like a thousand drums being played all at once.

Who needs shorts anyway?

Slowly creeping out my door, I step out of my room and make my way down the hallway. Hearing footsteps going up the stairs, I sprint back into my room and grab the closest weapon I have at my disposal. *A giant, black flashlight.*

Taking it in my hands, I hold it like a baseball bat.

Oh my God, what if it's an intruder? Or maybe even a kidnapper? I'm screwed either way.

I'm standing behind the door, lifting my flashlight because I'm ready to kill this son of a bitch. As I'm ready to wack this shadowy figure, I notice it's no longer a shadow.

It's a person.

Oh shit, it's Noah.

He screams. I scream.

I lower the flashlight as my face heats up with anger. "Are you fucking kidding me?"

noah

I lean against the doorway of Dani's childhood bedroom, her eyes glaring like they're about to set me on fire.

The palm of her hand rests over her heart. "Knock on the front door next time, jackass. You almost gave me a heart attack."

"Why would I have to knock?"

"It's the courteous thing to do considering you don't live here."

"I *actually* do."

"What the hell are you talking about?"

"Your mom wants me to stay here. *With you.*"

"And why does she think having you stay here with me is a good idea?"

"Beats the shit out of me."

She whips her head back. "You have to stay in the guest bedroom."

"That's so sweet of you to offer me an actual room to sleep in. And here I thought you'd have me sleep on the roof."

"Oh, fuck off." She rolls her eyes. "You might end up sleeping on the roof if you annoy the shit out of me."

I look down, seeing she's holding a flashlight. "A flashlight. What were you going to do with that? Blind the shit out of me?"

"Now that I think about it, it would've been better if I used it to murder you with."

"You really think that could be an effective murder weapon?"

She gestures to me step closer to her. "Why don't we find out?" She flips me off after I wet my lips with my tongue.

This is when it hits me.

Dani is standing here in nothing but a tank top and underwear.

Fuck me.

I'm having heart palpitations which are traveling all the way down to my shorts.

I clear my throat so loud it startles her, my hand spazzing out as I point to her. "Shorts."

"What?" The anger on her face dissipates and transforms into confusion.

"Y-you're...not wearing any s-shorts," I stutter.

Chills travel through my entire body. My shoulders feel tight. I roll them in a backward motion a few times.

She looks down, noticing she's only wearing underwear. "Oh...shit."

She's unable to meet my eyes, her cheeks all flushed. Grabbing her jean shorts, she runs into the bathroom and slams the door behind her.

I see Archie, her ginger tabby, sprawled out on his back. Our shouting and bickering startled him, but not to the point where he wanted to leave the room.

I go over to pet his soft fur, a whimper escaping his mouth. He's too lazy to give me a full meow.

Standing in Dani's childhood bedroom is a mind trip.

Her walls are still teal like they were five years ago.

There are Polaroid posters of albums that cover the wall

next to her closet, going six down and ten across. Those weren't there the last time I was here.

Walking over to them, my eyes land on *The Dark Side of the Moon* by Pink Floyd. I gulp deeply, feeling a rather large lump go down my throat. My eyes wander over the posters for *Currents* by Tame Impala, *Night Visions* by Imagine Dragons, and *Pure Heroine* by Lorde.

Her book collection has grown massively. My feet drag themselves over to her bookcase.

No fucking way.

Kneeling down, I notice Dani has her own collection of mysteries and thrillers. Some of which I notice are the same books I have. A breathy laugh leaves my mouth as I look up at her knockdown ceiling.

The bookcase is filled to the brim with romance books. There are books messily stacked on top of each other.

Whipping my head around, I see the journal I got for her sophomore year of high school sitting on her desk.

Holy shit, she kept it. And she's been using it. I thought she would've thrown it away.

It's pretty beat up, but she's kept it in good condition considering it's around eight or nine years old. Opening it up, I skim through it and read through some of the shit she's written in it.

I forgot how beautiful her handwriting is.

After, my eyes shoot to the bulletin board above her desk with a quote on it.

Remember to breathe.

A few photos of her, Bella, and Sage are pinned on there. There's one of the three of them at our high school graduation. Another one at Loggerhead Beach.

There's a photo strip of her and my mom from Sweet & Salty's grand opening. Goofy faces take up three of four photos.

Rolling my eyes, I laugh.

Making my way over to her dresser, I pick up the velvet box that screamed at me to be nosy and investigate.

Oh, fuck.

There's an infinity ring inside. The one my dad gave to Dani after her father, Jacob, passed away.

I remember what Dad said when he gave the ring to Dani. It serves as a reminder that her father's love for her will always be infinite. And that he'll always be there, watching over her.

Slamming the drawer shut, I rush over to the bed with the ring box buried in between my thighs.

She's been in the bathroom for a solid ten minutes now.

I wouldn't be surprised if she's having a full-on panic attack right now because I almost scared her to death and the fact that I saw her in her underwear.

The thought of her freaking out in there makes me want to see if she's okay.

I know what it feels like when your mind is playing tricks on you.

CHAPTER ELEVEN

I lean against the bathroom door, breathing heavily.

What are the odds he'd be here as I'm getting dressed? I mean, seriously. Are you fucking kidding me?

I take my hand, placing it on my chest. My thumb rubs the area in a circular motion. I breathe in and out.

My shorts are on my body in no time.

What the hell is going on with me?

This is the second time Noah's almost seen me naked.

What's next? My bare ass, that's what.

Shit, I hope the universe didn't hear that.

Once I collect myself, I slowly open the door.

Noah's sitting on my bed with his head down. I can't get a read on him. I can tell he's embarrassed though. Boy, I can't imagine why.

"Hi," I say.

His head lifts while his hands are resting in his lap.

I meet his gaze, his blue eyes burning a hole into me.

Oh God, I can't breathe.

I run my fingers through my hair because I don't know what else to do.

"You still wear this?" He digs out the ring box that's hiding in between his legs, taking out what's inside.

I lean against the doorframe of my bathroom. "Did you go through my shit without asking my permission?"

His mouth opens, lips flattening and eyebrows furrowing. "Curiosity got the best of me." He shrugs his shoulders.

I sit down next to him, snatching the ring out of his hand. "I've been wearing this ring for the last eight years. I never take it off unless I need to shower because I don't want to get it wet. Water will wear down the silver."

He stops me before I can slide the ring onto my finger. "Give me your hand."

Barely moving a single muscle, I narrow my eyes. I'm reluctant to give him my hand.

He reaches out, gently yanking it in his direction.

He looks up at me then down at my hand as he slides the ring on my finger. This would be a proposal if he was sliding it onto my left hand.

Thank God, it's not.

Even though it's on my finger, Noah doesn't let go of my hand.

My brain is short-circuiting as I take a deep gulp, swiping my hand away as fast as I possibly can. "Um...so...you're staying at the house?" I tilt my head, staring into his eyes just enough to make him uncomfortable.

He meets my gaze. "I thought we already established this."

He's so close to me I can feel his body heat, staring deep into my eyes.

The hairs on my arms are standing up, and my body feels limp. I slide farther away, creating some distance between us. "Well, then, if you'll excuse me, I have some writing and editing to do. Get the hell out." I shoo him out of my room.

He stands behind the doorway. "If you need me, I'll be here."

"Trust me, I won't need you."

I slam the door in his face, sitting down at my desk. I need to get some writing done, but all I can do is stare at the blinking line on Google Docs.

Fuck, not this again. Stop mocking me, you piece of shit.

I've been sitting here for an hour now, still staring at the dumb blinking line. My fingers aren't tapping on any keys because there aren't any words flowing out of my brain.

How is it that I can't write right now? My brain is a jumbled mess, that's why.

Getting up off the chair, I close the lid to my laptop pretty hard out of frustration because I can't get any words onto the page.

Time to go out and find some inspiration in one of my favorite places to exist.

The bookstore.

CHAPTER TWELVE

I'm sitting in the car in front of the Just One More Chapter bookstore, banging my head on the steering wheel. Not to the point where I could get a massive headache, but to the point where I'll definitely have a mark on my forehead later.

The last time my writing block was this bad was when Dad passed away.

Actually, it was worse. I couldn't write for months. It was a chore to do schoolwork. All I wanted was to do was sleep in my bed and never leave.

Getting out of my car and locking it, I head into Just One More Chapter.

I have no idea what I'm looking for. I knew I had to get out of the house and clear my head.

When I walk inside, it's hard not to notice the giant arched windows in the back of the store that have rolling shelves in front of them which are full of books.

There are a few people here and there.

Two girls that look younger than me are hanging out on the sofa in front of the store and a group of high school girls are scouring through the romance section.

Sunlight is reflecting off the white paint from the bookshelves that are located all over the store. The walls are white with abstract blue waves painted across the bottom of them. There aren't any signs for genres anywhere, but everything's organized. It's just a matter of knowing what you're looking for.

I don't see any employees I know since I haven't been here in years.

I didn't visit Just One More Chapter that often during my high school years since I used to be a frequent visitor of Sweet & Salty.

The fact that we even have a romance-only bookstore is incredible to me. I've been seeing them pop up all over New York and Chicago.

It warms my little romance reader's heart.

My eyes gravitate towards *Beach Read* by Emily Henry, sitting on a small table display with the rest of her books in the middle of the store near the small romance section they have.

I read *Beach Read* during my freshman year of college and it was life-changing. Emily Henry perfectly encapsulated what it's like to be a writer. Gus Everett quickly climbed to the top of my book boyfriends list.

"Dani, is that you?" A high-pitched voice calls out.

Turning around, I see Violet Prescott standing before me.

I haven't seen her since high school when chaos erupted like a volcano for her. We were never really close and part of me regrets we weren't, but shit happens.

Her blonde hair is in a braid and she has a pair of sunglasses sitting on top of her head. She's wearing a white tank top with spaghetti straps, gray sweatpants, and beige sandals.

"Wow, it's weird seeing you here," she says.

"I could say the same. I'm so used to seeing you at Sweet & Salty."

"Yeah, same here." She pauses. "Hey, I'm so sorry about Ben. When Noah texted me, I couldn't believe it."

"When Noah texted you?"

"Yeah, I've been keeping in contact with him for the past several years."

Say what now?

"Oh."

"Enough about me. How are you?"

"I don't even know. I came here because I needed to get out of the house. My mom is making Noah stay at my house with me. It's a nightmare."

"Wait, you two have to stay in the same place with each other? For how long?"

"I have no idea, but he might be dead before I am."

She laughs. "Yeah, that doesn't surprise me."

"Why are you here at Just One More Chapter?"

"Sage wants me to pick up *The Silent Patient* for her because she's too lazy to go out and get it herself."

Out of all the mysteries and thrillers I've read, that book is one of the only ones I haven't read yet. Solely because I know everything that happens in it.

I remember when Mom and Laura would play catch-up with each other.

Laura would talk about how obsessed Noah was with that damn book. It would be to the point where she'd give out major spoilers like they were free samples you'd get at Costco.

I snap myself out of my thoughts. "Sounds like Sage. She's always been lazy as hell."

"By the way, if you ever need someone to talk to, I'm here. I know we've never been close, but I really want to be. Closer to you I mean. Sage is my only friend, if you want to call her that. It would be nice to have more." She grins. "Hand me your phone," she sticks her hand out in my direction.

Giving her my phone, Violet types out her phone number and hands it back to me.

"Thanks." I smile. "Why is it you've been keeping in contact with Noah?"

She takes a deep breath. "I've been having him update me about Grayson."

Oh boy, I opened a can of worms. And I can't take it back.

"And Grayson doesn't know about this?"

She shakes her head. "No, and I don't want him to know. Please don't tell him."

"I won't. You have my word."

"Thanks." She pauses for a few seconds. "I should go and get this before Sage has my head. Don't hesitate to text me if you need anything. And I mean anything," she says as she reaches out to grab my hand.

I nod, feeling my eyes getting glassy. Using my ring fingers, I wipe away the wetness off my face.

Violet walks away from me to check out Sage's book.

Why does she want updates on Grayson?

The last time I saw Violet Prescott, it was my senior year of high school.

I was on my way to my English final and saw the two of them walking past each other.

Her eyes were glued on Grayson the entire time, but he didn't even look at her. It was like she didn't exist. Her face had heartbreak written all over it.

The rest is unknown and I'm too tired to think right now. This is all making me dizzy.

Watching Violet walk out the door takes me back to when I used to see her all the time at Sweet & Salty.

She exclusively reads romance. That I do remember because it was the one thing we sort of bonded over when we'd run into each other here. And nothing else.

I hope we can become friends and it's not just because she said that she needs more.

I want to go home, but I know Noah's going to be there.

Seriously, what the hell was my mother thinking? Why would she have the guy I've hated since I was a kid stay with me in our house? Does she not recall our *War of Words*?

Noah's the last person I'd want to be stuck at home with.

Honestly, he's the last person I'd want to be stuck anywhere with.

BELLA

ME

meet me at kailani's?

BELLA

Be there in 10

Should I ask why we're meeting there?

ME

nope

BELLA

We'll talk when I get there

Walking out the door, I head to my car and slip into the driver's seat.

I pull my hair up into a ponytail. I feel like I've been transported back into the 1980s with Tame Impala blasting through the speakers.

Closing my eyes, I take a deep breath before I back out of my parking spot.

The drive there is a mix of me jamming out, internally freaking out about running into Violet, and not wanting to go home because I'll have to deal with Noah.

When I pull in front of Kailani's, I head inside and find a table.

Bella walks in, heading straight for me. "How the hell did you get here so fast?"

"I was at Just One More Chapter because I needed to escape my house."

"You look like shit," she says, sitting down on the seat across from me.

I huff. "Thank you for that."

"I'm sorry. What's going on? Why did you want to meet me here?"

"I ran into Violet Prescott," I blurt out.

She extends her neck out slightly. "You what?"

"I saw Violet at the bookstore," I repeat.

She takes a moment to process. "How did that go?"

"It was strange and she looked the same. She was getting a book for Sage."

"I think we need to take Sage's computer away from her, so she can go out and get things herself."

I laugh with my mouth closed. "We really do." I exhale. "Violet's been in contact with Noah for the past six years and Grayson has no idea."

"Secrets aren't secret once they're revealed."

I chuckle. "Yeah, that didn't come out like you thought it would, did it?"

"It didn't." She giggles and gets up. "Do you want anything? I'm buying."

"Bella, you're not buying."

"Yes, I am."

"Fine. Can I have an unsweetened iced black tea?"

She nods and walks up to the employee working the register. When she finishes ordering our drinks, she walks over to the pickup area.

Since it's late in the day, Kailani's isn't as busy as it would be in the mornings. There are a few people here and there, sitting in the corner of the shop.

"Bella, I have your unsweetened black iced tea and your tropical mango iced tea," a voice shouts a few minutes later.

Bella grabs our drinks and thanks the barista before sitting back down at the table.

"Thank you for getting me caffeine," I say, grabbing the drink from her

"Always."

We sip some of our iced teas and exchange awkward glances at each other.

I squint my eyes, grinning. "I have something else to tell you."

"Okay, shoot."

"My mom is forcing Noah to stay at the house with me."

She blinks, her eyes widening. "I'm sorry. What?"

"My mom doesn't like the idea of me staying in the house alone, so she thinks having Noah stay with me is a good idea."

She smiles. "So, what you're telling me is you two are stuck in your house together? Just the two of you? Alone?"

I roll my eyes. "Yes."

"Interesting." She leans her chin on her hands, resting her elbows on the table. "I think your mom is onto something."

"Elaborate," I say.

"I may not be a romance expert, but I have heard a lot of people say how hate sex is some of the best sex you can have."

I'm sorry, what?

My mouth hangs open before I start laughing hard. "That's funny because it sounds like you're suggesting that I should have sex with Noah."

"That's exactly what I'm suggesting."

"Is there something in your iced tea that they didn't put in mine?"

She leans back, crossing one leg over the other. "Dani, can you imagine how hot that would be?"

"I'm imagining myself throwing up right now." I roll my eyes, pretending to gag.

"You're so dramatic." She gently shakes her head. "Imagine you guys are arguing and he keeps staring at your lips."

"Okay, I'm going to need a barf bag." My body grows increasingly stiff as I gulp down a quarter of my iced tea.

"Now, you're staring at his lips. And bam! You guys start making out. And shit escalates from there."

Never going to happen.

"Are you sure you're not a romance author?"

"Unfortunately, no. That's your department."

A small smile appears on my face. "As much as I don't want to go home, I have to check and make sure Noah didn't destroy anything."

"He's not a dog," she says.

"I'm not so sure about that one."

I get up from the chair with Bella following suit.

We walk out of Kailani's and stand in front of my car.

"If you ever need to rant to me about Noah, don't. I'm just kidding. Rant all you want. I know your mom is looking out for you. She wouldn't have done this if she didn't think it was right."

"Yeah, I guess you're right."

She lowers an eyebrow. "I'm always right."

I get into my car, sitting in the driver's seat and rolling down the window. "I'll update you when I can."

"I'd appreciate that," she tells me.

I wave to her. "Bye."

"Bye."

My drive home is a bit more peaceful than the drive to Kailani's. That is until I pull up in my driveway and realize Noah's going to be inside.

What the hell is Bella thinking? Hate sex with my childhood rival? Oh God, I'm going to throw up. Figuratively. Not literally. Like, why would she suggest that?

Glancing out my window, the sky is full of pinks, purples, and oranges. The sunsets here have always been so beautiful.

This one feels more special.

Thanks for lighting up the sky, Ben. Thank you for everything you've done for me and my family.

Walking into the house, I see Noah sprawled on the sofa. My sofa.

"Glad to see you made yourself at home!" I shout.

"Jesus Christ," he mutters under his breath, taking his wireless earbuds out.

"Yeah, how does it feel to get scared shitless?"

He rolls his eyes and flips me off, licking his lips. "I thought you'd never come back."

"Yeah, well, I never thought you'd be in my space. But, here we are."

"Just admit you love me being in your space."

"I hate that you're in my space."

I head into the kitchen to see what we can have for dinner.

He follows me, leaning against the entryway and crossing his arms in front of his chest. "What are you doing?"

"If you must know, I'm trying to find something we can make for dinner."

"Hey, if you stare at the contents of the fridge long enough, maybe something will jump out at you."

I glare at him. "Or maybe you could come help me find shit instead of standing there and doing absolutely nothing?"

"Nah, watching you get frustrated is one of my favorite activities."

I close the fridge. "Do you realize how close I am to punching you in the face?"

"Do you realize arguing with me isn't going to help you

figure out what we should eat for dinner? We're wasting precious time."

God, I'm not going to survive this. Maybe I should just hit myself in the head with the flashlight.

I let out a deep exhale. "Really? I had no idea. Seriously, be a good boy, and come help me find something we can make for dinner."

His face lights up as he takes a moment to take in what I asked him to do for me. "Fine," he says.

Opening the freezer, I hear a loud thump.

What the hell was that?

When I close it, Noah's glaring at me. "Next time, look behind you to see if someone's following you!"

I scrunch my face. "Shit."

"What?"

"Your forehead."

"What about my forehead?" He waits for me to respond. "What the hell is wrong with my forehead, Solomon?"

CHAPTER THIRTEEN

Dani rushes me into her bathroom, so she can clean up my wound.

I'm sitting down on the floor and my eyes are tightly shut. I'm trying so hard not to focus on the pain, but it hurts so much. There's a decent-sized gash on my forehead and it won't stop bleeding.

I'm in so much fucking pain right now.

She sits down in front me with her legs sticking straight out. "Lean into me."

I don't make eye contact with her, but I lean closer to her. My entire body is shaking.

"Hold still." She takes the damp washcloth, dabbing it on the cut to slow the bleeding.

"It's hard to hold still when I feel like I just got hit in the face by a freezer door. Oh wait...I did!"

She scoffs. "*You're* so fucking dramatic."

"*I'm* fucking dramatic? Right. And *you* aren't?" I huff, plastering a fake smile on my face. "Hi, I'm Dani. And I cried my ass off—"

She cuts me off. "I dare you to finish that sentence."

My lips quiver, attempting to myself back from smirking like crazy. "And I cried my ass off when Noah got a better grade than me on the final essay for English class during sophomore year in high school."

"Oh, shut up. I deserved a way better grade than you. My essay was so much better than yours and you know it."

"Did it hurt when I showed you my grade? Did it really hurt?"

She punches me in the arm.

"Ow! Dude, what the fuck?"

"Do I look like a dude to you?" She breathes out. "And that was for being a jackass. Now stop moving. Unless you want to bleed to death."

I roll my eyes at her.

She tilts my head back a little to examine the cut on my forehead. We fall into an awkward silence for several minutes.

Fuck, her eyes are mesmerizing.

How have I never noticed them before? They're dark brown and you can barely see her pupils because they're so dark.

Hello, what am I saying?

Watching her prepare the items to clean my wound, I smile and shift my mouth to the side of my face.

This is when I start to feel her gaze on me.

She looks up and down at me repeatedly all while she's trying her best to tend to my wound. "What?" She grabs a Q-tip, unscrewing the cap off the tube of antibiotic ointment and applying it to the wound on my forehead.

I look deep into her eyes. "How are you so good at this?"

She answers me without meeting my gaze. "My dad was very clumsy. He'd always injure himself. Whether that was cutting or hitting himself on something. I was his daughter turned self-trained nurse."

Dani's face lights up as she smiles at me.

Oh, I don't know how to feel about this. Usually, when Dani

smiled at me, it meant she had something planned up her sleeve. And now, it screams innocence.

I do wonder how I ever found her smile to be annoying.

It's beautiful.

If I'm being honest here, she's the most beautiful woman I've ever laid my eyes on. I've always thought that she was beautiful, but I could never tell her that. Not even now.

She stares at me. "What?"

I gulp. "You know I wanted to reach out to you multiple times over the last five years. I never did because I had a feeling you'd hate me even more than you already do."

"I don't *hate* you."

"You don't?"

"I just find you *slightly* irritating."

I laugh which turns into me getting all choked up.

Her palm rests on top of my thigh, sending shivers down my spine. Looking away, my eyes are rapidly blinking as a physical response.

"Hey," she says. "You're going to be okay."

This cannot be happening right now.

Her gaze meets mine. "Yeah, you know why?"

Studying Dani from her eyes to her torso makes me realize something.

How was I so repulsed by this woman? I never knew I could be hypnotized by a woman who I fought with all the time.

She laughs, brightening up her entire face. "Why?"

"Because you're here. *With me.*"

CHAPTER FOURTEEN

I clear my throat, taking myself out of Noah's trance and getting up off the bathroom floor. "How's your forehead?"

He doesn't answer me.

Lightly brushing my finger on the area surrounding the scratch on his forehead, Noah shudders as he gets up and his body shakes like a tremor from an earthquake.

"Am I hurting you?"

His face softens as he moves closer to me. "No, you're not hurting me."

I don't feel like vomiting from the close proximity.

I look away for a few seconds to break the tension, but it doesn't work.

His ocean eyes are burning an invisible hole through the side of my head. "Now that I'm all fixed, we're going to have to discuss the whole dinner situation."

"Why, because we don't have anything here to eat?" I cross my arms in front of my chest.

"Exactly."

"And who's fault is that? Why didn't you run to the grocery store to get food?"

He shrugs his shoulders. "The thought never occurred to me."

"Of course the thought never occurred to you."

Idiot.

"I have an idea of what we could do."

I look up at the bathroom ceiling. "Oh, I can't wait to hear this brilliant idea of yours."

"We go get dinner and pick up groceries afterward."

I drop my head back down. "Where are we going to get dinner, smart ass?"

He shakes his head, rolling his eyes. "I don't care. Name a place."

Why is it that some guys can't make decisions? It's so irritating.

"Marina's," I blurt out.

Marina's Diner has been around for over eighty years. I remember when Dad and I used to go there every Wednesday afternoon for burger night.

"Fine. Let's go," he says.

"Here's something you don't understand. Women can't just go out somewhere. Sometimes we have to change our clothes. Shower. Put makeup on…"

"I know. I have a sister. I can say if you're not ready in fifteen minutes, I'm leaving without you."

I roll my eyes. "Okay, get out." I push Noah towards the door.

"You know I could just turn around…like I did this morning," he suggests, raising an eyebrow and smirking at me.

"Get. The. Hell. Out."

When I close the door in his face, I change my clothes.

Opting for an all black outfit that consists of a v-neck blouse with buttons and jeans, I throw them on my bed.

I've never gotten dressed so fast in my life.

I nod and exhale as I run to the bathroom to fix my hair.

God, the humidity really hasn't done my hair any favors.

Plugging my waver into the wall, I run it through my hair to calm the frizz.

I slip on a pair of black wedges on my way out of my bedroom, seeing Noah standing there in a button-down shirt, jeans, and a pair of black and white Converse.

What the hell is he trying to do to me?

noah

Dani's standing in front of me in a v-neck shirt that has buttons, except the buttons aren't buttoned all the way up. They're buttoned up for me to see a sneak peek of her cleavage.

Fuck, I can't stop staring at her.

"What the hell are you staring at?" She snaps me out of my daze.

I clear my throat. "Can we go already?"

"Awe, is someone hungry?" She grins, slinging her purse over her shoulder.

We walk out the front door and she locks it behind us.

"Are we taking your car or mine?" I ask.

"Mine."

She pulls her car keys out of her back pocket. I have to look away from her because her jeans are hugging her ass so well.

This is fucking torture, man. Why am I doing this to myself? More importantly, why is she doing this to me?

She throws me the keys and I catch them in my hands.

"You're driving," she says.

"I figured that out when you threw the keys at me."

"You're lucky they didn't hit you in the face."

"Well, you already hit me in the face with your freezer. I think that's enough for today, don't you?"

She gets into the passenger's side of the car and I step into the driver's side. Putting the key into the ignition, music plays right away.

"I didn't know you listen to Queen."

She turns to me, cocking her head. "There are a lot of things you don't know about me."

My eyes grow wide as I turn away from her, biting my bottom lip.

XANDER

XANDER

Hey, bro. Sorry for updating you so late. Nothing new to report, except Grayson was driving me fucking crazy so I sent his ass home

Anyways, we were waiting to hear from Dr. Miller for hours for an update about Lizzie. The nurse came by and told us that she's been backed up today, so she'll update us tomorrow. Don't worry, I got your back

ME

Have I ever told you that I love you?

XANDER

I'm flattered

BTW, how are you enjoying your quality time with Dani?

ME

If Grayson told you to ask me that, tell him he's a dumbass. Bye

"That was Xander. I told him to update me if anything happens while we're gone."

"Are there any updates about Lizzie?" The eagerness in her voice makes me hopeful that something positive is going to come out of this nightmare.

"He said they've been waiting for Dr. Miller for hours because she got backed up. They won't hear from her until tomorrow. He told me he'll let me know what she says."

She takes a deep breath and nods her head.

I have no idea what she's thinking about. I wish I could get into her head. Okay, maybe I don't.

Some things should remain a mystery, right?

CHAPTER SIXTEEN

Despite how much he drives me absolutely crazy, I can only imagine how Noah's feeling.

Seeing the sheer panic in his eyes not knowing what's going to happen to Lizzie makes fear grow inside me like weeds.

He's hurting, even if it's not obvious to people who haven't gone through losing a parent.

I can feel everything he's feeling, like a sponge soaking up water.

"Are you okay? I know this isn't easy. You know, not knowing what's going to happen to her and everything."

He swallows, his Adam's apple sinking low and bouncing itself back into place. He breathes out like there's a chill in the air. "I hate not knowing if my sister's going to be okay. I-I mean shit happens we can't predict all the time." His voice is shaky and his eyes have a glassy sheen to them. "But, this is different. This is my family."

I turn to face him. "Noah."

That's all that comes out of my mouth.

His name.

A name I couldn't stand to hear when I was younger. I don't mind hearing his name come out of my mouth anymore.

We're both looking deep into each other's eyes.

He has tears streaming down the smooth skin on his face. "Let's go," he says.

He shifts the gear into reverse and wipes away the remnants of the tears that are falling out of his eyes.

Why does my heart feel like it's breaking?

We pull up to Marina's Diner.

One thing that sets Marina's apart from other diners is that it overlooks the ocean. The sun has set and the sky is dark.

Looking out of the window, I see a cluster of stars and smile.

Marina's interior is full of retro teals and greenery with a jukebox leaning against the wall near the entrance.

It feels like I took a time machine back to the '60s and '70s.

"Why did you want to sit in this specific booth?" Noah wonders.

"My dad and I used to sit here when we came for burger Wednesdays after he'd picked me up from middle school. Sitting here feels like he's actually here with us. With me."

"Do you miss him?" he asks, looking everywhere else, but at me.

"Why are you asking me that?"

"I'm just trying to make conversation."

"Can we talk about something else, please?"

"I've never seen a father love his child like the way that Jacob loved you," he blurts out. "Your dad lit up every room he was in. Just like mine did. God, those two were unstoppable together. And honestly annoying sometimes. I remember when the Sunset Cove University stingrays made it to the finals when we were in our freshman year of high school." He pauses for a brief moment. "Basketball lingo."

I can't help but stare at him.

"When they won, our dads screamed so fucking loud that we got a noise complaint from the neighbors. Do you remember that?"

"Uh-huh."

My eyes aren't glassy anymore. Tears are streaming out of them now. Burying my face in my arm, I try to control myself because I'm aware we're in public.

A smile begins to form on his face, but we get interrupted before either of us can say anything else to each other.

"Dani Solomon, is that you?" A familiar voice asks, walking over to us.

"Hi, Marina."

Marina is in her mid-sixties. She has long, dark brunette hair cascading down her back, with emerald green eyes.

The diner has been in her family for generations. It all started with her grandmother. She's been running the place since I was a kid.

"I haven't seen you in a long time, kiddo."

"I know. College and writing has been keeping me busy."

"How's the book coming along?"

"Pretty good. I've been having the worst writer's block today, though."

Noah's eyes light up as he watches me talk to Marina.

She turns to him. "Ah, if isn't the troublemaker himself. I'm so sorry to hear about your dad. How are you holding up?"

"I honestly don't know how to answer that question," he says.

"Death is a fickle thing. I remember when I lost my mom. I had no idea what I was going to do without her. I knew she wanted me to run this place when I got old enough. It was terrifying because, by the time I took over, she was gone. I didn't have any idea what I was doing." She pauses. "The people who say time heals all are a bunch of liars because it's not the whole truth. It doesn't take time to heal an open wound. All it takes is you believing in yourself that you can make it through whatever life decides to throw in your face."

"You sound like my mom," Noah says.

"She's right." Her face lights up as she smiles at us. "I've held you two up long enough. What can I get for you?"

Noah gestures to me with his hand. "Ladies first."

Why is he being nice to me? This is freaking me out.

I turn my gaze away from Noah, directing it towards Marina. "The usual. I mean, if you remember."

"Oh, honey, I remember," Marina says. "What about you, Noah?"

He looks at me and looks up at Marina. "I'll have what she's having."

"I don't know if you want to do that."

"I'll risk it," he blurts out.

"Okay, suit yourself."

"God, I remember when you two were babies. Now, you're old enough to have babies," Marina blurts out.

"Marina!" I raise my voice.

"What? Lots of young people are getting pregnant early these days. You guys would make good looking babies."

I bury my face in my face to allow the redness in my cheeks to subside.

"Oh, I'm just kidding. I'll go put your orders in," Marina says as she walks to the touchscreen to input our orders.

"She's right, you know." He pauses. "We'd make beautiful babies." He breaks out into this laugh that shoots straight into my bones.

My hands make their way underneath my chin as my eyes meet Noah's. "Shut up." I shake my head, giggling.

He chuckles. "Hey, what's up with the writer's block? Maybe I can help."

I laugh so hard I start to choke. "Y-you want to h-help me?"

"People tell me I can be helpful."

"What people? Your mom?"

I look at him and he meets my gaze, goosebumps are prickling all over my arms.

"Hey, I'll have you know my mom thinks I'm one of the most helpful people ever." He leans back against the back of the booth, crossing his arms over his chest.

"Right," I say with sass pouring out of my voice. "I doubt you'll be able to help me, but let's give it a shot."

"When did it start?"

"Today. That's why I left the house. I went to the bookstore to see if I could get an inkling of inspiration. Instead, I ran into Violet which distracted me even more than I already was."

His eyes grow wide. "You ran into Violet? As in Violet Prescott?"

I nod. "I'm honestly surprised I haven't run into her until now. Sunset Cove is a pretty small town." I pause. "She told me she's been keeping in contact with you all these years to get updates on Grayson."

He nods. "Yeah, she has."

"You know he's going to kill you when he finds out, right?"

"You mean *if*."

"No, I mean *when*. This is a *pretty big* secret to keep from your best friend, Noah."

CHAPTER SEVENTEEN

"Okay, hold on. You're changing the subject. Let's go back to your writer's block. What triggered it?"

She takes a deep breath, staring deep into my eyes. "Your dad."

I swallow deeply. "Oh."

"Sorry, I didn't mean to blurt it out that way. The same thing happened when my dad passed away. It's like my brain doesn't want to work with me. I hate it so much. And...I never used to be such a pessimist like I am now."

"Hate to break it to you, but you've always been a pessimist."

"Hey!"

I shrug my shoulders. "What? It's the truth."

"You're such an asshole."

"Don't tell me something I already know."

I wink at her as Marina walks over to us with our food.

Her usual is a bacon cheeseburger. Of course, it is. This isn't helping with my conflicting feelings.

"See, I was nice enough to not subject you to any kind of torture."

Yeah, but you're finding other ways to torture me.

I should've expected a burger because she talked about how she'd come here with her dad on Burger Wednesdays.

I cross my arms over my chest, while my mouth parts and eyebrows lower.

She picks up her burger, but her eyes land on mine before she takes a bite of it. "What?"

"Nothing."

I dive into my burger and it's so fucking good.

I forgot how good Marina's burgers are. I haven't been here in years.

The last time I was here was with Mom, Dad, and Lizzie right before I went off to college. It's one of the most recent memories I have of Dad. A happy memory that makes me sad to think about right now.

To my surprise, Dani polishes off her burger first.

"Hungry, huh?"

She rolls her eyes. "No, you're just fucking slow."

"Hey, this isn't a competition."

"Everything's always been a competition with us."

"Maybe we can change that and...other things."

Her lips shift to the side of her face. "What are you proposing, Kaplan?"

"I know I can be an asshole sometimes, but I want you to know I'm always here if you ever need to talk to someone. I know it's hard to talk about this kind of shit. Trust me, I do. I didn't listen in the past, but I'm listening now." I take a deep breath, continuing my train of thought. "We can be human beings who have conversations without having screaming matches with each other. What do you say?"

Her face is full of contemplation and confusion. "I can *try* and get on board with that," she says as a smile slowly appears on her face.

"Try *really* hard."

"You're making me change my mind."

Marina comes over to us with a styrofoam box.

Dani and I look at each other.

"We don't have any leftovers," I say.

"I know," Marina says, gesturing to Dani to open the box.

She opens it and Dani's jaw drops. She's practically salivating.

There's a giant piece of chocolate fudge cake in there.

"Oh my God, I love you so much Mar," Dani says.

She leans in closer to us, whispering. "Dinner and dessert are on the house tonight."

I shake my head. "Marina, no."

"In honor of your dad. You have no idea how much he helped me when I started running this place on my own. Your mom, too. You're pretty lucky, Noah. Not everybody has parents who would do anything for their children and serve their community. Your dad was special and so are you. Never forget that." She gently pats me on the back and turns her attention to Dani. "And I know how much your dad loved this cake. You'd get it every single time you'd come in. You both deserve something sweet after all the chaos you've endured. Enjoy it."

"Mar, you're making me cry," Dani says through her tears.

"Hope to see you more often, kiddo. I missed you."

"I missed you too." Dani gets up to hug Marina. "Sorry if I got tears all over you," she says as she laughs.

"It's okay," Marina winks at her and walks away from us.

"I can't believe she just did that," I say.

"I can," Dani replies with a giant smile plastered on her face.

dani

Noah can't believe Marina gave us a free dinner and dessert, but I'm not surprised. That's the kind of person she's always been.

Getting in the car, I drop my purse by my feet.

Noah gets in, realizing how close he is to the steering wheel. "Are you really *that* short?"

"Don't make fun of my height."

"I'm not. I don't know if it's safe to be this close to the wheel."

"Awe, you care about my safety." I give him a cute puppy dog pout.

"I never said that."

"Your eyes did."

"Are you ready to go to the grocery store?" Noah asks, sticking his thumbs up like an idiot.

Sitting in the parking lot in front of Marina's Diner, I watch the moonlight bouncing off the ocean from here.

I haven't been to Marina's in a long time because it reminds me too much of Dad, but I missed going there. Seeing Marina and feeling my dad's presence was oddly comforting.

I never pictured myself being there with Noah. It was weird talking to him about Dad. My writer's block. Yet, it was kind of nice talking to him how normal people talk to each other.

"Yo, Solomon!" he shouts, snapping me back from staring off into space.

"What?"

"Grocery store."

I shrug my shoulders. "What about it?"

"We need to stock up the fridge," he says. "What's up with you? You're acting weird."

"It's just...I wish I could snap my fingers and wake Lizzie up. I wish I could rewind time to somehow put a stop to the car that hit them. I know they're your family, but I've always considered them my family too. I wish I could do more to help." My voice is shaky and broken up.

"You have no idea how remarkable you are, Dani. It's only been a little over a day. Why are you putting unnecessary pressure on yourself?"

I gulp down his kind words, absorbing them into my body.

Did he just say I'm remarkable?

My lips swerve to the side of my face and find their way back to where they were. A smile slowly grows on my face which is wet from my salty tears. "It's weird hearing you compliment me."

"You need to hear every compliment that exists. You put so much pressure on yourself. You always put others first. It's time to start putting yourself first for once in your life."

"I always assumed you got the impression I was full of myself."

"I did," he says, backing up out of the parking space.

"If we're both being honest, I was wrong about you, too," I confess softly.

He licks his lips, looking at me for a split second until we're on the road. Now he's concentrating on driving. "How so?"

"I thought you were a little egotistical." I lift my hand, pressing my index finger and thumb together like I'm pinching something. "I was convinced you only cared about yourself. I've discovered you'd do anything to protect the people you care about. I admire that about you."

His ocean eyes pierce through my dark brown eyes, cutting through all the noise. He smiles so wide, blinding me with his pearly white teeth.

Gravity doesn't exist on the planet I'm on right now.

"I'm sorry. Did you just say you admire me?"

I roll my eyes. "Get over yourself, Kaplan."

"No seriously, you complimented me."

"You just complimented me." I huff.

He shakes his head, rolling his eyes and laughing.

The grocery store is right across the street from the Promenade at Sunset Cove. It takes us around twelve minutes to get there.

When Noah turns into the shopping center, I can't help but think about the fact that I'm going to the grocery store with him. A dumb thing to overthink, but I'm interested to see how this goes because I've never done anything like this with him before.

It's strange how something so mundane feels incredibly different with him.

Noah finds a parking space near the entrance and turns off the engine.

"Wow, it's pretty quiet," I say.

"Makes sense considering that it's 8:30 at night."

"Did you write down what we need?"

"Nope."

My eyebrows lightly furrow. "Why?"

"I have it all stored in this bad boy," he says, pointing to his head.

"Is this something you've always done?"

"Yeah, pretty much."

"And how many times did your mom have to go back to the store to get something you forgot to mention to her?"

He looks around the car, avoiding any possibility of looking me in the eyes. "Maybe a lot."

Yeah, I'm lucky I brought a list. This should be fun. Not.

Once we make it inside, he grabs a cart and follows me as I head for the produce section.

Avocados. Check. Romaine Lettuce. Check.

He throws a bag of honey-crisp apples into the cart.

"You're going to bruise those when you do that."

"Okay, *Mom*."

Oh, he did not just call me Mom.

I put my hands on my hips. "Take that back right now."

He laughs malevolently. "Never."

When we finish in the produce section, I go to the dairy section.

"What's on the list?" Noah asks.

I narrow my eyes at him. "Organic milk, eggs, goat cheese crumbles, cream cheese, shredded parmesan cheese, and plain Greek yogurt."

He shakes his head, mouth gaping open. "I thought you said it was a *small* list.

"It is a *small* list."

He walks over to me, grabbing the list out of my hand. "This is two pages long, Dani."

"It's a small notepad."

"It's still *two pages* long."

"Will you just get what I told you to get?"

"It's a good thing you're not lactose intolerant."

"Noah!"

"I'm going."

When we're done getting what we need in the dairy section, I make my way to the deli which is on the other side of the store. We missed the cut-off to get freshly cut meat and cheese, but it's fine.

I'm standing in front of a refrigerator full of various meats and cheeses that are pre-sliced and packaged in Ziploc bags.

I turn to Noah. "What deli meats do you eat?"

"Does it really matter? I'm a guy. I'll eat pretty much anything."

"Oh, that's right. I totally forgot."

"How did you forget?"

"Sometimes you act like a *girl*," I blurt out and immediately cover my mouth with my hand.

"Take that back."

"I don't think I will."

It takes us around thirty minutes until we finally make it to the self-checkout line. Our cart is pretty full which is good because it means we won't have to come back here for a while.

I stand in front of the scanner. "Stand next to me."

"I am standing next to you."

"On the other side of me, dumbass. I need you to bag the groceries."

He sucks his lips inwards, looking up at the ceiling and moving to the other side of me. "Are you just going to keep staring at me or are you going to start scanning everything, so we can go back to the house?"

I bite down on my tongue and scan the groceries at lightning speed which I can see is making Noah dizzy.

"Okay, slow down there Wario."

"You said you want to get out of here," I say.

"Yeah, but I'm a human. I'm not a machine. I can only go so fast." His tone is high-pitched.

"Stop complaining."

Once I finish scanning the groceries and bagging them up, we head out.

When we make it to the car, I open up the hatch.

"I got it," he says.

"Are you sure?" I ask.

"I hate that you think I'm incapable of doing shit."

"I didn't say that."

A small grin appears on his face. "You don't have to. Your eyes did."

CHAPTER NINETEEN

Pulling up in front of the Solomon family's house, Dani looks like she's about to pass out.

Her head is leaning back on the headrest and her eyes are closed.

"Hey," I say.

She lifts her head. "I'm so ready to go to sleep."

"Then, get inside and go to sleep."

"What about the groceries?"

"I got them."

"Are you sure?"

"Go, before I change my mind."

"I'm going," she says as she gets out of the car. "Thanks."

She walks up to the door, unlocks it, and goes inside.

Why did I offer to do this? This is going to take forever.

I'm so fucking tired from being at the hospital all day yesterday and from grocery shopping. Now I know why I let Gray handle the grocery shit. It's. So. Boring. But, it's not boring with her.

All the groceries are put away. My exhaustion has hit its breaking point. I'm sprawled out in bed in the guest bedroom of my childhood rival's house.

I'm in Dani's house.

She's right down the hall from me.

I can't get the look on Dani's face when Marina told us about how we'd make good-looking babies out of my head.

Her rosy cheeks.

Her smile.

Her laugh.

The way she kept challenging me at the grocery store.

God, I need help.

DIPSHITS

ME

I need to talk to you

XANDER

And who are you referring to?

ME

Both of you

GRAYSON

I have been summoned. What's going on, bro?

ME

I'm sorry I didn't tell you guys about my dad. It just shocked the hell out of me. And my mom. I should've texted you

XANDER

Don't beat yourself up about this

ME

I'm just freaking out. What if Lizzie doesn't wake up? What if she ends up being stuck like this for the rest of her life?

XANDER

There are no ifs, Noah. She's going to wake up

GRAYSON

Hey, how's it going with Dani? You know, being under one roof together and everything

ME

Do you know how easily I can walk to her bedroom from my room?

We went out for dinner because there was nothing here we could make. And then we went grocery shopping. Kudos to you brother because I was ready to go back into the car and wait for her. It was brutal

GRAYSON

It's a different experience when you actually enjoy doing something

XANDER

I agree with you for once

ME

Holy shit, it's a fucking miracle!

It's getting late. I need to attempt to get some sleep

GRAYSON

Good luck with that

XANDER

I'll be back at the hospital tomorrow morning and give you updates when I get them

ME

Again, I love you bro

GRAYSON

What about me?

ME

Yeah, yeah. Love you too. Sometimes

I turn my phone off and close my eyes, hoping I'll get some sleep.

But I doubt I will because my brain doesn't want to rest.

Please fucking rest.

Fuck, I can't sleep.

I glance at the clock and it's 12:30 in the morning and I'm hungry.

We have that cake from Marina's. God, I love Marina.

I remove the covers off my body and quietly make my way into the kitchen. Turning on the light, I see Dani standing there with the styrofoam box in her hands.

We both scream.

"Fuck. Why do you do that?" she asks, her eyes widening and placing her hand over her heart.

"Like I knew you were going to be in here."

"You should. You seem to have a radar for when I'm around."

"I'm not a meteorologist."

She squints her eyes. "The next time you scare the shit out of me, it might actually kill me."

I walk closer to her, looking into the box. "What the hell?" I cock my head. "Marina didn't give you the cake, so you can hog it all."

"No, but I figured you don't like chocolate, so..."

"You know it's not nice to make assumptions." I shake my head, pressing my lips together. "Give it to me."

She backs away with the cake in her hand, inserting a piece of it into her mouth. "You want it?" She hides the box behind her back. "Come and get it."

I don't have the energy for this shit.

Boxing Dani in, I grab the container from her and then a fork from one of the drawers behind her. "That was unnecessary, don't you think?"

"That was perfectly necessary," she says as she giggles.

"You have chocolate fudge all over your face," I say.

She pulls her neck in slightly. "Do I?"

I nod. "Uh-huh."

"Where?"

I put some of the fudge on the pad of my thumb, swiping it across her forehead.

She's looking at me like she wants to kill me. "Asshole!" She grabs a napkin off the kitchen table and sits down to wipe the chocolate I swiped across her forehead.

"What are you doing up?" I sit down at the table next to her.

"I could ask you the same thing." She folds her arms underneath her breasts.

I can't help but glance at them before I answer her. How can I not? They're right at eye level.

"Can't sleep, you?"

She nods in agreement. "I was laying there for an hour and then I got hungry. I remembered we have the cake from Marina's and here I am."

"Me too. I think eating because you're nervous about something is an anxiety thing."

She rests her fist on the edge of her jawline. "I've had anxiety munchies since middle school. When I get anxious about something, I eat. It's not as bad as it used to be. The last time it was really bad was—"

I cut her off. "When your dad passed away."

"Yeah." She clears her throat, scratching the back of her ear. "When did you get the munchies?"

"I think I've always had the munchies, but it got worse in high school."

"Why?"

"I put myself under too much stress, trying to be the best in class and writing a book. It was too much shit."

"Speaking of books..." She trails off as she crosses one leg over the other.

"Yeah."

"You went into my room, didn't you?"

My mouth gapes open slightly. "How do you know that?"

"You have a radar for me, and I have a radar for you."

"When did you get into mysteries and thrillers?" I smirk.

"I figured you'd notice my collection."

"It was hard not to. You have two shelves full of them."

"I got into them in high school. Let's just say there was always a voice stuck inside my head which kept telling me I needed to read them."

"Did this voice sound like me?"

"It sounded *exactly* like you."

I grin, looking down at the table. "Well, I'm glad to be of service." I meet her gaze, studying every feature on her face. "Can I ask you something?"

CHAPTER TWENTY

"What?"

"Do you miss your dad?"

"Didn't we cover this already?"

"You never answered it."

I exhale. "Of course I miss him. I miss him every single day. Doesn't matter how much time passes by, I will always miss him."

He smiles. "Does it get any easier? Coping with the loss of a parent, I mean."

"I can't answer that. For me, I have days where I'm totally fine. And I have days where I just wallow in my anxiety." I breathe out. "You know how you said I can talk to you about anything?"

"Uh-huh."

"I want you to be able to talk to me about anything, too." I look deep into his ocean blue eyes. "What's going on in that head of yours?"

"You don't even want to know."

"Try me," I say as I lean back.

"Just warning you. It's fucking scary in there." He points to his head.

"Trust me, I'm used to scary things." I tilt my head. "Talk to me."

"Okay. I've lost my grandparents on both sides. And I thought that shit hurt, and it did. But this it's a different kind of hurt. It feels like someone stabbed me with a really sharp knife fifty times in a row." He pauses for a moment. "I thought Dad would see me graduate and get my degree. Be there when I release my debut. Be at my wedding. But he won't be." He gets all choked up, his eyes filling up with tears.

Without a second thought, I scoot closer to him and wrap my arms around him.

An embrace that feels so personal and unlike anything I've ever experienced. I've never hugged Noah before, so this feels foreign and yet so right.

He wraps his arms tightly around my torso.

My palms make circular motions on his muscular back. My hand makes its way up to his dirty blonde hair.

Wow, his hair is so fucking soft.

I'm starting to get the impression this is getting way too intimate.

Noah doesn't seem too bothered by any of it though which is interesting. The crying subsides, but his grip on me grows even tighter.

It's almost as if he doesn't want to let me go.

What if I don't want him to let me go? What the hell is happening to me?

I can't move.

My body is frozen in time.

His pain is permeating through me like water when it comes into contact with sand.

"I'm going to tell you this because you need to hear it." I loosen my grip on him. He backs up, so he can look me in the eyes. "Lizzie's going to make it through this. And I'm not just saying that to say it. She's one of the strongest people I know. She's not going to give up without a fight."

His eyes are glassy all while he smiles at me.

Butterflies are multiplying in my stomach. My chest is rising and falling. My heart is beating like the sound of a thousand drums.

He's never looked at me that way before during such a calm, intimate moment. We've never had these kinds of moments when we were growing up. All of the moments we had together usually consisted of shouting and swearing.

This is making me feel things I've never felt for him before.

I'm absolutely terrified.

CHAPTER TWENTY-ONE

"Well, that was enlightening," I say.

"Enlightening?"

"Sorry, I don't know what word to use."

She laughs. "We should go to bed. It's late." She walks over to the entryway into the kitchen, leaning against it. "Good night, Noah."

"Good night, Dani."

I make my way into the guest bedroom and lay back on the bed with my hands resting underneath my head.

I've never talked to anyone about my feelings like that. Let alone talk to Dani like that. It was nice to have a civilized conversation with her and not constantly be yelling at each other. I never thought I'd see this day coming.

I can't get over the way she kept staring at me.

I swear she almost put me under her spell with those goddamn brown eyes of hers.

The way she reacted to me putting the fudge all over her forehead. Her eyes grew wide and her eyebrows furrowed. Then, the disgusted expression that appeared all over her face made me think about covering her entire face in chocolate fudge and see how she'd react to that. But, I didn't want to see that play out in reality.

The way she told me I could talk to her about anything.

The way she hugged me.

God, I didn't want to let her go.

Grayson's right. It's so much more than an attraction.

Damn it, I'm so fucked.

DIPSHITS

ME

Code red. I repeat we have a code red. CODE FUCKING RED!!!

XANDER

Dude, it's 1 in the morning

GRAYSON

What is it?

I hit the FaceTime app, turning my volume down so Dani doesn't hear anything.

Pick up the fucking phone.

"Dude, I thought you said you were going to talk to us tomorrow," Grayson says.

"This can't wait." I take a deep breath, letting it all flow out like a steady river. "Okay, you guys know I'm not a fan of talking about my emotions."

Here goes nothing.

"I've never been in love before. What does it feel like?"

I look at Xander, his eyes opening wide like he thinks I'm crazy to ask him that question. "Why are you looking at me? I've never been in love."

Our eyes land on Grayson who's examining the wall behind him and pretending like he can't hear me which I know is absolute bullshit. Clearing my throat, I successfully grab his attention.

He turns his head around. "Why are you both looking at me like that?"

"You heard me, dumbass. I'm not going to repeat it." I stare at him.

"Well, I haven't been in love, so I can't answer your question. How unfortunate. We could reach out to random strangers and ask them instead," Grayson says.

Xander and I understand this is an uncomfortable topic for Grayson to talk about, but I want to know. I need to know.

He rolls his eyes in an aggressive way. "Fine. You want to know what it feels like?" He looks down, his face getting out of frame. "What does being in love feel like? Okay, I can do this. You can do this Gray," he whispers to himself, pacing back and forth.

"Dude!" Xander and I say in unison.

He's scratching the back of his neck with his fingers and getting up off his bed to walk around his bedroom. "Okay, okay." He pauses. "You want to know what being in love feels like? It's an addiction. A drug you can't get enough of. She consumes you. Her voice. Her laugh. Her smile. Everything reminds you of her. When you're around her, you can't help but smile. You're giddy, nervous, and distracted all at once. You're able to be your authentic self around her. One hundred percent yourself. She makes you fucking crazy. But, you don't want to lose her. You can't lose her. And you don't know how to deal with that feeling. It's both euphoric and dysphoric at the same time. It feels like you're losing your goddamn mind." He sits back down on his bed, zoning out into space. "It's like you're the only two people who exist on this planet. All you want is to be around her. There's truly nothing like it. Nothing." Grayson takes a moment to catch his breath, snapping out of his trance. He leans his head back, letting out a deep breath.

My mouth drops open as I take in my surroundings. Xander raises his eyebrows, puckering his lips out.

What the hell was that?

I've never seen Grayson so passionate before. Let alone open to sharing his emotions like that. I know that I'm not the guy who's not fond of sharing his feelings with his friends but he's much worse than I am. He can be very closed off which can be frustrating, but I understand why he's like that.

"Wow. That was beautiful. Just beautiful. You should've majored in inspirational speech giving, bro," Xander says with a hint of sarcastic undertones in his voice.

"Oh, shut the hell up," Grayson says to Xander before focusing his attention on me. "Did that answer your question?"

It takes me a minute to generate an answer because my head feels like it's spinning out of control. I think I have a headache now.

Then, it finally hits me.

I can feel the heat from the imaginary fireworks going off behind me. I pop up from the bed, bending my knees up to my chest. My arms rest on my knee. My chest rapidly rises and falls, and my mouth hangs open.

Grayson smiles like the idiot that he is.

Xander looks at him with a confused expression written all over his face. "Am I missing something here?"

"That, my friend, is the look of a man who realized he's in love with a woman he's known since birth. A woman who he thought was annoying as hell. Not anymore. Am I right?"

Fuck. He's right.

I didn't want to admit it to anybody. Most importantly, I didn't want to admit it to myself. I don't know why. Guess I thought it was crazy to be in love with Dani because she annoyed the shit out of me growing up.

She drove me absolutely insane. She still does, but in a different way.

There are so many words to describe Danielle Solomon. *So. Many. Fucking. Words.* But, I don't think there's enough time to do so.

"What the hell am I going to do?"

Grayson answers me immediately. "You're going to tell her how you feel. You have to tell her."

"I can't tell her. Do you know how weird it's going to be between us if I do? I know she doesn't feel the same way about me."

"How do you know? Have you even asked her?" Grayson asks.

"It's not exactly an ideal conversation starter. We're just starting to get along. I don't want to freak her out by confessing all these feelings I have for her. Feelings I've probably had since we were kids."

Xander decides to join in on the fun. "She deserves to know how you feel. You don't know how she's going to respond. She could reciprocate those feelings."

"Or I make a complete ass out of myself and she doesn't feel the same way."

"When the time is right, you should tell her how you feel. What have you got to lose?" Xander gives me a dose of inspirational romantic advice.

He hasn't been in a long-term relationship before, but he has always been a hopeful romantic. Yes, I said hopeful and not hopeless.

What do I have to lose?

She's what I could lose.

I've lost Dani once.

I'm *not* losing her again.

Grayson observes me and Xander talking until he finally decides to contribute to our conversation.

He doesn't say anything.

Are you fucking kidding me?

A breathy laugh escapes from my mouth. "You have nothing to say there, Romeo?"

He replies to me almost immediately, his dark brown eyes meeting my blue eyes. "Xander took the words right out of my mouth."

"Well, that was constructive," Xander says, awkwardly smiling at Grayson and me.

No shit, Sherlock.

It's so much more than an attraction.

I'm in love with Dani Solomon and I have no idea how I'm going to tell her.

CHAPTER TWENTY-TWO

The morning sun is shining directly into my eyes.

I'm sitting at my desk and trying to get my brain into writing mode. It still doesn't want to work with me.

Why won't you work with me?

"Ugh!" I grunt loudly.

SAGE

ME

hey, i think it's long overdue for me to update you on what's been going on

SAGE

oh, really? how thoughtful of you. and i thought you forgot i existed

ME

rude, i could never. it's just been so fucking crazy lately

SAGE

relax, i'm just busting your non-existent balls.
well, bella basically told me everything, so
there's no need to update me

ME

what's everything?

SAGE

she told me about ben. i'm really sorry, dani.
she told me how you and noah have been
flirting with each other. gross. oh and how you
two are in love with each other. again, gross

ME

hold up. we're not flirting and we're not in love
with each other. you were given inaccurate
information

SAGE

you keep gaslighting yourself there. anyways,
please keep me updated. i thought you got
murdered or something. don't ever do that to
me again or i will murder you myself!

ME

i promise. love you

I hear footsteps and then a knock on my bedroom door.

Opening the door, I see Noah standing in front of me giving me this smug look that's written all over his face.

"What do *you* want?" I ask.

"Cranky are we?"

"Oh, shut up." I snap my eyes shut and open them. "I can't write. Nothing is coming out. *Nothing*. The blinking line is still mocking me. I can't take it anymore."

He walks into my bedroom, slamming the lid to shut my laptop. "Come with me."

I follow him into the kitchen, standing in front of the refrigerator.

He leans against the oven, a smirk slowly appearing across his lips and staring at me.

"What are we doing here? Are you just going to stare at me until I dissolve into nothing? Oh, wait, I have an idea. Let's see who can dissolve who first. I bet you'll win because my brain feels like it's going to explode. And I'm tired as shit."

He walks closer, eyes glued on me.

The smallest of gaps is in between us, but no gap can deny the buzz I'm feeling in my bones and everywhere else.

"I've known you for a pretty long time. And I know you ramble when you're nervous. Am I making you nervous?"

Yes, you're making me fucking nervous.

Backing up into the stainless steel fridge, I jump from the cool metal meeting the skin of my back through the thin fabric of my top.

He's doing this shit on purpose.

I just know it.

CHAPTER TWENTY-THREE

She's standing opposite me, frozen like a beautiful ice sculpture. Her dark brown eyes are staring straight into my soul.

I think I enjoy making Dani nervous, and I don't know why.

I'm unable to catch my breath with the way she's looking at me.

"The fridge is *fucking* cold," she mutters under her breath.

I close the gap between us. Our lips are so close I can smell her breath, a combination of mint and iced tea.

"What the hell are you—"

I cut her off before she can finish asking me what I'm doing. "You have no idea what you do to me."

I hear broken breathing coming out of her mouth as she sucks in her stomach and holds her breath. She blinks her eyes rapidly like a toy trying to reset itself when it malfunctions.

When she releases her breath, her stomach falls back into place. "I need to get stuff out of the fridge, so we can make breakfast." She pushes at my arm to get me to move.

I put my arms out, elbows bent with my hands up. "Alright. Let me get out of your way, *Princess.*"

She looks around the kitchen, mouth slightly parting open. She's taken aback by what I just called her.

Princess.

Because she is one.

She's *always* been one.

She takes out the carton of eggs we bought last night along with goat cheese and a loaf of bread. "I know what you're thinking. 'Dani, I don't like goat cheese. Why are you taking it out?' Because it's for me. You don't have to have any."

"Sit down."

A confused expression writes itself all over her face. "What?"

"Sit the hell down," I command as I take her over to the kitchen table. "You're not making shit. I am. It's about time someone takes care of you for once."

She pouts. "People do take care of me."

"Not compared to the way that you take care of people." I pause. "How do you want your eggs?"

"Scrambled."

"Do you put the goat cheese in last?"

She nods. "I can help put—"

"No."

"Yes, I put it in last," she says softly.

"We're not going to the hospital today," I blurt out.

"What?"

"You heard me. We're going to get the fuck out of this house. And we're going to try and get you inspired to write again."

"How are we going to do that?"

"After breakfast, we're going to go to Sweet & Salty."

She bursts out into laughter. "You in a romance bookstore? Ha, I'd pay to see this shit."

"No payment needed. We're going to get lunch at Coastal Shores because I've been craving a fried chicken sandwich so badly."

"You got a little drool there," she says pointing to the corner of her mouth.

I'm looking down at my chest, but I can't see where she's talking about.

"Made you look." She giggles like a baby.

"And how old are we?" I laugh.

"But it made you laugh, didn't it?"

Yeah, you did.

"It did." I stare at her, getting lost in her eyes. "Thanks. I needed that."

"I know you did."

"Anyways, Sweet & Salty and Coastal Shores are definitely on the list. It'd be good for the both of us to get out and away from the hospital."

"I don't want to hear the word 'hospital' for the next few hours."

"You and me both."

"That looks really good, Noah," she says as I place a plate full of scrambled eggs and a piece of buttered toast in front of her.

"Did you think it was going to look horrible?"

"No, of course not."

"You're so full of shit, Dani."

She places both of her hands over her mouth, her laughter bouncing off inside them and crackling like flames in an open fire.

My mouth curves up into a devilish smirk. "I hate when you underestimate me."

"You love it when I underestimate you."

Okay, maybe I do.

"Oh, shut up." I walk over to the table with a plate of scrambled eggs without goat cheese crumbles and buttered toast.

"This is good," she says before she stabs her fork into the eggs and puts them into her mouth.

"I'm glad."

"You know the only other people who make meals for me are Mom and Bella."

"What are you trying to say, Dani?"

"It's nice to have a guy cook for me."

Once we finish eating breakfast, I wash the dishes and the pan I used to make the eggs.

Dani's still sitting in her chair.

I'm leaning against the front of the sink, studying her from head to toe.

She looks so fucking beautiful.

Her white top is made of thick material, so I can't see her nipples peeking through this time. I don't know whether to be relieved or disappointed. Her shorts are made of the same thick material. I'm assuming it's a matching set. It looks really soft too.

Fuck, I want to touch her.

I can't stop thinking about what it would be like to run my fingers up her arm, feeling the warmth of her skin under the pads of my fingertips.

She gets up off the chair and walks past me.

It's taking everything in my power not to pick her up by her perfect ass, throw her down on the counter, and kiss the shit out of her until she loses her breath.

And I thought it was a good idea to spend yet another day with her. This time is different because I finally admitted to myself and the guys I'm absolutely crazy about her.

My mind is on a constant loop, making me dizzy as hell. Like, how the hell do I act somewhat normal around her now?

Guess I'm going to have to try my very best because I'm not ready to tell her how I feel yet.

I stop her before she leaves by grabbing her hand.

She looks down and her eyes bounce back up at me. "Hi."

"Go get dressed."

"Right now?"

"Yes, right now."

"Anything in particular you want me to wear?" She threads her fingers into mine, smirking at me.

Oh, she's really testing me.

"You can wear whatever you want. If I'm being honest, you look pretty in every piece of clothing you wear."

Why did I just say that out loud?

The cutest smile spreads across her lips. "You think I'm pretty?"

I think you're the most beautiful woman I've ever laid my eyes on.

I nod, my eyes starting at her feet and working their way up to her face.

"I'll go get dressed," she says through a breathy laugh.

She walks away from me and into her bedroom, closing the door behind her.

God, I hope I make it through today.

CHAPTER TWENTY-FOUR

I'm not losing my mind.

Noah was checking me out again.

And he called me pretty.

This time feels different because I know I wasn't imagining it in my head. The way his eyes worked their way up my body made me feel like I was about to melt into a pile of mush.

I don't just find Noah attractive.

I have feelings for him.

I think I always have, but I never wanted to admit it to myself because how could I have feelings for a man I used to hate? I have no idea if Noah feels the same way about me.

He used to tease me all the time.

Why is the way he's treating me now any different? It's not, but it is. It's not teasing in a way where it's mean and cruel. It's really hot.

How am I going to survive through this entire day with him now that I've admitted my feelings for him? Well, internally, I mean.

BELLA

ME

you were right. i'm not just attracted to noah. i have feelings for him. THIS IS SO FUCKING BAD, BELLS!!!

BELLA

I told you so. Give me all the details. NOW!

ME

this is going to be a long ass text, just warning you

last night, we went to marina's for dinner and went grocery shopping afterwards. we both were up pretty late because we couldn't sleep. we talked for like an hour or two about books, my dad, and ben. this morning he made me breakfast. he's taking me to sweet & salty so i can get inspired to write again. then, he's taking me to coastal shores for lunch. he said everything's a mystery after that

BELLA

You're having writer's block again?

ME

yeah, it fucking sucks, but i'm hoping this trip to sweet & salty might help. or maybe just the entire day. i don't know

BELLA

It sounds like he's pretty crazy about you

ME

i love you, but please don't feed into my delusions

BELLA

You do realize the shit you read in romance books can actually happen in real life, right? You just have to find your own book boyfriend. But Dani, you already found him. He's been in your life this entire time. And you both spent most of your lives fighting over the dumbest shit. Take this opportunity to get to know him and I mean really get to know him. We don't find love, it finds us. Well…some of us

ME

wow, that was beautiful. i really hope you're not feeding into my delusions because i'm going to be so disappointed if you are

BELLA

Ugh, shut up, Dani

You both deserve time away from the hospital. time to decompress. Time with each other. And time to get to know each other in a different light. Like you said, everything changed when you took care of him when he had his panic attack. You deserve someone who wants to take care of you. You take care of all of us: me, Sage, your mom. You've been taking care of Laura, Lizzie, and now, you're taking care of Noah

Dani, you're my soul sister. After everything you've been through and after everything you've done for me, you deserve all the happiness in the world. Especially if that happiness is with Noah!!!

ME

i love you so much. i don't deserve you

BELLA

> I love you too. Like I said, you deserve the world. Stop texting me and go live out your own version of the romance novels you read. Update me when you can. I need to know what happens

We don't find love, it finds us.

I'm trying not to get my hopes up that there's a possibility that Noah could have feelings for me.

What if he doesn't? What if this is all in my head?

God, I hate being an overthinker. My brain is in a constant loop which never fucking ends.

Shit, I need to get dressed.

I look at my reflection in my floor-length mirror.

My hair is a fucking mess. I don't have the patience to make it look pretty so I just throw it up in a high ponytail. That, and it's hot as shit outside.

There's a knock on my door.

I open it to see Noah standing in a white t-shirt and gray sweatpants.

We're both looking at each other's outfits.

"I swear this is a coincidence," he says.

I purse my lips. "Yeah, a major coincidence."

"We're not matching exactly. You're wearing shorts."

"We're wearing the same colors though," I point out, looking down at my white tank top and gray cotton knit shorts.

"I can put on a different pair of sweatpants," he suggests.

CHAPTER TWENTY-FIVE

Fuck, she looks so beautiful.

Her hair is up in a ponytail, tendrils framing her face. Her shorts are highlighting the crap out of her insane curves. And she looks so good in white.

Honestly, she looks good in everything. She could wear a goddamn trash bag and look absolutely perfect.

"You don't need to change," she says before she breaks out into a small fit of laughter.

I literally can't help but smile when I'm around her now. Admitting my feelings for Dani, even though it's only been to myself, has unlocked this side of me where it's impossible for me to ignore the little things. I notice the crease she gets in between her eyebrows when she smiles and the different kinds of laughs she has.

"Do you want to take my car or yours?" I ask.

"Can we take mine?"

"You're answering my question with a question." I grin.

"I'm sorry." She fiddles with her fingers, looking down at the floor.

Her mouth gapes open until she presses her full pink lips together.

I put my hands on hers to stop her from playing around with her shaking hands.

She looks at my hands and meets my gaze.

"You *never* have to do that with me," I say.

When I would get in extremely uncomfortable situations at school or at home, I would fidget with anything I could get my hands on. Sometimes I would just play with my own hands.

I want her to know that she's safe with me.

I don't want to be a source of anxiety for her.

I want to be the calm before the storm.

I want to be her everything.

"Dani, are you ready?" I ask, standing in the foyer.

She comes out of her bedroom, purse slinging over her shoulder. "Yeah, I'm ready."

Archie comes running up to us, meowing up a storm.

"Hi, buddy." She smiles at him.

He rubs Dani's legs, looking up at her.

"Hey, Archie." I pick him up and he grabs onto my shirt.

"Archie!" She wrestles with him until she finally gets him off me, meeting my gaze after she puts him down on the floor.

She punches me in my right arm in a playful way.

"I told you to stop punching me."

"I barely touched you." Her nose scrunches.

I've never seen her do that before. If she ever does it again, I'm fucking done for.

"You don't listen very well, do you?"

"You know I don't listen, especially not to you."

I lick my lips, walking closer to her. There's only a sliver of a gap between us.

I'm looking at her face in pieces instead of as a whole.

Her freckles are peeking through the makeup on her nose. They fade out as you look under her eyes. Her eyelashes are long and thick.

She's even more beautiful up close like this.

"I think we can change that. Don't you?"

She rolls her eyes. "Good luck with that."

We're both breathing heavily and staring deeply into each other's eyes.

God, I want to kiss her so fucking badly.

I close the gap between us.

Her lips are barely grazing mine. And yet it's enough to send me over the edge.

She sucks her lips in, chest slowly heaving. "We should go."

She escapes the forcefield around her.

I shake my head, clearing my throat.

God, why did I do that?

"Yeah, we should." I stop her before she makes her way out the door. "Am I driving or do you want to drive?"

"*You* can drive."

I stick my thumbs up in the air as she walks out the door with me trailing behind her.

When we get into the car, my hands are gripping the steering wheel so hard I might break it.

"Noah."

"What?"

"Are you okay?"

"I didn't get a lot of sleep last night. All I could think about was Dad, Lizzie, and Mom."

And you.

"If it makes you feel any better, I didn't get enough sleep last night either."

"Guess we both have a lot of shit on our minds."

She nods. "Yeah."

I back out of the driveway, glancing at the backup camera to make sure there aren't any cars driving by or any people walking behind us.

Once the coast is clear, we're off.

It's been about five minutes since we left the house, which isn't too long. The Promenade at Sunset Cove is around a ten-minute drive from Crystal Harbor.

The radio blasts our ears with Lorde.

She goes to turn the volume down, but I gesture to her to keep it on. I extend my arm out, twisting the knob clockwise to turn the volume up.

"I didn't know you liked this song." She projects her voice, so I can hear it over the music.

"There are a lot of things you don't know about me." I glance at her, grinning ear to ear.

She smiles, turning away from me to hide her flushed cheeks.

"The chorus in the song is so freaking good. Here it comes." She waves her right arm up and down to the rhythm of the song and starts moving the upper half of her body.

She's dancing while sitting in the driver's seat. I can barely hear the music over Dani's singing. While it's not an award-winning voice, I can't help but smile the entire time she's singing the chorus.

I turn down the music a little bit, so I don't have to yell over it. She'll be able to hear me easier.

"You know if the whole author thing doesn't work out for you, I think singing might be a great second backup plan," I tease, even though my tone sounds serious.

She puckers her lips out and pulls them back, curving them up to create a smile that lights up that pretty face of hers. "Actually that's a horrible backup plan. I'm guessing you can't hear like a normal person. I wasn't blessed with good singing genes."

"I know. I'm just being nice." I burst out in laughter that becomes louder than the music currently playing.

"You're lucky I'm driving right now because you'd have a small bruise somewhere on your arm from me hitting it."

That's one of the reasons why I brought it up.

I'd do anything to get her hands on my body.

We're driving around the area where Sweet & Salty is to find a parking spot.

Why did I think coming here on the weekend was a good idea?

"There's one!" Dani points to a space on my left and wiggles her hand in my face.

"Can you not do that? I'm driving."

"Sorry."

Shaking my head, I lick my lips and smile away from her.

I pull into the parking space and we unbuckle our seatbelts.

Dani's sitting there staring at the sign for Mom's shop. Her eyes are growing wide like this is the first time she's been here when it's actually the millionth time.

"This is going to sound really cheesy, but I'm really happy that your mom opened Sweet & Salty. It's always been a safe space for me, but even more so when my dad passed away."

She looks away from me, but I reach my hand out to turn her face back in my direction.

I squint my eyes, my gaze fixating on her. "That's not cheesy at all. We all have our safe spaces. I know I do."

Fuck, her eyes are going to obliterate me.

"What's your safe space?"

"I don't want to tell you. You might steal it."

She scoffs. "I would never do that."

"Just like the time you said you didn't steal my phone on family game night when we were in sixth grade."

"I didn't steal your phone." She opens her mouth, closing it to conceal a laugh that's about to explode out of her.

"You're full of shit, Solomon."

I put my index finger and thumb underneath my chin. My index finger and pad of my thumb are resting on the edge of my jawline.

Dani shakes her head, rolling her eyes at me. "I'm getting out of the car now, so feel free to yell at me on the way in."

She closes the car door, and I slam mine.

She's looking at me like she's about to jump me and crossing her arms in front of her chest. "What?"

"What the hell did my car door ever do to you?"

I inspect the door to make sure they're aren't any dents, scratches, or marks. "It looks perfectly fine to me."

"It better be because you would've been paying for any damage you would've caused. Just saying."

How about the emotional damage you caused after you stopped talking to me?

She walks into the bookshop, with me trailing a few steps behind, and the bell dings as the door opens.

God, I haven't stepped foot in here since Mom opened the place.

It still looks the same. Bright white bookshelves filled to the brim with romance books. There's a ton of pinks and greens to make the space cozy and make sure people know that this is a romance bookstore when they walk in here.

You can't get a bookstore that's pure romance any more than Sweet & Salty.

Dani's smiling like crazy which is having a domino effect on me, causing me to smile as she walks aimlessly around the shop.

Her smile is blinding, but it's also incredibly beautiful. Her eyes are sparkling like fireworks lighting up the night sky.

She turns around to face me. "You know I used to work here full-time when I was in high school? Luckily, your mom let me come back to work here during the summer to earn some extra money."

"Yeah, she told me she offered you a job."

"Before working at Sweet & Salty, I called this place my second home because it was. And it still is. It's surreal I've had the opportunity to work here. I've learned so much about running a small business and found out about self-publishing during my time here. I'm thankful for your mom, Noah. You have no idea."

"She talked about you a lot. The way you'd light up when you had a book in your hand and when a customer would come up to you, asking for a book recommendation. She said you were in your element. And she isn't wrong. You're glowing."

CHAPTER TWENTY-SIX

"Do you think I look like Edward when he stepped out into the sun in *New Moon*?"

Noah's looking at me like he doesn't understand what I just asked him.

"Have you watched *Twilight* before?"

He flattens his lips, raising an eyebrow. "Of course I have. Lizzie watched it all the time when we were younger. I couldn't help but sit down and watch them because I'd get immediately sucked in."

I smile. "Yeah, those movies will do that to you."

"For the record, I said you're glowing. Not sparkling. There's a difference," he says.

"Whatever."

I'm standing in front of one of the bookshelves closest to the register.

I can feel Noah's presence behind me, lingering there like a shadow which has always been there metaphorically, but is physically here now.

"You're *much* prettier than him by the way," he whispers in my ear while his hands settle on the tops of my shoulders.

Goosebumps are popping up all over my skin.

I smile at the bookshelf I'm standing in front of, turning around to face him. "Am I really?"

He laughs. "Uh-huh."

"Thanks, I've *always* wanted to know if I'm prettier than a vampire who sparkles in the sunlight." Sarcasm is present all throughout my voice.

He rolls his eyes, lips twitching to stop himself from smiling. "Are you getting inspired at all?"

I shake my head, frowning. "Nope." I take a deep breath. "It sucks. This place used to be where I found all my inspiration and now I'm getting nothing."

"This is a bad case of writer's block you got there."

"Thank you for stating the obvious, smart ass."

He gently nudges me in the arm and I return the favor.

Taking out my phone, I turn it on to check the time. It's almost 3 p.m.

How the hell have we been here for this long and I didn't get any inspiration to write?

"Can we go eat now?" I ask.

"Yeah, we can."

Noah walks out of the shop first while I stand in front of the doorway for a bit, taking in all the memories running through my head like an old videotape.

When I walk out, the bell rings as the door closes.

He's leaning against my car, staring at me.

I suck in my lips, swiping my tongue across the top row of my teeth.

Why are guys so attractive when they lean on shit?

"Do I have something on my face?"

He looks around, a confused expression writing itself all over his face. "No, why?"

"You stare at me a lot."

"It's hard not to," he says as I walk closer to him.

"Why?" I squint my eyes, grinning like crazy.

"Do you want to see what a beautiful woman looks like?"

I cock an eyebrow. "Huh?"

He takes out his phone, opening his camera and shoving into my face. "Who's that?"

"Me."

"Exactly."

Maybe he does have feelings for me. No, this has to be all in my head. This isn't real. Can I make it a day without over-thinking about something? No, that's never going to happen.

I giggle, feeling my cheeks overheating. "You don't have to compliment me all the time."

"I've said it before and I'll say it again. You deserve to hear every goddamn compliment that exists."

My heart just feels like it just sunk down to my stomach. I can't move or breathe.

When I finally unfreeze myself, I make my way to the edge of the sidewalk.

Walking over the protruded edge, I stumble backwards into Noah. His arms wrap around my waist to catch me from falling on the searing hot ground.

His broad and muscular chest is pressing into my back.

"Thanks for not letting me fall on my ass," I say.

"Anytime, Princess. I'll always be here to catch you when you fall."

He winks his left eye while both corners of his lips curve up to produce a smile.

"You know this is what a prince does for his princess in romance movies and books. He comes to her rescue."

"I don't call you Princess for the hell of it you know."

A small chuckle escapes my mouth as my lips curve up. "Would that make you my prince then?"

"I would say that's pretty accurate." Noah breaks out into this laugh, one I bet the entire shopping center can hear.

Oh, he definitely has feelings for me. I think.

"Good to know," I say.

We both get into the car and he backs out of the parking space we were parked in. Coastal Shores is on the other side of the Promenade. It's not too far away.

Closing my eyes, I wrap my arms around my stomach and waist. I need to feel what it's like having Noah's arms around me again. It's not the same because my arms are much smaller than his.

We pull into another parking space that's closer to Coastal Shores and he turns the engine off.

I lean my head back up, opening my eyes and feeling a hole burning through the side of my head from him staring at me.

My lips twitch. "What are you staring at?"

"Someone's hungry, huh?"

"Maybe."

He turns to me. "You know how I know? You get all cranky. Your face scrunches up and you look like you want to murder someone."

"That can be arranged."

"What?"

"We can run back to the house and I can get the flashlight. I might need it in case you really annoy the shit out of me." I wink at him.

He chuckles. "It's my life's mission to annoy the shit out of you, Solomon."

"Glad we're on the same page," I say, getting out of the car and walking up to the front door to Coastal Shores.

Noah holds the door open for me and I look up at him.

"This is another thing a prince does for their princess. He holds the door open for her."

"I know," he says before he breaks out into this laugh that mesmerizes the crap out of me.

Once we make it inside, I make a beeline to two empty seats

at the bar. Putting my purse by my feet, I slouch down on the seat.

"Why are you putting your purse under your feet? You could trip over it and fall again."

"Well, you're always here to catch me if I fall. Isn't that right, Prince Charming?" The corner of my lips rises up as my eyebrow furrows.

"Alright, you got me."

"Is that who I think it is?" A female voice says as she walks towards us.

Tan skin glistens from the reflection of the sunlight peeking through the windows. Dark brunette hair that's perfectly straightened. Familiar hazel eyes meet my gaze.

Valerie Castillo-Ryder.

"Dude, what the hell are you doing here?" I ask her.

"Ronnie was looking for new part-time employees and I needed to make some extra cash so it worked out quite perfectly."

Ronnie is the manager at Coastal Shores and he's been running the place for decades. Most likely since before Noah and I were born.

"Bella didn't tell me you work here."

"My sister doesn't tell you a lot of things, but she did tell me about Ben. I'm so sorry about your dad, Noah."

A sliver of a smile appears on his face. "Thanks."

Valerie's eyes grow wide. "Life hasn't been fair to you guys, has it?"

"Life hasn't been fair to your family either," I say to her.

She nods. "True, but I'm past all that shit. Bella, not so much. Let's move on, shall we? What are we drinking?"

Noah gestures to me to order first. I glance at the drinks section of the menu and my eyes land on the peach sangria. "I'll have a glass of the peach sangria."

She doesn't make any remarks such as 'ah, it's one of those

days, isn't it' or 'isn't it a bit early to be drinking even if it's the early afternoon?' Instead, she winks at me. Her eyes land on Noah. "What about you?"

He glances over at the beers that are available on tap. His eyes meet Valerie's. "Sam Adams Summer Ale."

"Do you guys know what you want to eat?" Valerie's eyes move from me to Noah.

We both look at each other and shake our heads.

"Take all the time you need." She walks away from us to grab our drinks.

He gets off the bar stool. "I'll be right back. Going to the bathroom."

Valerie returns, placing my sangria in front of me and Noah's beer on the counter.

She stares at me, studying my face.

"What?" I ask her.

"I didn't want to say anything when Noah was here, but my sister told me about your feelings."

"My feelings?"

"For Noah."

God, she has such a big mouth.

I roll my eyes, throwing my head back.

"Do you want some advice?"

"I think Bella covered that for me, but sure. Why the hell not?"

She bends down slightly, resting her arms on the bar counter. "Sunset Cove is a small town. It's rare to find someone, especially someone you've known your entire life, that you immediately connect with. I know you and Noah didn't get along, but there's something's different between you two now. He looks at you in the way I want my future boyfriend to look at me."

"And in what way does he look at me?"

She leans in closer to me. "Like he never wants to look away."

"God, you sound just like Bella."

"I mean we're cut from the same cloth, so it's hard not to sound like her." She pauses, tucking a loose tendril of hair behind her ear. "The fact that the man you've known all your life is the first man you've fallen for says a lot about you and a lot about him. Bella and I have always known there was something between you two and it was never hatred. It's always been something more than that. Don't be afraid to let him in, even into the parts you don't want him to see."

Don't be afraid to let him in, even into the parts you don't want him to see.

I've been afraid of many things in my twenty-two years of living on this planet. Falling in love with Noah is the scariest thing that's ever happened to me, but it's also the most exciting.

I have nothing to say to Valerie, so I just sit there, leaning back and digesting everything she just told me.

Noah comes back, looking at us. "What did I miss?"

"Nothing important," Valerie says. "I know I distracted you from figuring out what you want to order, so I can come back..."

Noah shakes his head, grunting.

"Guess I'm not the only one who's hungry." My lips quiver. "I know what he's having."

noah

"Then go ahead and order for me then if you think you're so smart." I raise my eyebrows, looking away from Dani.

"Do you not recall telling me this morning what you've been craving from here for days?" She smiles and her eyes land on Valerie. "Fried chicken sandwich and curly fries."

"Everything on it?"

Dani nods at Valerie.

"I bet I know what you're going to get," I say.

"What does the loser win?"

"You get to buy me ice cream from Sunset Cove Creamery after this. If you win..."

I'll tell you I'm in love with you. Yeah, there's no fucking way I'm doing that.

"I'll buy you one of those big chocolate chip cookies from The Green Sea Turtle."

"Deal," she says as she sticks out her hand for me to shake, but I hold onto her hand under the counter for a little bit longer.

"She's going to have the club wrap. No ham or tomato. Ranch on the side instead of mayo. With curly fries."

Valerie looks at me while I shift my body in her direction. We're both waiting to see if I'm right.

Dani rolls her eyes. "Guess I'm buying you ice cream."

I pump a fist in the air, making a goofy face.

"You guys have fun. I'll go put your orders in." Valerie disappears, leaving Dani and I alone.

"How the hell did you remember that?" Dani asks.

I roll my eyes and laugh. "We came here a lot when we were in middle school and you used to get that every single time."

"I didn't get it *every* single time." She taps her index finger on the counter.

"*Almost* every single time."

Studying her face, she looks at me with her eyes moving from side to side.

I love when she's annoyed at me.

Dani's basket is basically a ghost town and so is mine.

I'm so full, but I want that damn ice cream, especially because she has to buy it for me.

Valerie walks over to us. "Guess you guys were hungry?"

"You could say that," Dani says.

"Ready for the check?"

We both nod and look at each other.

If she thinks she's paying for this, she's out of her mind.

Valerie goes over to the touchscreen to print out our check, setting it down in between us.

"You're not paying for this."

"Noah."

I shake my head. "Do I need to remind you again of what you've done for my family?"

"No, you don't."

"Besides, you're buying me ice cream. It's a win-win situation."

"Yeah, for you."

"You're. Not. Paying. For. This," I repeat.

"Fine." She furrows her eyebrows, sinking in her seat.

"You're not actually upset about this. Are you? If you are, I'd be happy to have you pay for lunch and my ice cream."

"No, you're offering to pay, so pay."

"You're mad."

"I am *not.*"

"You do this thing with your face when you're mad."

"Shut up. No, I don't."

"Yes, you do. Your eyebrows furrow, your mouth turns into a frown, and you cross your arms in front of your chest."

"Stop making shit up."

"You're doing it right now!" I laugh. "I know it's hard to not think about Lizzie. Having an intense case of writer's block probably doesn't help either. It's nice to spend time with you and not scream at each other."

"Yeah, I *guess* it's nice."

"You *guess?*"

"What do you want me to say, Noah?"

There are so many things I want to say to you.

"Just tell me the truth," he says.

CHAPTER TWENTY-EIGHT

noah

"Okay, it's nice spending time with you instead of wanting to punch you in the face," she admits.

"You *loved* punching me."

"I still do," she says as she punches me below my shoulder.

"God, you're strong."

"Maybe, you're just weak."

"Take that shit back."

She shakes her head, getting up off the chair.

I leave a tip for Valerie, sipping on the water she gave us after we finished our drinks.

"I'm glad I got to see you guys!" Valerie shouts.

"Us too!" Dani raises her voice.

Dani walks out the door first with me following suit.

Sunset Cove Creamery is on the same side as Coastal Shores in the Promenade. It's not far away at all but with the heat and sun blazing it feels like it's miles away.

Opening the door to Sunset Cove Creamery, a cool breeze slaps me in the face.

Fuck, that feels so good.

Dani goes in first and I follow.

It smells like heaven in here. The sweet scent of waffle cones and nostalgia hits me in the face. I used to come here a lot when I was a kid. Little Noah was obsessed with ice cream. Adult Noah still has that obsession.

"What do you want?" she asks.

I look in the giant cooler, inspecting all the flavors they have. My eyes gravitate immediately towards mint chocolate chip. I point to it with my index finger, so Dani can see what she's going to order for me.

"Hey, what can I get for you guys?" A guy that looks about our age with dark brunette hair asks us.

"He's going to have a scoop of mint chocolate chip."

"What size?"

"Medium in a waffle cone," I say.

"How about you?" He turns his attention to Dani, scanning her from head to toe.

Why is he checking her out? Nah, fuck that, it's annoying the shit out of me.

"A scoop of chocolate in a small cup, please."

"Coming right up. Hey, do you go to SCU?" His eyes are burning a hole through Dani's face.

"Yeah."

"Oh, cool. I'm starting my junior year this upcoming semester. What are you studying?"

"Creative writing and magazine journalism. I'm going into my senior year this semester," she says to him.

It's like I'm not here anymore. He's not even looking in my direction.

"Nice. So, you're going to be..."

"An author. I've been working on my debut since middle school, actually."

"Wow, that's pretty cool. What do you write?"

"Romance."

"I had a feeling."

"How so?"

"I don't know. You look like a romance writer."

He's making small talk with her while he's putting her chocolate ice cream in a small cup.

"Oh, why? Do you think I look like a romance writer?" Her eyebrows raise.

"I don't know." He pauses. "Hey, can I ask you a question?"

"Sure," she says as her lips form into a small smile.

I'm fiddling with my fingers because I need to do something with my hands. I think punching this guy in the face will be my next option.

"Are you a library book?"

She doesn't say anything. Instead, she's just standing there and waiting in anticipation of what he's going to say next.

"Because I'd love to check you out."

Where the hell did that come from? Okay, this guy crossed the line so far it's no longer a line. It's a dot. A fucking speck.

She chuckles, but not in the cute way she normally does. She's uncomfortable, and so am I.

I put my arm around her. "Sorry man, she's taken."

She looks up at me, a smile slowly spreading across her lips and her eyes blinking rapidly.

"I didn't know. Makes sense, though."

"Why?" she asks him.

"You're pretty and nice. I shouldn't have assumed you were single. I'm sorry."

"It's fine," she says.

No, it's not fucking fine.

He hands Dani the small cup of chocolate ice cream and my waffle cone with mint chocolate chip ice cream.

She pays for our ice cream, barely making eye contact with the guy.

We sit down at the table closest to the door. She digs into her ice cream, but I can't shake off how angry I am.

"Noah," she says.

"What?"

"Calm the hell down. You didn't need to rescue me with that guy. I can handle doing things myself. I was about to say something very snarky before you intervened."

"I'm sorry. It just made me uncomfortable."

Can I still beat the shit out of him?

"You still get these bouts of anger, huh?"

I have these moments when I get angry over the dumbest shit. Something in my body gets worked up. Sometimes I just have to let it out, or it just breaks me down bit by bit.

"You remember that?" I take a bite of my waffle cone.

"I remember one of our family game nights back in middle school and you completely lost it when I won. You ripped the game up and stormed into your bedroom, slamming the door behind you. Your parents thought it fell off the doorframe." She takes a spoonful of ice cream as I feel my phone buzz through the table.

DIPSHITS

XANDER

Hey, so, we haven't heard from Dr. Miller yet. I don't know if she's going to update us at all. We keep seeing gurneys being pulled out of rooms and into the elevators. She's swamped with surgeries, man

ME

Shit, how's my mom?

XANDER

She's alright. Dani's mom hasn't left her side since we got here this morning

ME

That doesn't surprise me. Speaking of Dani...

XANDER

Did you confess your undying love for her yet?

ME

No, you idiot. She's been having this really horrible writer's block, so I took her to Sweet & Salty to see if it'd spark some inspiration for her

XANDER

I'm sorry did you just say Sweet & Salty? As in your mom's bookshop. The one that exclusively sells romance…

ME

Yes, dipshit

After that, we went to Coastal Shores for lunch and ran into Bella's sister, Valerie, at the bar

XANDER

Who's Bella?

ME

Dani's best friend. You'd like her

XANDER

Maybe you should send me her Instagram handle

ME

Why? So you can fall in love with her on the spot?

XANDER

Oh, shut the hell up. What happened after you ran into her sister?

ME

We're at Sunset Cove Creamery now. The guy who helped us out was flirting with Dani

XANDER

Somebody sounds jealous

ME

Of course I was jealous. So, I stepped in and told him we were boyfriend and girlfriend

XANDER

Wait, you did what now?

Ugh…doesn't matter. I'm going to head back to the apartment and make sure that it's all in one piece

ME

Why? Do you think Gray destroyed the place?

XANDER

Wouldn't surprise me. Honestly, nothing he does surprises me anymore. Oh, by the way, ignore him when he does stupid shit. He's trying to make up for the lack of manhood he doesn't have

ME

Oh, shit

GRAYSON

You want me to beat your ass, Xander?

ME

Hey, look who finally decided to show up

GRAYSON

Sorry, I was taking a shower. I just came back from the gym. Did you know there are places guys can sweat in I never knew about until now?

ME

I had the same thought when Dani and I were walking to Sunset Cove Creamery. Dude, what the fuck is up with this shit?

GRAYSON

I have no idea

XANDER

I'd love to see you try and beat my ass, Gray

GRAYSON

Want me to set up a mat for when you get home then?

ME

Okay kids, this was fun and all, but I'm going to go now. Good luck beating the shit out of each other

I can't imagine how my mom is feeling.

Annoyed that Dr. Miller hasn't updated her yet.

Anxious.

Mad.

Upset.

And then there's Grayson and Xander who are total dumbasses. All three of us are roommates. We live in the same apartment which is located off campus. I can attest they beat the crap out of each other on a daily basis.

There's something that's bothering Grayson because he's been so testy lately. I don't want to pry it out of him. I'm just going to have to let him tell me when he's ready. It's something that took a long time for me to get used to with him. Having patience.

"Hey, are you okay?" Dani pulls me back into reality.

"Xander has been at the hospital with my mom. He said they haven't gotten any updates from Dr. Miller about Lizzie's condition."

I'm freaking the fuck out. What if she's going to be like this for months? Years? What if she doesn't wake up and she has to be hooked up to a machine for the rest of her life?

Throwing my napkin into the garbage, I rush out the door.

I need air.

I can't breathe in here.

Throwing my empty cup into the trash, I follow Noah outside. He's pacing back and forth.

"Noah, stop."

He's not listening to me, so I stop in front of him and place my hands below his shoulders.

He doesn't make eye contact with me. Instead, he's staring at the ground.

"Look at me." I tilt his face up, so his eyes can meet mine. "Look. At. My. Face."

Once his eyes land on mine, it's game over. They're glued on me.

He doesn't say anything, and neither do I. We're just staring at each other, speaking with our facial expressions.

I'm trying so hard not to cry in front of him because it hurts me to see him like this. I've never seen Noah so vulnerable and in so much pain.

"Please talk to me. Tell me what's going on. We told each other that we'd tell each other anything. Remember?"

He sucks his lips in, closing his eyes for a brief moment before opening them. "What if my sister doesn't wake up? What if she's going to be hooked up to a machine for the rest of her life? What if she's in a coma for several more months? Possibly even years. Goddammit, I should've been the one in that fucking car."

"What the hell are you talking about?"

"Mom sent Dad out to the grocery store to pick up some things. I came home for the summer to spend time with them. Lizzie volunteered to spend some quality time with him after I wanted to go with him. I let her go because she doesn't see him as often as I do. My dad is gone because of me. My sister is unconscious because of me. This is all my fault."

Helping Noah sit on one of the benches next to the creamery, I sit down next to him. His chest is heaving and his breathing is offbeat.

"Hey. Don't blame yourself for this. None of this is your fault. When my dad passed away, I blamed myself. There's this chemical in our brains that tries to convince us when something tragic happens, it's our fault. The irony is, it isn't. It took me a long damn time to accept that." I take a deep breath. "Do you remember what I told you in the hospital? The day of the accident?"

He nods, his eyes blazing their way into my bones.

"I really hated it when people told me it takes time to grieve and move on when you experience a tragedy. But, it's the truth. There's something Marina said to us I can't stop thinking about. I've been replaying it in my head. 'The people who say that time heals all are a bunch of liars because it's not the whole truth. It doesn't take time to heal an open wound, all it takes is you believing in yourself.' She's right on the money. You just need to believe in yourself that you can get through this, because you can. And you're not alone. I'm here, and I'm not going anywhere."

"I forgot how wise Marina is," he says.

Giggling with my mouth closed, I smile and slightly squint

my eyes. "You wouldn't believe the amount of advice that woman has given me over the years. She came to my dad's funeral and sat down next to me. She held my hand the entire time. She's a fucking superhero. I wouldn't have made it through that day without her. Without Bella and Sage. Without my mom. Without your parents and Lizzie." I cup his face. "Lizzie's going to wake up. She's one of the strongest people I know. She's hurt herself more times than I can count on both of my hands. She's resilient as hell."

I place the palm of my hand on his bicep which is pure muscle.

Damn, is there a part of his body that isn't muscular?

His eyes are glassy. "I know she is. It's just...my mind goes straight to the negatives, so my anxiety can take over. So, it can win."

"Tell your anxiety to back the hell off. Your sister is going to wake up. I just know it."

He pulls me in for a hug which catches me a bit off guard.

My head lands where his broad chest is.

We sink into each other, his pain transferring over to me and making me shed a few tears.

Closing my eyes, I don't want to let him go, and I don't want him to let me go either.

Everything is going to be fine.

At least, I hope so.

CHAPTER THIRTY

ONE MONTH LATER

Lizzie's still in the hospital, unconscious and hooked up to a ton of wires. Summer is flying by, I don't know how July is almost over already.

This isn't the first time my sister's been in the hospital.

When we were younger, she was always accident-prone. Bad luck followed her everywhere.

She was in her tomboy phase when she was in her early teenage years.

She got into skateboarding. Well, she tried to get into skateboarding. She took a tumble down the hill near our house when she was fourteen and sliced her knee open. It took months for that wound to heal.

It's hard to believe my sister is a detective now for the Sunset Cove Special Victims Unit, solving sex crimes and helping victims. It's something she's been passionate about since she was in high school, giving a voice to the voiceless and helping people who can't help themselves.

It's inspiring.

She's always inspired me to chase after my dreams and not let the assholes out there get me down. I should compliment her more often to her actual face, and not just in my head.

I do have to say Dani has been amazing through all this. She hasn't left my side since she got here.

I don't deserve her.

The more time I spend with her, the more I fall in love with her. It's hard not to fall in love with a woman like Dani.

Every time she walks into a room, it's so bright I'm blinded. If she was a witch, I would've been cast under her spell.

It's getting harder to be around her though without blurting out the truth about how I feel. I want to tell her when the time is right. She deserves to know how I feel even if there's a chance she may not feel the same way.

I blink my eyes multiple times to pull me out of my daze.

I'm sitting on one of the chairs in front of Lizzie's room.

It's the afternoon. We've all been here for hours, anxiously waiting for the moment when my sister wakes up from her prolonged slumber.

Dani fell asleep in the crook of my neck, holding my hand with her arm interlocked with mine. She looks so fucking cute when she's sleeping.

Mom and Celia are sitting inside Lizzie's room, talking about God knows what.

She wakes up, slowly lifting her head out of the crook of my neck. She's rubbing her eyes. "Shit, how long was I asleep?"

"I'd say like thirty minutes." I smile at her, staring into her rich dark chocolate eyes that make me melt.

Her eyebrows lightly furrow and she smiles back at me. "Why are you looking at me like that?"

"I'm getting deja vu. We sat in these very same chairs a month ago, and you asked me the very same question when I woke up from my power nap."

She laughs into my shoulder, her breath heating me from the inside out. "You're right. I totally forgot about that."

"You forgot about something that happened a month ago?"

"In my defense, a lot of shit has happened over the past month. My brain isn't functioning like it normally does, and neither is yours." She wiggles her pointer finger in my face.

I grab it, moving it out of my face and interlocking my fingers with hers.

I'm finding every excuse to touch her in some way whether it's holding her hand, hugging her, or putting my hand on her thigh.

The interesting thing is she doesn't seem to mind any of it.

She doesn't flinch like she did before.

Out of nowhere, I hear screaming and crying. Dani and I look at each other all bug-eyed. We get up and run into Lizzie's room.

Mom is hugging Lizzie, but Lizzie doesn't seem too happy about it. Celia is smiling at them.

I'm doing my best to hold back tears because I don't want to be the domino causing all the women in the room to fall.

"Hey," my sister says in monotone through a rasp, barely smiling. "Can I have some water, please?"

Mom runs out of the room to get some water for her.

When she returns, she has a styrofoam cup in her hand with a bendy straw dancing around inside it.

Mom walks over to Lizzie and puts the cup in her face.

My sister's lips wrap around the straw, sipping on the water. "Where the hell am I?"

Mom looks at me and back at Lizzie. "You're in the hospital, honey."

"Why am I in the hospital?"

Mom glances at the floor, closes her eyes, and falls onto the floor. Celia helps her up, guiding her to the chair pushed under the desk across from Lizzie's bed.

Celia sits down on the chair in the corner of the room.

"There was an accident," I say.

"Is Mom okay?" Lizzie squints her eyes tightly. "Wait, an accident? What kind of accident? Where's Dad? Is he here?"

My shoulders tense up as my chest constricts.

Dani walks over to me. "You need to sit down." Dani smiles at her mom as a gesture for her to stand with my mom.

Once I sit down on the chair that Celia was just sitting in, my chest heaves faster. Dani notices and she sits down on my lap.

No questions asked.

She gently places her hand on top of mine as she leans back, moving her mouth closer to my ear. "Breathe."

God, I love it when she touches me.

My breathing slows, getting back to normal.

Holy shit, Dani's sitting on my lap. Now is not the time to freak out about this. It's about being there for your sister. She's your priority. Focus, Noah.

"Dad's not here," I spit out.

A confused expression takes over Lizzie's face. "What do you mean he's not here?"

"What's the last thing you remember?"

"Dad and I were in the car on our way to the grocery store and now I'm here."

I gulp hard. "You don't remember anything?"

She shakes her head as a silent answer to my question.

"That's okay." I take a deep breath and let it out. "You and Dad got into a car accident. Dad's injuries were really bad. He was in critical condition when he arrived here like you were. Unlike you, he was on the receiving end of the impact. He got more of it." My hand is shaking as I'm looking at the bed. "Dad's gone, Lizzie."

Her eye twitches. "You're lying." She scratches underneath her ear, lips trembling. "Noah Matthew Kaplan, tell me the truth." She looks at Mom. "He's lying, right? Please tell me he's lying."

I find my eyes gravitating in Dani's direction because I can't bear to look at my sister right now.

This is why I was terrified to tell her.

She's fractured on the outside and now she's completely broken on the inside like I am without the fractured part.

I'm just broken.

Leaning back on the top edge of the chair, I take Dani with me and wrap my arms around her even tighter.

"It's going to be okay," she whispers in my ear.

I slowly close and open my eyes, breathing in and out.

Mom's jaw vibrates, and her eyes blink rapidly to stop more tears from pouring out, but it's no use.

Celia answers for her before she runs after Mom when she leaves the room. "I'm so sorry, honey. Your brother is telling the truth."

"So, y-you're telling me I-I came in here with a father...and I'll be leaving here without o-one?"

I nod. "Yes," I whisper.

God, I hate that Lizzie has to go through all the stages of grief on top of getting back to her old self.

Sometimes life fucking sucks.

CHAPTER THIRTY-ONE

My mom took Laura outside of Lizzie's room to help soothe her.

Lizzie has her face buried in her hands and leans back on her pillow. My heart is shattering inside my chest as I watch a multitude of expressions fill her face.

Noah starts talking to her. "I know this is a lot to process. I still haven't fully processed any of it. Something I wish I did was scream when Dr. Miller told us about Dad." He pauses. "Do it. Pretend you're not in a hospital full of people." He backs up and leans on the back of the chair, taking me with him. "I'd cover your ears if I were you. She's a pretty loud screamer."

I do what he says, pressing the palms of my hands to my ears to filter out the noise.

Lizzie opens her mouth against her pillow, releasing muffled screams.

Hospital workers are looking into our room, trying to figure out what the hell is going on. I don't blame them.

Her screaming changes to sobbing in a matter of seconds. She face-plants into the bed. Her body shakes as muffled sobs are being filtered out from the material of her pillow.

I take my hands off my ears.

One of the nurses comes rushing in with Mom and Laura following her.

"Is everything okay?" the nurse asks.

She's in her early thirties, wearing scrubs. Her blonde hair is tied up in a low ponytail, bringing out her emerald-green eyes.

"What the hell is going on here?" Laura asks her son.

"I told her to scream to release some of the pain. It's something I wish I did when I found out about Dad's passing."

"Noah, we're in a public place. Don't do that again. Sometimes I wonder if you're actually an adult."

He shakes his head, focusing his attention on Lizzie.

His sister is sitting and staring at the wall across from her. "How did I survive? Why couldn't it have been me instead of him?"

"Oh, honey. Dr. Miller told us your injuries weren't as severe. Please don't blame yourself. This isn't your fault." Laura's doing her best to console her daughter.

This is exactly how I felt.

I thought Dad's accident was my fault even though I wasn't in the car with him.

I felt guilty I wasn't there. If I was, I would've tried to do something. Curse out the asshole who hit him. I could've saved his life or prolonged it for as long as humanly possible.

His death will scar me for the rest of my life as an open wound. I don't know if it will ever heal. That's the thing about losing someone who meant the entire world to you. It doesn't feel like they're gone forever. They're just taking an extended vacation without you.

I wish I had the power to take Lizzie's pain away and heal her broken heart. I'd heal Noah's pain and broken heart too. And mine.

But unfortunately, I don't have the power to heal people.

It would make life so much easier if I did.

"How is this not my fault, Mom? I was in the car. I wish I was the one in the driver's seat. I killed him. I killed Dad."

Tears are falling out of Lizzie's eyes. She's trying to catch her breath.

"Don't say that," I say to her, tears welling up in my eyes.

"How can I not say that, lioness? I shouldn't be here right now," she says.

My eyes narrow. "What are you talking about?"

"I don't want to talk anymore. I just want to be alone. Please," she pleads.

Noah's breath makes contact with the skin on my neck, causing me to breathe in and out.

His arms wrap around me even tighter than they were previously. I cave again, putting my hands on top of his. They're freakishly large, accentuating how dainty my hands are.

Goosebumps form on top of his hands, making my body jolt. His thumb gently rubs against mine.

I smile, knowing my touch is not only making him lose his mind, but because I'm calming him at the same time.

Noah seems to calm down when I touch his skin, especially when he's on the brink of having a panic attack or when he's in the middle of one.

I noticed it when I helped him for the first time a month ago, and when we were at the Promenade outside of Sunset Cove Creamery.

The weird thing is I calm down too when I feel his skin on mine. The same thing happens when I look deep into his eyes.

Here I go rambling on about Noah again. My mind can't seem to get rid of him. He's like a video that never stops replaying.

I wonder if he thinks about me in the way I think about him.

CHAPTER THIRTY-TWO

"We should give Lizzie some space," Mom suggests, gesturing to us to get the hell out of the room. Dani gets off my lap, looking at my sister as she walks out.

Celia and Mom are the next ones to leave the room, leaving Dani and I alone with my sister.

This is all too much for me.

Dad.

My sister.

Mom.

The only good thing to come out of all this is Dani. I wouldn't be able to get through any of this without her.

I need to get out of this hospital.

Home sounds good right about now, but I can't drive in the current state of mind I'm in.

My head is spinning. Everything is blurry.

I try to sit down on one of the chairs in front of Lizzie's room, but I miss it. I land hard on my ass. "Fuck," I mutter to myself.

"Noah, are you okay?" Dani asks.

I'm unable to meet her gaze.

Her hand is on my back, moving in circular motions.

"I need to go...home to check on S-Sammy, b-but I don't think I can d-drive," I stammer.

Dani walks off to talk to Celia before she heads back over to me. "Alright, my mom is going to take my car home. I'll drive you to your house so we can check on Sammy." She slides her hand into mine.

The way her skin touches mine drives me wild, it's sort of therapeutic. Her touch is healing me in ways I've never thought could be possible.

"Look at me." She reaches her hands out and cups my cheeks, turning my face in her direction.

Her brown eyes are even bigger close-up.

"Tell me about the novel you're writing." She brings me back to reality.

"What?"

"You know. The book you're writing and publishing," she says to me as we're walking to the elevators. "The book you've been working on since high school."

I swallow. "I-it's about a woman who moves to a small town. A-and she becomes the senior detective for the t-town's police department. She g-gets assigned to solve a decades-old cold case."

The elevator doors slide open.

We walk into it, standing side-by-side.

She meets my gaze so intensely it feels like this elevator could catch on fire at any given moment. "Tell me more."

"Um...a man who's a part of the prominent family she's re-investigating willingly teams up with her to solve the case. He wants to find out who murdered his parents."

Her distraction is working. My anxiety is subsiding like storm clouds disappearing when the sun comes out.

"There's a slow burn romance involved," I add.

Ding. Level 3.

Her eyes light up after I say that. "Noah Kaplan, did you just say romance?"

I roll my eyes. "Let's not make a fuss about it, okay? Before they can even act on their feelings, she discovers a deadly secret that ruins any chance of them ever getting together...Or does it?"

"Well, I know one thing for sure."

"What's that?" I ask.

"I'll be one of your first readers," she tells me all doe-eyed.

I smile. "Tell me about your book."

"You really don't care. It's a romance. I—"

I box her in, staring deep into her eyes. "Tell me about it," I demand.

"O-okay. Um...it's a college sports romance about a basketball captain and a gymnast. The basketball captain is the brother of the gymnast's best friend. They cross paths at a party and she's immediately turned off by him. He's smitten with her from the get-go."

Ding. Level 2.

I'm watching every part of her face move from her eyes to her lips. She's fucking mesmerizing. The passion and dedication she has for the craft is attractive as hell.

"That's all you get, Lover Boy."

"Do you know how attractive you are when you talk about writing? The way passion radiates off your body, shooting straight through the person you're talking to."

Shut the fuck up, Noah. Why did I just say that? I'm just going to dig a hole, jump into it, and never come out of it.

She raises her eyebrows, looking around the elevator in disbelief.

When we arrive at the lobby of the hospital, we head straight for the sliding glass doors.

There's this deafening silence, consuming the air around us. It's making sweat drip down from my forehead to my chin.

My heart is beating so damn fast.

Please make it stop.

She opens her mouth to say something to me, slightly cocking her head. "You think I'm attractive?" she asks, smirking before she bites on her tongue to rile me up even more.

Consider me riled over the goddamn edge.

Fuck, the things I want to do to her.

I want to make her pay for torturing me this past month with those beautiful brown eyes of hers. The way her smile lights up every goddamn room she walks in. Her laugh has become my favorite sound. But most importantly, those full pink lips. It's taken everything in my power not to push her up against one of these hospital walls and have our lips collide.

We make it out of the hospital and walk towards my car.

She has my arm slung around her neck, dangling at the level of her shoulder. I wait to answer her until we reach my car.

She digs for the key in my back pocket. I didn't even tell her that's where it is. Feeling her hand dig around back there is the closest I'm going to have her being intimately close to me.

God, she's really digging in there.

If she keeps this up, I'm definitely not afraid to kiss the fucking shit out of her on top of my car until she's unable to breathe like a normal human being.

How the hell am I going to answer her question? Don't sound desperate, you idiot.

Maybe I'm the captain of The Idiot Club instead of Grayson.

"I said the way you talk about writing is attractive. I didn't say you were."

I can immediately see the hurt written all over her face. She huffs out a soft breath, walking ahead of me.

You blew that one, jackass.

I speak up again, hoping that more dumb shit doesn't come

spewing out of my mouth. "I'm sorry. None of that came out right."

"Yeah, it didn't."

I don't know how to respond to her. I'm frozen, wishing I could turn back time to steer this conversation in a more positive direction.

The original plan was to keep all this shit to myself until I found a time that was right to tell her how I feel about her.

I don't know how much longer I can go through with this plan.

CHAPTER THIRTY-THREE

Noah told me he finds me attractive.

Am I dreaming or is this actually real? The irony is he's trying to play it off like he didn't actually say it. I mean he technically didn't, but I'm counting it.

I'm debating whether or not I should tell him I find him attractive too or say if I should say a quality I find attractive about him like he did with me.

I'm going to go with the second option. Let's just hope I don't regret it after this.

Noah and I are standing in front of the passenger door of his car.

I remove my arm from his neck, moving in front of him so he can't get in.

His eyes are looking around the parking lot, trying to figure out what I'm doing.

You got this, Dani. Tell him what quality you find attractive about him. Don't fuck it up. No pressure or anything.

"If we're playing this game, do you want to know one of the things I find the most attractive about you?"

He's staring at me in disbelief.

We're so close I can feel his body heat sizzling its way through every layer of my skin. Our lips are only a few inches away from each other.

I take a gulp and clear my throat as quietly as possible. "The way you care so deeply about your family. Honestly, just the way you love people unconditionally. It's an admirable quality in a person."

A big smile grows on Noah's face, lighting it up like candles on a menorah. "You want to know another thing I find attractive about you?" he asks, closing the gap between us.

I thought I would be safe from the Florida heat by wearing my hair in a high ponytail, but I didn't account for my body getting hot because of a guy.

Not just any guy, but because of Noah freaking Kaplan.

I wet my lips, my heart beating so loud it wouldn't surprise me if he could hear it. "What?"

"The fact that I can make you blush so damn easily," he whispers in my left ear, swiping the pad of his thumb over my cheek.

A small breathy giggle escapes my mouth.

His hot breath finds a home on the skin in between my neck and shoulder.

"Get in the car, Kaplan," I demand, glaring at him.

"Move your ass out of my way so I can get in the car, Solomon."

"I'm not moving. You'll just have to walk around me." I stand proud and tall, crossing my arms in front of my breasts.

He scoffs. "Fine, have it your way."

He extends his arm to open the passenger door and pulls the handle with his hand, but he can't open it unless I move out of the way.

"Don't even think about it," I say firmly.

"You don't even know what I'm going to do."

"I know you better than you think I do."

"Oh yeah?" He slings me over his right shoulder.

A little scream leaves my mouth. "Put me down. Right now." My hands are flailing all over the place as he secures me by holding the back of my thighs.

He places me down in front of the driver's door.

After all that, he managed to open the car door for me like a gentleman. I guess that's his way of apologizing to me for being an asswipe.

I sit down on the gray-colored fabric chair. The length of half of a basketball court is in front of me. That's what it feels like at least.

He sits down on the passenger seat, as I search for the bar to slide my seat forward.

His eyes plant themselves on me all while studying my face. "What the hell are you doing?"

"I'm trying to find the stupid adjustment bar thing. It's not underneath the seat."

He notices the frustration growing on my face, but doesn't fail to laugh at me in the process. "The adjuster is located on the side of the seat, not underneath it." A smug smile appears on his face.

"Well, look at you, Mr. Fancy Pants."

He's holding in a laugh. All grins and no big smiles. I can tell he's struggling because his lips are quivering. He folds his arms underneath his broad chest, muscles bulging.

Why is every inch of his body so muscular? It's so annoying. And distracting as hell.

I press and hold the black engine button for a few seconds, pushing my foot down on the brake pedal to start the car.

"I'm impressed you know how to start my car."

My tongue sticks up to the roof of my mouth. I proceed to bite down on my bottom lip. "Oh, shut the hell up. I'll have you know my dad had a car just like this one."

"Then, you should know where the mechanism is to move

up the seat. Isn't that right, Princess?" Sarcasm breaks through his voice which makes me grin like an idiot.

I turn my head towards him slightly.

"Eyes on the road!" he shouts, gesturing to the view in front of us.

"My eyes are on the road. You're distracting me!"

You're always distracting me.

I can see him wetting his lips out of the corner of my eye. "What if I told you I enjoy distracting you?"

He thinks he's so smooth, but it's not working for him this time.

We're on Sunset Cove Boulevard, overlooking the ocean which is to the left of us.

Even though this window is closed, I can smell and taste the salty ocean air. Tall palm trees scatter the sides of the road.

We pass a couple of neighborhoods on the way home. Breakwater, a neighborhood full of manufactured homes. Lighthouse Estates, the neighborhood for the wealthy, is further down the street.

Silence fills up the car like water filling up an inflatable pool.

We haven't talked since we left the hospital. I used to live for moments like this with Noah, but I absolutely hate it now.

After passing the clear blue ocean, we make it to our subdivision, Crystal Harbor. I bear right, turning into our community. Tall palm trees divide both sides of the road in a straight vertical line.

Pulling into Noah's driveway, I shift the gear into park.

We sit in the car for a few minutes. Noah's beautiful eyes are drilling a hole through the side of my head.

"Can I help you, sir?" I whip my head to properly face him, meeting his gaze.

He squints his eyes, unbuckling his seatbelt. Leaning his elbows onto the medium gray console, he places the palms of his hands on his cheeks. "Can I admire your beauty without comments or questions from the Peanut Gallery?" He moves his hand to his lips, brushing them with his thumb and index finger.

Who are you calling the Peanut Gallery, dipshit?

Heavy breathing takes over until Noah's eyes wander to my lips, leaving me breathless.

"There will always be comments and questions from the Peanut Gallery."

I break out of his trance and unbuckle my seatbelt. "You should go inside. Sammy probably missed you." I smile, blinking my eyes in slow motion.

He moves his hand away from his cheek while the other hand shifts from his lips to his chin in a swift motion. "You know I bet Sammy has missed you a lot. I think you should come in with me and say hi." His eyebrow lifts up and he grins at me.

"Fine, I'll come in with you and say hi."

I get out of the car and so does Noah. The car doors slam shut.

I walk to the front door, observing the porch.

Noah walks up to me with hands in the pockets of his shorts.

I look at him. "I guess my mom is still taking care of the landscaping."

He cocks his head. "What makes you say that?"

"Everything's alive." My voice goes up an octave, giggling with my mouth closed.

"Are you accusing my family of being plant murderers?" He bites down on the corner of his bottom lip.

"Maybe I am. Maybe I'm not. You'll never know." I hold in a laugh, grinning ear to ear.

As we step closer to the front door, I can hear loud barking from inside the house.

I point to him. "I want you to know Sammy is the only dog I tolerate. No dog will ever compare to him."

I have never been a dog person. I don't hate them, but I don't love them either. I've had cats my entire life, so I gravitate towards them more.

"I know how much you love dogs, so it means a lot to me you're here to visit him. I know it means more to Sammy though." Sarcasm rings throughout his voice.

He puts his hand on his upper chest, eyes closed and lips spread as a flat line.

Inserting the key into the lock, he turns it until it makes a clicking noise and twists it so the door opens.

Sammy comes running out and heads straight for me.

His tail wags back and forth, breathing heavily to express his excitement. He's gotten so big since the last time I saw him, which was in my sophomore year of high school.

"Look who it is, Sammy boy. It's Dani. You remember her, right?"

He gives me a nudge in the ass and comes back around. He sits in front of me, panting with his tongue sticking out.

"Hi, buddy." I pet his head, feeling his soft fur underneath the palm of my right hand.

I meet Noah's gaze like magnets that stick on a refrigerator.

This is how I'm going to be murdered.

By looking into Noah Kaplan's eyes.

noah

I know why death stares are called death stares, but the way Dani is staring at me tells me she doesn't want to kill me.

I'd love for her to do other things to me that don't involve killing me. Okay, I'm getting way too ahead of myself.

I follow her into my house and stand next to her.

She's taking in the interior of the house. The last time she was here was when we were teenagers.

When I come out of the bathroom, I hear a noise coming from my bedroom.

Dani is sitting on my bed, looking around the room.

I stare at her. "What the hell are you doing in here?"

"The last time I was in here was when we were fifteen. Everything's pretty much the same." Her eyes land on my bookcase.

Getting off my bed, she walks over to it. "Holy shit!" she shouts.

"What?" I walk over to my bookcase, standing behind her.

I get a whiff of cool mint and sweet peaches.

It's fucking intoxicating.

Just like her.

And I bet you that's what she tastes like.

I'd give anything to taste her right now.

She's running her fingers along the spines of the books that are on the two shelves that are at eye level. She picks up Things We Never Got Over with one hand. "Noah Kaplan, how do you explain all this?"

Crap, she knows my dirty little secret now.

"Tell me one thing," she says.

My right hand is covering my forehead. "Maybe I will. Maybe I won't. Depends on what you want to know."

"What got you into romance?" her mouth parts open, chest heaving.

"Not a *what*, a *who*."

"Okay, *who* got you into romance?" she asks in a sarcastic tone.

"The fact that you're asking is surprising to me. Shall we play the guessing game? We both know you're good at it. Look in the mirror."

She puts the book back on the shelf.

My hands are on her shoulders, guiding her to the long mirror on the other side of the bedroom.

She huffs. "What's the point of this?"

"Look in the mirror."

She drops her head down. "Why?"

"Just look in the *goddamn* mirror, Dani. Are you ever not going to be a pain in my ass?" I demand, standing proud and assured.

CHAPTER THIRTY-FIVE

His hands are still wrapped around my shoulders and both of his thumbs are making their way underneath the thick straps of my tank top.

I'm going to die being seduced by this tall, blue-eyed guy with dirty blonde hair who obviously belongs in a romance novel.

Holy shit, that's it. Noah Kaplan is a man written by a woman. That explains so much.

I pick my head up and look at my reflection in the tall mirror. "Why are we standing in front of your mirror, smart ass?"

"You asked me who got me into romance. Take a good look in the mirror, Sweet Peach."

Okay, where the hell did that come from?

It takes me a hot minute to realize I'm the person who got him into romance. I should win a medal for getting this guy into romance. A gold one that athletes win at the Olympics.

"Wait." I pause. "I'm the person who got you into romance?"

His hands move down to where my biceps are.

I'm shocked goosebumps aren't popping up all over my skin right now.

Ah, there they are.

His breath is hot against the back of my neck. He chuckles, staring right at me in the mirror. "Yeah, I went down the romance hole and never came out of it thanks to you."

I smile proudly, raising my eyebrows up and down a few times. "You're welcome. I have to say it's impressive you told me the truth. I thought you were going to lie out of your ass and say they're your sister's books."

"Why the hell would I do that?" His grip on my upper arms gets tighter.

He's not angry.

He's trying to get a reaction out of me.

And it's working. A faint noise comes out of my mouth. Faint enough that Noah can't hear it.

His hands move back to my shoulders. "You're very tense."

"What the hell are you talking about? I'm not tense."

"You have a lot of knots in your shoulders."

Oh God, he's massaging my shoulders.

"Well, I like my knots, so you can leave them alone," I say to our reflections in the mirror, sass pouring out of my voice.

He whispers in my ear. "I bet you do. But I'm going to loosen them a bit. Tell me to stop, and I'll stop."

Just fucking kiss me already. Throw me down on your goddamn bed. I'm begging you to put me out of my misery.

"Don't do it so hard." My body twitches.

"Stop being such a baby. I'll be gentle. I promise."

Remember when I said he was going to kill me by looking into his eyes?

No, that's not how I'm going to die.

This is how I'm going to die.

CHAPTER THIRTY-SIX

Dani's body keeps shuddering as I'm massaging her shoulders.

I never would have guessed I'd be massaging my childhood rival right now and be so turned on while doing it.

Her skin feels so good underneath the palms of my hands. It's soft and smooth like silk.

Fuck, I could do this forever.

"Do you want me to stop?" I ask softly.

I can't tell if she's under my spell or if she's uncomfortable.

She looks to the side, parting her mouth open and lips forming into a small circle as her jaw clenches.

Her gaze meets mine in the mirror as her lips rise up to form a seductive smirk.

I bite down on my bottom lip, struggling to keep my composure. I take my hands off her shoulders, dropping my arms to both sides of my body. "What the hell are you trying to do to me?"

She giggles. "I'm not trying to do anything."

I roll my eyes and laugh. "Bullshit! You were smirking at me."

"And your point is?"

"I didn't think this through."

"I can see that," she says.

We both burst into laughter.

The way her face lights up when she smiles or laughs is absolutely everything. I'll do everything in my power to make her smile or laugh because I love seeing her happy.

"Why are you looking at me like that?" Her index and middle fingers are twirling a small tendril of hair.

"Like what?"

"Like that." She lifts her pointer finger, wiggling it at my face.

I grab her finger to move it away from my face.

"Hey!" Dani yells, extending her hand out just enough for me to intertwine my hand with hers.

I pull her closer to me. There's no gap between us to have space for us to breathe.

Who needs space anyway?

I look down at her.

She's glaring at me.

"You know, you're *really* cute when you're angry."

Her lips shift the side of her mouth after she runs her hand through her beautiful dark brunette hair. "Oh, shut up."

"Never."

CHAPTER THIRTY-SEVEN

My eyes bounce over to the album posters that cover the wall over Noah's bed.

You can definitely tell a teenage boy used to live here.

"I don't remember all these posters."

He looks around the room. "Yeah, I had a few of them in middle school, but the collection grew in high school."

"I have to say you definitely have amazing taste in music." I sit down on the edge of his bed which faces his closet.

"Really?" he asks, sitting down next to me.

"Yeah," I say. "My dad introduced me to indie and alternative music, so I listen to a lot of the bands and artists that cover your wall back there." I point to the wall behind us.

"Dad got me a portable music player as a bar mitzvah gift. It was loaded with songs by Pink Floyd, Guns N' Roses, Queen, and Alanis Morisette. It led me to the music I listen to now."

I smile. "My dad loved Pink Floyd so much. He discovered them back in college. He introduced them to me when I was around twelve years old. Back then, I didn't understand the lyricism and deep meanings behind the songs. As I got older, I fell in love with how atmospheric and meaningful their songs are.

The Dark Side of the Moon is an album I've been listening to on repeat since Dad passed away. Feels like he's still here with me when I listen to it."

He takes a moment to digest what I just told him, taking in a deep gulp. Licking his lips, he smiles at me sweetly. "I totally understand how you feel. Music was one of the things my dad and I bonded over, especially Pink Floyd. And I know both of our dads loved *The Dark Side of the Moon* almost more than they loved us." He laughs. "I'm just kidding, but sometimes it felt like they loved that album more than us. Anyways, I-I'm glad we have music to connect with them. Even though they're not physically here anymore."

Getting off the bed, I rummage through the drawers of his desk.

"What are you doing?" he asks.

"Do you have earphones with a cord attached to them?"

He nods "Yeah. I've been meaning to get rid of them too."

We sit back down on the bed, inserting the cord into my phone and putting one of the earbuds into my ear.

Noah puts the other earbud into his ear.

I whip out my phone from my back pocket, and open Spotify. The pad of my thumb taps on my playlist, *Never Admit Defeat*, which is full of Dad's favorite songs which have now become some of my favorite songs of all time.

Pressing play on *Brain Damage* by Pink Floyd, our ears are flooded with its atmospheric melody which would sound even better if we were high right now.

At first, we look away from each other, but we eventually meet each other's gaze.

A smile appears on my lips for a brief moment as I look away from Noah, feeling his ocean eyes burning me from the inside out. Threading his fingers into mine, he rubs my thumb with his in a gentle vertical motion.

My heartbeat speeds up, becoming offbeat with the melody of the song. Gulping hard, I stare at Noah.

Oh God, he's staring at my lips.

My shoulders tense up and I can't move the rest of my body. Licking my lips, I prepare myself internally for what could come next.

He starts leaning into me just enough that our lips lightly brush against each other. His hand is resting on my neck and our foreheads are leaning against one another.

I close my eyes.

My phone vibrates through the bed, putting this intimate moment between us on hold.

I pick up my phone and see a text from Mom light up my lock screen. I barely read the preview, tapping on it right away.

MOM

MOM

Hey Sweet Girl, I want to update you and Noah about what's been going on

Dr. Miller finally came to talk to us. She said that she feels confident to release Lizzie from the hospital tomorrow afternoon. That is as long as everything goes okay for her during the night and in the morning

That being said, I'll be helping Laura with Lizzie because I know she can't do all this on her own. She needs help even though she'd never ask for it. Anyways, I hope you and Noah are okay. Have you kicked him out of the house yet?

ME

no and i don't plan to

MOM

I'm so happy to hear that. How's he doing?

ME

he's been blaming himself for what happened to ben and lizzie, but i'm helping him work through his emotions

MOM

That's good. I'm happy to hear you two are getting along. I'm on my way to drop Laura back at her house and then I'll be coming back to our house to pick up some things I didn't need at the time but now I do

ME

okay, we're on our way back to the house now

MOM

Remember to breathe, honey. I love you

ME

i love you too

The constant reminder to just breathe has been the usual for me since middle school.

My first panic attack was scary as hell. I was sitting in class when my vision suddenly turned all blurry. A knot so tightly wound in my chest that wouldn't go away. I couldn't see straight so my teacher sent me to the nurse's office.

I ended up spending hours there because I didn't want to go back into that classroom. The nurse ended up calling my mom to come and pick me up.

We had a long talk in the car about what we were going to do because I couldn't stay in public middle school any longer. She homeschooled me for a few months until she found a private middle school that worked for the both of us.

I don't know what I would've done with my mom. I don't know where I'd be or who I'd be right now. I'm so grateful for her. Dad was busy with his job at the time, but he still found time to take care of me when Mom needed a break.

I can't imagine how draining it was for them, not knowing what was going to happen with me.

Mom found a therapist who specializes in helping kids and teenagers with anxiety, depression, and everything in between. Dr. Jennifer Price, whom I referred to as Jen, saved my life.

When *Brain Damage* finishes, I pause my playlist and rip the earbud out of my ear, so I can tell Noah the good news.

I stare at him for a moment to catch his attention.

He takes the earbud out of his ear, eyes widening. "Is everything okay?"

I smile, tears bubbling up in my eyes. "My mom just gave me the best update." I pause. "Lizzie's coming home tomorrow."

Noah bursts into tears, burying his face in between his legs.

Now, I'm crying and rubbing his back.

When he lifts his head up, he looks at me for a couple of seconds and hugs me. His hands wrap tightly around my waist as his fingers run through loose tendrils in my hair.

"I'm so fucking happy," he says into my ear.

"Me too."

I try to free myself from our embrace, but it's no use. His grip on me grows tighter. I can feel all the muscles in my body getting crushed to death.

"As much as I'm enjoying this, we need to go home."

"Why?"

"So we can regroup and figure out what we want to make for dinner."

"Okay." He releases me from his grasp as he gently wipes away any remaining tears off my face with the pad of his thumb.

I return the favor, wiping tears off his face with the pads of my index and middle fingers.

We get off the bed one by one.

Noah puts his earbuds back into the drawer inside his desk.

Putting my phone in my back pocket, I stand in front of the doorway of his childhood bedroom.

Strong hands rest on my shoulders, sending chills straight down my spine.

"I'll meet you in the car." He removes his warm hands from my shoulders and walks away from me.

Thanks for the memories. The times when Noah and I screamed at each other when one of us won family game night. And for the moment we just shared now. It's one I'll cherish for a long damn time.

I make my way out of the house.

"How long have you been standing out here?"

"Not too long," he says.

He waits for me to move away from the front door, so he can lock it. When he does, we get in the car and head back to my house.

We pull up in front of the garage and I shift the gear into park.

"What?" I ask.

"Nothing," he says as he opens the door and gets out of the car.

I get out of the car, and press a button on my car keys so it locks. When I unlock the front door to the house, I turn the light on.

"Well, I don't know about you, but I'm going to go work on my book." He smiles at me before he goes into the guest bedroom to get his computer.

God, that smile is going to be the death of me.

CHAPTER THIRTY-EIGHT

I'm sitting on the big chair in front of the big window in the living room inside my house while I'm endlessly scrolling on Instagram to see what posts I've missed.

I haven't been on social media that much lately. That's crazy to even think about considering I'm usually on Instagram every single day—for hours at a time.

Is it unhealthy? Yes, of course it is. Do I care? No.

It's hard to not be on social media, especially promoting a book.

One of my favorite things about this community is being able to engage with readers and fellow authors. I love receiving sweet messages from readers about how excited they are to read my book.

I've spent years fine-tuning my debut romance novel.

It hasn't hit me by this time next year, I'll be a published author.

Fucking insane.

I hear the sound of the garage door opening which means Mom's home. I don't get up because I'm too lazy to.

Noah's still at the kitchen table, writing his heart out and wearing those Buddy Holly glasses that make my heart skip a beat.

The laundry room door slams closed.

"I'm home." I hear a sweet voice that belongs to my mother, traveling its way into the living room.

I decide to get up, running over to her. I just about knock her down like a bowling ball knocking down a bunch of bowling pins. Wrapping my arms around her tight like a Grandma does with her grandkid, I hear her huffing.

"What's the occasion?" Confusion fuses with happiness in her tone.

"I know I don't say this enough but I love you and I appreciate you so much."

"I love you too, Sweet Girl."

I take in her scent. A combination of florals and the sea.

She releases me, looking at me with admiration.

I narrow my eyes slightly. "What?"

"I'm so proud of you. Some days I can't believe you're my daughter."

"Thank you but...what the hell are you talking about?"

"You have this drive I never had when I was your age. You're inspiring, Dani. Look at the community you've built on your social media platforms. You're a leader. You always have been. I'm just so proud of you."

Don't cry. I've cried enough today.

Reaching out to grab her hands, I interlock them with mine. "Thank you."

I glance in Noah's direction. He's totally unaware that Mom is home because he has his wireless earbuds in. His head is bobbing around to the beat of whatever song he's listening to.

From where I'm standing, he looks like an idiot.

A very cute idiot.

CHAPTER THIRTY-NINE

There's something about music that transports me into the world I'm writing about.

I'm sitting at Dani's kitchen table, editing my debut novel for the millionth time. Okay, maybe not the millionth time, but it sure as hell feels like it.

Editing is something I was excited to tackle in the beginning, and now I want it to end. It never stops. It keeps going on and on.

I do enjoy it when I'm able to refine the story and take out unnecessary scenes that don't make sense for the characters or the story.

Nobody warned me how intense the whole self-publishing process is.

It's not just writing and editing the damn thing, but you have to market that shit like your life depends on it. I don't think a lot of people realize that independent authors wear a lot of hats, figuratively not literally.

We're writers.

We're editors.

We're social media managers.

We're social media content creators.

We're cover designers.

Despite how exhausting it can be, it's all worth it to get our stories out in the world.

It's funny because I'm horrible at making content to market my book.

I knew the person I wanted to reach out to and make content for me right away.

Violet Prescott was the only person to pop into my mind because I've seen her posts. She loves what she does and it's evident through her content.

When I asked her to create content for my book, she jumped at the chance. She was one of my first readers because I wanted her to see if she'd like it first since she's typically a romance reader.

I remember when I asked her to do this for me and she asked me if there was any romance in it. She was sold when I told her there was, and she actually enjoyed it which surprised the hell out of me.

Violet started out making content for me for free which I was grateful for at the time, but now I pay her on a monthly basis. She deserves it because she does admin and design work for me as my personal assistant.

I don't think I would survive without her.

On the flip side, I've discovered how challenging mystery thrillers are to write. It's ironic considering they're so much fun to read. It's such a different experience when I'm reading someone else's story versus when I'm writing my own because I'm reading someone else's words rather than reading my own as I write.

I've learned a lot about what makes a mystery thriller good from all the books I've read.

Twists and turns are essential, but foreshadowing is vital. It doesn't have to be anything major. Subtle hints here and there are enough because you don't want to give away the entire plot to the reader.

I knew when I wanted to write *Expect the Unexpected* that I'd need to plot first. I needed to see where the story would take me, so I plotted out each chapter and what scenes I wanted to be in them.

As I sit here and edit, I can feel Dad's presence lingering over me.

If I can place the blame on someone for my addiction to the mystery and thriller genres, it would be him.

I was in middle school when he introduced me to the genre. I became obsessed with how immersive these books can be and how they have you on the edge of your seat from start to finish.

When I told my dad I wanted to write one, he was incredibly supportive. There was never a time when he told me I couldn't do it or that it would be impossible.

I've been struggling with my dedication for my debut, but now I know what I want to do.

I'm dedicating this book to my dad because it wouldn't exist if it wasn't for him.

If you're here Dad, this book is for you.

Everything I do has *always* been for you.

dani

Sneak attack.

Target acquired.

I let go of Mom's hands, tiptoeing my way into the kitchen and sneaking up behind Noah.

Mom is trailing behind me as slow as a snail.

"Hey, Lover Boy!" I shout, pulling the earbuds out of his ears.

It takes him a minute to notice me behind him.

When he does, he jumps and rapidly blinks his eyes. "Don't do that shit to me! You wouldn't like it if I did that to you, right?"

I do a little dance, scrunching my nose. "You deserve it after all the times you've scared me."

"I have to say. I didn't think you had it in you."

And the happy dance comes to a screeching halt. "C'mon, can you just let me have this win?"

"Haven't you learned by now that I don't admit defeat?"

Asshole.

My mouth drops open, and a grunting noise comes out of it. "You're not going to get a reaction out of me."

"I just did." He gives me the side eye.

It's hard to hate him because he's still wearing those glasses that make him look so fucking hot. I don't know what it is about men and glasses, but it's such an attractive combination.

For some reason, Noah makes it even more attractive.

He runs his fingers through his perfectly tousled dirty blonde hair.

God, I want to run my fingers through his hair.

I roll my eyes, letting out a deep breath.

"Well, it's nice to see you two arguing for a change." Mom interrupts our mini edition of *War of Words*.

It's weird to hear her say it's nice that we're arguing for a change. We did it all the time when we were younger. We haven't argued about anything in the past month. I originally didn't want to come because I knew I'd see Noah and have to deal with him for God knows how long.

I'm so happy I came.

For Laura and Lizzie, of course.

Noah is just a happy accident.

He's a happy accident that makes butterflies flutter around in my stomach, turns my cheeks bright red, calls me cute nicknames, and compliments the shit out of me.

Oh God, he's my happy accident.

Mom's voice brings me back to reality. "Honey, is everything okay?"

My eyes land on Noah who meets my gaze in an instant. "Yeah, everything's fine."

"Well, I'm going to go grab some things I forgot to bring with me the first time around. I can always come back home if I forget something again. It's not that far away. Get some sleep tonight. Tomorrow's a big day."

Her shoulder bumps into mine.

She winks at me, kissing me on the forehead. "Love you,"

she mouths to me before she disappears into the master bedroom.

It takes Mom an hour for her to pack up the things she needs to bring over. Well, her essentials. She just walks out the laundry room door, slamming it behind her.

MOM

MOM

You two better be on your best behavior

ME

i'm not a child anymore and neither is noah. we're both adults and we've been getting along just fine

MOM

Sorry, force of habit. Don't forget to eat if you haven't already. Good night. Love you

ME

love you too!

Did she forget Noah's been in the house with me for a little over a month now? And the fact I told her that I don't have the urge to murder him with the damn flashlight anymore.

If anything, I want nothing more than to run into his arms and kiss him until he takes my breath away.

The thing is he takes my breath away without even trying.

CHAPTER FORTY-ONE

Dani pulls up a chair next to me and I get a whiff of her signature scent.

Sweet peaches.

I'm a fucking goner for her.

I'm sensing she's about to punch me in the arm. I don't know why. I just feel it in my bones. I'm not in the mood to have another bruise on my arm.

I deserve a medal for putting up with this shit.

"Don't even think about it," I say as my face and body stiffen.

I watch her wet her lips with the tip of her tongue. "I have no idea what you're talking about."

"Sure you don't." I cross my arms in front of my chest, leaning back in the chair.

She gulps so deep that the veins in her neck are popping out. "You don't scare me."

Challenge accepted.

"I might not scare you, but I know for a fact that I make you nervous."

She smacks her lips together. "You keep talking about how you make me nervous."

She moves her chair closer to me, her thighs sliding in between mine.

Fuck, I'm a dead man.

I'm instantly hard. I don't know how Dani doesn't see the obvious bulge pressing against my shorts.

"Let's talk about the fact that I make you nervous."

There's no question that you make me nervous.

"I have no idea what the hell you're talking about."

She leans into me putting her features on full display.

This is when I notice that the freckles on her nose trail all the way to the tops of her cheekbones. Her eyes are dark brown and I can see her pupils this close up.

A small smile grows on her lips. "Yes, you do."

"If you come any closer, I swear I'm going to—"

"You're going to what?" She lifts her head up, lips forming into a pout.

"I'm never going to let you go. You're going to be stuck with me for the rest of our lives."

She looks down and smiles at the floor, but my eyes are glued on her.

Every moment I'm with Dani, it feels like I'm underwater. I'm drowning and I desperately need to come up for air.

I'm going to tell her how I feel before school starts back up. I can't keep this bottled up inside me forever.

"Earth to Dani."

She snaps back to reality, meeting my gaze. Breathing in and out, she opens her mouth. "I've never told anyone this. I mean I don't think I have before. I don't know."

Dani's eyes are glassy. She pauses what she's about to tell me.

God, I hate it when she's sad.

Her thighs slide out from in between mine. She sandwiches in her hands in between them, dropping her head down.

"Hey, look at me." I tilt her head up with my index finger and thumb in one gentle motion. "Please talk to me."

Tears fall out of her eyes. "It's been hard for me to get close to people. I haven't made any new friends at SCU. I've always prioritized writing and school over being in a relationship. I keep losing people I love. My dad. Your dad. We almost lost your sister. I don't want to lose you too."

"I *promise* you're not going to lose me."

She huffs. "I hate that word."

"What word?"

"*Promise*. It comes with too many attachments."

"Well, I'm going to change your mind about it. Trust me."

She giggles, hiccuping and sniffling like crazy.

Her leg is violently shaking up and down. She stops shaking it the very moment my hand comes into contact with her skin, looking at me with those big brown eyes of hers.

I take my free hand, wiping away the wetness on her cheeks with the pad of my thumb.

She closes her eyes, smiling.

Is it fucked up to say she looks pretty when she cries? But it kills me when she gets teary-eyed. It's a double-edged sword.

"There's something my mom used to tell me all the time when I was growing up. We have to make our way through the darkness in order to get to the light." I take a minute to clear my throat. "I want you to know we're going to get through this...together."

She brings her hands up to her face, wiping away any remaining tears lingering on her cheeks and underneath her eyes. She sits back on the chair, not breaking eye contact with me. "Well, I guess we know what you can do for your backup plan if the author thing doesn't work out for you."

"And what's that?"

"Motivational speaking."

"I'm hanging out with Grayson and Xander too much, which is pretty easy to do since I live with them."

She tilts her head on a slight angle, grinning which lights up her face like the sun on full blast. "I didn't know you lived with them. That must be fun."

"Oh, it's a fucking joy. They're always threatening to kick each other's asses whether it's over text or in person."

"Really?"

"Yeah, but they do this shit all the time, so I'm used to it. Living with them is like having a bunch of toddlers running around the apartment."

She's laughing so hard her entire body is vibrating like a speaker on full blast.

"You know if I had to pick between Grayson and Xander to live with, it'd be Xander. No question."

She giggles. "Awe, poor Gray."

"Xander's a lot more chill when it's just me and him. He doesn't drive me as crazy as Grayson does. Don't tell him I said that. Although, he probably knows how much he annoys me so I guess it doesn't matter."

She sits there, studying my face and body language.

Yeah, I need to tell her the truth before summer ends.

If I don't, I never will.

CHAPTER FORTY-TWO

"What do you want to eat for dinner?" I ask, getting off the chair.

"What are our choices?"

"Maybe if you get your lazy ass off the chair and look in the fridge, you'll find out."

"Well, excuse me." He gets up from his chair and walks over to the refrigerator. He opens the door and weighs our options. "There's turkey, eggs, cheese, lettuce..."

"Stop listing shit and pick something."

"Calm down, woman." He grabs a package of tortellini out of the deli drawer, presenting me with it like the adorable dork that he is. "Is that okay with you?"

I walk over to him, leaning on the island behind us. An idea is brewing in my head.

"A woman on a mission," he blurts out.

I raise an eyebrow. "Excuse me?"

"You do this thing with your face when you're fueled up."

I fold my arms. "I have no idea what the hell you're talking about."

"You're doing it right now as we speak." He cages me in, his strong arms creating a forcefield around us. "Your eyebrows furrow and your lips flatten out into a straight line."

"Whatever. I'm a woman on a mission to make dinner. Unless you want to skip straight to dessert."

I cannot believe I just fucking said that.

He bites down on his bottom lip.

Oh God, not the lip bite. It's making me want to bite his lip with my teeth until it swells up like a balloon.

"We could if you want to, but I think it'd be better for our health if we don't do that."

I escape the forcefield he brought upon us, opening the fridge to search for the ingredients that are a part of my brilliant idea.

Pesto. Grated parmesan cheese. Greek yogurt. Cream cheese.

I haven't made this in months, so I hope this comes out good.

If it comes out like shit, we might be having eggs for dinner.

Or maybe we might be skipping straight to dessert.

noah

I have no idea what's going on. I'm just rolling with the punches here.

"What are you doing there, Picasso?"

"Don't you trust me, Heart Eyes?"

More than you'll ever know. Wait, did she just call me Heart Eyes? The nickname gives me whiplash. She pulled that one out of her fine ass.

"Of course I do." I scan over the ingredients sitting out on the counter next to the stove. "You're making a pesto cream sauce, aren't you?"

She claps her hands together, mocking me. "Good job. You figured it out. Can you take out the large nonstick pan that's in the bottom cabinet near the stove?"

"Is it on my left or right?" I gesture with my hands.

"On your left." She shows me with her hand which bottom cabinet the pan is in.

I open the cabinet door, grab the pan, and leave behind a conglomeration of loud noises which make my ears hurt.

"Sorry." I shrug my shoulders, sticking my hands out with my palms facing up.

She wets her lips with the tip of her tongue and grabs all the ingredients with her hands, placing them all on the countertop next to the stove.

"Do you need any assistance, Chef Dani?"

Her lips sway to the side of her mouth. "Are you actually going to help or are you just going to stand over me the entire time and supervise?"

Sweat is building on my forehead and other places I won't name.

"Tell me what you need me to do and I'll do it."

God, I love it when she bosses me around.

There's no doubt in my mind she gets off on bossing me around because her eyes sparkle like a freshly clean countertop when she does it.

"I need you to get garlic powder, onion powder, and Italian seasoning from the pantry."

I give her a military hand salute. "You got it, Boss."

Walking over to the pantry, I'm immediately overwhelmed by the shelves on the inside of the door. They're filled to the brim with dried herbs and spices. I'm searching for the shit she told me to find, but I can't find them.

A finger taps on my shoulder. I turn around to see Dani smirking at me. She finds all the ingredients seasoning within seconds.

"You did that shit on purpose."

"I don't know what you're talking about." She covers her mouth with one of her hands, hiding the fact that she's laughing at me.

"Alright, smart ass. Can you give me something I can actually do? I want to help."

"Fine. Go grab a pot and fill it up with water. Just before the silver circle that's on the inside of it."

After several minutes pass by, the pot is full of boiling water. Once the bubbles rise to the top of the pot, I hit it with a healthy dose of salt. I dump the tortellini in slow motion, so I don't splash us with boiling hot water.

She's watching me while she's making the sauce. "I don't remember seeing you cook before," she tells me, eyes widening and mouth slightly gaping open.

My eyes narrow. "Why would you?"

"Sorry, I didn't mean to say it like that. I just meant we've never spent this much time together. We couldn't even be in the same room when we were younger."

"Yeah, I know you didn't mean to say it that way. And I guess that's because we've grown up and realized there are more important things in life than trying to murder each other with words."

Her lips sway to the side of her mouth, her focus shifting back on finishing the sauce. "Right."

"Dani," I say as I stir the pasta clockwise with a giant black, plastic ladle.

"What?"

"That smells *so* fucking good."

"It does?" Her tone goes up an octave.

"You can't smell that?"

"Yeah, I can smell it."

"It smells like Nonna's Italian restaurant in here."

Nonna's is a local restaurant in Sunset Cove. It's one of the only Italian restaurants in this town.

Fuck, my mouth is watering. I don't know if it's from the food or the gorgeous woman standing in front of me.

She shakes her head. "You're just being nice."

"I'm serious."

She's stirring the pesto cream sauce in the pan with a wooden spoon. "Do you want to taste the sauce? Or do you want to be surprised?"

I want to taste you instead. Your lips. Neck. Clavicle. Chest.

Cleavage. Breasts. Let my mouth find a home in between your thighs. Fucking God, Noah. Pull yourself together, man.

"Surprise me. Um...how long do you want to cook the pasta for?"

"The package says two to three minutes, so let's start with two."

"Got it. How do I know if they're ready? I've never cooked tortellini before."

She looks into my eyes. "They float to the top when they're done."

Cooking with Dani is something I can picture doing more often. We have this rhythm in the kitchen, anticipating what the other is going to say before the thought escapes their mouth.

My mom did most of the cooking when I was younger.

I didn't inherit the Kaplan family cooking gene. My sister did. Lizzie helped Mom in the kitchen until she left for college. She couldn't even reach the countertop without a stool when she was a kid.

We spent a lot of hours in the kitchen when it came to the Jewish holidays. Passover and Hanukkah were big holidays in the Kaplan family household. My mom always invited Dani and her parents, as well as our extended family.

Dad wasn't the best cook, but he was a master at the grill. I remember we'd have family BBQs with the Solomon family pretty much every weekend.

I'm taken out of my memories as Dani grabs ceramic bowls for both of us.

"Can you turn on the faucet for me?"

"Yeah, sure." I go over to the sink, running my hand underneath the water. The chill is taking off the edge of the heat expanding throughout my body.

She turns the heat off where the pot was, bringing the

boiling hot tortellini over the sink. The woman is dumping out most of the hot water.

I tilt my head, raising an eyebrow. "Aren't you going to save that?"

"Some of it, so I can thin out the sauce. I mean I can leave all the water in there. That way we can have mushy tortellini for dinner, if you want." Her hands land on her hips, a smirk growing on her beautiful lips.

I put my hands up. "I'm good."

"When I put the tortellini in the pan, can you stir them into the sauce for me?"

I'd do anything for you.

I nod my head, signaling to her that I understand what she just asked me to do.

I make my way over to the hot stove. The sauce is bubbling, thickening up as it sits in the pan.

She puts a few generous spoonfuls of the tortellini into the pan. "You don't need to ask my permission to start stirring, you know."

"I wasn't going to."

"Yes, you were. I'm not the only one that makes weird facial expressions, Noah."

I squint my eyes together, sticking my tongue out. Picking up the wooden spoon, I start combining the pasta with the sauce.

She moves to my side, resting her elbows on the counter with her palms on her cheeks.

I watch her facial expressions and body language.

A smug look appears on her face before her lips form a cute smile. She's standing upright with her arms crossed in front of her chest.

"Are you going to pick on every little thing I do that doesn't measure up to your standards?"

She exhales. "I'm just observing. I have to say for someone who doesn't really know how to cook, you're pretty good at it."

"Growing up with a home cook for a mother and a sous chef for a sister will do that to a person."

That gets a cute little giggle out of her.

I swear I will do everything in my power to make Dani laugh. I want to listen to her laugh on repeat for the rest of my fucking life.

"Are the bowls ready to go?" she asks.

I nod, pointing behind me at the island.

She swipes them off there, placing them next to me. "You can sit down if you want. I can fill up the bowls with the pasta."

"Is that an order or a suggestion?"

"If it was an order, I would've told you to go sit your ass down at the table. Did I do that? No, I didn't. You can do whatever your little heart desires."

What if my little heart desires to pick you up, throw you on the counter, and kiss the shit out of you until you come apart screaming my name at the top of your lungs?

I re-adjust my shorts to make the bulge less obvious. "I'm going to sit down, then."

She shoves her hands in my face, giving me a thumbs up.

As I sit down at the kitchen table, she brings over a bowl of tortellini. There are pieces of shaved parmesan cheese and ribbons of basil on top.

It's a goddamn masterpiece.

"It's so pretty. I don't want to eat it."

"Then go ahead and starve," she says, going back to the counter to fill up a bowl for herself and bringing it over to the table.

"Quoting *Beauty and the Beast* I see. Seriously though, that was uncalled for."

She gets bit by the chuckle bug, covering her mouth. "I'm not even sorry."

"I know you aren't. That's the sad part."

She changes the subject. "Hey, you barely moved from that chair earlier. Did you actually get up off your ass at any point?

"I got up."

She crosses her arms, pushing her breasts up. "To do what?"

Don't look at her breasts. Don't do it. Concentrate on her face, man.

"To go to the bathroom. I can be more specific if you want me to be."

Her mouth shifts to one side before she presses her lips together. "I'm good."

"I told you I was editing my book."

"Oh, you were in your editing cave." She leans back against the chair, crossing her arms and putting one of her legs over the other.

"My what?"

"Well, it's like the writing cave, but it's not, since it's editing. Wait, you don't know what the cave is...at all?"

"I've never heard that term in my life."

"It's like a blackhole you can't escape. You're hypnotized by your computer screen and keyboard. And you can't bring yourself to do anything else."

"Ah," I say as I pick up my fork, stabbing a piece of tortellini onto it and putting it into my mouth.

Fuck, that's good.

I roll my eyes so hard it feels like they've fallen into the back of my head. "Where the hell did you learn to cook?"

"Why?"

"Did you even eat any of it yet?"

"I'm getting there."

I watch her as she picks up a piece of tortellini, but her eyes meet mine before she shoves one into her pretty little mouth.

"Can I help you?"

"Sorry." I let out a small chuckle.

I nonchalantly glance at her while she puts the pasta in her mouth, raising one of my eyebrows up.

God, I wish I was that piece of tortellini right now.

I clear my throat, anxiously waiting to hear what she thinks of the meal she made for us.

"Yeah, that's pretty good."

"No, Dani. It's better than if I would've had it at a five-star restaurant."

"Really?"

"Yeah and you never answer my question. How did you learn to cook like this?"

"My parents. My mom loves to cook, and so did my dad. I learned more from my mom though. And I have a best friend who's better at cooking than I'll ever be."

"Ah, the cooking gene. That one skipped me. Wait, which best friend is better than you? Bella or Sage?"

"Bella. She learned from her mom and Abuela. That's the ultimate cooking gene."

"She'd get along really well with Grayson. I've been learning a lot from him about the art of cooking, especially traditional Jewish cuisine. Seriously, ask me anything about Jewish food."

"Are you sure?"

"Yeah, ask me."

She bites her lip, looking up at the ceiling. "Okay, what's a latke made out of?"

"Grounded up potato, flour, and egg. C'mon, give me an actual challenge, Solomon."

"Fine. What ingredients can go into matzo ball soup?"

"That's a trick question."

She narrows her eyes. "Why?"

"Because you can put different ingredients in matzo ball soup. Chicken, carrots, pasta, different types of seasonings."

She's stunned to say the least. Her face freezes, mouth dropping open.

"You're going to catch flies with your mouth open like that."

She stretches her lips out, rolling her eyes at me. Her annoyance quickly turns into amusement. "I hate you."

"Sure you do."

We sit in silence for a while, so we can finish dinner.

My thoughts are so fucking loud. I'm surprised that she can't hear them. I'd be in so much trouble if she could.

CHAPTER FORTY-FOUR

When we finish our meals, I feel Noah's eyes peering at me.

My eyes pull in his direction.

There are those dreamy ocean eyes I've succumbed to.

He studies my face, making his way to my lips. "You got a little pasta sauce on your face."

I go to reach for my napkin, but he stops me and puts his hand on my arm.

"I got it."

He swipes the pad of his thumb across the corner of my mouth, bringing it up to his lips. He inserts it into his mouth, sucking on it.

This man is eating the leftover pasta sauce he wiped off my mouth.

I have to look away, so I can catch my breath. I thread my fingers through tendrils of hair from my ponytail.

What the fuck was that? That was the hottest shit I've ever seen in my life.

"Are you malfunctioning over there?"

I turn my head back in his direction, collecting myself by taking a deep breath in and out. "I'm fine."

Yeah, I'm the complete opposite of fine.

The urge I have to tell him to pick me up and throw me on the kitchen counter is real.

I sit criss-cross applesauce, realizing heat is spreading in between my thighs.

"You sure?"

I grin. "Uh-huh."

He gets up, grabbing his bowl and mine along with our utensils. He walks over to the sink, turning it on and washing the dishes.

Noah's done washing the dishes which probably took him twenty minutes to do. I would've been in here for a solid hour because I'm not skilled in that department.

I don't know what it is about men and washing dishes, but I find it so attractive.

I look at the pan we used and it looks brand new. Everything is stacked perfectly in the drain board. The dishwasher is organized with plates, bowls, and other items in their own respective places.

God, I want to marry this guy.

He's standing in front of the sink while I'm leaning against the island.

"Tell me a secret," I say.

He whips his head around. "What?"

"How are you so good at washing dishes and organizing them?"

"I'll tell you my secret for washing dishes if you teach me how to be a better cook. Do we have a deal, Princess?"

I stick out my hand in his direction, gesturing to him to

shake it. He does, but he holds onto my hand for a bit longer than he has to.

And I let him.

"You know I could get used to this."

"Used to what?" A sliver of a smile grows on my face.

His lips curve up, eyes lighting up like stars brightening the night sky.

My heart is beating fast like a race car driver driving in the Daytona 500, anticipating his answer.

"*This*." He points to us, using his index fingers on both hands.

"You need to be more specific."

He wets his lips, pressing them together. "Do I *really*?"

"You *really* do."

His jaw twitches, his Adam's apple bobs up and down. "I've had more fun with you this past month than I have with anyone in a long time."

How is it that Noah Kaplan has this incredible ability to take my breath away with just the words that come out of his mouth?

I change the subject because I have no idea how to respond to what he said to me. "I snuck some fresh blankets on the bed in the guest room."

"Thank you for your hospitality."

"Anytime. I'll be here. All day and all night just for your hospitality needs," I say as I curtsy for him.

That gets a laugh out of him, causing me to laugh with him.

I don't think I've laughed this much with anyone except for Dad. He knew how to make me laugh. He told the best Dad jokes. They were so bad that they were good.

I miss him so much.

"Well, time to get back to work. Then, I'm going to sleep. My brain might shrink down to nothing if I don't. That would suck." He smiles at me.

"Guess I should get back to my editing cave too."

He starts walking into the living room, turning back around to face me. "Hey, Dani."

"Yes, Noah."

"Hope you get a lot of editing done." He winks, smirking at me in the process.

I'm restraining myself from running into his arms and kissing him so hard his lips bleed slightly from me pulling on them with my teeth.

Pull yourself together, woman.

"Thanks."

I walk into my bedroom, shutting the door behind me.

How am I going to focus on editing when Noah's not even a foot away from me?

The kitchen is farther away, and so is the living room.

He's doing this shit on purpose to test me and my hormone levels.

Thank God I'm not on my period.

I bend my elbows and clench my fists. Closing my eyes, I breathe in and out multiple times in a row.

Time to dive back into the editing cave.

My fingers are finally working their magic, typing all the words that are flowing out of my brain.

Although the story I'm writing isn't as taxing as what's unfolded over the past month here, it does have moments of emotional intensity.

The female main character suffers from PTSD and panic attacks. It's oddly therapeutic writing about anxiety from a character's perspective because I'm also taking into account that it's actually me saying these things.

No matter how hard I try to focus though, my mind keeps shifting to Noah.

I have no idea what the hell he's doing. And it's stressing me out. I mean I know he's editing, but still. A girl needs to know these things.

Sitting back on my office chair, I glance out the window to see birds sitting in the tree in front of the house, chirping away.

The sky is gradually getting darker as time goes on. The view outside my window is nice and serene.

Why don't I feel serene?

I need a drink. Too bad I don't drink alcohol that often. Caffeine is the answer to my problem.

Wait, I can't drink caffeine right now. What the hell am I thinking?

See this is the problem. I'm already wired. Caffeine will only make it worse.

Music. That's what I need.

Music will calm me down and allow me to regain my focus.

I grab my wireless earbuds, sticking them both in my ears. I maximize the window for Spotify, finding my playlist that has my current favorite songs on it.

It's hard to miss because of the title.

Good Shit.

Pressing the play button, a big smile grows on my face when I realize Olivia Rodrigo's voice is in my ears.

I'm finishing up the edits I've been working on for the past month, courtesy of my lovely beta readers. They're a sweet group of people and they've been incredibly helpful in providing me with constructive feedback on my book.

It's no secret I'm an adult.

Maybe I don't act like one all the time, but I am.

It's surreal to relive my teenage years through Olivia Rodrigo's angsty and emotional discography. No, I didn't experience heartbreak or have a life-changing relationship.

But, it's cool to imagine I did both of those things through her music.

The irony is it hasn't been that long since I was a teenager. It just feels like it has.

Time is such a common yet foreign concept. Sometimes it's slow. Sometimes it's fast. There never seems to be any in between. Not in my personal experience, at least.

For instance, it feels like my dad passed away only yesterday, but he actually passed away nine years ago. I can't believe it will be a decade next year.

I blink my eyes three times in a row to stop the tears from welling up.

My bat mitzvah was one of the last times I had a heart-to-heart with him.

I studied the shit out of my Torah portion, but anxiety got the best of me before I could even walk into the temple.

My dad pulled me aside.

I remember the exact words he said to me.

You're going to do great, pumpkin. If you feel those nerves trying to take over when you're up there, just picture everybody in their underwear. Works like a charm. You studied so hard for this. You can do this. I know you can. You're a strong girl because you're my girl. My daughter. You're a Solomon. And we never back down from a challenge. We never admit defeat.

That last part always echoes over and over again in my head like the inside of my head is incredibly hollow.

I'm brought back to reality when I notice how late it's getting. "Shit, I need to get ready for bed," I mumble to myself.

Removing the earbuds out of my ears, I put them back into their case.

I do a quick change out of my clothes into my pajamas.

Once I open my bedroom door, I walk to the bathroom.

Before I can open the bathroom door, Noah comes out.

He's standing there, but that's not the main thing I notice.

The man isn't wearing a fucking shirt.

You wouldn't know it by looking at him right away when he's wearing a t-shirt. But, wow. I had a feeling he was muscular underneath because I've felt his biceps and chest.

Fuck, he's ripped.

I study his chest and toned stomach, taking in the beautiful sight. I'm biting my bottom lip so hard it might bleed.

He takes his sweet time, scanning me from head to toe.

He's kerosene, lighting my body on fire. I'm hot everywhere.

"Hi." He leans against the doorframe, crossing his arms with a smirk across his lips.

Why is it so attractive when guys lean against door frames?

"H-hi," I stutter.

"Are you okay because it looks like you look like you just saw a ghost?"

I flatten my lips. "Everything's just *peachy.*"

I'm shocked I'm able to get any words out.

I'm not the type of girl who weighs physicality over personality.

Noah's the entire package. He's smart, creative, talented, charming, and funny. To top it all off, he's so fucking handsome.

"Bathroom's all yours. Good night, Dani."

He slowly walks away from me. I'm engulfed by his signature scent. Ocean, orange, and minty goodness.

"Night."

I walk into the bathroom, slamming the door shut. Sitting on the edge of the bathtub, I cover my face with my hands.

I can't do this anymore.

I think about Noah all the time. I dream about him for Chrissakes. I need to do something about this now or I'm going to regret it later.

Getting up from the edge of the bathtub, I walk over to the

sink. I rush through my usual night routine, taking a cold and hard look at myself in the mirror.

I can't believe I'm saying this, but I admit defeat.

"You win, Noah Kaplan," I say to my reflection in the mirror. A deep breath comes out of my mouth. "Fuck it."

I storm out of the bathroom, catching up with him before he goes into the guest bedroom.

I can't believe I'm doing this.

Grabbing his hand, Noah turns around with a confused expression written all over his face.

He lowers his eyebrows. "Forget something?"

A long stretch of silence occurs. At first, I hesitate to act on my attraction to him—until I don't.

I grab his face, planting a kiss on his lips.

When I pull away, he looks at our surroundings with widened eyes and meets my gaze like he can't believe what happened.

He stares at my lips for a moment before gently grazing them and running his tongue along them.

He requests entry into my mouth.

I accept his request without any hesitation.

The palm of his hand lands on my cheek and the other slides down to grip my hip.

His lips are warm and soft. They taste like mint and the ocean.

My body wants him so fucking badly, but my brain is telling me something entirely different.

The chronic overthinker is determined to take over.

Wait a minute, what am I doing? This is wrong.

I pull away, realizing I just kissed Noah fucking Kaplan.

He stares at me like he can't believe what just happened, his mouth gaping wide open. He looks like he's going to say something, but he doesn't. He's frozen like a statue in an art museum.

My breath hitches, growing heavier by the second.

I try to rub my arms in an attempt to get rid of the goose-bumps but it's no use. They've become a regular thing when I'm around Noah. I should be used to them by now.

I take a deep gulp, almost choking on the saliva going down my throat. "I'm sorry."

I sprint into my room, slamming the door behind me and having a borderline panic attack.

CHAPTER FORTY-FIVE

She kissed me.

She. *Fucking.* Kissed. Me.

I should've said something, but I froze.

She tastes like sweet peaches. One kiss wasn't enough. I need more.

I sprint over to her bedroom, knocking on the door.

The door swings open.

Dani stands there, her chest heaving. Beads of sweat outline her gorgeous face. Her face could be covered in shit and it'd still be the most beautiful thing I've ever laid my eyes on.

All I can think about right now is how much I want to make her sweat in other places.

"I'm sorry. I shouldn't have done that," she breathes out.

"You're right. *You* shouldn't have done that."

Her lips part open slightly, staring at me in disbelief. I can see the look on her face that she's convinced our kiss was a mistake.

I'm going to prove her wrong.

"I should've," I finally say.

Grabbing her face with my hand, I aggressively pull her

body weight into me. Our lips crash into each other like ocean waves crashing onto shore. My tongue gently slides into her mouth, meeting hers in the process.

My hand dances its way to her neck with my thumb settled on the edge of her jaw.

I push us into her bedroom, kicking the door closed with my foot in one smooth motion.

Our lips are in sync, moving together like they're one unit. Instead of slamming her down on the bed, I push her up against the wall that's next to her bookcase.

My lips let go of hers for a brief moment. "Raise your arms for me, Sweet Peach."

She raises her arms high in the air. "Like this?"

"Just like that."

I pin them up against the wall, interlocking my hands with hers.

"You're about to ruin me, aren't you?" She looks at me in a way that knots my stomach so tight I can't breathe.

Her eyes are steady on me. The corner of her lip rises, melting me like a lit candle.

"You've already ruined me. It's only fair that I return the favor."

"Oh, yeah?" Her tone is playful.

"You have no fucking idea."

We're both breathing heavily.

Her eyes bounce from my eyes to my lips repeatedly. "Noah, I'm losing feeling in my arms."

She most certainly is. I can feel how limp they are just by holding her hands. The only reason she's able to keep her arms up is because of me.

"I thought you worked out." I smirk, my tone coming out as playful.

She bats her long, black eyelashes at me. "You're going to regret that."

I move closer to her, our lips brushing lightly against each other. "You're going to regret talking back to me like that."

"I'd love to see you try," she says into my mouth.

"Are you challenging me?"

"Maybe." Giggles escape her mouth, making me feel like I'm floating and witnessing this moment from above.

Releasing my hands from hers, I free her arms from my grasp.

I cup her face, pulling it closer to mine. Within seconds, our lips make their way back to each other. My heart is beating so loud it could explode out of my chest at any moment. I don't want to waste another second because I'm craving to taste more of her lips which taste as sweet as she is.

I'm fueled by pure adrenaline and raging hormones at this point. I groan straight into her mouth. To my surprise, she lets out a faint moan which is so fucking hot. My pulse is quickening as I attempt to steady my breathing patterns. I'm growing harder by the second. I don't think I'll be able to last any longer.

When she thinks we're about to get deeper into this, I pull my mouth away from hers.

"Is something wrong?" She lightly furrows her eyebrows.

I walk over to her bed, sitting down with my legs hanging off the edge. "Sit on me."

Her eyes roam around the room, avoiding the possibility of meeting my gaze and crossing her arms over her breasts. "What?"

"Sit on my lap, Dani," I demand.

Her body jerks, but she listens to me. She's strolling over to me like she's walking in the park on a sunny day.

Hurry the fuck up, woman.

I grab her by her hips, guiding her onto my lap.

When she sits down, I hear a whimpering sound come out of her mouth.

"Do you feel that? Do you feel what you're doing to me?" I murmur into her ear, smiling into her neck.

I lean my head forward to get a glance at her face.

Her cheeks are bright red.

My girl is blushing.

She leans forward, bringing her legs up to her body and burying her head into her arms.

"You can't hide from me."

"How am I turning you on right now? I'm not even doing anything."

"Let's call it the Danielle Solomon effect. You have this crazy power to turn me on just by looking at me with your hypnotizing brown eyes."

She lifts her head back up, placing the palms of her hands on her flushed cheeks.

"You have no idea what you do to me, but you're about to find out." I trail my hand up her arm which is covered in goosebumps. When it reaches her shoulder, I slide my thumb underneath the strap of her tank top.

Touching Dani is fucking addicting.

The way her skin melts into my fingers when I touch her makes me feel like an erupting volcano, seeping molten lava through its cracks.

I wet my lips, pressing on them so hard that I can feel my teeth.

My lips swiftly find their way back to her neck. I move a few stray tendrils of her ponytail out of the way so I can get to work, nibbling on the soft and smooth skin on her neck.

"Noah," she says through a quick breath.

"Is this okay?"

Her head moves, but I can't tell if that was a yes or no.

"I need to hear a yes or no come out of your mouth, Princess."

"Yes."

"Good girl."

She gets up off my lap, standing in front of me. "Are we really doing this?"

"Stop talking, Dani." I scoot off the bed, immediately gripping onto her hips.

This kiss is different from the others. It's not soft or sweet. It's desperate and needy. We're devouring each other like predators hunting their prey.

She sways her hips back and forth.

I reach down, picking her up with my hands resting on her ass.

She wraps her legs around my waist, grinding against me.

Our lips are an entangled mess. There's no way they could escape one another now.

Her arms are wrapped around my neck. "Noah," she moans into my mouth.

"Fuck, don't do that."

"Please put me out of misery and throw me on the damn bed already."

I do what she says because she knows how much I want her. I want to feel her body weight under mine. God, I want to be inside her.

I throw her down onto the bed.

She scoots back, bending her knees to her chest. She spreads her legs open, one at a time.

She's going to kill me I swear.

I crawl to her and throw the stupid, decorative pillows off the bed.

"I'm in charge now," Dani blurts out.

I swallow hard, grinding my teeth. "Wait, I thought that—"

"It's my turn to have a little fun of my own."

CHAPTER FORTY-SIX

I study his chest all the way to the deep V shape that goes down into his shorts, running my fingers over his chest, down to his abs.

V shapes are so fucking underrated and hot as hell.

He's smiling hard to hide his flushed cheeks, his pearly white teeth blinding the shit out of me. I can feel his eyes blaze their way inside of me, melting my core down to nothing. "I need to tell you this now because if I don't tell you now, I never will." He grabs me by my waist, pulling me onto his lap with his hands settling there. He clears his throat, and the muscles in his jaw are flexing. "I've been consumed by you for years, Dani. I want you. All the time. I think about you. *All. The. Fucking. Time.* I'm surprised I can get any work done on my book because I know you're always there, lingering in my mind. I can't escape you. I don't want to escape you." He leans into me, cupping his hands on my face.

"Noah. I-I don't know..." My chest heaves, causing every part of my body to vibrate.

I. Can't. Breathe.

"I'm not done."

Of course, he's not done. When is he ever done?

"Do you want to know how I've been for the past five years?"

My eyes flutter like butterfly wings flying in open air.

"Shitty." He pauses. "It took every fiber of my being to not message you on Instagram when I found your author account. Do you know why I didn't? Because I knew you'd block me. And I couldn't bear to lose you. I wanted to know what you've been up to since I last saw you. To feel close to you again."

I move my hand behind my neck. I can't believe what I'm hearing.

He smiles at me like he's seeing me for the very first time.

The butterflies are back, swarming my stomach so much it's almost painful. A pain that I don't mind suffering through if it's because of Noah.

"I haven't seen the guys because I'd rather spend time with you. They're tired of me talking about you all the time."

He's been talking to Grayson and Xander about me. Oh my God.

He stares into my eyes. "Those romance books I have in my room, they remind me of you. I thought you hated me, but I'd buy them and read them anyway. It felt like I was there with you."

I stare at him.

I've never been so hypnotized by this man until this very moment.

"I felt closer to you through the books you read," he breathes.

Oh, fuck.

"You've been talking to the guys about me?" I hiccup.

My eyes are glassy. I can feel the tears that are begging to be released.

"That's what you got out of this whole thing? Me talking about you to my friends?" He grins, turning into a smile.

I lean my head into his chest for a brief moment as air comes out of my nose.

"Remember how much of an asshole I was to you in sophomore year? When I said all those horrible things to you on the day of the one-year anniversary of your dad's passing?"

I nod. "Uh-huh."

"After you stormed away from me, I felt so fucking bad. I knew I had to do something to make it up to you."

"What did you have to do?"

"My dad wasn't the one to send you the box."

"What box?"

"*The box.*"

What box is he even talking about? The box. Wait...Oh. My. God.

I remember coming home from school the day after Noah blew up at me. There was a cardboard box sitting on my bed with a note taped onto it.

Hey Dani,

Noah's really sorry for what he said to you at school today. It was completely inappropriate and heartless. Don't worry, he's in trouble. Big trouble. I hope the items in here make you feel something. I'm always here for you. Always.

Love, Ben.

"It was *you.*"

He nods. "It was *me.*"

"I don't understand."

"I told my dad to write out the note and plaster his name on it because I knew you would've thrown the box out. Set it on fire. Stomp on it. I knew you wouldn't have opened if my name was on the note."

I chuckle. "I still use that journal to write down book ideas. Well, pretty much anything that has to do with my books. The mini Kit Kats were a nice touch by the way." I wink at him. "You know, my addiction to Kit Kats started because of my dad. He used to buy the regular-sized ones all the time. Mom hated having that shit in the house, but Dad didn't care because they made me happy."

You make me happy.

He laughs, sitting there and studying my face. "Do you know women like you are hard to come by?"

I blink my eyes repeatedly to register the random subject change.

My lips pucker out, flattening into a semi-curved line, and my eyebrows lower themselves. "Women. Like. Me."

"Yes, women like you. It's hard to find a woman who's not afraid to be brutally honest with you even if it might hurt. You already know how attractive I find that quality about you. So, that's enough of that." He moves on to something else. "You have one of the biggest hearts I've ever seen. You knew how inevitable it was that you were going to run into me at the hospital. You knew you'd have to deal with my bullshit antics. For who knows how long. And yet...you still came."

I can't get one word in because my brain doesn't want to connect with my mouth.

Letting Noah ramble on is the best solution.

I'm slowly melting into a pile of mush, hearing him talk about me. *He's talking about his feelings. For me.* Tears are pouring out of my eyes. I can't control it, so I let them fall.

"You didn't think I'd end this without mentioning your talent for words, did you?"

I laugh through my tears.

"You have a gift for writing, Dani. A lot of people wish they had your talent. I don't know anybody who writes like you. You have this incredible ability to immerse readers into a story.

Many of them can see themselves through the characters you write and your book isn't even out yet. It's fucking magic what you do." He takes a moment to catch his breath, his eyes working up to my face. "God, you're distracting."

"And you don't think that you are?"

He tugs on my shirt, his hands gripping tightly on my waist. "We're talking about you. Not me." He smiles, the fire in his eyes dissipating as his pupils dilate. "When I'm around you, I have this indescribable out-of-body experience. I'm floating in the sky. Dani, you're right there with me. My sunshine. The light that scares away the darkness inside of me. I need you in my life. I need my sunshine."

Fuck me, that was the most romantic shit I've ever heard.

His hands return back on my face, cupping it like a gentle giant.

I put my hands on top of his. Breathing in and out, I do my best to slow down my rapid heartbeat. Once I calm down, I know I have to say something. This is my chance to tell him how I really feel about him. "Before we go any further, I need to tell you something."

"Okay, Sunshine."

He removes his hands from my face, giving me the space to move around if I need to.

"I'm sorry to tell you this but..." I pause out of curiosity to see how he'd react.

His facial expressions are unreadable. He looks around the room, trying to figure out what he did wrong.

God, this is all real.

Bella did tell me to go live out my own version of a romance novel.

This is it.

"You've been reading too many romance books, my friend."

A sad expression appears on his face as he looks away from me. He's avoiding every possibility of looking at me right now.

"That's not even remotely funny," he says through a breath, looking down at the floor next to him.

"Hey, Lover Boy."

He doesn't reply, so I resort to returning my hands to his cheeks.

Sitting in front of him, I tilt his head up so I can see his handsome face. "You know what you are?"

He shakes his head, grinning ear to ear.

"The best thing that's ever happened to me. Yes, I knew I'd run into you. It was inevitable. But, you know what? If I didn't come back home, I would've missed out on all this. All these feelings. Being there for your family. Being there for you. You drive me absolutely insane but in the best possible way. My body always craves to be in close proximity to yours. I want to be around you. All. The. Damn. Time."

He looks at me, listening intently.

"You're *my moonlight*. The moon is just a mere shadow of the sun and for years, I thought I hated you for always being around. But even then, you were always there in the back of my mind. So goddamn persistent, too."

He's breathless and wholeheartedly mesmerized by me.

"I've never met a man who cares so deeply about his family and his loved ones. You're the only man who makes me blush just by looking at me. I've never laughed or smiled so much in a long time." I smile which turns into a breathy laugh. "You can't have two halves without a whole. I need you in my life, Noah. I need my moonlight."

I reach over and grab the glass of water sitting on my bedside table, gulping the entire thing down my throat.

After several minutes of me spilling my guts out, Noah finally says something to me. "Are you done?"

"Yup."

"Okay, before we do this, you need to promise me this can't

be a one-time thing. If we do this, that's it. *You're it for me.* There's no going back."

I used to despise the word 'promise.' Noah is giving it an entirely new meaning now.

His hands grab onto my hips, tugging me closer to him.

Tilting my head, my hands wrap around his neck as I smile. "I *promise.*"

He aggressively grabs me by my waist, our lips come into collision so hard I might wake up with a nice bruise on my lips tomorrow.

"Lie down flat on your back for me," Noah tells me.

He slithers down to the lower half of my body like a snake with his hypnotizing eyes on me the entire time.

My pulse staggers, latching onto every imperfect heave coming out of my chest.

He tickles the skin on my stomach with the string from my shorts. "I'm taking these off. Is that okay?"

Fuck, yes.

"Yes."

I let out a smooth breath, staring at the ceiling.

He slides them down my legs, throwing my shorts off the bed. His eyes land back on me. "Lift your arms for me."

"Hey, I thought I was in charge." I frown, my voice going up several octaves like I've been sucking on a helium balloon for several hours.

"You're on a brief intermission."

I open my mouth, letting out a gasp.

He takes off my shirt without any issues, proceeding to examine my chest area and smiling up a storm.

"What?"

His eyes relocate to my face. "You're wearing a bra this time."

I cross my legs, raising my right eyebrow and tilting my

head with my eyes firmly planted on his. "I couldn't make it *too* easy for you. You're going to have to work for it."

"You should know it turns me on when you challenge me." He bites down on his bottom lip as he checks me out.

His dreamy ocean eyes wander to my chest and down to my stomach.

"Are you okay over there?" I smirk.

"No, I'm just overwhelmed that a woman like you exists. Dani, you're a fucking masterpiece."

I place my hands on my flushed cheeks.

Noah is the only guy who knows how to make me instantaneously blush, and I can't seem to get enough of it.

"Oh, shut up, Heart Eyes."

"I mean, look at you. Get up and turn all the way around for me." He gestures to me, moving his index finger in a circular motion.

"Are you kidding me?"

"Does it look like I'm kidding?" His face is expressionless.

Okay, I'm getting up.

I get off the bed as fast as I possibly can, moving my body so my backside faces him. I turn around as slowly as possible to make him sweat.

"Fuck, how are you even real?"

I'm staring at him in disbelief because I never thought I'd hear those words come out of Noah Kaplan's mouth.

"Come here," he urges.

I meander over to him, running my fingers through his hair.

He grabs me by my ass with his hands, pulling me closer to him.

My body jolts from the sudden movement change.

Wow, that feels so damn good.

He kneels before me.

My head shifts backward, chest heaving. "What the hell are you doing?"

"I'm worshiping you, Princess."

I swallow hard and deep, feeling a lump go down my throat.

He looks up at me, wrapping his hands around the back of my legs and feathering searing kisses on every inch of exposed skin.

Shit, shit, shit.

"You're torturing me," I whine.

He looks up at me. "Baby, you've been torturing me for years. I'm going to torture you for a little while longer. Let's see how you like it."

He plants rough kisses all over me before he stands up in front of me, smiling.

There's a fire in his eyes that's burning so bright. It transfers over to my body, mixing with the chills going down my spine.

He goes in for the kill, taking my lips with him. "Dani."

God, I love how easily my name rolls off his tongue.

His lips move to my neck, collarbone, and back up my lips again.

I've waited so fucking long for this.

"If I do anything you don't like. Tell me, and I will stop," he says as he meets my gaze.

"Okay, I can do that."

"That's my girl." He gets up and slams his lips into mine.

Pressing his body hard against mine, he thrusts into me gently which allows me to feel how hard he is.

A whimper escapes my lips.

Fuck, I don't think I'm getting any sleep tonight.

CHAPTER FORTY-SEVEN

noah

She's my sunshine.

I'm her moonlight.

Fuck, I love this woman.

I can't get enough of her.

I've tasted Dani's lips, tongue, and mouth. Now, I'm craving to taste the rest of her.

"I need to see all of you." I bite down on my lip.

She has this vicious look in her eyes and it's so hot.

She's so fucking hot.

Her nerves have transformed into this fearless confidence, making me want to scream so damn loud the entire neighborhood can hear us.

I sit back down on the bed, scooting back until my back leans up against her pillows. Crossing my legs, I lift my arms up and rest them behind my head.

Dani stands in front of the bed, obeying my request as she reaches up to unhook her bra.

Sticking her arm out, the bra dangles in her hand. She drops it on the floor and her eyes soften as she meets my gaze, taking my breath away.

I know how I said I hated it when she teases me, but I lied. I love it.

Her breasts are in full view, leaving little to no room for my imagination which makes me the happiest guy in the world. I've been going to sleep for the past month, dreaming about what her naked body looks like.

This is so much better than my stupid, fucking dreams. And so much better than all the romance books I've read.

I swallow deep and clear my throat. "Fuck." My heartbeats are louder and faster than the speed of light. "Dani, you're the most gorgeous woman I've ever seen in my entire life."

She glances at me and turns away, staring at the floor with rosy cheeks and smiling. "Shut up," she mumbles as she moves closer to the edge of the bed.

A magnet pulls me closer to her, causing me to change out of my current position.

I firmly place both of my hands on her breasts, massaging her pink nipples with my fingertips.

She arches her back, letting out this insane moan. "Noah," she says my name in one breath.

"I told you you'll know when I moan, didn't I?"

"Y-you did," she stutters as I stop massaging her nipples, bringing my mouth closer to her breast.

I start to suck which makes her moan even more, pulling her weight onto my lap for easier access. My tongue swirls around her nipple before I pull away to examine her facial expressions, seeing how she's reacting to what I'm doing to her.

Her back is still arched and her neck is curved, rolling her eyes so damn hard they might pop out of her sockets.

This is fucking bliss.

She brings her head back down, staring at me with this intensity that could disintegrate me in a matter of seconds. "Your turn, Lover Boy. Take off your shorts now."

I'm rushing to untie my shorts, but I can see in her face that her patience is wearing thin.

"I don't have all night," she growls.

"I'm going as fast as I can, baby."

Once the shorts are off, she sticks her arm out at me, wiggling her hand. "Give them to me."

When Dani's in charge, there's this effortless confidence that radiates off her. It's absolutely scrumptious. Just like she is.

She bites her lip, taking her sweet time to admire the visible bulge coming out of my boxers. She looks away, throwing my shorts across the room.

What the hell is going on? Why is my heart beating so damn fast? Am I having a heart attack? Am I dying? Am I already dead?

I can't balance myself, but somehow I stumble my way so I'm fully on the bed before everything comes crashing down.

"Noah, are you okay?"

"Y-yeah, I'm f-fine. I'm f-fine."

My back is facing her, my hands are shaking, and my breathing is getting sparse.

Not now. Please, not now.

Anxiety always makes an appearance at the worst times.

Dani runs to my rescue like the amazing woman she is. "You're not fine." Her face circles its way around to see mine, grabbing it with her hands so it's at eye-level with hers.

She stares at me, grabbing my hands. "Take a deep breath. You're going to be okay."

I close my eyes, breathing out at first and breathing in as slowly as I can.

When I open my eyes, Dani is all I can see.

She's every guy's dream, but she's always been mine. The thing is, she isn't a dream at all. She's real and she's standing in front of me right now.

Fuck, I can't breathe.

"What's going on in that beautiful head of yours?"

"I'm fucking nervous. I've never...I've never had sex before." I gulp hard, making my lips quiver.

She takes me by my hands, pulling me over to the bed. We sit down at the same time before she climbs on top of me.

This skin-to-skin contact isn't helping with my raging hormones or my massive hard-on.

"I haven't either," she reveals.

"I don't want to fuck this up. I'm prepared. I did research."

The cutest smile spreads across her gorgeous lips right before she gets bit by the giggle bug.

I'm so in love with this woman.

"You did some research?"

"Does that surprise you?"

She shakes her head. "Would it surprise you if I told you I did some research of my own?"

"No, it wouldn't surprise me at all."

Her face softens. "We can take it slow. If it's uncomfortable or painful, we'll stop. Okay?"

I nod. "Okay."

How can someone be sweet and sexy at the same time?

Her hands cup my face, traveling down to my abs. "How the hell have you been hiding all this from me?"

"I could ask you the same question."

Fuck you, anxiety. You're not ruining what's about to be the best night of my life. Let's do this.

CHAPTER FORTY-EIGHT

"Out of curiosity, what did you use for your research?" I ask as Noah climbs on top of me, his body weight feeling so good on top of mine.

I'm going to have to borrow that cologne sometime, so I can douse myself in it. Honestly, I might not have to after we're done here.

His lips meet mine with a sense of urgency. He kisses me fiercely, pouring all of his emotions into this kiss.

Desire.

Lust.

Desperation.

I gasp as he gently tugs on my lower lip with his teeth.

He takes it as an opportunity to shove his tongue into my mouth, marking his territory inside.

I put my arms around his neck and grab his face.

He pulls away from my mouth, studying me with this intensity that's making my insides melt like tempered glass.

Amusement is visible in those mesmerizing eyes of his. I can feel his breath as he moves closer, brushing his lips against the tip of my ear. "I think you already know the answer to that question."

I swallow, hard and deep. "You read spicy romance books," I blurt out before I can register that those words just escaped my lips.

He stares back at me, amusement taking over his face again. And if I'm not mistaken, hunger.

He read spicy romance books for research. God, I love him even more now.

I stare back at him.

"I can take it from the look on your face you were surprised by that."

"Uh-huh." My heartbeats are increasing at a rapid speed.

"Remind me. What's the name of the book you're reading? One that has smut in it, perhaps?" His voice and intense gaze are sending shivers down my spine.

I clear my throat, unable to comprehend what he just asked me. I'm smiling up a storm and blushing so hard my cheeks might overheat. "Why?"

"What book is it?"

"Noah."

"Tell. Me. The. Name," he commands.

"I'm re-reading one of my favorite romance books right now."

"Oh?" He peppers kisses along the side of my neck.

I'm officially a mess.

As his kisses deepen on my neck, I delicately run my fingers through his hair while my other hand brushes against his cheek.

His kiss softens, slowly sliding his lips over to mine and brushing them ever so slightly.

"I-I'm in a...r-reading slump," I stammer, barely a whisper and almost sounding like a cry.

His head lifts, eyes directed towards my face. "Why are you re-reading one of your favorite books?"

"Sometimes it helps me get out of a slump when I re-read my favorite books."

"What is it called?" He rasps, his voice full of desire.

I squeeze my eyes shut as he bites and tugs on my bottom lip. "*Icebreaker*," I say.

My eyes snap open to the realization he's the only guy I've ever allowed to touch me and kiss me. I mean, he's the first guy I've ever kissed. And hell our first kiss was perfect. *He's perfect.*

He smirks, his gaze setting my skin on fire.

"Why the hell are you looking at me like that?"

"You want to know the authors I read?" He locks eyes with me.

My breath catches in my throat as I stare into his eyes, drowning in them. It's as if the planet stopped spinning on its axis and he's the only thing I see.

My heart is pounding hard inside my chest. All I can feel is his hands on my skin and his breath.

His voice brings me back to reality as a smirk materializes across his lips. "Elsie Silver, Lucy Score, and..." He moves closer to my ear, his hot breaths convulsing off my skin. "Hannah Grace."

My mouth drops open, my eyes blink rapidly for a few seconds.

Lizzie must have given him a list of my favorite romance books. Maybe that flashlight might come in handy after all.

"Indeed, I did. So...if you ever wanted to test out the waters, I'd be happy to oblige."

"Test out the waters?" I stifle out a laugh.

"We can make those spicy scenes you read about all the time a reality. I'm going to use every goddamn opportunity to get you to scream my name so fucking loud the neighbors are going to hear you."

Damn, that was hot.

"Noah, I-I, that was s-so…"

Before my thoughts have the slightest chance of traveling out of my mouth, he crashes his mouth onto mine, ravishing it.

Sucking.

Licking.

Biting my lips.

Just when I think it can't get any better or worse, he tilts my head so he can deepen our kiss.

I grip onto his shoulders for support since my knees are starting to give out. That's when he bounces my body up, earning a gasp that escapes my mouth.

I wrap my legs around his thighs, circling my arms around his neck.

I don't even know what's right or wrong anymore.

He gently places my body on top of the bedsheet and there's no space between us.

The way he's kissing me is enough to send me into overdrive and I believe it's having the same effect on him. I can feel his groin which is hard as a rock through the thin fabric of my underwear.

He has me under his spell and I can't help but succumb to it. The moment he starts to grind against my soaked clothed clit, I release a desperate groan and my toes begin to curl.

Meanwhile, he's still kissing me like I'm the only source of oxygen left for him to breathe out carbon dioxide.

He's not wasting any time because he moves down to the lower half of my body, taking my underwear off.

He travels back up my body, kissing every inch of bare skin. Leaning back on his knees and feet, his blue eyes darken as he looks up at me. "Can I touch you?"

I nod. "Yes."

Noah takes a deep breath as he reaches out to touch me.

The initial contact of his skin in between my thighs sends shockwaves all throughout my body.

After he moves his way up towards my clit, I release a spontaneous moan.

He lifts his head up to meet my gaze, smirking. "God, Dani. You're fucking soaked for me."

I roll my eyes, licking the inside of my cheek. "Oh, shut up." Extending my arm to open the drawer of my night table, I pull out a condom.

He licks his lips, smirking. "And how long has that been in there?"

"Do you really want to know?"

He runs his fingers through his hair. "Just wondering if it's going to be able to do its job."

"It will." Giving him a fake laugh, I narrow my eyes as he ditches his boxers.

I glance at the ceiling with my fist resting on my lips before my eyes gravitate in Noah's direction.

My mouth hangs open when I see his dick.

How the hell is that going to fit inside me?

I distract myself by watching him as he rips open one of the packets with his teeth.

"Are you a dog?" I cover my mouth in an attempt to contain my laughter.

"You think you're so funny, don't you?"

"I think I'm hilarious actually."

His mouth makes a home on mine.

Heat floods all over my body, especially in between my thighs.

"Who's laughing now, huh?" He rasps.

I swallow, my anxiety escalating at an insanely quick rate. My shoulders are tightening. I close my eyes, exhaling a few times in a row.

Back in high school, I remember when Bella told me about her first time.

The first time can hurt. Like fucking hell. But then it gets better.

As if sensing my anxious thoughts, Noah cups my face and gives me a passionate kiss. He pushes me down onto the bed again with him on top of me. He pulls his lips away from mine, staring at me in a way that makes my heart triple in size.

"Are you okay?"

"Yeah. I'm just preparing myself. That's all," I breathe out.

"If it's uncomfortable or painful, tell me. *Promise*?"

I nod, giving him a silent answer that I'm going to be okay.

Somehow, I know I will be. *Because I'm with him.*

Looking up at the ceiling, I begin to dwell on the fact that I've never had sex before. Noah and I have already established this, but I'm so fucking nervous.

My chest is rising and falling really fast.

Calm down, Dani. Just breathe.

He wraps his arms around me and I hug his back, feeling how rock-hard he is against me, so I swallow hard.

I pull my head back down. "I don't know if you're going to fit, Noah."

He looks at me, studying my face. "Is there anything I can do to make sure it doesn't hurt?"

"Yeah, I've used a vibrator before. Just go slow."

He blinks his eyes, looking around the room before meeting my gaze. "Fuck, don't say shit like that to me."

A smile tugs on the corners of my mouth. "Why?"

"I'm going to come and I'm not even inside of you yet."

A wicked smile grows on my face.

He's talking dirty to me and making sure I'm taken care of at the same time. Yeah, this man has been reading too many spicy romance books.

"Ready?" He studies me, starting at my face and making his way down to my ankles.

"Yeah, I'm ready."

He positions himself in between my legs.

I start to breathe like a normal person.

"I'm going to need you to relax for me. It's going to be okay. I got you."

I let the tightness in my shoulders roll off my back, loosening up as best as I can.

He slowly guides his dick in, allowing me to adjust to the size of him with each push until he's fully seated inside of me.

"Are you okay?"

I nod, staring at him and taking a deep breath. "Yeah, I'm okay."

He continues, pushing in and out.

Oh my God.

This is unlike anything I've ever experienced. It's weird and different experiencing sex in real life than experiencing it through romance books.

I mean, duh, of course it is.

Romance books are fictional.

This is happening right now.

Holy shit, this is so much better than books.

Sweat trickles down the temples on his head as I watch him attempt to control himself, so he doesn't thrust all the way inside of me. It appears it's as hard for him as it is for me. And I find the sight oddly comforting.

I'm exhaling so much that I might lose the ability to breathe properly. I'm rolling my eyes so hard they're starting to feel nonexistent.

A tear streams out of my eye and down my face.

Instead of whispering soothing words into my ear to calm me down, Noah kisses away my tears. A simple but effective gesture.

He continues his thrusts before he peppers soft kisses on my cheeks, lips, and neck.

Our gasps mingle with each other, becoming one. It's like we were always meant to fit together.

His tongue touches his top lip, pulling it back into his mouth. "Is this okay?"

I want him to hear all the dirty thoughts that are running rampant in my mind right now. Like how much I want him deeper inside me or how I'm about to lose all my self-control.

"God, yes," I whisper.

His thrusts get deeper and harder.

A little moan escapes my mouth before his lips slam into mine.

"Fuck, Dani. You're taking me so well."

He reaches down right above where we're joined and my grip on him grows tighter. His finger circles my clit, my nails scraping his back.

Moans escape my lips as I cling to him.

He kisses me on the mouth like a man who's starved. It's as if he hasn't eaten in weeks, possibly months.

He's peppering more kisses starting on my cheek, and working his way down my body.

Jaw.

Neck.

Collarbone.

My toes curl in anticipation of what's about to escape out of Noah's dirty mouth next.

"Fuck," he says. "Do you think you can come for me, Sweet Peach?"

I can't answer him.

My body is floating in the stars of the night sky because of the way he feels inside me like he belongs there. He has *always* belonged there.

He doesn't force me to answer him.

Instead, his thrusts get even rougher and more profound,

causing me to let out the biggest moan that's ever come out of my mouth.

I'm sweating like crazy.

To my surprise, he straightens up and lifts my legs. He puts them on his shoulders. The new position allows him to enter me deeper as he continues fucking me, rubbing my clit.

My orgasm is on the brink of a sweet release.

Shit, shit, shit.

"That's my good fucking girl."

For a man who I described as sweet, Noah's not so sweet in bed. He's the complete opposite, actually. He's confident and straightforward. But most importantly, he's so fucking hot.

Moaning from the base of my throat, I roll my eyes. "N-Noah." The biggest smile grows on my face.

He leans closer to me, capturing my lips in a messy and passionate kiss as he takes everything I can give him.

He collapses on top of me before he rolls off to the side, landing beside me. We're panting and attempting to catch our breaths and compose ourselves before either of us speaks.

I'm trying to slow my intense, rapid heartbeats while my interlocked hands are resting on my stomach. "Fuck me."

Shit, did I just say that out loud?

He turns his head toward me. "I just did, but we can go for round two if you want." He pulls me closer to him, our noses barely grazing each other. His eyes are full of contentment as a tender smile spreads across his lips. "Thank you, Dani," he whispers. "For giving yourself to me."

He gives me a sweet peck on the lips.

"What?" His lips twitch before they break out into a gorgeous smile.

I bite down on my bottom lip, sucking it in.

I have to say I thought I'd be freaking out over his dick more, but here I am about to pass out from his round, tight, and muscular bare ass.

I gulp down on some residual saliva sitting at the base of my throat.

"Do you do ass workouts or something? Because...holy shit!" I fold my arms, raising one of the covers over my breasts.

He puts his boxers back on, turning around to face me. "You like my ass?" He's back on the bed, planting a wet kiss on my forehead.

"Uh-huh."

"Want to know a secret?"

I nod, smiling so big my face might freeze like this forever.

"I *love* your ass." He cups my face with both of his hands.

His lips cover mine hungrily, sucking all the air out of my lungs.

"You haven't even seen my bare ass though," I say.

"It's only a matter of time, baby." He winks at me, smirking before he wets his lips with his tongue.

I get out of bed to put my underwear and bra back on. Grabbing a pajama shirt and bottoms out of one of the drawers in my dresser, I slip them on.

"So much for not being allowed in your bed, huh?" he asks, doing his best to hold in a smile.

"You planned this, you sneaky little shit. You purposely chose to sleep in the guest room because you knew this was going to happen."

"Like you said. We were inevitable. It was going to happen sooner or later." he smirks at me.

We're in bed together. My bed.

This is wild.

"Dani, that was fucking mind-blowing. Best sex I've ever had."

"You mean the only sex you've ever had."

"Oh, shut up." He rolls his eyes. "You know what I mean."

"Make me."

He places his hand on my cheek, pulling his body closer to mine.

I love the way he kisses me. The way he praises my body. The way he makes me feel. He makes me feel like I'm the most beautiful woman on the planet.

His lips let go of mine. "Oh, shit."

"What?"

"How could I forget about Lizzie? I'm such a shitty brother. Why out of all the nights we've been together did we decide to have sex the night before she's getting released from the hospital?"

Shit, he's right.

"I guess we just needed to be a little selfish tonight."

"You guess?" He breathes into my neck.

"Noah, there honestly wouldn't have been a proper time for us to do this. Tell each other how we really feel about each other. See each other naked for the first time. Have sex for the first time. I guess that brings me to ask you this question. And I'm honestly terrified to ask it..." I trail off. "Do you regret it?"

"Why the hell would you even ask me that? Of course, I don't regret it. I would do it all over again. And again and again. Tonight was the first night I didn't feel alone. I didn't feel like the world was crashing down around me. Because you're here with me. Dani, you make me the happiest guy in the entire fucking world."

A sigh of relief washes over me.

I never want him to leave.

CHAPTER FORTY-NINE

My eyes slowly open as I stretch my arm out to the space next to me. The empty space next to me.

Noah's gone.

Was all that stuff he told me last night bullshit? Did he just use me so he could lose his virginity? No, that can't be it.

I hope it's not. If it is, he's the same asshole I remember him being all those years ago.

I rub my eyes, turning my head towards the windows, I see sunlight sneaking into the room through the curtains.

Why did Noah leave me? Did I do something wrong that made him upset or angry with me?

When I'm with him, I don't feel alone. It's a strange feeling to have because I'm used to being on my own.

I don't like this feeling of loneliness because it's making me feel unwanted.

Here's the thing about anxiety.

No matter how hard you try to have the mindset of not wanting something to happen, anxiety will always convince you that it will happen. It will screw with your mind so much that you start to believe it.

Blinking my eyes rapidly to take myself out of my thoughts, I find a folded piece of white paper sitting on my bedside table. "I don't remember this being here," I mumble to myself.

I stretch my arm, grabbing it with my hand and opening it.

Good morning, Sunshine.

I didn't want to wake you because you looked so peaceful. I did want to leave you a note and tell you I'll be back soon. I promise.

Noah

Rushing over to check my phone, there's a text from Noah lighting up my screen. I press on the preview, so I can read the entire text.

NOAH

NOAH

I wanted to text you in case you didn't read my note. You're probably freaking out right now because you woke up and noticed I wasn't there lying next to you

ME

i did read your note

you did scare the shit out of me

NOAH

I'm sorry, I didn't mean to scare the shit out of you. Please don't hate me

ME

i don't hate you

NOAH

Okay, good

I can't stop thinking about last night

ME

oh, really?

NOAH

Uh-huh

ME

you're very lucky

NOAH

Why's that?

ME

i was about to take out the flashlight and have it by my side, so i can beat your ass with it when you come home

NOAH

God, you're cute when you're angry

ME

oh, shut up

NOAH

I'll be home soon. Going to run a quick errand.
Try not to miss me too much

ME

don't worry about me, i'll survive

My anger quickly subsides as my lips curve up into a smile.

I'm dreading telling Bella about what happened between Noah and me last night, but I'd much rather she hear it from me than someone else.

Sage isn't going to give a shit. She really won't because she's not a fan of hearing about people's love lives. Let alone their sex lives.

Shit, how am I going to tell Lizzie that I just had sex with her little brother? Oh, that conversation is going to be awkward as hell. I'm going to prolong that one as long as I can.

BELLA

ME

please don't freak out and make a big deal of what i'm about to tell you

BELLA

Okay, but why would I freak out?

ME

pretend i'm sending you eggplant emojis

BELLA

Why the hell would you send me eggplants?

ME

you're impossible

BELLA

It's hard to guess what you're talking about when you send me a bunch of eggplant emojis. Just spit it out!

ME

noah and i had sex last night

BELLA

WHAT? YOU'RE JOKING. NO FUCKING WAY. YOU AND NOAH. SHUT THE FUCK UP. You're joking, right? You're not serious

ME

oh, i'm serious

My phone lights up immediately with a FaceTime call from Bella.

I'm not in the mood for this shit right now, but I accept the call.

Her face pops up on the screen of my phone, skin glowing. Her caramel hair is carefully placed over her shoulders. There's no makeup on her face.

She looks like she's sitting on her bed at the Castillo-Ryder family house. The house she grew up in. The house I spent a lot of time in when I was younger.

She smirks at me. "You had sex with Noah? Please tell me you're shitting me!"

"I'm not in the mood for this."

"You're the one who texted me, remember?"

"I told you to not freak out."

"How can I not freak out about this? Do you know how many years I've been waiting for this to happen? Awe, my best friend is no longer a part of the virgin club."

I roll my eyes. "Oh, shut up."

"Well...how was it?"

"Everything that led up to it was amazing. The sex itself was mind-blowing, considering it was my first time. It did feel weird at first. Before we lost our virginities to each other, we told each other how we really feel about each other. I found out he used smutty romance books for sex research. He called me his sunshine and I called him my moonlight. Bella, I've never felt this way about a guy before."

She looks around, smiling up a storm.

I pull my face into my neck. "Why are you smiling like that? Please stop doing that."

"You're *in love* with him. Head over heels in love. The kind of love you read about in romance novels and watch in rom-coms. You. My. Friend. Are. In. Love."

My face goes blank as my mouth gapes open. Bella Castillo-Ryder just made me speechless.

What are the odds?

I thought I was kidding myself when I kept saying I was in love with Noah, but I'm not kidding myself at all.

I'm in love with Noah Kaplan.

"Hold the phone. You said our virginities. He's a—"

I cut her off before she can finish her train of thought. "He *was*," I tell Bella as a goofy smile appears on my face.

She changes the subject. "Are you going to tell him you love him?"

"I was, but I really thought he was going to tell me first. And he never did. I just don't want to sound desperate."

She put her hand on her forehead. "Dani, does it really matter who tells who first? What matters is that you love him. You. Love. Him. Sometimes you don't need to hear the word 'love' out loud. You just need to feel it."

Sometimes you don't need to hear the word 'love' out loud. You just need to feel it.

"You're right."

"I'm always right."

I laugh, closing my eyes.

The front door slams shut.

I go into full panic mode until I see Noah standing in the doorway. My eyes lift up to fully meet his gaze.

I hear Bella laughing through her breath. "Say hi to Noah for me."

My mouth shifts to one side of my face. "You can say hi to him yourself."

I flip the camera around, so Noah's in the frame. He waves to the camera with a goofy smile slapped across his cute face. "Hi, *Bella*."

"Hi, *Noah*." Her eyebrows raise up and down, making a kissy face at me.

My eyes wander around the room to avoid the awkwardness that's happening right now, but they keep landing back on Noah.

It's hard not to look at him and it's so much harder to look away.

For starters, he's dripping in sweat. The front of his t-shirt is soaking wet, showing off his stupidly muscular torso. He's in gym shorts with a backward baseball cap on his head.

I nod my head, flattening my lips. "If you two are done reacquainting yourselves, I'm going to hang up now."

"Noah, Dani has something to tell you!" Bella shouts out of the speakers from my phone.

"Bye, you idiot." I roll my eyes and shake my head.

"Bye!" She winks at me.

I hang up the FaceTime call, feeling relieved and anxious all at the same time.

"What is it you have to tell me?" He licks his lips in anticipation of my official love confession that's not happening.

Not right now, at least.

"Bella was just being her usual annoying self. It's nothing."

Biting down on my tongue, my eyes roam all over his wet torso until my eyes bounce up to meet his.

He folds his arms in front of his broad chest. "Are you done yet, Sunshine?" He seductively raises his eyebrows a few times in a row.

My lips curve up to form a smirk. "Not just yet."

"Come over here, get your fine ass out of bed, and fucking kiss me already."

Ripping the covers off my body, I run into his arms.

Our lips crash into each other. His face is full of sweat, but I don't care. My hands cup his flushed, sweaty cheeks. He picks me up by my ass, my arms wrapping around his neck.

I pull my lips away from his. "What was the errand you had to run?"

"I told you not to miss me too much." He smiles into my mouth.

I huff. "That's not funny. I was scared when I woke up and

saw you were gone. I thought you used me, so you could lose your virginity."

He backs his head away and has the most irritated look on his face. "If you thought that, then you don't know me at all. I'm sorry I scared you. I just went for a run around the neighborhood. I go for morning runs sometimes because they help clear my mind. Then, I went to pick up something for breakfast."

"Breakfast, you say."

A smug look takes over his face. "Uh-huh."

His palms secure a tighter grip on my ass which makes me roll my eyes and exhale sharply.

"Before we eat, I need to take a shower." He puts me down feet-first on the ground. "Care to join me?"

Oh, hell yes.

Noah bites down on his bottom lip, waiting for me to respond.

I don't even hesitate to answer his question. "Your sweat is all over me now, so I guess I have to take one."

We're walking into the bathroom, taking turns removing each other's clothes.

Before we strip completely naked, he attempts to turn on the shower by twisting and turning the knob.

"You're going to break it. Just turn the handle to the left." My hand is on his, showing him the correct direction the handle should be turned. "That's it. Just like that."

"You're talking dirty to me, already?"

I smile, feeling my cheeks turning red. "Oh, shut up."

Sayonara boxers.

Goodbye to my underwear.

And hello to Noah's bare ass.

He stretches out his arms with his hands laid flat out, gesturing to me to get into the shower. "Ladies first."

I step into the shower and get attacked by the hot water streaming from the shower head.

He's in the shower now, his hot breath seeping deep into my skin.

My backside faces him before I turn around. Licking my lips, I move closer to him. "Your move, Heart Eyes."

He grabs my face, his tongue requesting entry to meet mine.

"You know we both *actually* need to shower," I say in between kisses.

He moves under the shower head. Water drips down his face, running all the way down to his legs.

My eyes bounce back up, so I can meet his gaze.

"Stand in front of me with your back facing towards me."

I turn and move in front of Noah, looking around the shower waiting for what's going to happen next.

There's a clicking sound of a shampoo bottle opening.

"What are you doing?" I ask, confusion fusing into my tone.

"You said we're here to shower. So, that's what I'm doing."

The bottle is squeezing out shampoo.

Noah is lathering it in his hands under the hot water to suds it up. "Lean your head back for me, would you?"

His hands make contact with my head, massaging my hair and scalp.

Oh, but it feels so good. He's being quite gentle with his fingertips.

"That...feels...nice."

"Yeah?"

"Uh-huh," I say through a short breath.

I'm rinsing out the two rounds of shampoo I massaged into Dani's hair with my fingertips as gently as possible.

My fingers smell minty fresh like my breath.

She really thought she was going to be doing all this herself? Washing and conditioning her hair. Washing her body.

Hell, no.

I want to do everything I can to please her and make things easier for her. She seems pretty pleased to me. That's what it sounds like out of her pretty little mouth, at least.

Grabbing the conditioner, I squeeze some into the palm of my hand. I work it up to my fingertips, putting it all over the ends of her hair. It smells like green tea and roses.

After I'm done, I smile against the back of her neck.

This is the part I've been impatiently waiting for since we stepped into the shower.

My hands move her wet hair over to one side of her head, so it doesn't get loaded with peach-scented body wash. Starting at her legs, working my way up to her breasts, and wrapping my hands around both of them. I'm massaging the body wash in, so they get extra clean.

This was a really bad idea. And I mean a horrible idea. My hard-on is massive, so I need to speed this shit up.

Her head leans into the crook of my neck. "Fuck, Noah. Hurry up," she whimpers.

I can't help but think about how I'm being intimate with the one person I've known most of my life. I never imagined that we'd be so vulnerable with each other.

And here I am getting the chance to witness the way the water cascades down her back.

When I'm done washing her body, I slam her against the shower wall. Her lips taste like morning breath since she just got out of bed. And I don't mind one fucking bit.

When I release her lips from mine, she looks at me in a way that obliterates me in a matter of seconds.

I grab the shower head, spraying it all over her.

She's yelping from the hot water running down every crack and crevice of the back of her body. Her shoulders, back, ass, and legs. She turns around and I aim the shower head at her opening.

Her mouth drops open, a grunting noise coming out of it. She runs her fingers through her soaking wet hair. And that's not the only thing that's soaking wet.

"Warn a girl next time, will you?"

She grabs the shower head from me and douses me with it. When she's done, she puts it back where it belongs.

I can't see anything because of all the water dripping into my eyes.

When I gain my sight back, I see Dani standing there. She's shaking her head with a seductive smirk plastered on her lips.

"Guess I deserved that."

She walks over to the windowsill, picking up the container of body wash. Squeezing out some into her hand, she lathers it under the steaming hot water.

"Turn around with your back facing towards me," she commands.

Her hands are massaging the body wash into the skin on my back.

"What the hell are you doing?"

"Making sure you get extra clean," she whispers.

Fuck, yes, please.

Closing my eyes, I feel her fingernails digging into my back before they work their way down to my ass. She squeezes both cheeks with her fingers.

I moan, breathing heavily.

What did I do to deserve this?

She places the container back on the windowsill.

I press my body weight into her backside so she can feel what she's doing to me. Turning her head to face me, she looks up at me and smiles.

I tilt her head and kiss her lips which have captivated me beyond comparison.

"I'd happily drown in you for as long as humanly possible," I confess.

Her mouth parts before she gets a small case of the giggles.

I move her hair out of the way, so I can plant a soft kiss on her neck.

After I turn the hot water off, I kiss her full pink lips and slap her ass as she walks out of the shower. Her body jolts as a soft moan escapes out of her mouth.

She turns around and squints her eyes at me, wrapping herself in a towel before walking over to the mirror that's hanging above the sink.

"I don't think my hair has ever been this clean. Even my hairstylist doesn't clean my hair this thoroughly."

"Well, I'm glad to hear that." I wrap the lower half of my body in a towel.

Walking over to Dani, I snake my arms around her waist and kiss her neck.

She glances at my reflection in the mirror. "Hey, Noah."

"Yeah?"

"Where's your cologne?"

"Why?"

"Go get it," she demands.

Sprinting to the guest bedroom, I swipe my cologne off the bedside table.

Back in the bathroom, Dani's still in front of the mirror until she hears me walking in.

She struts over to me with a giant smile on her face. "Hand it over," she says as she sticks her arm out in my direction, wiggling her fingers.

When I go to give it to her, she reaches out to grab it, but I pull it back into my chest. I do this until a cute, angry expression takes over her face.

Kissing her forehead, I tilt my head down so we're at eye level. "If you want to smell like me, you could've just asked. I'd be happy to rub my scent all over you. I thought that's what I did last night."

She looks up at me, her big brown eyes staring right into my blue eyes. The cutest fucking smile expands across her lips. She can't help but look away from me with rosy cheeks and adorable dimples.

How is this woman real?

"Can I have it now?"

"I'll spray it on the inside of your wrist first. Let's see if you *really* like it before you *bathe* yourself in it."

"Fine." She rolls her eyes and stretches out her arm, flipping it over and making a loose fist, so I can see the inside of her arm.

I run my index finger up and down her forearm. "How are your forearms so smooth?"

"You ask the most random questions."

"How much do you want to bet you love my random questions?"

She ignores me because she's adamant about getting my cologne all over her body, but I need to make sure that's what she really wants.

I press down on the top of the cologne bottle, releasing a steady stream onto the interior part of the skin on Dani's wrist.

She lifts her arm up to her nose, inhaling the fresh scent. "Give it to me, so I can douse myself, Lover Boy."

"Are you sure?"

The corner of her lips twists up. "Oh, I'm sure."

I sway my head from side to side, flattening my lips.

Giving her the bottle, she sprays it several inches away from her body and shimmies through the transparent cloud that's expanding in the air.

My nose picks up hints of mint, orange, and the ocean.

Why does it smell even better on her than it does on me?

She's back at the sink, combing her damp hair.

I walk up behind her, grab the comb out of her hand, and place it down on the countertop. My arms hug her waist, making their way around her stomach.

She looks at our reflections in the mirror, closing her eyes as the biggest smile takes shape on her beautiful face.

My chin is resting on her shoulder.

Her eyes open and meet mine. "Can I help you?"

My lips make contact with the nape of her neck.

She turns around and extends her arms out, running her fingers through my wet hair.

She furrows her eyebrows, sliding her hands out of my hair. "I need to get dressed. And so do you." She jumps up to kiss my forehead, but she kisses my nose instead.

"Fine. Get dressed. When you're done, come into the kitchen. You'll see what I picked up for breakfast while I was out." I plant a kiss on her cheek before walking out of the bathroom.

As I make my way to the doorway, Dani says something to me with her warm and welcoming eyes.

She makes me feel weightless because gravity doesn't exist when I'm with her.

I never want this feeling to go away.

I'm in the kitchen, preparing breakfast. I'm cutting bagels I picked up from Kailani's on a giant cutting board.

There aren't any Jewish delis in Sunset Cove, so we have to settle for Kailani's. They're not bad, though. They just don't have the authentic Jewish touch.

If I ever get a craving for pastrami or latkes, I'd have to drive all the way to Orlando, which is forty-five minutes to an hour away—depending on traffic.

I never have the time or energy to do that.

Scallion cream cheese is sitting on the countertop next to the stove along with a glass bowl, four eggs, butter, and a spatula.

Being with Dani doesn't feel real. It all feels like a dream. One I never want to wake up from.

My mind keeps replaying last night like a recorded videotape.

It's hard not to think about it.

Seeing Dani naked for the first time. The look on her face when she came when I was inside her. How she reacted to me kneeling before her as well as kissing her neck and thighs. The way she moaned when I was sucking and licking her breasts.

"Noah Kaplan!" she shouts, bringing me back to reality.

I re-adjust my shorts, so my bulge is less noticeable.

She's standing in the entryway to the kitchen.

"Why are you yelling?" I ask.

She walks closer to me, pointing to her neck. "Look what you did to me. I look like I was bitten by a goddamn vampire."

I burst out into laughter, covering my mouth with a vertical fist.

She looks like she's going to kill me. "This isn't funny. What am I going to do?"

"Does it really matter? You just *bathed* yourself in my cologne."

"That's different. When Lizzie asks me about it, trust me, you know she will. You know what I'm going to tell her?" She pauses. "*Hey Lizbug. You're probably wondering who gave me this giant ass hickey. It just so happens that it was your baby brother. Surprise! Why is it so dark you may ask? Oh, he sucked me bone dry. You want to know what else he sucked...*" Her voice is high-pitched.

"Don't you dare finish that sentence." I notice she isn't dressed. "Hey, what is this?" I gesture to her body.

She's wearing a white tank top that is hugging her gorgeous curves and underwear that's ruffled on the edges.

"What? I'm wearing clothes." She presents herself with her hands.

"You're wearing a tank top. That's about it."

"Look who's talking. You're not even wearing a shirt." Her hands are placed on her hips.

"I didn't feel like putting on a shirt yet."

Her lips slightly pucker out. "Just admit I win, and you lose."

I stand against the island in the middle of the kitchen.

She boxes me in the same way I did to her a few days ago. Except, she's got this sparkle in her eye that tells me she's not messing around.

"Why? Because you finally admitted defeat last night?"

"I'm not the *only* one who admitted defeat last night, Heart Eyes," she says as she places her fingers above my chest. She works her way down to the hem of my waistband, tugging at it.

"I'm guessing you didn't notice the bagels on the counter over there."

"I did." She wraps her arms around my neck.

"Do I need to put the eggs back in the fridge?"

"What do you think?" Her eyes narrow before her lips quiver into this unbelievably sexy smirk.

"I'll take that as a yes."

I grab the eggs and put them back into the fridge as Dani leans against the island. She still has that smirk written all over her gorgeous face.

It's driving me insane.

My turn to box her in.

She's not nervous, confidence is radiating off her like it's nobody's business.

"What do you want me to do?" I ask.

"You know what I want you to do."

My hands pick her up by her ass, setting her on the island. Her legs are brushing against mine.

I pull her closer to me, leaning into her.

Once my lips meet hers, it's over. Her hands cup my face before her arms make their way around my neck.

This is a hungry kiss. We're swallowing each other. Dani more so than me. Surprising considering I'm usually the one who does more of the swallowing.

I pull my lips away from hers.

"Is everything okay?" Her pupils dilate as an adorable little frown appears on her beautiful face.

"Everything's fine. C'mon, we should eat."

"Are you sure?" She crosses her legs.

I wasn't lying when I told her that I'm okay. My concern at

the moment is making sure she gets fed because I know how she gets when she's hungry.

I nod, kissing her on the forehead. "How do you want your eggs?"

"Scrambled."

After helping Dani off the counter, I take the four eggs I took out several minutes ago again.

She looks at the eggs. "Four eggs? Are you feeding a small army?"

"Yeah, you're the small army I'm feeding."

Her nose scrunches as she playfully nudges in the shoulder.

God, I love when she does that. It's so cute.

Dani's the perfect combination of sexy and cute.

It's actually ridiculous how she's able to act all cute and innocent and swiftly change to sexy and sinful.

I don't know which side I love more. I love all of her sides if I'm being honest.

I'm so in love with her that it hurts.

I didn't tell her that I'm in love with her last night. It never slipped out, but I wish it did.

"Screw you!" she shouts.

"I mean we already have."

She bites her bottom lip before licking her top and bottom lip. "Shut up."

"Why don't you come over here and make me?"

She wraps her legs around my waist, waiting for me to pick her up.

When I do, she gives me a show-stopping kiss.

After she's done, she kisses my cheek and I plant her back down on the tile floor.

I separate the eggs, putting two groups of two together. "Okay, there are two eggs for you and two for me. That's why there are four eggs."

"You know I suck at math."

"We learned this in kindergarten."

"You're so goddamn annoying." She rolls her eyes. "By the way, I want one egg. Two is too many."

"You got it, Boss."

CHAPTER FIFTY-ONE

"Will you go put on a shirt, please?"

"Can't *handle* me shirtless?" He raises his eyebrows three times in a row.

"I can handle you *just* fine. Thank you very much. I really don't want to take you to the hospital for third-degree burns or some shit like that." The hot butter he's melting in a skillet splatters.

He looks up at the ceiling, eyes wandering around and breathing in and out. He brings his head back down, so his eyes line up with mine. "Fine. I'll put on a shirt. Just because you asked."

His eyelashes flutter like butterfly wings as he walks away.

I watch him walk out of the kitchen and smile like an idiot.

Walking over the air fryer oven, I plug it in to turn it on and stick a plain bagel on the rack.

Feeling big strong arms around my waist, I jump. "Why do you do that?" I turn around, punching him in the arm.

"You know, I don't like it when you punch me."

"Don't scare me like that, and maybe I won't punch you." I

move a small, glass bowl closer to him. "Will you just crack the eggs, please?"

He salutes me. "Yes, Chef Dani."

I close my eyes, letting out a deep exhale.

Noah keeps his hands to himself as we prepare breakfast.

Our bagels are almost done toasting, the edges gradually turning golden brown.

He plants a wet kiss on my forehead. "They're perfect."

He grabs the tongs out of my hands and pulls out both halves, placing them on the small plastic plates that are sitting next to the oven.

I place one of my hands on my hip. "Aren't you forgetting something?"

He presses down on his lips after sticking out his tongue, but only a touch. "Want me to kiss you on the lips, Princess?"

"No, dumbass." I roll my eyes, laughing. "Don't forget the eggs are on the stove."

"Oh, shit!" His voice raises as we both run over to the stove.

He's scrambling the eggs with a small, plastic spatula.

They're fine.

You think I wouldn't be freaking out about eggs, but here we are.

As I zone out, I take the time to realize what happens today. We're bringing Lizzie home.

My heart is bursting with so much joy.

I'm hoping everything goes smoothly for Noah's sake. I can't bear to watch him experience another panic attack. Last night freaked me the hell out and this is coming from someone who has anxiety.

It's different when you're the one experiencing anxiety versus watching someone else experience it.

Sometimes it feels like you're walking down a dark alley and have no idea where it leads to. It threatens to take over everything.

I can only imagine what he must feel.

Noah splits the scrambled eggs, putting half on my plate and the other half on his. He spreads the scallion cream cheese he picked up from Kailani's on his bagel before he hands the tub over to me.

"I wonder what my dad would say if he was here right now. You know because we're getting along and the fact that we're actually together." Noah fully snaps me back to reality.

"He'd lose his shit," I blurt out.

"Not exactly."

I stare at him, cocking my head to the side.

"Dad always rooted for us to get together," he says.

I slightly purse my lips until a small grin forms on my face. "I remember when we had our last family game night with my dad before he passed away. Ben pulled me aside when you weren't paying attention. He told me you need someone like me in your life. Someone who challenges you, but secretly cares about you. I thought he was crazy at the time."

"Then, he'd just blurt it out in front of the both of us all the time. You'd get so pissed off when he did that. Your cheeks would turn bright red."

"I have *no* clue what you're talking about." I cross my arms in front of my chest, standing my ground.

"Yeah, you do."

"No, I don't."

"Yeah, you—"

I cut him off. "No, you're not listening to me. Your dad never upset me. You have no idea how much I looked up to him. He became my father figure after Dad passed away. He freaked out when I got into SCU. I loved your dad more than you'll ever understand." I get all choked up. "So, in a way, I've lost two dads. Not just one. You will *never* understand what I'm going through."

God, I can't believe he's not listening to me. He doesn't

understand how close I was with Ben because he never paid close enough attention.

"Please don't follow me." I walk away from the island and head for my bedroom.

"Dani." He nervously chuckles. "I was just..." He tells me as he follows me out of the kitchen.

The tears are falling like leaves do when it's autumn in states that experience seasons.

My feet are heavy.

Inhale. Exhale. Repeat.

Fuck, I had to open my big mouth about Noah's anxiety. And I completely invalidated my own.

This shit sneaks up on you when you least expect it.

Ending up in front of my bedroom, I attempt to make it inside, and fail spectacularly, might I add.

I fall onto the floor and I see Noah rush over to me.

He sits down next to me and stretches his arm out, wrapping it around my shoulder. He moves his hand onto my back, rubbing gentle circular motions.

My lips are dry until my tears moisten them. My hands are violently shaking. My heart is beating so fast it feels like it could explode out of my chest any second now.

I'm panting like an animal who just went out to hunt for its prey.

I hate that he's seeing me like this.

God, I hate myself more for exploding at him the way I did.

He didn't deserve that.

My head nuzzles into the nape of his neck, his arms are fully enclosing around me. He's warm and gooey like freshly baked cookies that just came out of the oven.

When I give into his touch, my anxiety begins to evaporate into the thin air that surrounds us. The way his skin feels against mine is enough for me to catch my breath and make me realize I'm safe. It's all because I'm with *him*.

His silence isn't deafening.

It's comforting.

I shut my eyes, finally gaining the ability to breathe again.

"Can you talk, Sunshine?" he asks me sweetly.

I open my eyes. "I-I think...so. Aren't you going to a-ask me...what happened?"

"You get brain fog too? I thought it was just me. Do you know what just happened?" His tone is kind and patient as he pays close attention to my facial expressions and body language.

This is the face of a guy I've fallen deeply in love with.

"Brain fog? I didn't know it had a name." I struggle to get a chuckle out, but it eventually comes out.

He runs into the living room to grab the tissue box and hands it to me. "Dani, I'm sorry. I had no right to assume I knew everything about your relationship with my dad. I know we've already established this, but I was an asshole back then. *I really was.* I was living in my own perfect world where I didn't give a shit about anyone or anything. Fuck, I wish I was there for you when you lost your dad. I'm so angry at myself. For not being there for you. For not providing you with the comfort you've been providing me."

Lifting my head out of Noah's neck, my eyes meet his. "There has always been a part of me that wished you came to my rescue the day my dad passed away. That you were the one holding me and listening to sad music with me. If you were there to hold my hand and help me with my panic attacks." I take a moment to collect myself. "We can always wonder about these things. We can be angry with ourselves. There are so many things we both wish that we did, but I'm just happy to be here with you. Right now."

He looks down at me and plasters a cute smile on his face. "Let me be here for you now. You're going to be stuck with me for a long ass time, Solomon."

All of this got me thinking about something I've secretly known for a long time.

I smile down at the floor before meeting Noah's gaze. "You know how people say home isn't a place, it's a person?"

"Uh-huh."

"You're my home. You may be my moonlight, but there's no doubt in my mind that sunlight runs through your veins because of the way you radiate this gentle and loving warmth. There's no other way to explain the way I feel when I'm with you, except that it feels like I'm coming home. To you."

My words take him by surprise because he's speechless.

He's staring deep into my eyes, branding me and claiming me as his. My hand interlocks with his, our fingers fitting perfectly together.

Fate and destiny brought Noah back into my life. I can't imagine the people we used to be anymore. There's no price tag when it comes to what we have now.

"I should've told you this last night, but I was a chicken shit. Here it goes. Dani, I..."

Fuck, seriously?

His phone buzzes in his back pocket. The screen lights up with a text as he pulls it out to face him. "It's my mom."

He's typing his heart out while I wait patiently to see what updates Laura has in store for us.

He places his phone onto the floor beside him when he's done. "Mom says hi."

"What did she say?"

"Dr. Miller called her to tell her we can take Lizzie home in a few hours. Talked about how she's going to have intense physical therapy. A PT will be coming to the house until Liz is able to go to the hospital for PT herself. That's about it."

"That's good news, isn't it?"

"Yeah. It's great news. I mean if you look at it that way."

"PT will help her regain her strength and get back to her old self. It's awesome news."

"You're right."

His eyes are distracting the hell out of me, so I resort to changing the subject and turning on the Danielle Solomon branded charm. "Hey, do you know what my favorite color is?"

He chuckles, his facial expression shows he's surprised by the sudden subject change. "What's your favorite color?"

"Whatever color your eyes are. Ocean blue. Teal. Turquoise. I don't know."

He wets his lips with his tongue, letting out this deep breath that almost takes my breath away. "You're so fucking cute, you know that?"

My cheeks are warm again. What a surprise.

Leaning my elbows on my knees, I cover my flushed cheeks with my hands.

I don't know why I even do this anymore. He knows he can make me blush just by looking at me. It's a normal reaction I give when someone compliments me.

He puts his hands on mine, delicately pulling them away from my face and holding onto them for dear life.

My skin is tingling like pins and needles from his touch.

He's sitting in front of me now, scooting me closer to him. "You never have to hide from me."

"Sorry, it's a reflex."

"I'm going to stop your reflexes every chance I get."

"Sure you are," I say.

"Try me, I dare you."

"Please tell me you're joking. We're not kids anymore, Kaplan."

"The fire in your eyes says something entirely different, Solomon."

"You *really* are an idiot."

"And I'm a proud member of The Idiot Club along with

Xander. Grayson is the leader because he's the biggest dumbass out of the three of us."

Looking to the side, I close my eyes and get a very bad case of the giggles.

I love the way this man makes me laugh. He's the king of distractions in all of its forms. Curse or a blessing in disguise?

I'd have to say both.

CHAPTER FIFTY-TWO

She's laughing.

It's amazing to me how she can just sit there, laugh, and look so fucking beautiful. Her entire face glows like light does when it's surrounded by darkness.

She's the most beautiful woman I've ever laid my eyes on.

Dani keeps telling me how she worries about me all the time but what about the other way around? I worry about her too. All. The. Time. I knew something like this was going to happen. It was bound to happen. That's what happens when you have anxiety. It's always bound to explode out of you when you least expect it.

"You know what my favorite color is?"

Her lips struggle to form a smile. "What's your favorite color?"

I lean closer to her.

Her freckles are prominent. Long, thick black eyelashes flutter upwards. Her pupils exist when I get this up close and personal. It's hard to see them from a normal distance because her eyes are the color of dark chocolate, but without the bitterness.

"Dark brown," I say with no hesitation.

"Hmm, really?" She smiles into my mouth.

"Do you know how gorgeous you are?"

"Enough with the compliments already."

"It's never enough. You're going to be showered with a shit ton of compliments, whether you like it or not. Deal with it."

Her lips graze mine.

It doesn't even bother me that her breath smells like scallions and scrambled eggs because mine probably smells exactly the same way.

I cup her face and kiss her.

When I kiss Danielle Solomon, my heart rate increases tenfold. Adrenaline kicks into high gear. And the way my kisses make her breathless only makes me want to kiss her even more.

She makes me breathless.

Oxygen enters my bloodstream as I breathe out carbon dioxide.

When her tongue dances against mine, I groan hard and deep. "Don't. Do. That."

There's a wicked look in her eye, telling me she's not going to listen to me. She's going to continue to torture me with her soft, pink lips and her dancing tongue.

Fine with me, but she's going to regret it, especially after I'm done with her.

I get up off the floor with her hand in mine, taking her with me.

"Where the hell are you taking me?" She whines.

Walking into her bedroom, I take her over to the white plush chair in between her bedside table and dresser.

Her lips pucker out enough that a cute little smile lights up her face. She sits on my lap, her body aligning horizontally and tucking loose tendrils of hair behind her ears. "We can't be one of those couples who have sex all the time."

"Wait, since when are we a couple?" I ask.

I've been wanting to ask her to be my girlfriend, but I've been wanting to wait because this is all happening so damn fast.

She bites her top lip while her eyes search around the room in order to avoid eye contact with me. "It just slipped out. I didn't mean anything by it. Really. I—"

I cut her off, even though I adore it when she rambles. "Dani."

"What?" Her tone is high-pitched.

"Look at me, Sunshine."

She turns towards me, looking up at me with those big brown eyes. Embarrassment is written all over her face, but she's not blushing. "What are we if we're not a couple?" she asks, biting her lip.

"It's hard to be a couple when I haven't asked you if you want to be my girlfriend yet." I wait to see if she responds, but she doesn't. She's waiting for me to ask her the question, so I ask it. "Do you *want* to be my girlfriend?" I grin.

After last night, I assumed we're dating, but I've learned to not make assumptions when it comes to Danielle Solomon.

"Eh," she says.

"What the hell do you mean by eh?"

She laughs like an evil villain does in a cartoon movie. "Ah, it's so easy to get a reaction out of you."

"You want to know what else is easy?"

"What *else* is easy?"

"The fact that I can make you blush with one glance and laugh by saying the dumbest shit to you. But, my favorite is how fast I can make you come."

I'm running my fingers along her arm which is prickling me with the goosebumps forming on her skin.

She's breathing heavily.

Oh fuck, she's moaning deep from the base of her throat.

Just kill me now.

I've never heard a woman moan like that in my entire life. Hearing Dani moan like that is making me lose my goddamn mind.

My hard-on is massive. The more she lets those insane moans escape her hypnotizing mouth, the bigger it gets.

"Shall we test my theory?" I raise my eyebrows up and down over and over to get my point across.

"I have a feeling I can't say no since I can feel you under my ass."

"Hard not to do considering all you're wearing is underwear."

"Don't start with me," she says.

"I'm not starting anything."

"Will you kiss me before I change my mind?" Irritation trickles throughout her tone.

"You can always change your mind with me."

"Stop being sweet and just fuck me, Noah."

The mouth on this woman.

"You know I want to, but..." I trail off.

"Oh, trust me. I know you want to."

She slips her freezing cold hand up my shirt. Her fingers trace the outlines of my abs.

"Your hand feels like you just stuck it inside a freezer." I take her hand and place it in between both of mine, rubbing my hands to help warm it up.

"How is it you can switch from being incredibly sweet and cute to irresistibly charming and sexy in a matter of seconds?"

"You think I'm sexy?" I smirk.

"That's what you picked up from all that?"

"Dani, you're so unbelievably sexy it blows my fucking mind." I trace the edge of her jawline with my thumb making my way down to her neck.

My lips meet the smooth texture of her neck.

Before I get to work, she stops me. "No more hickies!"

"I need to even it out. It'll look weird as hell if you have a hickey on one side of your neck and not on the other."

She rolls her eyes, grinning so big it makes my heart grow ten sizes. "You're so full of shit, making dumb excuses when I know you're just going to continue doing it anyway. You don't need to mark me up to stake your claim on me, Noah. I'm already yours."

"Not if you don't want me to and not if you're uncomfortable. By the way, I'm not staking my claim on you. Wait...hold on. You're already mine?"

"Of course, I'm already yours. I've *always* been yours." Her hand works its way up to my chest. "Have at it, Heart Eyes. You know what—"

I interrupt her. "You talk too much."

I shut her up by crashing into her mouth with mine.

How the hell am I going to survive without being able to touch her around everybody today? This is going to drive me insane. Just her being in close proximity to me makes my skin buzz.

I walk over to the bed, sitting on it. I move so my back is against the pillows.

She sits there, staring at me.

"Come here," I command.

She struts over to me, jumping onto the bed and landing right on top of me.

I grunt. "I said come here. Not jump on me and crush the shit out of me."

"My bad." She laughs.

She's sitting on my lap, facing my direction. "Lift your arms for me, Heart Eyes."

She takes off my shirt and throws it onto the bedside table.

She goes to take off her tank top, but I stop her. "Allow me."

"I'm totally capable of taking off my own shirt."

"I know, but you're going to have to get used to the fact that there are people who want to take care of you. Let me take care of you."

I free her hair out of that high ponytail of hers. It all falls down, framing her face like a painting that belongs in The Louvre.

"Why did you just do that?"

"You're beautiful when your hair is up, but you're even more stunning when your hair is down."

She smiles, her cheeks getting redder with each fleeting moment.

"Hey, um...There are these scenes in *Flawless* that I haven't been able to get out of my head since I read them."

Her lips twitch before she wets them with her tongue. "Ah, the whipped cream scenes."

"How the hell did you know that's what I was talking about so damn fast?"

"I haven't been able to get those scenes out of my head either."

I stare at her in a way that causes her look away from me.

When she meets my gaze again, she kisses the tip of my nose. "Unfortunately, we don't have whipped cream."

"Lucky for you, I have an even better idea of what we can use to replace the whipped cream."

CHAPTER FIFTY-THREE

noah

I get off the bed, sticking my index finger up in her direction. "Give me a minute."

Sprinting out of the bedroom, I open the fridge and grab a peach out of the bottom drawer.

I make my way back into the bedroom, leaning against the doorframe.

Dani's sitting there with her head down in her bra and underwear. She's staring at the covers on the bed.

God, I can't wait to get her fully naked.

"Hey, Sweet Peach."

She lifts an eyebrow. "Is that what I think it is?"

"You bet your ass it is."

"What the hell are you doing with a peach?" She shakes her head, pursing her lips.

"I'm glad you asked." I throw the peach up in the air and catch it in my hand. Walking over to her, I sit down on the bed in front of her. "Because you're about to find out."

"Please tell me you washed it." A look of disgust writes itself all over her face as she sits on my lap and wraps one arm around my neck to support herself.

"Of course I washed it." I roll my eyes and laugh before my face becomes emotionless. "Now, I want you to listen to every word that comes out of my mouth. And I mean really listen because we both know how much you love listening to me."

"Okay." She nods, covering her mouth to hide the giggling noises coming out of it.

Enclosing an arm around her waist, I tug her closer into my body. "You're going to do everything I tell you to do. Do you understand?"

"Yes, sir." She salutes me.

"Good girl," I say as I hand her the peach.

She takes her time to feel the peach with her hand. "What do you want me to do with it?"

"Put it up to your lips as slowly as you possibly can."

She brings the peach up to her lips, barely grazing it.

"Take a bite of it," I say.

"Like a normal bite or...?"

I exhale. "Pretend it's my ass."

She seductively raises her eyebrows, smirking at me. "It would be my pleasure."

She swirls her tongue on the skin, taking a small bite of the flesh.

I'm watching every move she makes and her eyes are on me the entire time. My chest is heaving intensely as I lick my top lip.

Savoring and swallowing the flesh she consumed, she stares at me. "How was that?"

"Perfect," I say. "Take a bigger bite out of it now. As much as you can fit into that pretty little mouth of yours."

"My pretty little mouth? I'll have you know my mouth isn't little. You should know that, shouldn't you?" Her tone is loaded with sarcasm.

"Will you stop being a brat and do what I told you to do? If you're not going to listen to me, I'm going to have to punish you."

"You're going to have to punish me? I'd pay to see that."

"Dani, will you just eat the fucking peach?"

"Alright, calm down." Her brown eyes darken as she bites a bigger piece of the flesh. It takes her a bit longer to swallow it.

A dribble of juice drips down her neck. My lips make contact with the juice, my tongue traveling its way up to where the dribble begins.

Once I get all the juice licked off her neck, my sticky lips make a home on hers. "Give me the peach."

She hands over the round piece of fruit to me.

I bite off some of the flesh where Dani's bite marks are.

There's a line of peach juice going down my cheek.

"Swipe your thumb across my cheek," I demand.

Running her thumb over the skin on my cheek, she holds her thumb up in the air.

By the look in her eyes, I can tell she knows what I'm going to do.

I bring her thumb up to my lips, slowly sliding it into my mouth and sucking on it.

She whips her head away from me.

I lean forward to see what she's doing.

She's rolling her eyes and breathing out deep. "What is it about you and sucking on my thumb, huh?"

There are other places I'd love to suck.

I release her thumb from my mouth, licking away the residual liquid remaining on my lips with my tongue.

"What do you want me to do now, Heart Eyes?" she asks, her eyes making every bone in my body ignite.

I smirk. "Lie on your stomach with your ass sticking up in the air."

She does what I tell her to do. "Happy?"

"Oh, yeah," I say with enthusiasm.

Ripping off her underwear, I'm breathing heavily.

"You're lucky those didn't cost a lot of money because I'd be kicking your ass right now if they did," she says.

"You can kick my ass anytime."

I move her hair out of the way, squeezing some liquid from the peach with my hand onto her back. It's trailing its way down to her ass cheeks.

I make sure it doesn't end up anywhere it's not supposed to.

She huffs. "What the hell are you doing?"

"You'll see." I pepper rough kisses down her spine, my tongue darting out and soaking up the dribble I doused her in. Traveling my way to her ass, my tongue makes contact with it.

"Noah," she moans under her breath.

"Do you want me to stop?"

She moans, her hands gripping the comforter. "Hell no."

After I finish biting and licking her ass cheeks, I kiss her on the back of her neck. "I'm going to wash my hands. Don't move."

"What if I need to—"

I cut her off. "Don't. Move."

Washing my hands in Dani's bathroom, I look at my reflection in the mirror. I close my eyes and exhale, my chest rapidly rising and lowering itself.

Breathe, man.

Storming out of the bathroom, I slam the door behind me.

She's still lying on her stomach and her bare ass is sticking up in the air. She jumps when she realizes I'm standing in front of her as her eyes scan me from head to toe.

"As much I love it when you fuck me with your eyes, I'd love to do the real thing."

"Oh, I bet you'd love that, wouldn't you?" A wicked smirk appears across her lips as her dark brown eyes link with mine.

I nod, swallowing deep. "Uh-huh."

"You want me?" she asks, spreading her legs open one at a time. "Come and get me."

Holy. Fucking. Shit.

I can see everything and I mean everything.

My heart is beating so fast. I swallow deeply and take a brief moment to collect myself, taking a deep breath and letting it out.

Running like my life depends on it, I land on the bed sprawled out on my back before I lift myself up and flip her over, so she's lying flat on her back.

I move her head so it's resting on a pillow.

"Can I take care of you?" I ask, climbing on top of her.

She narrows her eyes. "How are you going to do that?"

"Let me surprise you."

"I don't like surprises."

"You're going to love this one." Confidence takes over my tone.

"Wanna bet?"

I plant a rough kiss on her lips to shut her up, licking my way down to the skin above her waistline.

Her breath hitches as a gentle moan leaves her mouth, hands gripping the sheets. "Why did you stop?"

I stare at Dani's bra, tugging on the fabric in between her cleavage. "This needs to come off."

"Then, take it off."

"Are you sure?"

"You're the one who said it needs to come off. Noah, you may as well get the hell off me, so I can do it myself."

"Sit up," I say, my voice low and deep.

A seductive grin tugs at the corners of her lips as she raises one of her eyebrows. "I knew you needed a little push."

"God, you are a brat." Undoing the clasp of her bra, I throw it onto her bedside table.

She lies back down, but I take my time to run my index finger along the skin of her body.

She's a goddamn work of art.

The kind you have to study for as long as possible to take in all her beauty, but you're unable to form any words about how magnificent she is.

She has curves in all the right places and buttery smooth skin. With her perfect soft and round breasts, I can't help myself from wanting to bury my face in between them.

This woman is going to be the death of me, and I'll thank her for it.

"What are you going to do to me, Lover Boy?"

"What do *you* want me to do to you?"

She looks up at the ceiling for a few moments before locking eyes with me. "I want you to fuck me with your fingers," she blurts out.

Are you fucking kidding me right now?

Blinking my eyes in rapid motion, I attempt to process what Dani asked of me as broken laughter escapes out of my mouth.

A worried expression writes itself all over her face. "Shit, you're not malfunctioning are you?"

"Are you sure about this?"

She nods. "I'm sure."

"If you're uncomfortable or in pain, tell me and I'll stop. Okay?"

"Okay."

I slide down to the lower half of her body with my eyes on her the entire time.

Spreading her legs open wider, I kiss the inner part of her ankles. Making my way up to the inner part of her thighs, I run my fingers through her and get absolutely drenched.

I think I'm going to pass the fuck out.

Her chest is imperfectly heaving, her eyes closing, and her back arching.

Swiping some of her fluid onto my fingers, I raise them up in her direction.

"Seriously, how the fuck are you so wet?"

"Let's call it the Noah Kaplan effect," she says as she winks at me.

I glide my body back down to where she's dripping for me. Sweeping two fingers gently against her clit, her back arches to the point where her stomach collides with mine.

Soft moans abandon her sweet mouth.

"Are you okay?"

"I'm fine. Keep going," she says with impatience growing in her voice.

"Are you sure?"

Her nostrils flare. "If you don't fuck me with your fingers, I'll fuck myself with my vibrator instead."

Fuck, the mouth on this woman blows my mind. Yeah, there's no way in hell she's pleasuring herself without me involved.

I shake my head, huffing. "Has anybody ever told you you're ridiculously impatient?"

"Has anybody ever told you you're irritating as shit?"

"Yeah, you have. Like a million times."

Slowly rubbing her clit, Dani's moans become more frequent and loud. She's pulsating and tightening around me.

Oh, she feels so fucking good.

"You like that, don't you?"

"Noah," she whimpers.

"Dani," I say through a soft breath.

"Fuck, I'm so close."

"You look so fucking pretty like this, soaking wet for me and taking my fingers so damn well," I coo.

My words send her over the edge. Her tightness around me fades away as her muscles contract. She grips onto me, digging her nails into my back. "N-Noah."

"That's my girl," I say as I gradually remove my fingers from her center.

Meeting her dreamy brown eyes, I bring my index finger to my mouth.

The second her taste settles on my tongue I instantly get harder, which I didn't think was possible. It's even sweeter than kissing her soft, pink lips. I can't stop the moan that sneaks out of my throat.

Her mouth gapes open like she can't believe what I just did.

Sticking my middle finger up at her, she gives me a dirty look. "Are you flipping me off?"

"Suck," I say through a measly breath.

She shakes her head. "What?"

"Suck on my finger. I want you to see how sweet and delicious you taste."

"Noah," she whines.

"Suck. On. My. Finger," I command.

She nods as a lump travels down her throat.

I shove my middle finger into her mouth as her tongue dances around it with her eyes on me the entire time.

Jesus Christ.

She swallows, clearing her throat and licks her lips. Her gaze meets mine and I feel like I'm sinking into the ground.

Running my thumb across her lips, I kiss her hard and deep. I roll off her, threading my fingers into hers.

We both stare at the ceiling for a few moments.

She turns to me and smiles. "I'm out of breath."

"You and me both."

She gets off the bed, and walks over to her dresser. "Now if you'll excuse me, I need to go put on a new pair of underwear because you destroyed these," she says as she holds them up to me.

I'm doing my best to ignore how hard I am from fingering her because seeing her fall apart was more than enough for me.

I sit closer to the front of the bed.

She opens the top drawer of her dresser, grabbing a pair of black underwear.

Before she can slide them up her legs, I stop her. "I'm going to need you to come closer."

She crosses her arms. "Are you kidding me?"

"Come closer," I demand.

She backs up, standing right in front of me, but I don't do anything right away.

I can sense she's starting to get annoyed because she's huffing and her hands are resting on her hips. "Am I just going to stand here for the next hour? Or are you actual—" she yelps after I spank her hard on her ass.

"Sorry, I needed to get that out of my system."

She rolls her eyes at me, turning back around and reaching for her underwear. Scooting off the bed, I place my hand on hers to stop her from putting them on.

"Hey, I'm totally capable of putting on my own underwear." She narrows her eyes at me.

"Dani, your legs are wobbling like crazy. Let me help you."

"Fine." She licks her lips, placing her hands on my shoulders for support. She steps into her underwear and I bend down onto my knees, sliding them up her legs.

While I'm at it, I grab her bra and hand it to her. She puts it on and I hook it, so it stays in place.

"I love that you can dress and undress me." She turns her body, pecking a kiss on my cheek.

I smile, kissing her forehead. "I love dressing and undressing you too." I take a moment to study her. "Did you choose to wear these on purpose to torture me?" I ask, tugging on the fabric of her underwear.

She walks her fingers up to my chest. "My mission in life is to torture the hell out of you. If I'm being honest, I've completed my mission multiple times at this point."

My hands wrap around her waist and she leans her head back underneath mine, humming.

Switching her hair to one side of her head, I place a gentle kiss on her neck.

She grabs a tank top and a pair of shorts which are sitting inside her suitcase in the corner.

I lie back down on the bed, waiting for her to lie next to me, but she's not walking towards me.

"Where the hell do you think you're going?" I ask, sitting on the edge of the bed.

She whips her body around, squinting her eyes. "I'm going to the bathroom." Striding over to me, she squishes my face with her index finger and thumb and kisses me. "Don't miss me too much."

"I'll try not to, but it's not going to be easy," I say before my hand comes in contact with her ass.

Her body shakes. "Stop smacking my ass!"

"Hard not to when your ass looks like that."

"You're crazy."

I smile. "Crazy about you."

She shakes her head, winking at me as she walks into the bathroom and closes the door behind her.

Did all this shit actually happen or was it all a dream?

Dani's lying next to me in bed and looking more beautiful than ever.

"So, did you enjoy the peach?"

"Uh-huh."

"I have to say it wasn't as sweet as I thought it would be." I bite down hard on my bottom lip. "You taste much sweeter."

"Oh yeah?"

I nod, cupping her face. Her lips collide with mine as her fingers gently run through my hair. Her leg wraps around my thigh.

After she pulls away from my lips, I study every inch of this woman's beautiful face.

She smiles. "Why are you staring at me like that?"

"I'm not staring. I'm just admiring the view."

She shakes her head, breaking out into this adorable laugh which allows me to see her teeth.

Her cheeks turn a bright shade of red.

She rolls her eyes, turning away from me. "Yeah, whatever you say."

I run my fingers through the loose tendrils draping perfectly against her back. "You know I had a feeling your hair would be soft, but I didn't know how soft it would actually be."

This is when an idea hits me like a punch in the face.

"Can you sit up with your back facing me?" I ask, sitting upright with my legs spread out.

"Why?"

My lips form into a puppy dog-like frown. "Please," I beg.

"Fine." She rolls her eyes with her mouth partially open.

Scooting closer to her, I push her hair out of the way, so my lips can make contact with her neck.

Separating her hair into three even sections, I start crossing them into each other.

"Noah Kaplan, are you doing what I *think* you're doing?"

"Depends. What do you think I'm doing?"

"You're so annoying."

"And yet, you're still here."

"There's nowhere else I'd rather be than with you, Moonlight." Her tone is overflowing with sincerity.

My heart stops for a few seconds.

I lean my head against her back, smiling down at the top of the bed. "There's nowhere else I'd rather be with than with you, Sunshine."

CHAPTER FIFTY-FOUR

Noah's gently combing his fingers through my hair. Just when I thought I couldn't be more in love with him, he goes and does shit like braiding my hair.

I'm officially done for. How is this real life? I'm seriously living in a romance novel.

"Have you ever braided a woman's hair before?"

"Nope, you're the first."

"I guess that makes me lucky, huh?"

He presses his lips up against my ear, whispering into it. His breath melds into my skin. "No. I'm the lucky one."

He makes me breathless.

Noah Kaplan makes me lose my breath every single time he opens his mouth. I never know what to expect with him.

When he finishes the braid, he wraps a hair-tie around the end to close it off. His hands have a solid and delicate grip around my newly braided hair as I turn my head over my shoulder.

"I never answered your question earlier."

"Remind me what my question was again." He smirks.

"You asked me to be your girlfriend."

"You realize you just said a statement."

"Stop picking on my spelling and grammar imperfections. I never pick on yours."

"That would be because I don't have any."

I elbow him in the stomach.

"Hey!" He clears his throat. "You want to know how you answered my question? You said eh."

"For a smart guy, you can be pretty dumb sometimes." I smile. "Of course, I'll be your girlfriend." I giggle, sticking my tongue partially out.

He laughs and scrunches his nose, grabbing my face and crash-landing his lips on mine. His hand softly tugs at the braid he made and his thumb runs along the edge of my jawline, tilting my head up.

When our lips release one another, I meet his gaze.

My body ignites into a plethora of flames which are about to implode and explode. Just from the way he's staring into my eyes.

Blue represents confidence and sensitivity.

That's how I feel when I look into Noah's eyes. Confident because I know he'll always be there for me no matter what. He's sensitive and perceptive when it comes to my emotional needs.

Sometimes we have to do things that scare us because they have the possibility of turning into something incredible.

Take flowers for example.

They start out as nothing but a seed in the ground.

When they bloom, beautiful petals and green leaves overwhelm three of the five senses: sight, touch, and smell.

Love is a flower. It needs time to grow and evolve.

It may have taken me years to finally admit to myself how I feel about Noah, but I wouldn't go back and do anything differently. This is how it was supposed to happen.

"Why are *you* staring at me like that?" Noah snaps me out of my trance.

He believes he's the lucky one and he's not wrong about that. But, I'm lucky too. It's unfortunate this all happened during tragic circumstances.

Ben always knows how to work his magic, even if he's not physically here anymore.

If I'm able to distract Noah from his pain, it's worth it. *He's worth it.*

"A wise person once told me what I'm doing right now isn't staring. It's admiring the view in front of them."

He places his index finger and thumb underneath his chin, looking like the human version of the thinking emoji. "I wonder who this incredibly smart and handsome guy is."

I giggle like a bunch of middle school girls do when they're gossiping about cute boys.

He pulls me into his chest, wrapping his arms around my waist and kissing the top of my head. "Can we stay like this forever?"

My head is resting in the crook of his neck. "Hate to break it to you buddy, but we need to leave soon. Have you heard from your mom yet?"

"Not yet. The ringer on my phone is on, so you would've heard if she texted or called me."

"Right." His head leans down, lips inches away from meeting mine and my eyes search around the room. "Are you going to kiss me?"

"I'm thinking about it."

"Stop thinking about it and just do it."

"You know, you'd be a great salesperson for Nike."

"Oh my God, you're such a dumbass," I say, grabbing his shirt and pulling him into me.

A question pops into my head, so I break our kiss. "Can I ask you something?"

"Right now?"

"Yes, because if I don't ask it now, I'll forget."

"Shoot," he says.

"Why didn't you tell me about how you felt about me when we were in high school?"

"I debated it. More times than I could count. I knew you'd accuse me of trying to distract you from studying, so I could get a better grade than you. Or maybe I'm trying to mess with you. There was one thing I almost did because I had a lot of opportunities to do it."

"Oh, what's that?"

"Grab you by the hand, take you into an empty classroom, push you up against a wall, and kiss the shit out of you."

My body shifts, so I'm sitting in front of him, crisscrossing my legs.

God, I can't even imagine how teenage Dani would've reacted to that. Actually, I can. She would've tried to push teenage Noah away, denying her feelings. But, she'd give in. Just like Adult Dani has, but it wouldn't be such an easy feat.

Why am I speechless?

Noah licks his lips, making them glisten. "Are you okay over there?"

"Uh-huh. So...why didn't you do that?"

"Why didn't I do what?"

"The whole kissing the shit out of me thing."

"It wasn't just because of how I thought you'd react. It was also me. If there was a slight possibility of us starting something, I couldn't risk losing you. So, I decided not to act on my feelings then. I'm really glad I didn't."

"You don't regret waiting for me?" A cute frown grows on my face.

He shakes his head, pressing his lips together. "Never. I will always wait for you, Danielle Solomon. No matter how long it would take for us to make our way back to each other. *We're inevitable. You and me.* Sound familiar?"

A small chuckle escapes my lips as I wave around my middle finger in front of his face.

He grabs my hand, yanking me on top of him.

Taken by surprise, I let out a gasp. My eyes close and a big smile grows on my face.

"It's my turn to ask you a question now."

"This isn't a game, Noah."

"None of this is a game to me, Princess." He stares me down, his blue eyes hypnotizing the crap out of me. "Tell me the truth. Did you really hate me?"

"You were irritating, annoying, and full of yourself. But, no, I didn't hate your guts if that's what you're asking me. You just drove me crazy. Guess that explains why we stopped talking to each other."

"No, that explains why you stopped talking to me." His lips quiver, pupils dilating.

"Yeah...I just couldn't take it anymore. The constant fighting and competing with you got old. That's not the real reason why I stopped talking to you though..." I drift off, hoping that he doesn't want to know the truth.

His eyes tell me something entirely different. "Tell me why you stopped talking to me." He threads his fingers into mine, anticipating my response. "Please."

"We kind of talked about this already, but I can talk about it in more depth." I shrug my shoulders.

Noah nods, gesturing to me to continue anyway.

"Okay, it was our sophomore year of high school. It was the one-year anniversary of my dad's passing. And I know your mom kept you out of the loop, but you're whip-smart. I don't understand how you didn't figure any of it out. You know, what happened to him and how I missed most of my freshman year." I take a quick minute to catch my breath. "Anyways, I debated on going to school that day because I knew I wouldn't be able to focus on anything, but my mom insisted I go. So, I did. I distinctly remember you came up to me in the hallway by my locker. You said something to the effect of my dad being in a much better place because he didn't have to suffer by being in my presence every day anymore."

He closes his eyes, shaking his head. "Fuck...I'm so sorry. Do you know how much I pressed my mom to tell me what happened to your dad? I had to resort to asking Bella because she was the only person who was willing to tell me what the hell was going on. I was fourteen. I wasn't a child. I hated that my mom treated me like I was. Like I wouldn't have been able to *handle* it." He pauses, looking around the room to collect the rest of his thoughts. "That's why I sent you the box because I had to do something to make up for being a jackass to you, even if you didn't know it was me at the time. God, I wish I could go back in time and go to your dad's funeral. Be there for you like how you've been there for me. After everything I did to you, you came to my rescue all these years later. I don't fucking deserve you."

His eyes have a glassy sheen to them.

I cup his face, caressing the top of his cheekbone with my thumb.

He shifts his head away from my direct view.

"Oh, Noah. Now I know it was you who sent that box, it changes everything. Everything *has* changed." I breathe out. "I was so consumed by grief back then. I couldn't think straight for a while until I stopped talking to you. Junior year was when everything got better and I was able to focus on things again. I got back on track with my romance novel and discovered my love for freelance writing. I felt like myself again. I felt alive."

Did someone just inject me with truth serum?

"In the back of my mind, I knew the universe would bring us back together again. It believes we belong together. And I agree. Don't you?" I move his face back into view, but he's not making eye contact with me.

Tears are cascading down his face. My heart feels like it's made out of glass, shattering into a million tiny pieces, when I see him cry.

"Hey, Moonlight. I'm going to need you to look at me."

He doesn't budge, so I resort to something that I know that he won't resist. I get off his lap, turning him with my hands, so he's sitting on the edge of the bed.

Kneeling down on the floor in front of him, I interlock my hands and place them in front of my face. "I'm on my knees, begging for you to look at me."

If there's one thing I know about most men, they love it when a woman begs. I have to say women love it even more when men beg.

More than you could *ever* imagine.

CHAPTER FIFTY-FIVE

"You know I can't resist when a beautiful woman begs."

Dani reaches out her hands, wiping away any wetness lingering on my face from my tears.

My lips taste salty and they're wet.

Her eyes are firmly planted on mine.

Why the hell would I ever say her dad is probably happier because he doesn't have to deal with his daughter anymore? What the hell was wrong with me back then?

"Has anybody ever told you you're absolutely incredible?"

She licks her top lip with the tip of her tongue, grinning ear to ear. She doesn't tell me to shut up or stop with the compliments.

I'm surprised by what comes out of that beautiful mouth of hers next.

"What else am I?"

Grabbing her by the hand, I drag her back on top of me.

She wraps her arms around my neck, straddling my waist.

"You're entering *dangerous* territory," I say.

"Tell *me* what else I am to you," she demands through a whisper into my ear.

Irregular breathing patterns take over me as I bite down on the insides of my cheeks.

My hands squeeze her waist. A faint moan leaves her mouth, sending me over the edge.

I run circular motions on her shoulder with the pad of my thumb followed by my lips making contact with it. Then, my lips move to her neck, clavicle, and chest. Every fucking inch of exposed skin.

Her skin is my drug.

I can't get enough of it.

"You're so fucking beautiful, Dani."

She gulps so hard that I see a lump go down her throat. "N-Noah," she stutters my name as she arches her back.

My hands make their way into her shorts, running along the outline of her underwear. "Yeah?"

She moans again, but it's not as faint this time. "Don't you dare stop."

"Wouldn't dream of it."

I'm so hard right now I couldn't stop even if I wanted to.

My phone dings, lighting up with a text message from my sister.

I thought Mom would be the one to tell us that she was ready to be taken home.

Fuck, seriously? Why does my family have a radar when I'm about to have sex or right when I'm about to tell this gorgeous woman I'm in love with her?

LIZZIE

LIZZIE

Please come and rescue me. Mom is driving
me fucking crazy

ME

Has she officially driven you to insanity?

LIZZIE

I'm getting very fucking close. Dr. Miller
cleared me, so I can go home. Seriously, come
and take me home. Now!

ME

Calm the hell down. You're so fucking
dramatic!

LIZZIE

Oh, I hate to do this over text, but Mom made
funeral arrangements for Dad. She wanted to
tell you, but she didn't know how so I told her I
would tell you. It's in two weeks. I know she
didn't want to have it until I woke up from my
prolonged slumber. Well, I'm awake now…

ME

I don't even know what to say to that

LIZZIE

You don't have to say anything. I'm still trying
to absorb it. All of this

ME

Anyways, we're on our way to rescue you
Rapunzel

LIZZIE

You're the best brother a sister could ever
ask for

ME

Oh, cut the crap. We're coming. I'll text you
when we get there. Okay?

LIZZIE

THANK YOU. LOVE YOU BRO!

My brain is malfunctioning. I'm staring at the wall lined
with Dani's Polaroid posters, trying to digest the information
my sister fed me.

How does Lizzie end off our conversation with a friendly 'love you bro' after she just told me about how Mom made funeral arrangements for Dad? Why did she tell me over text and not wait to tell me in person? Why did Mom have her tell me about this?

I knew this was going to happen. How could it not? Mom wants to give Dad a proper send-off and I respect that.

I just wish it didn't have to happen at all.

"Was that your mom?" Dani asks.

"Lizzie, actually. We need to go before she murders my mom with her IV machine. And she told me Mom made funeral arrangements for Dad."

"She's annoying her *that* much?"

I nod.

"Noah, are you okay?"

"I don't think I've been okay for the past month. This is fucking icing on top of the cake I don't want to eat." I inhale and exhale. "Go get dressed. I mean it this time."

She kisses my cheek. "Yes, sir."

We're both dressed, scrambling to make sure we have everything we need.

My phone is in my back pocket.

Dani has her purse hanging diagonally across her body.

We're standing in the middle of the foyer, between the living room and dining room.

"Do you have everything you need?"

"I think so," she says.

"Double check, and make sure. I don't know if we'll have to come back to the house. I don't know how long we're going to be at the hospital. I—"

She cuts me off before I can finish my train of thought. "Hey Noah."

"What?"

She cups my face with both of her hands, staring at me with those big brown eyes of hers. "Breathe, baby."

I'm her baby now. I could get used to that.

Inhaling and exhaling, I stare deep into her eyes which are melting my core down to nothing and mesmerizing the shit out of me.

The color brown is often associated with resilience, dependability, and security.

Dani's one of the most resilient people I've ever met. I've been able to depend on her so much. She's provided me with a sense of security I've always dreamed of having with someone. I feel so safe when I'm with her. It's absolutely insane.

Her lips curve up to form a smile which naturally causes me to smile, too. She's breathing in and out with me. "You good?"

I nod, running my tongue along the top row of my teeth. "I'm good. I do have one question, though."

"What is it?"

"Where the hell is Archie?"

Her mouth drops open before her hand covers it. "Oh, shit. Maybe we scared him because we were being too loud last night so he went into hiding. I'll go look real quick."

"And by we, you mean you, right?"

"Hate to break it to you, but I wasn't the only one who was loud last night." She walks closer to me, invading my personal space and running her finger down to my stomach. "You talked about how badly you wanted me to scream your name so loud that the neighbors could hear me, right?"

"Uh-huh."

Her hot breath is melting layers of my skin away.

"Congratulations, you did just that. But guess what, Lover Boy?"

I cross my arms in front of my chest. "What, Princess?"

She leans into my ear. "Next time around it's going to be you screaming my name so goddamn loud the entire town is going to hear you."

"Don't say shit like that to me right now. For Chrissakes, we're on our way to the hospital to pick up my sister who's been unconscious for the last few weeks."

"You should've known something like that was coming," she says.

"Yeah, you have. Quite a few times actually." I smirk, licking my lips.

She rolls her eyes, shaking her head.

Right on cue, Archie runs towards us and meows up a storm.

Dani picks him up. "Hey, buddy, I'm so sorry I forgot about you. You can blame Noah for that."

I pet Archie's soft, ginger fur. "You know she's lying to you. It's bullshit and she knows it too. That's the sad part."

She puts Archie down, punching me in the arm.

"What the hell? I told you to stop doing that."

"Asshole." She doesn't break eye contact with me. In fact, her eyes are scanning me from head to toe.

"Stop doing that. We need to go."

She rolls her eyes and says goodbye to Archie. He meows at her, rubbing the back of the sofa with his body.

We rush out of the house, but now I'm standing in the driveway. "We're taking my car, which means I'm driving."

"Okay," she replies as she finishes locking the front door. "I could drive."

I shake my head. "Dani."

"Yeah?" Her nose scrunches.

My face softens. "Get in the car."

She walks over to the passenger's side.

Running over to her, I open the door. I have to treat her like the princess that she is.

She gets in, takes her purse off her body, and puts it on the floor in front of her. I close the door and rush over to the driver's side.

I'm sitting down in the car. And I'm dizzy. Things are spinning. It's not anxiety this time. I think I'm crashing. It's been hours since we've eaten.

I'm surprised Dani hasn't crashed yet. She ate less than I did.

A worried expression appears on Dani's face. "What's going on? You're scaring me."

"I think I'm crashing. We haven't eaten anything since breakfast. That was hours ago."

"Oh, shit. Um...switch with me. I'm driving."

"What?"

"You heard me. You can't drive like that. It's too dangerous." She walks around to the driver's side, and opens the door. "Can you walk?"

"Yes, I can walk."

I step out of the car, starting with one foot. I just about trip over the edge of the car with my other foot.

"Smart ass," she mutters under her breath.

I make it to the passenger's side, planting my ass down on the seat.

"Give me your phone." She sits on the driver's seat, pulling it closer to the steering wheel.

"Why do you need my phone?"

"Noah Matthew Kaplan, if you don't give me your phone right now, this isn't going to end well for you."

Oh shit, she just said my full name. She means serious business.

I give her my phone.

She takes a moment to admire my lockscreen. "I'm your

lockscreen?" Her lips turn into this adorable pout, making my insides transform into a tangled mess. "When did you take this?"

"This is going to make me sound like a creep, but I promise I'm not. I took it this morning before I left to go on my run. You looked so fucking beautiful and peaceful. I can change it if you think it's too weird."

"It's not weird. It's cute in a creepy kind of way." She shakes her head, grinning. "I need your passcode."

"060301."

"Your birthday. Really? I didn't think you would choose something that obvious."

"I know your passcode is your birthday too."

"How do you know that?"

"Everybody uses their birthday as their passcode for their phone. Okay, we're getting off topic here. What the hell are you doing?"

"I'm calling reinforcements."

"Dani, we don't have time for this."

"Guess what? We're making time for this."

dani

God, I don't know what I'd do if the favorites section on phones didn't exist. In situations like these, it's a necessity because I don't have to go through his contacts to find the one person I'm looking for.

Putting Noah's phone on speaker, the line rings for a brief moment.

"If you're calling to torture me by talking about Dani again, you can just forget it. I'm tired of this shit, Noah."

"Grayson, shut up. It's me."

Noah violently shakes his head. "No," he mouths to me and crosses his arms into the shape of an X.

"Dani? Why the hell are you calling me on Noah's phone?" Grayson asks, confusion flowing throughout his tone.

"Is Xander with you?"

"Yeah, why?"

"I need you guys to pick up some food. I literally don't care what it is."

"Hey Dani, what's going on?" Xander's sweet voice is soothing my anxiety.

"Noah's crashing. We haven't eaten in hours. Lizzie texted

him and said she was ready to be taken home. But, h-he can't drive like this. I know we're going to a hospital but I-I'm freaking out. I-I don't know what to do."

I hear Grayson's voice now. It's deeper than Xander's. "We're on our way. Hang in there buddy."

"Yeah, whatever dickhead," Noah shouts in my direction.

"Love you too, bro!" Grayson yells.

"Thank you," I say.

"Anything for you, Dani."

I roll my eyes. "You guys really are a bunch of idiots."

Noah nods his head up and down, closing his eyes and grinning at me.

"Idiots who are saving your ass," Grayson says.

"Do you know when you shouldn't say shit like that?" Xander asks Grayson.

"Can you two try to not beat the shit out of each other for like an hour? There's literally no time for this. Please go!"

I hang up the phone and Noah's giving me the side-eye.

"You know, even if I called Xander, Grayson still would've come. Just saying. He's going to have to get used to me being around. A lot more than he's used to."

"Fuck yeah, he is." He tilts his head, smiling at me and making my body feel like it's on fire.

Pursing my lips out, I let out a giggle that quickly turned into a laugh.

Every time I laugh, Noah stares at me. It doesn't make me uncomfortable. His eyes become full of curiosity and admiration. It makes me disintegrate.

"You're doing what you told me not to do to you back at the house. Quit it!"

"It's hard not to look away from you when you laugh like that. There's this invisible string that pulls me towards you and I can't stop it. I don't want to stop it."

"I can't handle romantic shit like this right now because I

might spontaneously combust in this car." A lump travels its way down my throat. "You're distracting me from freaking out."

"*Really*? I had *no* idea."

My legs are shaking up and down.

Patience is soon to become non-existent. I lean over to him, feeling his forehead. It's warm, but nothing to be alarmed about.

"What are you doing, Nurse Dani?"

"Checking to see if you're overheating."

"Don't be surprised if I am. And it's all your fault."

"How the hell is this my fault?"

"You sure as hell know why, Sweet Peach."

"Oh my God, you're not coming onto me right now, are you? We don't have time for this shit."

He leans onto the console, elbows resting on it. "Flirting with you is a reflex for me."

LIZZIE

ME

hey lizbug, we're running behind because your brother is having a sugar crash

LIZZIE

Shit, is he okay?

ME

yeah, he's fine. we're waiting for grayson and xander to bring him food. i promise we're coming

LIZZIE

Look, my brother can be a shithead sometimes, but I still love him. Please tell him to not freak out about rushing over to the hospital to bring me home. Tell him I care about his well being more than my sanity

ME

i will. hang in there!

"That was Lizzie," I say.

"Of course, you texted my sister."

"She needs to know what's going on."

He rolls his eyes. "You're right."

"You bet your sweet ass I'm right."

"You think I have a sweet ass?" He cocks an eyebrow while a sexy smirk grows in slow motion onto his face.

"It's just a figure of speech."

"You added the sweet part though."

"Can we just change the subject?"

"While we're on the subject, you have a sweet ass too," he blurts out.

"Cut it out!" I hit him on the shoulder with the palm of my hand.

Damn it, my cheeks are warm. Is there going to be a time when he doesn't make me blush? Nope. Never going to happen.

"We need to tape that mouth of yours shut, Kaplan."

"Is this going to be a new kink of yours, Solomon?" He raises his eyebrows.

Grayson and Xander need to hurry the hell up before I'm murdered by Noah's flirting tactics.

After twenty-five agonizing minutes of waiting for the guys, they finally pull up in front of us.

As I exit the vehicle, I stand in front of my side of the car and wait impatiently for the guys to make their way over to us to give us the food.

Noah jogs over to me, playfully nudging me in the shoulder.

We watch Grayson step out of the driver's side of a black pickup truck.

"What the hell took you guys so long?" I ask, huffing.

Grayson walks over to us with a to-go box which has the

Coastal Shores logo on it. There's a cartoon sandwich in between all the brown text. "Well, since it's hot food, they actually have to make it, heat it up, and cook it so we don't have a case of food poisoning on our hands."

Noah's demeanor shifts from playfulness to annoyance. "Oh, look who it is. The captain of The Idiot Club."

"Noah...not now," I say.

Xander gets out of the truck, making his way over to Noah. He's examining his face. "He looks fine to me."

"Thank you, Captain Obvious." He rolls his eyes at Xander before he turns his head towards Grayson. "If there's a fucking salad in here, I swear to God, Grayson Becker, I will make it my life's mission to make your life a miserable hell."

"I would *never* do that to you," Grayson says as he hands the box over to Noah.

I walk over to Noah, Grayson, and Xander.

Noah opens the styrofoam box, revealing a sandwich and curly fries.

"It's a fried chicken sandwich with the works. Lettuce, tomato, onion, and mayo. I know how much you love this sandwich, so that's why I got it."

"I love you so much right now."

So, you're telling me all I have to do is shove food into Noah's face for him to say that he loves me? Done.

"I love you too buddy. Sorry that I've been an asshole lately."

"You're forgiven...for now." Noah grabs my hand. "Take half, Sunshine. You haven't eaten in hours either. I honestly thought you'd crash before me. Just give me the tomato and the onion. And don't argue with me."

Sweat builds on my skin.

The guys are watching us.

Noah gestures to me to sit on his lap.

I shake my head. "No," I whisper.

"Sit on me," he mouths.

"Fine."

Walking over to the passenger side of the car, I sit on Noah's lap with the box of food sitting on top of my legs.

He has one arm secured around my waist, so I don't fall.

I take off the top bun, removing the tomato and onion. Before I bite into the sandwich, I feel two sets of eyes on us. They're burning holes through multiple layers of skin on our faces.

"What the hell are you guys looking at?" Noah asks the guys.

They're looking at each other, trying to comprehend what they just witnessed. Grayson speaks up first. "Uh, Sunshine? Sharing food. Dani's sitting on your lap. What the hell did we miss?"

"You guys...missed a lot," Noah replies as he licks his lips.

"What's a lot?" Xander adds.

"Do you want to tell them, or should I?"

I have a mouthful of food, so I resort to pointing at him because I can't respond by talking.

"Pretend I'm not even here," I say.

"I can't do that, Dani."

"Fine. I'll go eat on the step that's in front of the door to my house. Knock yourselves out. Don't talk about me too much, Heart Eyes. Grayson's head might explode off his body."

That gets a laugh out of Noah and Xander.

"Haha, you're so funny," Grayson says.

"You've got a little something on your shirt," I tell him.

Grayson looks down at his shirt, only to be met with my pointer finger hitting him in the chin.

I wink at the guys, walking away to go sit on the step so they can talk about me as much as they want to.

noah

"Do you guys want the raw or fluffy version?"

"Raw is the only answer here," Xander replies.

"Okay...um. Dani and I...We..."

"Spit it out, man," Grayson presses me.

Ah, screw it. I'm going for the raw and honest truth.

"Dani and I had sex last night." A smug look writes itself all over my face.

Xander reacts to the news first. "Holy shit, bro!"

Grayson is next. "I fucking called it."

"No, you didn't," Xander squints his eyes at Grayson.

"Yes, I did. I told you Dani would be the person that Noah would lose his virginity to. Remember? In sophomore year?"

"Don't recall any of that." Xander rolls his eyes.

"What the hell are you guys talking about?" I chime in.

"It doesn't matter. What does matter is our little boy is all grown up." Grayson has this proud expression on his face, causing me to roll my eyes in his direction.

"So...how was it?" he asks, raising his eyebrows.

"Over the past twenty-four hours, we've had sex in her bed. I've licked peach juice off her ass. And I've tasted her with my fingers. Does that tell you how it was? If it didn't, I can be more honest with you. I'm never going to have sex with anyone else. Dani's it for me."

"Damn, I wasn't expecting that. She's walking just fine considering you railed the shit out of her," Grayson says.

"Oh, trust me, that's not going to last for long though."

"Guess those romance books came in handy then, didn't they?" Grayson raises his eyebrows, making a kissy face.

My cheeks are warm, getting redder by the minute. "Hell yeah, they did."

"Wait a damn minute. You *licked* peach juice off her ass?" Xander raises his voice.

I hit Xander in the shoulder. "Will you shut the hell up? She's going to hear you."

"Who are you and what have you done with my best friend?" Sarcasm takes over his voice.

I shrug my shoulders. "Your best friend has evolved."

Xander scoffs, rolling his eyes. "Bullshit, you just lost your virginity."

"That's evolution for you," I tell him.

"That's not everything that happened. You're holding back something from us. Spill it." Grayson has a big, dumb smile on his face while Xander crosses his arms in front of his chest.

It's hard to look at Grayson's face when he's talking to me because my eyes dart right to the ink that covers his arms in their entirety.

His love for tattoos started when he was a teenager.

He was in his rebellious phase, but I think we all went through that phase if I'm being honest.

I'm shocked I can still see bare skin on his arms. I thought he would've had full sleeves by now.

Xander has a few tattoos here and there on his arms. Not as many as Gray has though.

Then, there's me. The tattoo virgin.

I've never thought about getting a tattoo until this morning.

When I went for my run, my mind thought of the idea of getting a tattoo. A black outline of the sun on the inside of my wrist. Fucking crazy to even think about this since Dani and I just got together last night, but I need a reminder that the sun will always come out after a monsoon.

"You look like your head is going to explode," Grayson says.

"Sorry, I was just thinking about something."

"Thinking about what?" Xander asks me, cocking his head.

"It's not important. On the other hand, I may have told Dani I'm in love with her."

"What do you mean by *may* have?" Xander repeats.

"I didn't actually say it, but I told her I can't stop thinking about her. How I want her all the time. I called her my sunshine. I don't know why I didn't tell her I love her. I'm such an idiot."

"Yeah, you are an idiot. But we already know that."

I shake my head, rolling my eyes. "You're so fucking helpful, Gray."

"Don't tell me something that I already know."

"I'm being sarcastic, dumbass."

Dani's walking back over to us like a goddamn model. She does this shit on purpose to torture me internally and externally.

"Shit, act normal," I whisper.

"Again, you're an idiot," Grayson makes his point even clearer.

Sticking my middle finger up at him, I smile at Dani who's standing in front of me.

"Are you boys done gossiping about me?"

"We weren't talking about you, Princess."

"I know you were, Heart Eyes. I could hear you guys all the way from where I was sitting." Her nose scrunches as a smile spreads across her lips.

Fuck, I'm never going to get tired of those adorable nose scrunches.

"Well, we're going to go and leave you two kids alone," Xanders says with his top lip covering his bottom lip.

"Thanks for saving my ass from passing out," I say to the guys.

"Anytime, buddy." Grayson puts his hand on my shoulder. "Anytime."

Dani walks closer to the guys. "Can I talk to you guys for a second?"

Grayson and Xander look at each other and nod in unison at Dani.

What could she possibly want to talk to them about? Can't be about the three of us talking about her because she knows what we discussed. I know she does.

I watch the guys while Dani walks over to Grayson's truck.

Anxiety is being put on the back burner because I want to finish this damn sandwich. It's so fucking good.

dani

"Thank you guys for coming. I'm sorry I was kind of a bitch on the phone."

"You don't need to apologize. Any person would've reacted like that if they were in the same situation," Xander says to me.

Dubbing Xander as the voice of reason, I can see why Noah is best friends with him. Xander brings you back to earth when it feels like you're looking down at it.

Grayson piggybacks off Xander. "He's right. And there's nothing we wouldn't do for Noah. There's nothing I wouldn't do for him. I've known the guy since we were kids. He's been there for me through the good, the bad, and the ugly."

"I know. And I know he's very grateful for both of you even if he might not say it enough," I say.

Grayson makes eye contact with me. "Since it appears the two of you are a package deal now, don't ever hesitate to reach out if you ever need anything. Seriously, I mean it. And I'm sorry for acting like an asshole to you. I've been trying to convince Noah that he's been in love with you for years. Took him fucking long enough to realize it. Don't tell him I told you this, but he was freaking out about how he should tell you how he feels about you."

"We thought he was going to have a heart attack," Xander chimes in.

"I've never seen him like this," Grayson says.

My lips twitch. "Seen him like what?"

"Noah's fucking crazy about you. He'd literally murder someone for you if he knew someone was trying to hurt you. He'd go to the ends of the earth to find you if he lost you. By the way, I know why you call him Heart Eyes. When you're around him, his pupils transform into little hearts like they do in cartoons." Grayson pauses to catch his breath. "He deserves to be with someone like you. Someone who will protect him and his heart. I hate being sappy and shit like this, but you two belong together."

Wow, that was beautiful.

I've never heard Grayson get all sentimental like this before and I've known the guy for a long time.

We were never really close because Noah and I couldn't stand to be around each other.

For some reason, I've always known he's a good guy. He is a good guy. Noah's lucky to have Grayson and Xander in his life. He needs them.

"Okay, I lost Noah. I can't lose you too. Who the hell is this person, Gray?" Xander asks.

Grayson rolls his eyes. "You're so fucking dramatic."

Xander sticks his middle fingers up, waving them in Grayson's face.

They walk towards the truck with me following them.

The guys get into the truck, slamming the doors shut and buckling their seat belts.

I walk around the driver's side, and knock on the window.

Grayson rolls down the window.

I look at both of them. "I'm going to do everything in my power to protect him, you know."

"I know you will." Grayson pauses. "Give me your phone, so I can put my number in it. Xander's too so you don't have to contact us through Noah's phone."

Giving Grayson my phone, he inputs his and Xander's numbers into my phone and hands it back to me. "Now, you can contact us yourself. Whenever you need us, we'll be there."

"Thank you," I say.

Xander peers his head at me. "I just want to say Noah's lucky to have someone like you in his life. He's not the only one who'd save you from a murderer. I know you'd save him if he was in the same situation. I mean you've hated the guy for years, but you came anyway because you knew he'd need someone to console and take care of him. It's admirable. Don't you ever let anybody tell you you're less than because Dani... you're pretty fucking awesome."

Closing my eyes, I absorb everything Xander just said to me.

God, this guy is pure sunshine.

I smile, placing the palm of my hand over my heart to show him his words meant the world to me without verbally saying anything.

I wave goodbye to the guys as they drive off, walking back over to Noah who is sitting in the driver's seat. "I'm driving," he says, oozing confidence.

"Over my dead body." I look around the car, coming to the realization I haven't eaten any fries yet.

Stupid thought to have right now, but I'm still hungry.

"Wait a minute, did you eat all the fries?"

"How dare you accuse me of such a thing?" He looks deep into my eyes, smirking at me.

God, that fucking smirk is going to be my cause of death.

He reaches over to the passenger seat, opens the styrofoam box, and shows one to me. "You mean these fries?"

I plant my ass in his lap while he continues to tease me with the fry, pulling it farther away from me. "Give it to me."

"We really need to teach you a thing or two about manners, Solomon." His tone is playful, but I'm not in the mood to play this game.

Rolling my eyes and wiggling my nose out of anger, I look everywhere else, but at him.

"Open your mouth," he commands. He inserts the fry into my mouth, allowing me to bite off half of it as he shoves the other half down his throat. "Sharing is caring."

"You're such an asshole."

"Yeah, but I'm *your* asshole."

We're both staring at each other's lips, anticipating who's going to kiss who first.

I decide to go in for the kill, planting my lips hard on his.

He's losing the ability to breathe properly. "Dani, we...n-need to g-go," he stutters, moaning while I pepper kisses all over the nape of his neck.

"Fine, have it your way." I kiss him on the cheek before I get off his lap, climbing into the passenger side of the car.

His eyes are melting me down to pure liquid. "Consider this as unfinished business. I'm not done with you."

Yeah, obviously. You were hard the second I started kissing your neck.

Heat is pooling in between my thighs.

No, it has to be sweat.

It does feel like one hundred degrees out here with the mix of the blazing sun and intense humidity.

"Let's go rescue your sister," I say.

He presses the button to turn on the engine, switching the gear into drive. Resting my hand on the console, he flips my hand over so he can thread his fingers into mine.

His thumb is rubbing gentle vertical motions on my thumb.

I shift my head towards the window so he doesn't see how red my cheeks are and allows me to smile without him knowing.

It's a fifteen minute drive to Sunset Cove Hospital from the house.

We spend the entire drive belting out songs by Gracie Abrams, The Cure, and Arctic Monkeys.

We're both horrible singers, but it doesn't matter. Singing with Noah is freeing, especially when his ocean eyes meet my brown eyes for a brief moment when we're at a traffic light that's located right across from the hospital.

The light turns green and Noah turns left, making a right into the hospital's main parking lot.

Seriously, I feel like I live here.

After driving around the parking lot closest to the entrance for several minutes, we find a spot.

Noah pushes in the engine start/stop button, moving the gear shift into park.

Removing the elastic holding together my braid, I comb through the loose waves with my fingers.

"Hey, you're ruining my masterpiece." He frowns.

"Sorry, I'm starting to get a headache and it's hot outside."

"It's hot in here too," he says as he raises his eyebrows.

I wet my lips, giggling like a schoolgirl. "Did I really ruin your masterpiece?"

His eyes trail down to my waist and back up to my face, causing my lips to twitch. He leans into me and runs his fingers through a loose tendril of my hair. "If I'm being honest, *you're* my masterpiece."

My nose scrunches, lips curving up into a dorky smile.

Did Noah hold my hand up until this moment? Yes, he held my hand the entire time. I love the way his hand fits in mine like it was made just for me.

He makes his way to my side, opening the door for me and sticking out his hand, so I can hold it again. "Let's go rescue Rapunzel from her tower, shall we?"

"We shall."

Once we breeze our way through security, we run to the elevator.

When the elevator doors open, he presses the button with the number four on it.

As the doors close, I gather my hair at the back of my head and secure it into a low ponytail.

His gaze is setting me ablaze.

"What?" My face scrunches before my lips shift to the side of my mouth.

Strutting over to me, he pins me against the wall. His lips make a crash-landing on mine, one hand cupping my face as the other wraps around my waist.

Ding. Level 2.

His mouth makes its way to my neck, gently tugging on my skin.

This cannot be happening right now. He's trying to freaking kill me.

Ding. Level 3.

"Noah," I groan through a faint breath.

His lips are soft and cushiony like a great quality pillow you'd get at a fancy resort.

Ding. Level 4.

He pulls his lips off mine and walks out of the elevator.

I stop to collect myself.

That was one of the best kisses I've ever had in my entire life. That says a lot because pretty much every kiss I've had with him has been life-changing.

Goosebumps cover the outer layer of my skin, visible for everybody to see.

He looks behind, noticing that I'm not following him. "You alright?"

"Uh-huh. I just...um...I need a moment," I say before letting out a smooth exhale.

A big smile appears on his face. "Took your breath away, didn't I?"

"You could say something like that."

"Just wait until tonight, Sweet Peach." He winks an eye, a smirk clutching onto the corners of his lips.

My eyelids rapidly blink. Brain attempting to process what I just heard come out of his mouth. *God, his mouth.* It's trouble in all caps.

My cheeks are overheating. They're most likely bright red.

"Your flushed cheeks aren't going to go away if you keep rubbing them. That's only going to make it worse."

"Oh, shut up."

"If you keep telling me to shut up all the time, you're going to have to make me. Every. Single. Time."

I exhale, rolling my eyes. "Let's go, Heart Eyes."

Walking over to Lizzie's room, Noah's speed-walking to catch up to me. When he does, we see his mom and my mom standing in the doorway.

"Hi, Mom," he says to Laura.

"We were beginning to think you guys weren't coming. Are you okay, Noah Bear? Lizzie told me what happened."

He goes in for a hug before coming back to stand next to me.

"I'm fine because I had my little helper with me." His hand hardcore squeezes my ass, making me jump.

"Everything okay, sweetheart?" Mom asks me.

I give him a death stare and turn my head back around to meet Mom's gaze.

"Just *peachy.*" I give Mom and Laura a fake smile and thumbs up.

Our moms walk into Lizzie's room.

"Are you guys coming?" Laura looks at both of us, waiting for an answer.

I nod. "Yeah, just give us a minute."

He's in *so* much trouble.

CHAPTER FIFTY-NINE

We're standing in front of the wall near my sister's hospital room.

Dani looks like she's going to murder me. Lucky for me, she doesn't have her giant flashlight in her hand right now to kill me with.

She hits me below my shoulder. "What the hell is wrong with you?"

My eyes grow wide. "Sorry, my hand spazzed out."

Sticking my tongue partially out, I burst out into laughter.

"Bullshit." She crosses her arms underneath her breasts, reminding me I've seen them bare.

In fact, I've seen her naked body. Getting hard as I keep thinking about it. Don't fucking go there, man.

She looks down at the bulge growing in my shorts, her mouth hanging partially open. "What the hell is turning you on right now?"

"You!" I raise my voice.

"Keep your voice down," she says quietly, her jaw vibrating and placing her hands on her hips. "How? I'm not even doing anything."

"It's the Danielle Solomon effect, remember?"

I'm not telling her I'm picturing her wet, naked body in my head. Why the hell would I do that? That's too weird.

"Right." She shakes her head, flattening her kissable pink lips.

She walks into Lizzie's room with me trailing behind her.

Lizzie's face is essentially a blank canvas. "Look who finally decided to show up."

I open my mouth to talk first. "We told you we were going to be running late, genius."

"I'm fucking with you, shithead." Lizzie's eyes land on Mom and she points to us with both of her index fingers. "They're taking me home."

"We're relieving you of Lizzie duty," I tell Mom. "Dani and I will meet you back at the house. Celia, can you take my mom home?"

"It would be my pleasure."

"Celia!" Mom shouts.

"Laura, just let the kids do this for Lizzie. Let them have their time to bond."

Bonding time. Yeah, maybe this isn't a good idea.

Celia senses Mom's hesitation. "Let's take this outside." She wraps her arm around Mom's shoulder, leading her over to the chairs hanging out in front of the room.

"I'll be right back," I say to my sister and Dani.

I run out of the room to catch up with Mom and Celia. When I do, I tap Mom on the shoulder and meet her confused gaze.

"Can I talk to you for a minute?"

"Of course," she says.

"I'll be waiting by the elevators," Celia says as she rubs Mom's back before she walks over to the elevators.

"How are you doing with all this?" I ask her.

"I don't even know how to answer that to be completely honest with you."

"That's how I feel."

"How is anyone supposed to feel when their husband and their child get into a car accident? And then their husband passes away." She closes her eyes, her lips quivering.

"Lizzie isn't a child though," I say in the hopes of stopping any tears from coming out of her brown eyes.

"Oh, honey, you're always going to be my children. I don't care if you're forty. I will still call you my child."

I chuckle. "Fair enough."

She studies my face and body language thoroughly. "There's something you're not telling me."

"What?"

"I know you're an adult, but you know you can talk to me about anything. You know that, right?"

I exhale, reaching my arms out and placing my hands on her shoulders.

"Dani and I are together."

She rapidly blinks her eyes, moving her head around. "So, that means you guys are..." She waits for me to finish her thought for her.

"Dating."

She nods in slow motion. "I see."

"You're freaking me out, Mom."

"It's a lot of information to absorb."

"How? It was one sentence."

She huffs. "Your dad knew this would happen. He told me you two getting together was inevitable."

Inevitable is beginning to become one of my favorite words ever.

"Seems like you and Dani have an affinity for the word inevitable."

She studies my face. "There's something else you're not telling me."

Guiding Mom over the chairs hanging out in front of Lizzie's room, we sit down next to each other and I face her.

Fuck, my heart is beating so damn fast.

I exhale. "I'm in love with her. And I didn't tell her when we were together last night. I wanted to, but I chickened out. I've never felt this way about a woman before. When I saw her standing in the middle of the fourth floor in this hospital a month ago, I thought I was hallucinating. I was convinced she wouldn't come, but she did, despite how she felt about me at the time." I pause to catch my breath. "I was stubborn as hell back in high school, not listening to Dad or Grayson because I couldn't wrap my head around the idea that I could be in love with a woman I couldn't stand growing up." I lick my lips. "When I'm with her, it feels like I'm underwater and I can't come back up for air. All I want to do is hold her hand, hug her, and touch her in some way. So, yeah. I love Dani Solomon and I don't know how to tell her."

Mom breathes out through her nose, blinking her eyes as a tender smile spreads across her lips. "You've got it bad, Noah Bear. Is that why your shelves are full of romance books? It's been to serve as a reminder of her after you two stopped talking?"

I nod, closing my eyes.

"Guess it's time for some words of wisdom from your mom, huh?" She gives me a loving smile. "Love has its way of finding us when we least expect it. It can be terrifying, overwhelming, and exciting all at the same time. It's like listening to a song for the first time and knowing right off the bat it will become a favorite of yours for a very long time."

"*Brain Damage* by Pink Floyd has become one of my favorite songs of all time," I babble. "We listened to it in my bedroom and the way she kept looking at me felt as if I wasn't in my own body. She makes me feel everything when I'm with her. All I want to do is take care of her because she's done so much for us. For her friends. For her family. She deserves someone who loves her unconditionally. Someone who treats her like a princess. Someone who worships the ground she walks on. Someone—"

Mom cuts me off. "I think you're talking about yourself, honey. She deserves someone like you." She pauses. "You know, sometimes I wonder if you're my son and if we're from the same bloodline. You have such a big heart and you care so damn much about people. Let Dani have a piece of your heart, and let her in, even in the parts you don't want her to see because I know she'll love them. I know she loves you too."

"How do you know?"

"Call it maternal instinct." She winks at me.

"Hey," Dani says as she walks over to us.

"I'll talk to you later," Mom tells me as she kisses my forehead.

Mom and I stand up and she walks over to the elevator. I watch her disappear with Celia.

Dani places her hand on her hip. "Is everything okay?"

Oh, you just missed me spilling my guts to my mom about how I'm hopelessly and desperately in love with you.

"Yeah, everything's fine. Just had some mother and son bonding time." I pause. "Where did you just come from?"

"I had to go to the bathroom after you chased down your mom." She licks her lips. "I can go into more specific detail about what I did in there if you want me to."

My mouth parts slightly. "I'll pass."

We make our way back inside Lizzie's hospital room.

"I thought you were never coming back. God, you almost missed out on me giving myself a concussion by banging my head on the wall behind me from Mom giving me the whole PT spiel and everything," Lizzie says.

"I would've paid to see that one," I reply.

"You suck." Lizzie sticks her middle finger up at me.

"Hey, Lizbug," Dani greets my sister.

"Hey, lioness. Ugh, I slept so shitty last night. It's not just that my back is killing me from the accident, but now it's going to be even more sore from sleeping on this damn bed for several weeks. How did you two sleep?"

Dani and I look at each other. I clear my throat excessively. "Sorry. Had a lump in my throat." She squeezes my ass just as I answer Lizzie's question, making me spring forward a touch. "W—we slept fine."

"You okay, little bro?"

I turn my head in Dani's direction, eyes widening. "Uh-huh." Turning away from me, she smiles at me. A goofy yet sneakily hot kind of smile.

"Oh my God. You two had sex!" Lizzie blurts out.

What the hell?

We both freeze in place.

"Shhhh," I say as I place my index finger over my mouth. "The entire fourth floor is going to hear you!"

"I knew it," she says, crossing her arms in front of her chest.

"How did you know?" Dani asks her, gently shaking her head.

"The energy between you two feels different. I felt it the moment you walked into the room. Noah, buddy, you were trying so hard to not look at Dani."

There's something else that's hard right now. And it's not me struggling to not look at Dani which doesn't matter anymore since Lizzie knows.

Well, she doesn't know everything.

"There's more," I say.

"More?" Lizzie asks.

"This isn't a friends-with-benefits type of situation. It doesn't even come close to it." My eyes land on Dani's. Her lips are partially open and she's listening intently. "I've been absolutely crazy about this woman since high school. This past month and a half has made me reevaluate my feelings for her. Admit how I truly feel about her to myself and to her."

This is it, Noah. Tell her that you love her. That you're in love with her. Just fucking do it.

Dani's holding her breath in anticipation of what I'm about to reveal. Yet, I feel like she already knows.

I just haven't told her I love her with actual words.

"I'm—"

"Is everything okay in here?" A nurse with dirty blonde hair and hazel eyes asks us. I can't make out her name tag.

Goddammit. Every time.

"Everything's fine. Sorry for being too loud."

"Yeah, so sorry," Dani echoes.

"Just checking. I'm glad you're going home today Lizzie."

"Me too!"

"You got this," the nurse says as she walks out of the room.

Dani and I peek our heads out into the hall to make sure nobody else is coming.

No more interruptions. I'm begging.

I pull Dani back into the room by her waist, twisting her around, so she faces me. I'm aware I'm staring at her full pink lips that hypnotize the shit out of me.

My sister is staring at the both of us. She's anxiously waiting for something to happen. "Don't mind me. Pretend I'm not even here," she says.

Breaking eye contact with Dani, I turn my attention back to my sister and change the subject. "Did Mom call for a wheelchair?"

"She called for a wheelchair an hour ago. One of my nurses said someone is on their way with one."

Just at the right moment, a female nurse with brunette hair rolls a wheelchair in front of the doorway. "Elizabeth Kaplan?"

"That's me."

The nurse nods her head, rolling the wheelchair further into the room. She helps Lizzie get into it.

I can't help but notice my sister is checking her out.

"You're very pretty..." She looks at her I.D. badge to get her name. "Leia. Like Princess Leia from *Star Wars*?"

"Elizabeth!" I shout.

"What?"

"I'm sorry about my sister. She's on a ton of pain meds."

Lizzie flips me off, causing Dani to burst out into laughter.

"No need to apologize. Let's get you out of here, Miss Elizabeth."

She gives Nurse Leia an extended salute. "Yes, ma'am."

I check around the room to make sure that we all have everything.

Once I see we have everything, Leia pushes Lizzie out of the room and towards the elevator.

Dani and I follow at a measly pace. Interlocking her hand with mine, Dani looks up at me with those big beautiful brown eyes of hers.

I'm such a goner for this woman.

Leia rolls my sister into the elevator, but there's not enough room for all of us to fit in there.

"Why don't you wait for the next one?" Lizzie smirks, licking her lips and raising her eyebrows.

My sister's a mind reader. I swear she crawls inside my head and finds out all the dirty things I'm thinking about. It's not only cruel. It's highly disturbing.

"Bad idea," Dani says in a hushed tone into my ear.

"Sometimes bad ideas are actually good ideas in disguise."

"See you guys downstairs," Lizzie tells us as her middle fingers dance in the air.

God, how many drugs is she on?

"You're such a..." The elevator door closes. "Moron."

I press the down button.

Dani steers clear at any chance of looking me in the eyes.

I can't take my eyes off her. The way her dark brunette hair frames her beautiful face. How her tank top is hugging every damn curve. How easy it is to make her blush, smile, and laugh.

The elevator doors open.

We step inside.

I can tell she's waiting for me to make a move. Tension engulfs the air swirling around us. It's so thick you couldn't cut it with a sharp knife.

To my chagrin, she walks over to me. Her hips are swaying back and forth just to test my raging hormones.

My heart sinks all the way down to my stomach. Nerves are radiating throughout my body. "You coming over to kiss me, Solomon?"

"What would give you that impression?"

"You're staring at my lips."

"That obvious, huh?"

"Just shut up and kiss me already if you're not all mouth."

Her body slams into mine, kissing me like she hasn't kissed me in days, weeks, or possibly months.

Ding. Level 3.

I'm going to miss these damn elevators because they're magical.

I pull away, realizing I need to tell this gorgeous woman standing in front of me I'm in love with her.

"Dani, I need to finish what I was trying to tell Lizzie in her room. The truth is I was actually talking to you."

She sees my chest heaving and notices I'm breathing heavily. "Are you having another panic attack?"

"No. There's something I've been wanting to tell you."

Ding. Level 2.

Her arms cage me in, brown eyes dissolving me like chocolate melting in the hot Florida sun. "Then, tell me already!"

"I'm in love with you. I'm sorry I didn't tell you last night. I wanted to, but it never came out. I knew you were anxiously waiting for me to tell you. It's just...I've never been in love before and didn't know what it felt like. Until I met you. When I'm with you, nobody else exists. All I can think about is you. All I want to do is be near you. Kiss you. Hold your hand. Make you laugh. Be your shoulder to cry on. I want to be your everything. I love you."

"You're in love with me?" She smiles.

"Of course I am. I've been in love with you since we were teenagers. Hell, probably since we were kids."

Ding. Lobby.

I walk out of the elevator, dragging her out with me. Her eyes are glassy. "Oh God, please don't cry."

"They're happy tears. I *promise*." She laughs through the tears, choking on them in an attempt to catch her breath. "Hey, Noah."

"What's up, Dani?"

"I'm in love with you, too. I've been wanting to tell you since this morning. Remember when Bella told you I had something to tell you? This is it. She thought it was ridiculous that I've been waiting for you to tell me you're in love with me. I didn't want to come off as desperate, so I kept my mouth shut. I'm not keeping it shut anymore. I love you."

Tears are trickling down her face. I bring my thumb up to her cheeks, wiping away the tears falling out of her eyes.

We're standing in the middle of the lobby.

I walk closer to her, sealing the gap between us.

All eyes are on us. There are a few elderly women sitting on the chairs behind us. A group of teenagers hanging out by the cafeteria entrance.

"Noah, people are watching."

"Let them watch. They're about to watch the best TV show of their lives. And it's in real time, baby."

"You're such—"

I cut her off. "An idiot?"

"Yeah."

"But you love me anyway?"

"Of course, I love you. Even if you're an idiot. *My* idiot."

Gripping onto her back, I dip her before I plant a kiss on her. My hand is cupping one side of her face. Her lips are soft and sweet. I'm high on adrenaline. The rush of all this feels addicting and fucking incredible.

My lips release from hers. I bring her back up, so she can stand upright.

One of the elderly women stops us on our way out. "That was quite something, wasn't it? Tell me who this handsome young man is, young lady."

"This handsome young man is my boyfriend."

The woman's eyes land on me. "Hold onto this one."

"I plan to keep her for a *very* long time." I smile, winking at Dani.

She grins at the floor, cheeks turning red.

We say goodbye to the group of women and make our way out of the hospital. My sister and Nurse Leia are waiting for us in front of the sliding doors.

"Well, you guys definitely put on a show there," Lizzie says with a big dumb smile spreading across her lips.

"You saw us?" Dani asks Lizzie.

"We both did. It's hard not to because the doors are transparent and you were both in perfect view."

"I'm going to go pull up the car." I kiss Dani's cheek. "I love you!" I shout as I walk away from her.

Running to the car, I feel so damn relieved I finally told Dani I'm in love with her and how I love her. The best part is she's in love with me too. *She. Loves. Me.*

I wasn't kidding when I told one of the elderly women we talked to in here. I'm keeping this woman for a long time. Or for as long she'll keep me.

Pulling in front of the hospital, I roll down my window. "Ready to go home?" I ask my sister.

"Does it mean I have to deal with Mom and her annoying antics?"

"Unfortunately, yes."

"I'd rather stay here."

"Lizzie, Dad's funeral is in two weeks."

"Please don't remind me."

I'm not ready to say goodbye to Dad. And I know that Lizzie isn't ready to say goodbye to him either.

God, I hope the next two weeks go by as slowly as possible.

CHAPTER SIXTY

TWO WEEKS LATER

I'm standing in front of Dani's mirror in her bedroom and wearing a suit I never imagined I'd be wearing to a funeral again.

Let alone my dad's funeral.

Since I was a kid, I've been to four funerals.

My grandparents on both sides of my family passed away before I started high school.

I swore to myself I'd never go to another funeral again, but here we are.

The Jewish religion has this tradition called sitting shiva. It's where you come together for seven days to provide a time of emotional healing and mourners join together.

It's fucking depressing as shit.

It's just a bunch of people you don't know and some you do, telling you they're sorry for your loss and reminiscing about the good times. People ask you about life updates.

It's awkward as hell when you have to answer questions

about your love life. Like, why are people I don't know asking me that? It's none of their damn business.

We did it for both sets of my grandparents.

We can't do it for my dad because there's not enough time. Lizzie and I begged Mom not to, even if Dad wanted it because sitting shiva would just make us all want to kill each other.

I think my sister would kill Mom first.

And then me.

My mom and Lizzie are like two peas in a pod but there are moments where they fight. It's never gotten physical. Just verbal. Typical mother and daughter shit.

Instead of sitting shiva, we're having a funeral reception for Dad.

Not to be confused with a wedding reception.

That's a *much* happier event.

Dainty hands wrap around my waist, pulling me out of my black hole.

I look up and see Dani's beautiful face staring back at me, dark brunette waves sitting perfectly over her shoulders.

I'm so happy she's here with me.

"Hey, Moonlight."

I force a smile, only lasting a few seconds.

I just want today to be over already.

She peers her head more, so I can fully see her reflection. "I'm not going to ask you how you're feeling because I know you can't feel anything right now and that's completely normal. If at any point you don't want to be there anymore, tell me. Just say the word, and we'll leave."

I turn around to look at her.

She's wearing a black dress with relatively thin straps and a small slit going up her thigh. It's accentuating the shit out of all her gorgeous curves and perfect breasts.

I can't stop staring at her. *My girlfriend.* God, I love saying that. *My. Girlfriend.*

"Are you trying to give me a heart attack?"

"What makes you say that?" She cocks her head, giving me a cute smile.

"Look at you. I'm blinded by your beauty."

She gestures to me with her hands, pretending to fake throw up. Meeting my gaze, she smiles at me.

"How do I look?" I ask, readjusting my tie and collar.

"Like you're mine," she replies, kissing the top of my hand.

My cheeks are warm and flushed. They're most likely bright red like a ripe tomato.

"I love you," I say.

Her face lights up, making the shadows in the room disappear.

She's so fucking beautiful and she's all mine.

I'm seriously the luckiest guy in the world.

"I love you, too," she says as she wraps her arms around my neck, planting a kiss on my lips. A sweet and tender one, making me crumble like old houses do over a long period of time.

"We need to go," she adds.

Getting on my knees, I wrap my hands around the back of her thighs. I pepper kisses up to where her dress stops. "Five more minutes, baby. Five. More. Minutes," I beg through a cracked whisper.

"Noah, we can't be late. We're going to your dad's funeral. This is wrong. And rude."

"What's rude is how sexy you look right now."

CHAPTER SIXTY-ONE

Fuck me.

Noah's lips are making my skin quake and my pulse quicken.

"Oh, G-God," I stammer.

"Do I look like God to you? No, I don't think so. You need to say my name, Dani." He pauses, eyes burning holes all throughout my face. "Say. My. Name."

"Noah," I moan under my breath.

"That's my good fucking girl."

I roll my eyes so hard it feels like they're going to roll back into my head.

His hand lifts up my dress, grabbing my ass.

This is so wrong on so many levels.

I should stop all this, but my body doesn't want me to. It wants more and I hate that it does because we're going to his Dad's funeral.

What the hell is wrong with me?

My phone rings, taking me out of my thoughts.

He lifts my dress up, exposing my stomach. "Don't. You. Dare." He kisses, sucks, and licks my bare skin.

I reach over to my bed, seeing my mom's beautiful face light up the screen. "H-hi, Mom."

Grabbing his face with my index finger and thumb, I lift it up just enough so he can meet my gaze.

I move my lips from the phone. "You're *so* naughty."

I bring the phone back over to my mouth.

"Where the hell are you guys? You needed to be here fifteen minutes ago. Ben's funeral starts in twenty minutes," she says.

"We're coming. I p-promise."

"Okay. Please, hurry up."

"I know. Love you."

"Love you too."

I hang up the phone, smacking Noah's shoulder blade. "You're really something, you know that? That was my mom. We needed to be there fifteen minutes ago. We need to go. Now."

Noah gets up as I fix my dress. "Do you know how hot you are when you're pissed off like this?"

"If you don't get in the car right now, you're sleeping in the guest bedroom tonight," I threaten him.

"I'm going!" He kisses me on the forehead and runs out of my room.

My purse is slung over my shoulder with my phone in the side pocket. I don't have time to say goodbye to Archie or time to look for him.

Booking it out the front door, I lock the top and bottom locks with my key.

I walk towards the car, Noah is sitting in the driver's seat. I plop my ass down in the passenger's seat.

"There's no goddamn way I'm sleeping in the guest bedroom tonight," he says.

"That's my good fucking boy." A devilish smirk grows across my lips.

He bites down on his bottom lip, wetting them afterward. "Oh, I could get used to that."

"Okay, let's go." I buckle my seatbelt, putting my purse down on the floor in front of me.

He stares off into space, his hands gripping the steering wheel so tight he could break it.

"Hey, baby." My hand intertwines with his, eyes locking on mine.

I know how hard today is for him. He hasn't said a word about today in the last two weeks. Not surprising because I know how difficult it is to talk about losing someone who meant the absolute world to you. And now you're saying goodbye. It's like they were never here in the first place.

I've got to hand it to him. He hides his grief well. Too well. I'm terrified that it's all going to blow up in his face. His mother and sister's faces. And mine.

"Do you want me to drive?" I ask.

He's staring at the garage door. "No, I'm fine."

"Are you sure?"

"You're the one who told me we need to go. Stop asking me questions that don't matter," he snaps.

"Forget I even asked," I huff.

There's this knot in my chest getting tighter. It tugs at my heart, attempting to pull it down to my waist.

He's hurting. Remember how you felt when you lost Dad and had to go to his funeral?

Struggling to hold back tears, I turn my head to look out the window. This is where I'll be for the next fifteen minutes, pretending like I don't exist.

"I didn't mean..."

"Just drive."

He reaches his hand out to thread it into mine. I pull it away, sandwiching both of my hands underneath my thigh.

I'm here to support Noah.

In all honesty, today is hard for me too. Hard since my mind wants to flash back to my dad's funeral.

It was at Sunset Cove Memorial Gardens. I told myself I never wanted to go back there. Relive the pain. The hurt. The devastation.

I need to be strong.

For Noah.

For Lizzie.

For Laura.

Noah and I don't speak a word to each other during the entire drive. The silence feels deafening, cold, and depressing.

We turn into the Memorial Gardens.

It's the same as I remember from almost a decade ago. Tall oak trees scatter the rather large plot of the land. Cars are packed along the side street.

Ironically it's called Memorial Gardens, when in reality, it's a cemetery. Guess they wanted to call it something pretty instead of something depressing as hell.

He pulls behind a car on the side street, shifting the gear to park.

My head finds a home in between my thumbs, rubbing curvy motions along my temples.

I'm trying not to lose my shit. My eyes feel heavy, glassy, and irritated.

"Are you okay?" Noah asks.

Now, I'm staring off in the distance.

Nine years ago I was here, sitting in Mom's car and bracing myself for what I was about to endure. I was saying goodbye to my dad. A man who didn't deserve to leave the world in the way he did.

He was in his late forties. He had so many years left to live. He won't see me graduate college or get married. My children won't have him as their grandfather.

"Dani?" Noah's voice takes me out of my own personal hell.

"What?"

"You didn't answer me."

"I'm fine." I rub my finger underneath my nose, moving a tendril of hair behind my ear.

"You're not fine. Talk to me."

"This day isn't about me. It's about you. It's about celebrating your dad. If we don't move our asses, our mothers are going to have our heads."

How is it people wake up every day and not worry about anything? You know, the people who don't have a million thoughts running through their heads on repeat. The kind of thoughts that consume you when your eyes are tightly shut and when your eyes are wide open.

I wish I could do that and not worry about every little thing, but that's not how my brain is wired.

I was young when I lost my dad, barely a teenager.

I had to bear the weight of the world, but also the weight of losing my best friend. Some days, the weight is still so heavy it could crush me. Other days, it lingers like it's waiting to attack.

My life since I was fourteen years old has been in black and white and not like the movies from the 1940s.

I thought I'd never see my life in color again, but I was wrong.

Noah Kaplan has given me the gift of seeing the world in color. The gift of laughing until I cry happy tears. The gift of making me blush so hard my entire body heats up.

He brought me back to life and I'm so grateful for everything he's done for me.

Stepping out of the car, I sling my purse over my shoulder.

The car door slams shut. And there goes Noah's door.

We're on our way to Ben's memorial site. I can see Laura and Mom from a distance. Lizzie's next to Laura in a wheelchair.

He stops, standing in front of me and placing his hands on my shoulders. "We don't hide shit from each other. I need you to talk to me. Tell me what's going on. Please."

I brace myself, exhaling deep. "I haven't been here in nine years. Memories keep flooding back. I keep telling myself I need to be strong. For you. And I can't do it. I can't do this. I can't be here. I—" He stops me from my emotional rambling by pulling me into his big, strong arms.

Whenever Noah hugs me, it feels like I'm home and I never want to let him go.

"You had your dad's funeral here."

"Yeah."

He's gently rubbing my back to calm me down.

How is it that I'm losing my shit and he's not? How is he so calm? I'd be an emotional wreck if I was him right now.

"Remember when you told me we'd leave if it gets to be too much for me?"

I nod as a silent response.

The tears are steady, pouring out of my eyes like no tomorrow.

His arms release me before his hands thread into mine. "You need to tell me if it ends up being too much for you. When it does, we're out of here. Okay, Sunshine?"

"Okay." Wiping the salty wetness off my face, my eyes land on his face that I've come to love so damn much. "How are you so calm right now?"

"I don't think I'm calm. I'm just numb."

"That's a valid emotion to feel," I say.

We speed-walk over to where Laura, Lizzie, and Mom are.

Once we make it uphill, Laura greets us. "What the hell

took you guys so long? The service was supposed to start ten minutes ago!"

"Traffic," he lies through his teeth.

"Your dad would be so disappointed in you."

"Really? How would you know? He's not even here!"

"Noah," Lizzie jumps in, rolling her wheelchair closer to us. "Don't!"

"Don't look at me like that, Lizzie. Who are we kidding here? What makes you think Dad wanted an outdoor funeral in the first place? Maybe he wanted his ashes shoved inside a drawer. Maybe he wanted to be buried in the ground, so his body could decay and turn into pure bone. Hey, maybe we could use him as a Halloween decoration next year!" His chest is heaving, breathing heavily.

"What the hell is wrong with you? That's sick!" Lizzie shouts.

"That's enough! Noah, go sit your ass down. Now!" Laura shakes her head as the muscles in her jaw vibrate.

Noah rolls his eyes, sitting down on a chair in the front row.

It's just the five of us.

Laura, Lizzie, Noah, Mom, and I.

No other family members are here. His grandparents would've been here if they were still around. The Kaplan's are a decent-sized family. Noah has Aunts, Uncles, and cousins. I guess I'll find out if they're coming to the reception at the house.

Sitting down next to Noah, I can feel the anger coursing through his body.

The second I hold his hand, his anger cools down. "Take a deep breath."

He does what I tell him, closing his eyes. His mouth is shaped as a small circle and his shoulders are rising and falling.

I look at him. "You know that was totally uncalled for, right?"

"I know…It's just I don't get why Mom keeps saying Dad would've wanted this. He wouldn't have wanted any of this. I've never heard him tell us he'd want an outdoor funeral when he passes away. I hate that she keeps making shit up."

Feeling a hand on my shoulder, I turn around to see my mom. "I know how hard it is for you to be here, Sweet Girl. It's hard for me too, even if it's been several years. There's no alternate universe we could live in where I wouldn't have been here for Laura."

"I know," I say as I look away from Mom and Noah to stop myself from crying.

Noah turns around to get in on our conversation. "Thank you for everything you do for my mom. For staying with her at the house and helping her with Lizzie. I know it means the world to her. It means a lot to me."

She leans closer into him, cupping his cheeks with her hands. "Oh, Sweet Boy, you never have to thank me for anything. I'd do anything for your mom. I don't know if I would be here right now if it wasn't for her and my beautiful daughter." Mom takes a deep breath. "Dani's right about that outburst you had. That was the last thing your mom and sister needed right now. They're hurting and I know you are too. But, there's absolutely no reason to project more pain onto them."

He looks down at the floor, taking in what my mom just said to him. He meets her gaze. "You're right, I'm sorry."

"Let us begin," the rabbi says standing next to the shiny, wooden coffin.

Roses scatter the top of it. A plaque with Ben's name is plastered in the center of the top of the coffin.

God, I hope we both make it through this.

The funeral service lasts approximately forty-five minutes.

Laura and Lizzie give their eulogies. Noah doesn't. I knew he wasn't going to. He told me last night he couldn't do it. His mom understood his reasoning behind why he couldn't.

I spent the entire funeral service with my arm tucked into his and my head leaned into the nape of his neck.

Time to go back to the house and talk to people I don't even know. People who will ask me what I'm up to and other bullshit that's none of their business. I just need to plaster a fake smile and deal with it.

Maybe I should bring that giant black flashlight with me just in case.

Never know if I might need it.

CHAPTER SIXTY-TWO

Dani has no idea what's going on in my head and I don't want to subject her to any of it.

The darkness is slowly taking over my mind and body. It's like my humanity is wilting away like a dying flower.

I feel the warmth radiating from her hand. Her arm is nestled around mine. Even after I snapped at her when we got here, she stayed.

I *don't* fucking deserve her.

She deserves *so* much better than me.

Here's where it gets complicated. I'm never letting her go. She's stuck with me until we're gray and old. I'm going to marry her. It makes me so fucking happy to say that even if it's in my head.

She lifts her head out from my neck, looking up at me with those gorgeous eyes of hers. "Ready to go?"

"As ready as I'll ever be, I guess."

Dad's casket is in full view and I can't stop staring at it.

God, I hope he's not in there. I hate funerals. So. Fucking. Much.

"Hey, Moonlight. Eyes on me," Dani says.

My eyes land on her.

Her face is glistening from the sweat bordering the outline of her face.

All I want to do is rip that dress off her body. It's maddening how much she consumes me. I want her. All. The. Time.

I really can't get enough of her.

We're at my dad's funeral. What the hell is wrong with me? Why am I like this?

Getting up off my chair, I help her up.

Her lips brush against mine, making my pulse go absolutely wild. Her breath feels hot on my skin. Cupping her face, I kiss her. Her hands grab my waist, so she can balance herself.

My lips let go of hers.

She gives me the sweetest smile that makes me smile in return. "Time to go get tortured," she says.

We pull up down the street from the house and get out of the car.

She holds my hand, gripping on it like she doesn't want to let go. And I don't want her to.

Why the hell are there so many cars here?

My dad didn't know this many people. At least, I don't think he knew this many people.

Let's just say he wasn't the most popular guy. Although, he was the life of the party.

He made everybody around him laugh. Not just laugh, but laugh so hard you'd cry.

He had the biggest heart and cared so much about people. He'd do everything in his power to make sure Lizzie and I were loved and taken care of.

Dad was my best friend.

We'd watch basketball games together. Sometimes Grayson would get in on the fun. We'd all have the best time, screaming at the TV when our home team made a three-pointer or missed a shot. We'd eat burgers or hot dogs on game days.

It pains me that I can never talk to him about books, writing, and our love for basketball.

I can't talk to him about Dani. God, I talked to him about her all the time.

He's not going to see me walk across the stage and receive my bachelor's degree, see me blossom as an author, and be at my wedding. My kids won't have him as a grandfather.

A life without Dad is an emptier one, but Dani somehow fills that void for me.

I don't know what I'd do without her. Dad would've loved her. I mean he did, but he would've loved her as *my girlfriend*.

There's no doubt about that.

He's proud of me and proud of who I've become.

I can feel it deep in my bones. I want to continue to make him proud. I want him to know I'll never forget him and that he'll always be a part of me.

"I'm going to go to the bathroom. I'll be right back. I promise," Dani says, kissing me on the cheek.

I watch her head upstairs to the bathroom.

Why are there so many people here?

I have no clue where my mom is. Or Lizzie. Or even Celia.

I'm losing my balance. The room is spinning. Leaning against the wall nearest to the living room, I place my hand over my heart. It's beating faster than speeding bullets.

My hands are violently shaking and my mouth is dry. I can't breathe. I need to get the fuck out of here. Somewhere far away, so I can clear my head.

Running out of the house, I unlock the car and shift the gear into drive.

I don't know where I'm going.

I just know I need to get as far away from the house as possible.

I need air.

CHAPTER SIXTY-THREE

I finish up in the bathroom, washing my hands thoroughly.

God, it's so loud in here.

I didn't know that Ben knew so many people. He probably didn't even know half of the people here. This is what happens when you have a funeral reception. Even when you sit shiva, random people show up for absolutely no reason.

Unlocking the door, I make my way downstairs.

Frantically searching for Noah, I look in the living room. He's not there. Next up is the kitchen. Shit, he's not there either and he wasn't upstairs.

Luckily, I run into Lizzie. "Lizbug, where's your brother?"

"I don't know," she says.

"We came in together. You haven't seen him in the house at all?"

"No. I don't know where he is."

Fuck.

"Where would he go if he needs to clear his head?"

Lizzie looks down at her feet, taking ages to answer my question. Patience doesn't exist for me right now.

"Lizzie, where the hell would he go?"

She meets my gaze, an idea hitting her like a bolt of lightning. "Try Loggerhead. He used to go there a lot to think when his panic attacks got really bad when he was in high school."

This is the safe place he wanted to keep a secret from me. Not anymore.

"Have you guys seen Noah? I couldn't find him. I checked everywhere." Laura asks, concern writing itself all over her face.

I place my hand on Laura's shoulder. "I'm going to find him. Tell my mom where I'm going, okay?"

Laura nods as Lizzie follows me out the front door. "Be gentle with him."

"Don't worry. I got this!" My heart is beating so damn fast. Adrenaline is pumping.

I'm trying my best not to panic because there's no time for that.

It takes me five minutes to get to my house. I'm so happy that we live right down the street from them. Unlocking the front door, I search for my car keys. They're hanging on the key holder next to the door.

Once they're in my hand, I rush to get in the car. My hand shakes as I unlock the door to the driver's side.

Loggerhead Beach is a ten-minute drive from the house. Maybe less than that if I drive over the speed limit, but I'm not risking getting pulled over today. The gear shifts into drive and I'm off.

What the hell is he thinking, disappearing like that and scaring me to death? Is he okay? Is he alive? Oh God, he better be. I can't lose him too. I just can't. Why would he do this? Doesn't he know I'm here for him and that he can talk to me about anything?

I arrive at Loggerhead, feeling my heart is about to fall out of my ass.

There's a parking spot right next to the entrance.

My high heels are coming off. I'm walking in the sand bare-foot. My feet keep sinking with every step I take.

Searching frantically around the beach, Noah's nowhere to be found.

My chest is heaving so heavily that it feels like I could go into cardiac arrest right this very second.

Please be here.

Instead of going further east, I make my way west. It's closer to the bridge that overlooks the ocean.

A guy with dirty blonde hair who's dressed in a suit catches my attention.

When I get closer to him, he turns his head.

It's Noah.

I wet my lips with my tongue, running over to him and placing my hands on my knees to catch my breath. "What the hell is the matter with you?"

He rolls his eyes, getting up off the sand to walk away from me, but I follow him.

We make it as far as to where I started my search for him.

"I thought you were dead. You scared the shit out of me. Will you please talk to me?"

He ignores me.

"Stop walking away from me!"

"You have no idea what I'm going through. Just leave me alone," he says.

"You did not just say that to me!"

He keeps walking, but I keep up with his pace.

Standing in front of him, I get in the way of his path and stop him in his tracks. "In case you forgot, I lost my dad when I was in high school. He passed away in a car accident. I had to attend his funeral and sit shiva. So, don't you dare tell me I don't understand what you're going through."

I'm so angry I could punch him point-blank in the face. Maybe I should. But, I won't.

I love his stupid face too much.

noah

Loggerhead Beach has been my safe place since I was a teenager.

It's where I'd go to clear my head when shit hit the fan.

When I was driving, I knew I was coming here without a second thought.

I knew Dani would come after me because that's the kind of person she is. She's determined and incredibly relentless. She'd stop at nothing to make sure I was okay, always putting my needs above her own.

The way she's looking at me right now is killing me. She's standing in front of me, anger fueling her up.

Distraught over all of these emotions racking my brain, I fall onto the sand in a crouching position.

She sits down in front of me with a look of concern.

I think she knows there's a chance I could drown myself in my sadness and pain.

I meet her gaze. "I'm sorry I said that to you. I'm sorry I keep blowing up in your face and snapping at you. I don't even know why you're here, sitting in front of me. I'm such a fucking mess. You deserve to be with someone who has their shit together."

She shakes her head, huffing. "I'm a mess, too. I don't want to be with someone who has their shit together. All I want is to be with you. You have no idea what was going on in my head when I couldn't find you. I thought I lost you for good. Fuck, the thought of losing you hurt so much. It felt like a million tiny knives were stabbing me all over my body. Don't you ever do that to me again." She crosses her arms underneath her breasts, brows furrowing. Tears are pouring out of her dark brown eyes that I love so goddamn much. "*Promise* me," she politely demands.

"I *promise*."

"We can be broken together and help each other heal over time." She takes a moment to look at me, wiping tears off my face. "I love you. I just want you to be okay. I care about you too much."

"I know." I smile at her like I'm seeing her for the very first time. "I love you, too."

We both get on our knees to hug each other, landing back on our asses because the sand is too hollow.

After I tuck a stray tendril behind her ear, I crash my lips into hers.

I will follow this woman to the ends of the earth. There isn't a world that exists without her in it. She's it for me.

It's unfortunate that we were brought back together this way, but I believe my dad did this on purpose. He knew Dani would come to the hospital. He knew she'd take care of me, comfort me, and love me in a way that feels like a dream. A dream I *never* want to wake up from.

Thank you for everything, Dad. Thank you for bringing Dani back into my life. I'm going to miss you so fucking much.

We're sitting on the sand in front of the ocean, waves crashing onto that shore with a humid breeze swirling around us. The sun is setting, filling the sky with a variety of pinks, purples, and oranges.

"It's beautiful, isn't it?"

"Yeah, it's beautiful," I say, looking at her.

Dani has *always* been a beautiful view. *My beautiful view.*

She turns around. "You're missing it."

"I don't need to see it. I have a gorgeous woman sitting next to me."

Her cheeks are flushed and she's giggling like a lunatic. "Here we are. Together as boyfriend and girlfriend. Life knows how to throw crazy shit at us, doesn't it?"

"It definitely does. Like you said, we were inevitable."

"Indeed we were." She smiles, her eyes twinkling.

I lean into her, our lips meeting one another. My tongue requests entry into her mouth. She happily grants it.

Eventually, I pull my lips away from hers. "I can't wait to take you home."

"Why?" Her lips curve up to form a seductive smirk.

I study her from the neck down, bringing my eyes back up to hers. "So, we can finish what we started before we left the house earlier. That's all I've been thinking about. Ripping your dress off your body and kissing every inch of your bare skin. Prepare yourself because it's going to be a *long* night."

"I love you." She pauses. "I can't wait for you to ruin me tonight." She smiles into my mouth.

"I love you, too." I return a smile into her mouth.

Everything about this moment is perfect, being here with Dani. How her head fits perfectly into the crook of my neck.

I never want to leave. I just want to stay here with her forever.

I can't wait to see what life has in store for us.

I'm not going to lie when I say I'm slightly terrified, but there's something I learned from these past two months that makes me feel a bit more at ease.

Life loves to throw horrible shit at us, but we can't let that stop us from living. We just have to keep moving, even if it's difficult and takes time. There's always going to be someone who's in your corner who supports you, loves you, and tends to your wounds—even if they aren't physically visible.

After all this time, we made our way back to each other. I'm so grateful we did. I can't imagine my life without her in it.

Danielle Hope Solomon has always been in my corner and I'm never going to let her go.

epilogue

TWO YEARS LATER

"You've been staring at your computer screen for hours," Noah says, kissing my neck with his hands resting on my shoulders. "You *deserve* a break."

"This book isn't going to write itself, you know."

"True, but it's not going to be written at all if you burn yourself out."

"I just need to finish this chapter."

"That's what you always say," he says as his arms wrap above my chest area. "And you get sucked right back into your goddamn hole."

Crazy how I'm sitting at my desk in my childhood bedroom with my former childhood rival turned long-term boyfriend standing over me.

We love coming back home for the summer and spending time with our mothers. For some reason, every time we come back to Sunset Cove, it feels foreign. It's almost like we never lived here. It's a strange feeling.

The last two years have been a whirlwind. I can't tell if they actually happened or if they were a dream.

After six months of dating, I moved out of the apartment I shared with Bella and into Noah's off-campus college apartment. The one he used to share with Grayson and Xander. I felt so bad for them when he kicked them out.

Three months after we graduated college, Noah and I moved to Cedar Springs. A small town located in the heart of Central Florida. We wanted a change from the salty ocean air and tall palm trees.

Noah wanted to be closer to his sister. Lizzie moved to Crescent Falls last year because she got an amazing job offer with the police department there. She wanted an escape when she regained her strength and mobility back after the accident.

When the one-year anniversary of Ben's passing rolled around, we visited him at Sunset Cove Memorial Gardens. I visited my dad because it was the ten-year anniversary of his passing. It was a lot for Noah and me, saying goodbye to both of them all over again. We went to Loggerhead Beach afterward to clear our heads. It's not just Noah's safe place anymore, it's *our* safe place.

I became a published author in August which was one of the main highlights of that summer.

Laura held a special event on release day at Sweet & Salty for my debut, *Balancing Act*. She advertised it like crazy months before on social media and the store's website.

God, I remember how I was overcome with an abundance of emotions when I walked into the store. There are three that stick out to me: anxiety, excitement, and gratitude.

There was a table set up for me to meet readers and sign a copy of my book for them. It felt like a dream because there was a line that stretched down to Just One More Chapter.

It was insane to see my book in a bookstore and special because it's in a bookstore very near and dear to my heart.

My editor texted me that my book made it to number five in the Sports Romance category and number eight in the New Adult & College Romance category. I cried for hours because I couldn't wrap my head around it.

I can't believe I get to write about flawed characters falling in love as my career every single day.

Something I've loved to do since I was a little girl.

It's absolutely absurd and surreal.

Noah was by my side the entire day of my debut's release and the days that led up to it. I don't know how it's possible, but I fall more in love with this man every day. He's so kind and patient with me. Sometimes I feel like I'm sleeping, but my eyes are wide open.

Noah became a published author in October of last year.

Just One More Chapter held a release day event for his debut, *Expect the Unexpected*.

He let me be one of his first official readers after he completed his manuscript. His writing is immersive as hell and incredibly detailed. He sucks you right into the story and writes incredibly complex characters.

I won the lottery with him.

Before he released his sophomore novel, he hired a literary agent named Julia and she's a superstar. She helped Noah send out his manuscript to various traditional publishing houses last year.

He accepted an offer with Voyager Press, a major traditional publishing house based in Florida, but they have offices world-wide. It was a four-book deal which he completed in the spring of this year.

He's now working on a murder mystery duology.

Voyager offered him a deal for the duology, but he ultimately turned it down. He had a great experience with them, but he wanted to indulge in the self-publishing experience.

I'm so fucking proud of him, and I know his dad is, too.

Noah snaps me out of my daze as he glides the strap of my tank top down to my upper arm with his thumb.

Rolling my eyes like a broken record, I moan. "Don't. Do. That."

He kisses the top of my shoulder before he runs his tongue from side to side.

Is he trying to kill me?

"Tell me to stop," he says.

I'm trying to type, but my body keeps shuddering, so I slam my laptop shut.

Getting up out of the chair, I grab his face and smash my lips into his.

He picks me up by my ass and takes me into our bedroom, throwing me down on the bed and removing my top. Laying me down on the top of the covers, he climbs on top of me and studies my face.

My lips flatten as my eyes narrow. "What?"

"I'm never going to get over how stunning you are. You belong in a museum, so people can worship you, the ground you walk on, and the fact that a woman like you exists."

Fuck me, that was romantic as hell.

"You know what happens when you say shit like that to me!"

"What happens?"

"It catches me off guard."

"I love catching you off guard." He plants a tender kiss on my lips. "And as much as I'd *love* to fuck you right now, you have a hair appointment in fifteen minutes."

"What if I don't want to go? Can't I just stay here with you?" I pout, giving him puppy dog eyes.

"You have no idea how much I want you to stay here with me, but you need to get dressed, baby. You deserve a little pampering. Plus, your eyes need some rest from staring at your computer for several hours straight."

I roll my eyes. "Are you taking me to my appointment?"

He shakes his head, flattening his lips. "Nope, I asked Bella to take you because she ended up booking an appointment fairly close to the time when yours is."

"Why the hell did you take my shirt off then if you knew we weren't going to end up doing anything?" The corner of my lip quirks up, eyebrows furrowing.

"Why not?" A wicked smirk spreads across his lips.

I laugh, flipping him off.

Sliding off the bed, I rummage through my suitcase for something to wear. My eyes land on a dress I don't remember packing. A white lace mini dress with a flared skirt.

I take it out, presenting it to Noah. "Did you sneak this into my suitcase?"

His mouth shifts to one side of his face. "Maybe."

"Noah!" I raise my voice, narrowing my eyes.

"Yes, I snuck it in your suitcase. I want you to wear it today."

"Why?"

"It's one of my favorite dresses you own and you look like a Greek goddess when you wear it."

This is the dress I wore to my release day event for *Balancing Act* at Sweet & Salty. Guess it's been ingrained in his brain since then.

I scrunch my nose, rolling my eyes. "Fine, I'll wear it." After I slip into my dress, I stretch out the strings in the back. "Can you tie me up?"

"Oh, I'd love to tie you up," Noah says as he wets his lips with his tongue.

"The strings to secure my dress, dumbass."

He grabs onto the strings and crisscrosses them into each other, tightening them so my dress is secured. "Is that good?"

"Uh-huh."

He secures me by placing his hands on my hips, moving my hair so he can kiss the back of my neck.

Once he's done, his eyes start at my legs and work up to my face.

BELLA

BELLA

Waiting in front of your house

ME

i'm coming!

BELLA

You better be

I cross my arms underneath my breasts. "Are you seriously fucking me with your eyes right now?"

"It's hard not to when you look like this, especially how you look in this dress."

Rolling my eyes, I giggle. "I'm going."

Before I can walk out of the bedroom, Noah grabs me by my hand and pulls me by my waist, cupping my face with his hands to kiss me.

"Noah, I need to go."

"You said you didn't want to go."

"I changed my mind, and I don't want to be late for my appointment."

"What if I changed my mind?" He pouts, giving me goo-goo eyes.

"God, you're such a pain in the ass."

"But you love me anyway?"

I shake my head, grinning. "Of course, I love you."

I run out the front door, waving to Noah and running to Bella's car.

I hop in and she looks at me.

"Ready to get our hair done?" Bella asks, scrunching her nose.

"Yeah, let's do it." I chuckle.

After forty-five minutes of girl talk and hair makeovers, Bella drops me off back at the house.

When I open the front door and walk into the house, Noah's standing there, wearing a white button-down shirt and black pants.

He's staring at me, taking in the dramatic haircut I decided to go for.

My hair lands right at my clavicle now.

"Wow," he says.

"You don't like it?" I ask, whipping my head back and forth.

He laughs, taking a moment to admire me. "It's short." He pauses. "I assumed you were just getting a trim."

"I wanted a change. It was getting way too much for me to manage."

He walks over to me, running his fingers through my hair. Meeting my gaze, he smiles at me. "I love it."

"Don't lie to me."

"I'm not lying."

"You really like it?"

"I don't like it, Dani. I love it."

"I can go back to the hair salon and have them reattach my hair."

He shakes his head. "No." Kissing my forehead, he grabs me by the hand. "There's something I want to show you."

He guides me into the bedroom.

Holy shit. My jaw is on the floor.

There are lit candles filling up every square inch of my childhood bedroom, except the area near the bookcase.

I love him.

I go over to smell one of the candles sitting on my dresser, bringing it up to my nose and zooming it out, so the label is in clear view.

"Peach Bellini, huh?"

"You know my mom has an obsession with Bath & Body Works." He chuckles. "The candle smells good, but it doesn't compare to the way you smell. God, you always smell so good."

I giggle, placing the candle back to where it was.

This room is full of so many incredible memories.

Noah and I had our second-first kiss in here and had sex for the first time. I remember the time when he licked peach juice off my ass and the residual dribble that dripped down my neck.

Note to self: remind Noah about peach foreplay.

We've been staying here since my mom forced him to stay with me two years ago because she was terrified to leave me alone. At the time, I hated her for doing that.

Looking back on it, I'm so happy she did because I don't know if we'd be together right now. I've thanked her for her service more times than I count on two hands.

When I whip my head around, I see Noah sinking one knee on the cold, tile floor which brings me back to reality and makes me feel like I'm flying in a dream.

Oh my God, I can't believe what I'm seeing.

My eyes grow wide. "What the hell are you doing?"

"What does it look like I'm doing?" He pulls out a velvet box from his back pocket, opening it to reveal a ring.

Stumbling backward, I bury my face in my shaking hands. Every part of my body is vibrating. Tears line the rims of my inner eyelids, waiting to pour out.

I manage to smile, sucking my lips in.

"Are you okay?" he asks, his eyes growing wider by the minute.

Does it look like I'm okay?

I shake my head.

"You're going to have to try and bear with me because this is going to take a little while."

Nervous laughter comes out of my mouth as I'm violently nodding my head.

Noah grabs my hand and threads his into mine, smiling at me. "Dani, the last two years I've spent with you have been the best and craziest years of my life. I've dreamt for so long to be with someone who loves the damaged parts of me, but is willing to help me put those parts back together." He clears his throat. "We've known each other since we were born. Our mothers tried so damn hard to get us to be inseparable like they are, but it didn't work. We spent so many years competing with each other using words. It got so bad you stopped talking to me which broke my heart."

Fuck, cue the tears.

"But, look at us now. We're published authors. I mean, we're writing for a living. It's insane." He breathes out as his eyes begin to have a glassy sheen to them. "We're living the dream together, and I wouldn't want to live this dream with anyone else but you."

My lips quiver, dropping my head down and lifting back up, so I can look at his handsome face.

He lets go of my hand, so I have the freedom to freak the hell out if I want to.

"You're incredibly driven. Look at what you've built over the last few years. Tens of thousands of readers and authors who see your talent for words. Your ability to connect with them on a personal level is special. Not many people have that gift. Hell, I don't think I'll ever be able to do that. You should be proud of yourself because I am." He inhales and exhales. "God, you're brilliant. You're never afraid to say what's on your mind. You're resilient. You care so deeply about the people you love. And you're the most beautiful woman I've ever seen."

Wetting my lips with my tongue, I blink my eyes in rapid motion as a smile slowly appears on my face.

"You've always been in my corner, and I'm never going to let you go. There isn't a world or alternative universe I could be a part of that doesn't exist without you in it. I want to spend the rest of my life with you." He raises the ring closer to my face. "Danielle Hope Solomon, will you marry me?"

Frozen like an ice sculpture, I'm standing here and blinking my eyes like I can't believe what I'm hearing.

This doesn't feel real.

"Are you going to answer my question?" He laughs nervously.

"Give me a minute."

"Please take all the time you need. It's okay if my knee becomes permanently numb after this." Sarcasm embeds itself into his tone.

He's studying me as I break out into laughter which echoes throughout the bedroom, bouncing off the walls.

"Why are you laughing?"

My laughter gradually dies down. "I can't believe this is actually happening."

Ah shit, the tears have returned.

"Well believe it, baby."

"I love you, Moonlight."

"Is that a yes?"

"Yes," I breathe out.

He hoists himself up and crashes into me, one arm enveloping around my waist and one hand working its way through my hair. When he releases me, he cups my face and plants a tender kiss on my lips.

He slides the ring on my finger and I take a moment to admire it.

It's a round half-carat diamond with four prongs and single mounting, dripping in white gold.

Oh my God, it's perfect. He's perfect.

"I love you so much, Sunshine." He walks away from me, whipping his phone out of his back pocket and placing it on the bed. He's on a mission to do something, but I can't figure out what it is.

He taps a button and *Brain Damage* by Pink Floyd floods out of the phone speakers.

I grin at the floor.

Noah tilts my head up, so I can meet his gaze.

Sticking his arm out in my direction, he smiles at me. "Dance with me."

Sliding my hand into his, he brings me closer to his chest which presses gently against mine. I place my head into the nape of his neck. Our arms are bent with our hands intertwined. His other hand is resting on my back.

We're dancing to our song. A song we first listened to together in his childhood bedroom and almost shared our first kiss because of it.

This moment will be one I will never forget and one I will cherish for the rest of my life.

God, I'm the luckiest woman in the world because I fell in love with a handsome, tall, dirty blonde, and blue-eyed mystery and thriller author named Noah Kaplan. A guy who happens to be my former childhood rival. A guy who makes me feel seen and validated. He makes me feel like I'm the most beautiful woman in the world.

He's the kind of guy who belongs in a romance novel, one specifically written by a woman.

He has this incredibly dirty mouth which makes me lose my mind every time we're intimate. I can say with utmost certainty I don't want to be anyone else's Sweet Peach, but his.

After all this time, we found our way back to each other and I wouldn't have it any other way. I can't wait to spend the rest of my life with him and I can't wait to see what the future has in store for us.

acknowledgments

I've been writing fictional stories for as long as I can remember. Most of them live between the lines of college-ruled paper. There's a possibility I might revisit them or maybe they'll never see the light of day. Guess you'll have to wait and see.

I cannot believe you're holding my debut novel in your hands right now. It's surreal that I'm a published author with a book out in the world.

After All This Time wouldn't be in your hands if it wasn't for the people who were involved in the process from the very beginning all the way until the very end. Stick with me because this might take a while.

Mom, thank you for being the best "momager" I could ever ask for. Thank you for always supporting me and allowing me to follow my dreams. I love you.

Dad, thank you for constantly pushing me to the best version of myself that I can be. Thank you for always supporting me in everything I do. I love you.

Granni, thank you for supporting my passion for writing stories since I was a kid. I love you. Thank you for everything you've done for me.

Thank you to my author friends for your guidance, friendship, and support. I'm so grateful for every single one of you.

Thank you to my alpha readers for your constructive feedback and unhinged comments. This book would've been a chaotic mess without you.

Thank you my beta readers for making this book what it is

today and for cheering me on. Getting to witness your reactions in real time meant the world to me.

Jess, thank you for creating the adorable and stunning cover for my book. I had no idea what I wanted this cover to look like. You brought Noah and Dani to life better than I ever could've imagined.

Ellie, thank you for enhancing Noah and Dani's story and allowing my words to leap off the page.

Katie, thank you for bringing my book to life with your eye for design. I've learned so much from you and I'm so grateful for that. I love being able to talk to you about our shared love for graphic design and how crazy our cats are.

Maria, thank you for lending me your talent. It's surreal to see Noah and Dani in your beautiful art style as well as seeing them with my own eyes.

I want to thank you, the reader, for taking a chance on a new author and for reading Noah and Dani's story. I hope you enjoyed it. Feel free to stick around because there's so much more to come.

about the author

Jessica Sydney writes romance that makes you feel every emotion that exists. It's something she searches for when she reads books. She wants you to able to see yourself in the characters she writes.

Jessica has been writing since she was young. She fell in love with the way that writing is able to transport her into alternate realities.

If she's not writing, you can find Jessica watching her favorite TV shows, listening to her Spotify playlists, or chaotically mood reading her way through her TBR.

Join Jessica on her author journey by following her on social media. You can sign up for her newsletter for updates on upcoming books and unhinged chaos.

www.jessicasydneywrites.com

www.ingramcontent.com/pod-product-compliance
Lightning Source LLC
Chambersburg PA
CBHW060614300726
48975CB00005B/1559